A Scent of Violets

by

JENNY SANDLE

Best wishes
Jenny Sandle

HORSESHOE PUBLICATIONS . WARRINGTON . CHESHIRE

ISBN 1 899310.13.4

British Library Cataloguing in Publication Data
A catalogue record for this book is available from The British Library

First published 1997 by
HORSESHOE PUBLICATIONS
Box 37, Kingsley, Warrington,
Cheshire WA6 8DR

Book cover designed and illustrated
by Philip Jackson of Cheshire

Printed and bound in Great Britain by
Print Express Services Ltd
Frodsham, Cheshire, WA6 7HL

PROLOGUE

The agent's board had collapsed into the undergrowth. The pole moss grown, the name barely discernible. Long tendrils of clinging, shiny green ivy grew over the fallen post almost obscuring the name. What should have been an open and welcoming magnificent gateway was almost indiscernible from the rest of the perimeter hedges.

Inside the neglected grounds nature had run wild for six years. Unchecked by man the nettles had taken over and were almost three feet high. Brambles prickled their way into every possible avenue, ready to tear and snag at the unsuspecting legs of the unwary intruder - for intruder one would surely feel in this rank garden. Trees had shed their leaves for six autumns without the sweeping, burning gardener's hand; bushes had overstepped the boundaries of their once neatly defined borders. The main avenue to the house was deep in moss and rotten leaves; small twigs littered the ground; no-one could approach the house unheard. The only evidence of occupation were the occasional clusters of rabbit pellets; the frequent rustlings in the dense undergrowth.

Beyond barriers grown by nature lay the house. Brabage Vicarage was a double-fronted brick house of the style so loved by Victorians. The no-nonsense appearance of rectangular windows and doorways seemed at variance with the elaborately scrolled porch; mock doric columns each side of the blistered and peeling double door. A symmetrical arrangement of windows - two each side of the front door on the ground floor, five on the first floor - presented a hostile appearance for they were black in the reflected gloom of the surrounding gardens. Standing away from the front door one could just see three attic windows peeping over the edge of the rotting and collapsing guttering.

To one side of the main building was what had obviously once been a stable block converted, in more recent times, to a garage.

The house did not invite inspection. A curtain wall joined stable and house. Set in the wall was a rusting gate, an effective barrier since it had collapsed on its corroded hinges and become tightly wedged in undergrowth. Beyond the gate lay the rear of the house - the kitchen regions. Several windows were boarded up, as was the door.

To the other side of the house lay the ruins of a once elegant terrace. Its terracotta tiles were cracked - lifted and sunken in places. Railings had collapsed.

A stately conservatory filled part of the wall, many windows now gaping holes, others patched with tape, plastic sheeting or hardboard. Another curtain wall linked the conservatory corner with the perimeter wall. The brick archways in this wall were intact; the doors solid against prying eyes. Beyond lay the kitchen gardens.

The extensive grounds were bounded by a high stone wall, collapsed in places. Now, after years of rampant growth, large sections of the grounds were impenetrable. Secret places were screened by dense trees and prickly shrubs. The once inviting walks were sadly overgrown. Who would have guessed, looking at the deep thicket to the left of the house, that once a pleasantly gravelled path had wound its way between the bushes to open eventually onto the edge of a small lake, on the shores of which stood a now rotting summerhouse?

The vicarage presented a challenging face - defying anyone to dare to approach. Brooding, and in its way, belligerent, it had lain unsold and neglected. Prospective purchasers had been deterred, not only by its ruinous aspect, but also by its atmosphere. Gloomy and hostile: it was difficult to imagine the sun ever shining on the dank, dark Brabage Vicarage. Viewers shuddered and turned away to more welcoming prospects. The house sat back on its haunches, a beast waiting to pounce on its prey.

PART ONE

LIZ

CHAPTER ONE

Liz snapped herself into her seatbelt and eased her car into the slow crawl of homeward commuter traffic. The stream leaving Manchester this evening seemed even heavier than was usual on a Friday night. All three lanes were at a standstill. Resignedly Liz sighed. Seventy-three miles to go. But at least this was the last time she would have to drive it. At that thought she smiled quietly to herself. A young man driving in the next lane grinned, clearly interpreted her smile to be at him. He reached out to blast his stereo - LOUD. If the road ahead had been clear Liz knew that he would have roared off in a screeching of rubber in order to impress her. Her lane began to inch forward.

Liz passed the young poseur again. He grinned; she smiled, less at him than because she was so happy. The car in front stopped. Liz braked. Young Lancelot went crawling by attempting to look nonchalant, pretending that he wasn't looking at her, but actually watching her all the time. Liz switched on the radio. The comforting tones of Brian Perkins were announcing the latest unemployment figures. Hard to show concern in her present mood of exhilaration. She passed Lancelot again. He was now trying to impress someone else, gesticulating at what appeared to Liz to be an oversized candy-floss perm perched on thin shoulders driving an Escort convertible. So much hair! There must be a head underneath it - somewhere!

All three lanes were once more at a standstill. Lancelot, between Liz and the driver she had unkindly dubbed "Perm-On-A-Stick", looked smugly at each woman in turn. "Christ! He looks at us as though we were all in bed together," Liz laughed to herself. "What a nerve! Still, in the era of AIDS I suppose it could be described as the ultimate in safe sex: each of us isolated, secure inside our glass and metal bubbles!"

Liz was startled by the sudden blast of a horn behind her. She was

daydreaming and had allowed a gap to open up. Lancelot looked across at her, so did "Perm-On-A-Stick". Liz laughed, really out loud this time when she saw the wrinkled face below the candy-floss. The result of too many sessions on a sunbed! Make-up apparently put on with a JCB; hideously flashing tombstone teeth between over-glossy red lips. Lancelot caught Liz's eye, shrugged his shoulders and raised his eyes in a gesture of resigned despair - the joke shared. "You win some, you lose some!" muttered Liz, driving on suddenly as her lane began to move once more.

She was on the motorway now. It was beginning to go dark. Looking ahead Liz saw tail lights stretching as far as she could see. Odd, the illusion that cars some distance in front are stationary. She could feel herself almost hypnotised, entranced by the red, dancing patterns on one carriageway and the flashing white headlamps on the other side. Blip, blip, blip as they passed the motorway crash barrier. It was little wonder that people fell asleep at the wheel. She should be used to it. Here it was the beginning of March and she had been commuting - correction, she had commuted - for almost a year. The beautiful summer and golden autumn evenings had all been swallowed up by the road. Winter had been just horrible: ice; snow; rain; motorway pile-ups; roadworks. She never wanted to live through that period in her life again. When she had eventually arrived home she hadn't even the energy to eat, just a long, hot bath and falling exhausted into bed. Well, tonight was the last time she would do that. She looked ahead and relished her future, planning out the days to come, days that she would spend at home, doing all the things she'd never had time to do.

At thirty-two Liz had never had a break from her career. Most women have time out in having children, even if only a year or so here and there. Not Liz. She and her husband Paul had no children.

At first they had not wanted children, always forced to justify their position, to fight their corner by an intrusive world that couldn't bear to see a happily married couple without children. Laughingly and in a determined way Liz and Paul would parry curious questions by stating their determination to make their marks in their individual careers before reproducing. Lately though the questions had begun to annoy Liz. What right did people think they had to be able to pry into every corner of your life?

Over the past year Liz and Paul had acknowledged that they would like a child. Like so many people they had assumed that once they stopped using contraception it would just happen. It hadn't - not yet anyway. There was plenty of time before having to worry about it. Still, Liz did wonder why she wasn't yet pregnant.

Liz's thoughts were interrupted by an urgent pulling on the steering wheel. Something was wrong. The car was lurching dangerously to one side. "Shit!" she thought, "it would happen tonight of all nights!" She pulled the car safely onto the hard shoulder, switched on the hazard lights and got out. The front nearside tyre was almost flat. Liz knew that the spare was in the boot, knew that she was perfectly capable of changing the wheel; she just didn't want to. Who would? The nearest emergency telephone was a long way away. By the time she had walked there and back she could have sorted out the puncture and be on her way. Better get on with it then!

Lights illuminated her periodically. Tools out of the boot; loosen the wheel nuts; jack up the car. Lights passing. Lights stopping. Car on hard shoulder in front of her; car reversing (strictly against the law she thought!); man getting out.

"Hi! Got trouble?" He smiled at her, rather wolfishly Liz thought.

"Nothing I can't cope with!" snapped Liz, angry at herself for being grateful that he had stopped. The man was standing over her now, looking down. He looked OK really. Perhaps it would be nice...

"Here, let me." He took the wheelbrace and spun the wheelnuts off. Liz stood back. "Saw you stuck. Recognised your number."

"You did? How? Do I know you from somewhere?" Liz was wary now.

"You travel regularly on this motorway don't you?" Liz paused before answering him.

"Up to now, yes. This is my last night. But how did you know that I travel this route?"

He replied, nonchalantly, "Oh, just a game I play, to pass the weary hours behind the wheel. I notice car numbers, make words from them, phrases, anything to amuse myself and keep me awake.

"That's how I know your number. Nothing sinister I promise you." But the laugh he gave as he said this was very sinister indeed. "I usually see you about here, plugged into the motorway and driving mindlessly like the rest of us." He was about to go on, to continue the casual conversation when there was a flash of blue lights. A Police car pulled in behind. One glowing jacket got out, one stayed inside, talking on the radio.

"Everything OK here?" The policeman leaned against the side of the car and looked intently at Liz and the stranger.

"Yes Officer. I had a puncture. This chap has stopped to help me."

The chilly night air crept around Liz's ankles. She stood away from the car.

The grass verge was muddy and she felt her heels sink. The policeman and the stranger were chatting. "Thank God," she thought, "that I won't be facing any more of this!" If she had experienced any trepidation, any anxiety about leaving her well-paid publishing job in the city this puncture would have settled them. Looking back she wondered how she had managed to commute for so long. No wonder she was worn out! Still, it had all been worth it. Her mind drifted back to the previous year when they had first seen the old house. It had all been an accident really. They'd been on their way from their Manchester city apartment to visit friends in Shrewsbury. They weren't expected before evening, she remembered.

It had been Paul who had insisted on travelling the minor roads; the "scenic route" he had called it. They had seen some of the sights on the way; a snack at Knutsford, on to Jodrell Bank and a quick look at Beeston and Peckforton castles. They were negotiating the narrow, twisting Cheshire lanes, looking for somewhere to have coffee when Liz had finally given up on reading the map and admitted that they were lost! The countryside had been beautiful, very picturesque, but deserted. They could find no-one to ask for directions. After more than half an hour of trusting to luck at each road junction, Paul had finally pulled over and studied the map

It was as they had resumed their way that they had seen it - the agent's signboard struggling to be seen in dense undergrowth. The driveway could hardly be seen, almost closed over by spreading shrubs.

"Let's go and take a look," Liz had said, excitedly, always ready to explore, to seek adventure.

"We can't Lizzie. What would we say if we were caught peering in through windows? They'd think that we had plans to burgle the place!"

"Oh, come on Paul! The place is deserted, it must be. Look at the way the hedges have grown across the gateway. Look at the nettles for goodness' sake! No-one could have been through that gate for years!"

"What's the point? Even if we do take a look, there's no way we would want to move out here. We must be sixty or seventy miles from Manchester. Anyway, we could never afford it!"

"Oh, come on! Don't be so ... so ... middle-aged!"

As they pushed through the final curtain of tangled undergrowth they had both gasped. Liz had been amazed, overawed by the old house. She was drawn to it immediately. Paul gasped for a different reason. He could see no further than the boarded-up windows, the sagging gates, the jungle of the garden. Liz had been

intrigued and had stepped forward to explore the old house. Paul had had no option but to follow.

At the end of an hour, all thought of coffee forgotten, Paul had reluctantly agreed that they could collect the keys from the agent and take a look inside. Thrilled with this agreement Liz had thrown her arms around him and kissed him. As she did so the sun came out, penetrating even the dark depths of the old kitchen garden. Liz caught the scent of violets, pervading the air around her.

It was weeks later when they were paying one of their now regular visits to the house that she had caught an echo of that same fragrance at the bottom of the stairs leading up to the old attics. She called to Paul, asking if he too could smell violets.

"Oh Liz, you are fanciful! There's always odd smells around these old places." And, ever the pessimist, he had added, "Knowing our luck, it's probably dry rot!" He had insisted that he could smell nothing.

Of course, they hadn't been able to afford the place, at least not without a struggle. Selling their apartment just as the property market began to take an upturn had been lucky. Also fortuitous was the fact that no-one else seemed to be interested in the dilapidated old place. When the sale had finally been completed the agent had breathed a sigh of relief.

That was when the really hard work had started. They'd needed both salaries to fund the basic renovation. A gruelling time of early mornings and late nights, hardly seeing each other except at weekends, had followed. Paul had eventually managed to find a post nearer home in Nantwich, but Liz had continued the punishing drive to Manchester. That was all over at last! With only the decorating left to do, and one or two other jobs within Liz's capabilities at DIY she was going to stay at home and finish off the house. She would ...

"That should do it then!" A voice broke into Liz's reverie. In a moment she was back in the uncomfortable present, back on the hard shoulder of the motorway; cold mud penetrating her shoes. "All done!" The stranger smiled engagingly at Liz and then, rather ingratiatingly at the policeman.

"Thanks so much. It was really good of you to stop."

"Don't mention it." The man walked back to his car, got in, started up and drove off, waving over his shoulder as he pulled onto the carriageway.

The policeman opened the car door for Liz. He remained standing on the hard shoulder, his jacket glowing in the gloom, until she pulled back into the stream of traffic.

It wasn't until she had resumed her route home that Liz realised just why the

officer had stood there during the entire wheel changing. It hadn't been to protect the stationary vehicles with his flashing blue lights, nor yet for the opportunity to fill a quiet half hour with some casual conversation. He'd been keeping his eye on things, afraid that Liz may have been in danger. Liz recalled that it had only been a short time ago that a lone woman driver had been abducted from her broken down car. Things fell into place. Liz shuddered. Thank goodness she was giving up commuting!

It had been dark for some hours when Liz at last pulled her car between the gateposts and heard the tyres crunch over the gravel drive. She pulled up at the front door - the garages weren't yet completed. She ran up the steps and as she did so glanced with feelings of warm belonging at the slate house nameplate, illuminated by the overhead light. "Brabage Vicarage". Key in lock. Open door. "Paul! I'm home!" she called to the welcoming hallway.

CHAPTER TWO

Cold moonlight silvered the bedroom. Liz stared around her, startled out of sleep. What had awoken her? It was quite a wild night. She could hear the wind threshing the trees in the garden, feel it battering the front of the house, snatching at the windows, trying to prise the frames loose from the walls. Somewhere a door was banging and in the distance farm dogs were barking. What a contrast to city life where the traffic never ceased, even in the early hours of the morning.

Blearily Liz looked at the illuminated clock, 2.30 a.m. She turned over and settled once more, snuggling down under the quilt, close to Paul's back. Just as she was drifting back into sleep she was startled once again, opening her eyes wide. Moaning; low moaning. She listened for a moment, sure that the noise was the wind around the old chimneys. Satisfied she nestled snugly into the warm bed.

Moments later she was wide awake, sitting up in bed and staring wildly around her. Someone had grasped her shoulder. She was sure, yes, she had felt a powerful hand shake her to consciousness. The room was a patchwork of silver moonlight, draining the colour from all it touched, and deep, black patches of velvet darkness. As she became aware once more of the moaning a stab of fear lanced through her. She could feel herself being drawn, up and out of bed, across the carpet to the door. With her hand on the doorknob she stopped.

"What the hell am I doing?" she thought. She turned to walk back to bed. As she did so the low moaning gave way to a deep, heart-rending sobbing. The sound seemed to fill her head, the room, the house. Like an automaton Liz turned, grasped the doorhandle, turned it and opened the door.

On the landing all was dark and quiet. Liz, eyes glazed, walked forward. Her bare feet did not register the change from carpet to rough boards as she stepped on the bottom tread of the attic stairs. White-knuckled, her hands held the banister to steady herself. She mounted the stairs to the top floor of the house.

The attic storey was totally unrenovated. Piles of builders' materials stood about, waiting to be used. Almost magically Liz walked through the clutter, her unseeing eyes not even registering obstacles. A rusty nail, protruding from rough floorboards brought her to an abrupt halt. She cried aloud in pain, bent to examine her injury. Her eyes cleared; she looked around confusedly. She was on the attic floor. What was she doing here in the middle of the night? Wiping away the blood on her fingers she stood up and turned taking a step towards the top of the staircase. As she did so she stopped, suddenly recalling the moaning, the sobbing

noises she had heard. That must be why she had come up here, to investigate! Liz could feel the coldness of the unheated stairs stealing around her. Cold fingers of fear rippled up and down her spine; her heart felt gripped in an icy claw. She must be mad, coming up here by herself in the middle of the night.

She looked around the gloomy staircase. Wisps of shadows fled maddeningly just out of her field of vision. Pools of inky blackness lay everywhere, and yet as she stared into them, hard, they boiled and tumbled, seething with movements she couldn't quite discern. She was gripped by a sudden panic, an urge to run; to flee back to the warm bed she shared with Paul. Yet she couldn't run; something held her there, held her against her will. Whatever it was, she knew it was behind her. She could feel it there; feel the power, the force of it holding her. She knew that she would have to turn, have to face it, whatever it was. But she was afraid. She spoke, aloud to herself, out into the darkness.

"Come on Elizabeth Graham. You have never been afraid of anything, and you're not going to give in to that feeble imagination of yours now! Get a hold on yourself; turn around and face it, whatever it is!" Taking a deep breath she let go her grip on the banister rail. She began to turn, feeling the compulsion inside her drawing her round. She paused, afraid once more. Her resolution began to waver a little. Her treacherous memory reminded her that she had indeed been afraid of many things.

Away at boarding school, while her parents had been stationed abroad, she had listened in wide-eyed horror to the other girls' tales of grey ladies, phantom horsemen and headless courtiers. She had swallowed them all indiscriminately, for hadn't her grandmother fed her with the sure knowledge that such things as ghosts existed and that her own family was particularly psychic?

Liz looked down at her trembling, white-knuckled hands. She tried breathing deeply to steady herself. She reasoned with herself. She either gave in to her fear, returned to the bedroom and admitted that the noises were all due to the wind or she went forward, along the attic landing to find out just what had been making the moaning, sighing, sobbing noises that she had heard.

She had no choice. As she stood at the head of the stairs she felt something push past her. Nothing was visible, but a cloud of icy coldness engulfed her and everywhere, pervading the air all around her, was that elusive smell of violets. She was swept along, drawn by a compulsion she could do nothing to resist.

There were three doors on the attic landing. Each was firmly closed. The house was silent. Liz listened. Imagination! It must have all been her imagination. No sooner had this thought entered her mind than she became aware of breathing,

quite close to her. The breathing seemed to be coming from behind the centre door. Liz approached. She stood with her ear close to the peeling paint of the old wood. She listened. The breathing became a moaning; the moaning a sobbing. The sobs grew louder seeming to fill all thc air around her. With no awareness of what she was doing her hand reached out, reached out to turn the door handle. She tried to pull it back. She couldn't. She had no control over her movements. Whoever, or whatever, was making that noise, was forcing her, forcing her forward, forcing her to turn the handle, to enter the old attic. She fought hard, but her arm would not obey her. Fascinated, she watched her hand grip the handle and begin to turn it. Immediately the door was snatched inwards, Liz firmly grasping the handle. She was pulled into the dark heart of a maelstrom.

Wild sobbings, moanings, whimpering, round and round. Horror, grief, and yet the conflicting emotions of joy, love and happiness were all flying around the room; whirling in a great surge of sound, light, darkness. Shadowy faces, half glimpsed figures, ghostly fingers caressing her face. Liz was drawn in and whirled around like a miniature rag doll, a plaything, tossed about by the hurricane breath of a reckless giant child.

Everything went black.

* * * * * * *

In the warm nest of the bed Paul stirred. He turned over and reached out to curl his hand familiarly over Liz's hips. A cool emptiness met his seeking arm. Sleepily he moved further over, expecting to meet the welcome of Liz's body. Instead he moved into a cool, hollow void. Her place in the bed was empty; Liz was gone. It took a few moments for his fuddled brain to take in the fact of Liz's absence. She had probably gone to the bathroom, he thought as he settled down, warming Liz's patch of thc bed in readiness for her return.

Paul was worried about Liz. She seemed to be enjoying her new life at home, her break from the punishing tyranny of her career, but she was different somehow. Ever since she had first seen the vicarage she had changed subtly. Her determination to buy the place, to come and live here had carried them through a seemingly hopeless maze of renovation work; plans; regulations; recalcitrant builders, joiners and plumbers. Now they were here. There was still quite a lot to be done, but they had managed so far. He had expected Liz to relax the pace a little once they had moved, and yet she seemed more intense than ever, more fired with determination than she had ever been. It was almost like being married

to a different person sometimes. It could probably all be put down to hormones!

Paul tried to shrug off his concern. When had he ever not been worried about Liz? When both of her parents had been killed in an accident in Africa, shortly after he and Liz had married, he had thought that Liz was going to have a nervous breakdown, but she had come through it all. True, she tended to work much too hard in her job, but then she was ambitious -or had been. At the moment she just seemed to want to stay at home, reluctant to leave the vicarage, fanatical about the work left to be finished. She hardly met anyone these days. Maybe he should suggest a party? They could assemble a group of friends and colleagues, put them up for the weekend - those who wanted to stay anyway. The old place was certainly big enough. They could show off all that they had done to Brabage Vicarage to date. Yes, a party. That was a very good idea. He would suggest it to Liz as soon as she got back to bed.

As soon as she got back to bed. Where the hell was she? She must have been gone for ages. He listened. He could hear nothing, only the wind moaning in the old chimneys. Strange how it sounded like sobbing. If he didn't know better he'd think that someone was weeping bitterly, up in the old attics. He lay, listening, for several minutes and then decidedly threw off the duvet, placed his feet on the cold carpet of the floor and went off to look for Liz, padding through the silver pools of moonlight.

* * * * * * *

She watched the unconscious form of Liz lying so very still at the foot of the attic stairs. She had rushed things. Too much, too soon. Hadn't impatience always been her besetting sin. She may have ruined everything now by her impulsiveness. Liz was the first person she had found who could provide a link, the first person who could help her. Now she had spoiled it all.

In the bedroom Paul lay asleep. She tried everything, cold breath, moaning, sighing. Maddeningly, he slept on. She kept trying, doing her utmost to get through to his inert mind. Finally he stirred, turned over and reached out. After a few minutes of moving about, he settled once more. It was no good.

Back on the landing, Liz was still unconscious. The shadowy black form bent over her, almost willing her to return to consciousness. She began to weep.

* * * * * * *

The bedroom door opened. Paul emerged onto the landing. Into the silence he called Liz's name. There was no reply. He switched on the lights and instantly the colours that had been bleached by the moonlight sprang into relief. Shadows fled. Paul walked along the landing towards thc bathroom. He had to admit that this house spooked him. He teased Liz when she had told him that there was an atmosphere, almost as if the house possessed an identity of its own. But up here, in the middle of the night, it was rather spooky. Shadows; pools of darkness where no darkness should be. At the bottom of the attic stairs, for instance, there was no reason for that shadow. He peered at it. "Liz!" he cried, and ran forward.

* * * * * * *

She saw him, saw the concern, the deep love in his eyes. She could not watch as he gently bent over, stroked Liz's face, lovingly lifted her and carried her back to bed. She fled.

Hours later, comforted by coffee with a dash of whisky, released by telling Paul of her experiences, Liz lay still. Paul reached for her and held her close to his chest. She was OK. No damage, just extremely shaken. He felt the relief flood through him. As he held her he felt her stir, reaching her face up from the warmth to kiss him. She kissed him hard, urgently. He responded.

Their lovemaking was different from anything he had ever experienced before; tender and at the same time driven by a savage intensity, a hunger to be satisfied. Both were so caught up in the ferocious whirlwind of their passion that they did not heed the dark, shadowy figure at the door, were not aware of the gasp that became a grief-stricken sobbing as the figure turned and dissolved from sight, leaving behind only a delicate scent; a scent of violets.

CHAPTER THREE

The party was going extremely well. Paul looked around the room. Everyone seemed to be enjoying themselves. He was relieved that Liz's ex-colleagues and his new ones were mixing. On so many occasions such as this the guests fell into two groups, finding it difficult to step outside their familiar cliques. Throwing the party had presented him with the opportunity to build a few bridges, let his working relationship with new people consolidate itself into friendship. Also, of course, it was good to see those old familiar faces from Marshall's Publishing. Just because Liz was taking time out didn't mean that she had to lose touch altogether, and it really did seem to be doing Liz a lot of good.

Paul watched his wife, across the other side of the room, talking animatedly with Simon, her former boss, and Simon's friend, introduced earlier to Paul as "Roger from Chester archives". Roger had smiled and shaken Paul's hand warmly, but Paul had not yet had chance to talk to him. Liz seemed to be making up for it though; just look at her. He hadn't seen her that lively for so long: Not since they had moved into the vicarage in fact. Paul quelled a fleeting moment of jealousy. Liz was attractive, tall and dark haired. Her shining hair hung to her shoulders, her dark eyes sparkled as she made conversation with Simon and Roger. She was so elegant, so slim. Wasn't she a little too thin though. Since she had been at home full time she seemed to have lost quite a lot of weight. Not enough to worry about - not yet anyway - but something to watch nevertheless.

Paul circulated, topping up glasses, making conversation and introductions. He was enjoying himself: In fact he was happier than he had been since they had moved to Brabage. He should be delighted to be living here in the Cheshire countryside. It was something he and Liz had dreamed about for years, but ... but, the problem was, Liz.

Since they had moved to Brabage Liz had changed. She rarely wanted to go out, hadn't met most of the village as yet. Look around in here, Paul thought to himself, not one person from the village among the fifty or so guests. She seemed content to spend her time inside the house.

Moving about the room, a bottle of red wine in one hand, a bottle of white in the other, Paul found himself at Roger's shoulder just in time to overhear the words "salt mines". He stopped in mock alarm.

"Hey, we moved to Brabage, not Siberia!" Simon, Roger and Liz all laughed. Roger explained.

"Ah, hello there Paul. I was just telling your lovely wife about all the local attractions. There's so much to see and do in Cheshire. It's a vast county, and a most interesting one. It seems that you and Liz don't know too much about it. For instance Liz didn't know that the crown jewels were stored in the salt mines here in Cheshire during the last war!" Paul allowed himself to look suitably impressed with this snippet of information. Roger went on.

"I know that you are both familiar with Chester - who in the region isn't? Also the castles at Beeston and Peckforton, but there's much more to Cheshire than the tourist traps. Now, take the period of the Civil War for instance ..."

Simon interrupted what had threatened to become a lecture on local history.

"Yes, I was telling Liz, she ought to get out and about, learn about the place. This house for instance, I would bet a pound to a penny that it has an interesting history. Liz could knock together a little guide to the area, places of interest, potted histories of the old houses, you know the sort of thing. We would be able to sell something like that. What about it Liz?" He turned to Liz.

"Oh, I don't know, Simon. Since I've stopped commuting I seem to have my hands full just with the jobs left to do in the vicarage. I can't really ..."

"Nonsense Liz. You should get out and about. I've been telling you that for ages. You have let this place dominate you, it's as though a tyrant has entered your life - DIY at Brabage Vicarage!" Paul laughed; Simon and Roger joined in, but Liz looked uncomfortable.

Simon sailed in. "A dog, that's what you should have Liz. All country people have a dog. That would get you out and about, walks and so on. Soon bring the roses back to your cheeks."

Later, as Paul climbed into bed beside Liz, he found himself agreeing with Simon. A dog would be a good idea. It would keep Liz company, stop her brooding on that nonsense about there being "something" in the house. He snuggled down, determined to do something soon about acquiring a dog.

* * * * * * *

Sunday morning. The sun was shining; a glorious spring day as Liz and Paul saw Simon to his car. The last of their guests to leave he thanked them most profusely.

"Wonderful party. Can't remember when I last enjoyed myself so much. I must say Liz, when you first took on this place we all thought that you were mad. Now though, I can see that you are really getting somewhere. But, don't bury yourselves out here. Don't leave it so long until we see you again."

Simon got into his car. He paused as he was closing the door. "Oh, and Liz, don't forget what I said. A guide to this area would go down very well indeed." Liz began to protest, but Simon slammed the door and started the engine.

The car had begun to move when he wound down the window and called back,

"By the way, don't forget to let me have back the rest of those photos you were using, the ones of the soldiers from the Great War."

Liz looked puzzled.

"I left all those behind at my office, to be returned to their owners." Liz's final project for Marshall's had been a collection of poetry, postcards and letters from the First World War. She knew that she had left all the material at the office, in fact she had never brought any of it home to Brabage.

"I think there may be some bits and pieces still lying about. In fact I saw a small framed photograph on the wall of the attic stairs, a soldier and his wife, sweetheart or whatever. Anyway Liz, check on it will you, there's a love."

Before either Liz or Paul could respond, Simon was gone, his tyres crunching through the gravel at the gateway. They regarded each other in silence for a moment, each sure that they possessed no such photograph as that described by Simon. Liz ran inside and up the stairs.

There it was. There was no doubt about it. A handsome young man in military uniform stood holding the back of a chair. Seated was a young woman in ankle length skirts. Both were smiling happily at the camera. Liz lifted it down from where it hung on the wall. She was white and shaking.

"Paul, I don't know how to explain this, but this wasn't here before. It doesn't belong to us and it most certainly is nothing I have brought from the office!"

"Come on Lizzie, it's just something that's slipped your mind!" Paul was quietly patient, trying to calm Liz's trembling.

"No, Paul it's not! It wasn't here before, I tell you." Liz was beginning to get a little hysterical.

"Look Liz, it obviously belongs to us. Look at the woman in the picture. She's the spitting image of you, in fact she looks very much like your mother."

Liz scrutinised the picture, her trembling hands beginning to calm.

"But it isn't Paul, it isn't anyone in my family. You know what it is don't you? This is a message, a message from whoever it is haunting this house." A tear began to trickle slowly down her cheek.

"Stop it Liz! Stop it! How many times must I tell you that there's absolutely nothing haunting this house, nothing but your imagination!"

"And the scent of violets. How do you explain that away Mr.. Clever?"

"Liz, stop it! Don't cause a row between us. I've told you about that scent. When my aunt had been dead for more than thirty years, her house still smelt of the lavender furniture polish she had always used. Smells linger, especially in old houses."

"Well, Roger believes that the house is haunted."

"Hmphh! Roger. He's the expert is he?"

"Working in the archive office he hears of all sorts of funny things. And he's quite open minded about it. He thinks ..."

"Sod what Roger thinks!" Paul was angry now, the green ire rising.

"Roger will say anything to flatter you. He fancies you something rotten." Liz's jaw had dropped in amazement.

"Fancies me? Whatever gave you that idea?"

"You should have seen yourselves last night. It was sickening. You were like a big schoolgirl, listening to every gem that fell from his lips.

"That's not fair Paul. I was interested in what Roger was talking about. He's a fascinating man."

"He's a fascinating man!" Paul parodied, pouting his displeasure. Liz was silent for a moment, she didn't want to have a row, but Paul's accusations were unfair. "You're only being like this because Lucy couldn't make it!"

"Lucy! Lucy! You must be joking. It was a relief when she said that she couldn't come!" Lucy was an ex-colleague of Liz's and had made no secret of the fact that she thought Paul was wonderful. Over the years she had taken every opportunity to fawn and flatter, to lure and tempt. Paul, so much in love with Liz had always been totally impervious to Lucy's charms.

Liz took a deep breath. This was no way to carry on. What point was there in having a row with Paul. That wouldn't solve the mystery of the photograph. She looked down at it.

"Paul!" was all that she managed to gasp as she fell to the floor in a cold faint.

* * * * * * *

Some time later, in the kitchen over a pot of strong coffee, Paul and Liz looked at the picture. Both knew what they had seen; indeed, Simon too had seen the photograph, but now what was in the frame was merely a blur, a sea of sepia mud through which no image could be discerned.

"Well, now do you believe that there's something odd going on in this house Paul?" Liz regarded him through tears. Paul sat tight-lipped for a few moments,

unwilling to accept the evidence before him. He knew that once he accepted that there was indeed some sort of supernatural presence in Brabage Vicarage all his defences would come tumbling down. But what was he to say? The photograph frame was on the table between them; the picture that he knew he had seen, faded from sight.

"Yes Liz, yes," he said reluctantly. "There must be something." An expression of relief passed across Liz's features. At last Paul believed her. She wouldn't have to keep on fighting to convince him. Her relief was short-lived as Paul added,

"Yes Liz, definitely something. But what? And, more importantly, what are we going to do about it?" He stood up and went around the table. Leaning one hand on the back of Liz's chair, almost in imitation of the photograph both had seen, he bent forward and folded his other arm around her. She raised her face to his. They kissed. Somewhere in the house there was a long sigh.

CHAPTER FOUR

"Yes Roger, of course I understand."

Pause.

"Well then, I'll book a place for next week then, if that's OK? Monday. A week today."

Pause.

"Yes, anything really about the area, but at the moment I'm limiting my research into the house itself, Brabage Vicarage."

Pause.

"That would be splendid. If you get together all that you have and I'll see you next week. Thanks."

Pause.

"Yes, I think everyone enjoyed the party. See you next week then, and thanks for all your help."

Pause.

"Yes Roger, I think I know where Duke Street is. I know Chester quite well. 'Bye for now."

Liz replaced the telephone with a sigh. She had really hoped that she would be able to get along to the County Records Office today. She hadn't realised that she would have to book a place a week in advance. Still, Roger was being very helpful. At least when she did get there next week he would have most of the relevant material assembled. Sometimes it could be very useful to have an inside contact!

Liz walked through to the kitchen and made coffee. Yesterday she and Paul had decided that Liz would try to uncover as much information about the house as possible, The Records Office was the first step, and even Paul had agreed that Roger could prove extremely useful. Now there was to be this delay. What should she do in the meantime? Liz didn't want Paul to cool off, just as he had agreed on this investigation. Liz cradled her coffee mug and thought.

* * * * * * *

Hugging her coat tightly around her, Liz set out to walk the mile to the village shop. "Get out and about!" Paul had said, "meet a few of our neighbours. It's not good for you to be here, all alone, day after day." So she was off to the

village. No need to acknowledge that her prime aim was to do a little digging about the house and its former occupants. Here she was enjoying the short walk. Spring flowers were just beginning to make their appearance. Dog violets and primroses grew side by side, nestling under the shelter of the new growth of comfrey, dandelions and deadnettles.

Brabage was a small village, an anachronism really. It was almost entirely owned by a large estate. Most of the inhabitants were tenants of the estate, agricultural workers for the most part. The fact that the estate had built the majority of the houses in the village at several different periods in its history lent a certain uniformity to the main street that was oddly pleasing. The doors of the older buildings opened straight onto the pavement. Tenants made up for the lack of front garden by making good use of window boxes and tubs, holding the promise of Brabage being a blaze of colour in a month or so.

In common with many villages, the population of Brabage was falling, victim to the lack of employment in the countryside and the lure of the large towns. It was too far away from the major conurbations for all but the most hardy to consider commuting. This was no new phenomenon. Liz knew that the population of the village had been falling steadily since numbers were first decimated during the Great War. Even the church did not maintain a presence. After it had merged the two parishes of Brabage and the nearby Framley, the Establishment had sold the church and the vicarage.

Brabage was lucky to still maintain its village shop and Post Office. "Probably due to the temperament of Mrs. Allinson, the shopkeeper," thought Liz. "No one would dare to defy her and do their shopping anywhere but Brabage!" More than once Liz had been the recipient of hostile looks and cold words as the meagre contents of her basket were taken to the till.

The day was cold and Liz clutched her coat more tightly around her. The wind carried rain in its teeth. Liz was thankful to at last reach the shelter of the shop. She went in, closing the door behind her with relief.

"Morning Mrs. Graham," said the plump and brisk archetypal shopkeeper.

"Morning Mrs. Allinson. I notice that you omit the 'good'- intentionally I suppose?"

"What was that Mrs. Graham?" Mrs. Allinson had clearly not understood.

"I said, the weather's awful!" Liz compromised.

"Certainly is! Often turns out like this early March. Bet you're glad you're not travellin' to Manchester now eh?"

"Too right! But, please call me Liz. You've known me for almost a year now!"

Mrs. Allinson regarded Liz steadily from under suspicious eyebrows. The look conveyed the distinct impression that a year was a mere nothing in village time. Liz may as well have dropped from Mars yesterday.

Liz noted that Mrs. Allinson did not reciprocate her gesture by offering her own Christian name. Clearly it was all a matter of status, village hierarchy, and Liz had put her foot in it. She covered her embarrassment by picking up a basket and moving purposefully around the shelves, taking down things that she didn't really need. She had to get Mrs. Allinson talking about the vicarage. How to start was the problem!

"Oh, I'd better have some handcream too," Liz said, turning back to the shelves, "my hands are in a dreadful state!"

"Bound to be with all that decoratin' Plenty to keep you busy there I expect."

"Yes, every single room needs complete re-decoration. We expected it of course, with the house lying empty for so long."

"Not only that though. They was weird, them folks what had it last. Don' expect they dun much in the way o' decoratin' They was always so spooky an' quiet. Used to come in my shop now an' then. Give me the willies, I can tell you!"

This was the part of the vicarage's history with which Liz was familiar.

Brabage Vicarage had once belonged to an odd American cult. They had moved in during the early seventies in order to attempt communal living. Unfortunately they had discovered that the principle of everyone being responsible for everything had resulted in no-one taking on responsibility for anything: each person assuming that someone else would undertake the job in question. Repairs went unattended; the garden (except for the kitchen plot which was utilised fully) was permitted to revert to the wilderness that had greeted Paul and Liz.

Liz thought that part of the reason for the vicarage lying empty for so long had been not so much its state of disrepair but rather the complicated and protracted negotiations required in order to effect a sale with the labyrinthine cult organisation in the States. If they hadn't been determined most people would have given up. Liz had been extremely determined.

"What about before that though Mrs. Allinson?" Liz prompted, for once the shopkeeper had set off on the topic of the cult, she could keep going all day, her imagination scaling greater and greater heights as immoderation, exaggeration and speculation filled the gaps in her knowledge of the cult's activities.

"Well, I suppose it was a bit neglected as a school, leastways towards the end. I believe that it started up beautiful, all polished wood and tiled floors. By the time it were sold it was all green distemper an' lino!"

"I know, I've uncovered it, several layers down!" laughed Liz.

The bell clattered as another customer entered the shop, greeted Mrs. Allinson and began to move around the shelves.

"And before the school, it really was a vicarage?" Liz was determined to keep to her subject.

"Now you're going back many years, almost as far back as the First World War. Well beyond my time! There's not many people in Brabage as'd remember that!"

"My granddad remembers it!" chimed in a voice from behind Liz. Liz turned. A young housewife was waiting to pay for the groceries in her wire basket. "Granpa remembers all about them days. Can't tell you what 'e 'ad for 'is dinner but can tell you all about the school 'ere, the church, the vicar ..."

"The vicar!" Liz exclaimed, seizing the first opportunity that had been presented to discover anything about the people who had lived in the vicarage.

"Yeh! The vicar. Ses 'e wus a right bastard an' all!" Mrs. Allinson's face registered the proper disapproval towards a young person using such language, especially about a man of the cloth. Liz felt herself on the verge of giggling.

"What was vicar's name then, Mrs. Jenkins?" asked Mrs. Allinson.

"I don' know. Granpa Shipton will though! Many's the time 'e's moaned about bein' stuck out in the church porch fer not learnin 'is piece o' scripture fer Sunday school, or bin caned fer bein' naughty in prayers!" Liz's interest had been aroused.

"May I come and see your grandfather please Mrs. Jenkins?"

"Could do. Can't guarantee you'll get any sense out of 'im though!"

Mrs. Allinson interrupted, talking across Liz to Mrs. Jenkins.

"I meant to ask you, have you heard anything about what's happening to the estate? "

Liz knew that the owner of the estate had recently died and its future was uncertain. The village was a ferment of rumour, that the estate would be split; that certain parts would be sold; that a foreign business consortium was going to buy it and make huge changes.

They chatted for some time about the subject before Liz finally managed to make her escape.

"I'll give you a ring then Mrs. Jenkins, about talking to your grandfather."

"Yes, any time. I'll be 'appy to 'ave the ol' man kep' busy!"

The bell clanged as Liz closed the shop door behind her.

Mrs. Allinson and Mrs. Jenkins watched her retreating back.

"Well, she's a funny one an' no mistake!" Mrs. Allinson commented.

"Shouldn' be surprised if she weren't writin' a book. Someone like 'er don' come livin' in a place like this fer nothin'. You tell your granpa to watch that one. She'll write down everythin' he ses, write it in a book an' make a fortune out of 'im. You mark my words Mrs. Jenkins!"

"Seems OK though. I like that 'usband of 'ers. Funny they got no kids. My Tom ses they bin married about six or seven years."

"Not everyone 'as kids straight away Mrs. Jenkins," answered Mrs. Allinson, speaking from the expert knowledge of her widowed and childless state.

"Yeh, but six or seven years! Maybe things aren't, you know, aren't right between them."

The two women exchanged significant and eloquent glances. They leaned closer in order to indulge themselves in the ancient and time-honoured popular village pastime known universally as 'a good gossip'.

* * * * * * *

Liz fairly skipped the mile back to the vicarage. The rain had stopped and she hardly felt the wind at all. She hugged to herself the first real piece of knowledge about the past inhabitants of the vicarage. The vicar was a bastard! Liz giggled. She would go to see the old man, get him talking about the old days. He must be a mine of information.

Liz enjoyed the vigorous walk back to the vicarage. Paul was right, she didn't get out enough. Before they moved here they used to go walking almost every weekend. Now, though, now she was reluctant to leave the house for any length of time. There was always that fear, apprehension she felt, that something may happen in her absence.

She knew that she had changed since their move to Brabage, and Paul had told her so frequently enough during the past few weeks. But how could she explain to him the compulsion she felt inside, the fascination with the house. Often she would spend hour after hour just looking out of the windows, dreaming of what the place had been like in the old days when it was a proper family home. In spite of all that Paul had said, it wasn't an obsession; Liz was sure that it wasn't an obsession. She just felt caught up in the atmosphere of the house. There was something there; a presence from the past, and she, Liz Graham, would find out what it was. She had taken the first step now, she was on her way!

* * * * * * *

She watched from the vantage point of the middle attic window as Liz made her way towards the vicarage. She could see the entire sweep of the drive, from the gateway to the front door. Things were being put right. The nettles which had so overwhelmed the house had been cut but the dense undergrowth choking the path leading to the summerhouse had not yet been tackled. Pity! Daffodils were in bloom beneath the old oaks, their branches bare as yet. Here and there the celandines were showing their faces to the new spring. The daffodils were almost flattened by the strong gusts of wind, but as soon as it dropped they righted themselves, their delicate appearance belying their inner strength. They stood boldly to attention, ready to face the next onslaught. Liz looked excited. The watcher knew that Liz was her link; Liz was the person she had been waiting for. Things were going to be alright again. She waited, with keen anticipation, Liz's homecoming.

Liz walked briskly up the gravel drive. Ten yards from the house she stopped. She didn't know why she stopped. She looked up at the facade of the house. Just for a moment she had felt that she was being watched. She looked hard at every window. Nothing! Some window frames had been replaced, others repaired. Very few boasted curtains as yet, just the main living room and bedroom. Liz contemplated all the work ahead. Her mind was alive with colour schemes and plans for various rooms. She looked at each window in turn, seeing in her mind's eye the completed job. Her scrutiny paused at the attic windows. Was that a trick of the light, a reflection, or was there a figure standing at the centre window? Liz stared hard trying to make out the shape. Fascinated, she approached the house. The figure disappeared. 'Must have been a reflection' she thought. She went back to her former position but was unable to regain the illusion. She looked up at the sky. Dark grey clouds were being pushed along by a savage wind. The light was changing from moment to moment.

Satisfied that what she had seen was a reflection, that her eyes had been deceived by the scurrying clouds, she mounted the steps and put her key into the lock.

CHAPTER FIVE

It was only just after four in the afternoon when Liz heard the scrunch of tyres on gravel. She went to the front door and was surprised when, on opening, it revealed Paul's car. She ran down the steps.

"Paul, you're home early!" and she threw her arms around his neck, kissing him. It had been a long afternoon, and she was bursting with her news about the prospective interview with 'Granpa'.

Extricating himself from her embrace Paul spoke excitedly, "I had to come home early. I picked up a special present for you, look!" and he indicated the back seat of his car.

A crossbreed dog (collie and labrador Liz thought) sat staring dolefully out of the car window. The dog was mainly white with a black patch over one eye and ear; the other ear was partly black and partly spotted. The dog regarded Liz solemnly, its deep brown eyes watching her apprehensively.

"She's called Sally, is about two years old, fully vaccinated, house-trained and I got her from the RSPCA." Paul's words were stumbling over each other in his anxiety. He so wanted Liz to like Sally. He had only met her himself a couple of hours ago, and already she had wrapped herself firmly around his heart. He needn't have worried. Liz was opening the car door, eager to make a fuss of their new pet.

"She's had a horrible life, according to the girl in the kennels. Her first owner got rid of her because she couldn't be bothered taking her for walks. The second owner emigrated and didn't think it a good idea to take a dog. Her last owner was an old lady. Unfortunately she died. Poor old Sally was left in the house with the old lady for a day and a half before her howling alerted the neighbours. Quite a traumatic short life eh?"

But Liz didn't appear to be listening. She had got into the car and was busy making friends with Sally. She spoke from the back seat.

"Of course you realise that people will tell us that Sally is just a child substitute."

"So what. It doesn't matter what people say. I thought that you needed a bit of daytime company, and when a baby comes along Sally will love it just as much as she loves us." Liz noted that Paul had said 'when' not 'if'.

Her face clouded. She didn't think she'd ever get pregnant!

Sally licked Liz's face as she fastened the lead to the collar. She guided the

dog out of the car and towards the front door. Already the dog was firmly attached to Liz and didn't intend to let her out of its sight.

"Faithless hussy!" Paul exclaimed as Liz led Sally in. "I thought that it was me you loved. Remember who rescued you from the kennels!" But his light-hearted words belied his anxiety as he watched Sally closely. If there really was something supernatural in the house, surely the dog would sense it.

He sighed with relief as Liz led the dog into the hall. No hesitation at all! He stood back and watched as Sally eagerly explored the ground floor of her new home. He admitted to himself that he had started to have his own doubts about Liz's 'spirit' but they were being laid to rest by the sight of that confident tail, held high and buzzing through all the rooms.

* * * * * * *

They were awoken in the middle of the night by a long, mournful howling coming from downstairs.

"We'll have to go down to her," muttered Liz, her voice thick with sleep.

"No, I'll go. You stay here. No sense in both of us getting cold," replied Paul.

"I'd rather come with you," insisted Liz, the old familiar feelings of apprehension creeping over her.

Downstairs they found Sally sitting bolt upright on her beanbag bed, nose pointing to the ceiling. As they entered the kitchen another long howl rumbled deep in Sally's throat.

"Thank God we've got no near neighbours!" said Paul, approaching the dog bed. "Quiet now Sally. It's OK" He patted and stroked her; she looked up at him apologetically. "I know, I know, it's your first night in a strange house. You'll settle. There's nothing to be afraid of here!"

"I suppose that we were warned that she was a howler," put in Liz. "What do you think? Shall we take her back upstairs with us?"

"You know what the RSPCA said - her own bed and make her sleep in it!"

"Well, she belongs to us now, not the RSPCA. Personally I'd prefer her to sleep in the bedroom. After all she is supposed to be keeping us company! Will you bring her beanbag?"

"OK then. I don't mind where she sleeps as long as I'm not pushed out onto the beanbag by the Aga. Cosy it may be but it's not my idea of comfort!"

Liz called Sally to her. The dog entered the hall fearfully, looking around timidly. With lots of encouragement from Liz she did climb the stairs, albeit

reluctantly, ears down and belly close to the floor. As she entered the bedroom a ridge of hair bristled down her spine, her hackles came up and her ears flattened against her head. She emitted a low growl. Liz reached down and fondled her ears. Heartened slightly, Sally began to wag her tail. Liz got back into bed. There was an immediate 'thump' and Sally landed alongside her. She pressed close to Liz.

"Alright Sal, nothing to be afraid of!" But as soon as she uttered these words Liz knew that there was indeed something in the room; that hard to define presence that she felt so frequently.

Paul came through the door clutching a huge armful of dogbed. He put it down close to their own bed.

"Oh, I see that you won't be needing this. Sally's already chosen her spot!" He pretended to be stern but he was really secretly pleased that this dog had adopted them so readily. He got into bed, reaching out to tickle the dog's ears. Sally seemed to forget her earlier fear and responded to the attention.

They lay for some time, both trying in vain to get back to sleep. The noises in the night had unsettled them more than they cared to admit. Sleep seemed very far away.

"What about a hot drink? We're obviously not going to get back to sleep easily," said Paul eventually.

"I can't see me being able to get back to sleep without a cup of tea," responded Liz, relieved that she was not the only restless one. "Should I make it?"

"No, you stay here with Sal. I'll only be a couple of minutes."

As soon as Paul had gone Sally began to scrabble madly at the quilt. Liz lifted one corner. Sally immediately disappeared down to the bottom of the bed. From the landing Paul caught the movement.

"Very unhygienic you know, having a dog in bed, even if you did bath her earlier!" he called, his indulgent tone giving the lie to his stern words.

"I'll move her when you get back," said Liz, knowing full well that Sally would probably spend all night in the bed.

Liz heard Paul's steps descend to the kitchen. She looked through the open bedroom door, out onto the landing. In spite of being well-lit she thought that she saw a shadow out there, just about the size of a cat. She stared at it, trying to puzzle out exactly what was creating that small patch of darkness.

As she stared she realised that the shadow, the blackness, was growing. She shook her head, trying to convince herself that it was all an optical illusion. Because she was mesmerised, transfixed by what was probably an ordinary pool

of shadow, she was imagining the increase in size. She closed her eyes. What made her open them again, suddenly, was a long exhaled sigh, right next to her. In fact she felt the breath blow into her face. She became aware that Sally was whimpering and pressing hard against her legs, quivering so much that Liz half expected to see the entire bed shaking.

The sigh was repeated, but this time it tailed off into the sound of sobbing. Liz looked towards the sobs. The shadow was now much larger. It most certainly was not her eyes playing tricks. It was growing rapidly now and as it grew so the sobbing intensified. Liz's eyes widened in fear. She willed herself to turn away, but she could not: she was totally transfixed. The patch of darkness seethed only yards in front of her. It attained the size of a slight adult and ceased expanding. Whatever it was began to glide nearer to the bed. Liz was paralysed with fear. She could see that it was a figure, although she could not discern details. As it approached she could do nothing but watch its progress. She heard a whimper and, with a shock she realised that the sound, the sound of fear, had escaped from her own mouth. The figure halted. This was the pause Liz needed. The trance was broken. Without hesitation she dived down to join Sally beneath the safety of the covers.

She lay in her dark cave. The sounds outside, muffled through the quilt, grew in intensity. What could she do? Instinct told her to yell her head off, scream, call for Paul. Intellect told her that whatever the nature of the apparition it most certainly could not hurt her. Wasn't there supposed to exist some verbal formula for use in banishing spirits? Liz attempted to reason with herself.

There could be nothing there. It was only her imagination. Her own logic countered that argument by evidencing the behaviour of Sally. Caught up in her own thoughts it took Liz some time to realise that the room had quietened. All was still. She felt a firm hand on her shoulder. During her musings, her dithering, Paul must have returned and assumed that she had fallen asleep. Confidence restored, she threw back the quilt.

The room was empty: no Paul: no shadow. There was only the feeling that someone, something was there; watching and waiting.

Without warning Liz was engulfed, enfolded in insubstantial arms. She was being stifled, suffocated in overwhelming blackness. The scent of violets was everywhere. Liz could hear, or rather feel the figure which had swamped her being racked with wild sobbing. She wanted to scream. She opened her eyes but all she could see was blackness. Once more there was the feeling of being caught up in a maelstrom, being swept around in a whirlpool. She became one

with the grief-stricken figure. Her head spun; her heart was being torn apart. She felt no malevolence, only deep sorrow. She was like a puppet, a lifeless and broken doll being rocked backwards and forwards by a power which she was unable to comprehend. She was helpless. All was blackness.

"Lizzie! Lizzie! Wake up!" Paul was back. "And you said that you wouldn't get off to sleep again without a cup of tea!" He had brought two mugs of tea and a handful of dog biscuits on a tray.

"I ... I ... didn't fall asleep Paul."

"Just resting your eyes, I know!" Paul began to tease but realised that Liz was very upset. Tears trickled down her cheeks. She began to sob, biting her lower lip between clenched teeth. Paul put his arms around her.

"Come on Liz. What's wrong?"

"Paul, it - she - was here, here in this room! Whatever it is in this house is just so full of grief and sorrow."

"Oh, Lizzie," Paul interrupted, "you must have been dreaming, having a nightmare. You're awake now, and remember, Sally's here. She'd know if there was anything - anything supernatural about. I guess that she'd be howling the place down!"

On hearing her name a shamefaced Sally emerged. Her ears lay close to her head, her eyes were downcast. Paul reached out and stroked her. "Come on Sal, tell Lizzie that there's nothing to worry about."

Sally nuzzled into Liz who cradled her in her arms: a warm embrace so different from that last. At the recollection she shuddered.

"Lizzie love, you're shivering. Drink this tea and let's get snuggled down and back to sleep."

"Paul! Are you seriously trying to tell me that you heard nothing?"

"I heard a few bumps, which were obviously you larking about with Sally."

"I wasn't 'larking about' with Sally. Didn't you hear the crying?"

"Crying? Of course not. I'd have come straight back upstairs if I thought you were upset."

"Not me, I wasn't upset. It was her crying! She was weeping, sobbing. It filled the house. Couldn't you hear it?" Liz was getting very close to hysteria.

Paul shouted, "Liz, there was nothing, I promise you!"

"There WAS Paul, and I was in the middle of it. Such grief, such loss."

Liz closed her eyes. Her mind seemed to be drifting. "Rachel, weeping for her children, and she would not be comforted ... "

"Liz! Liz!" Paul was beginning to panic. Liz took no notice. She was in a world of her own.

"... Because they were no more." Liz finished.

Paul took a firm hold on his wife's shoulders. He squeezed. Hard. "Liz!"

As though she were surfacing from a deep, dark pool she opened her eyes and stared at Paul.

"Liz! What are you saying?"

"Wh-wh-what?" Liz was clearly bewildered.

"Rachel, weeping for her children and so on. Where did that come from?"

"It's from the Bible I think." Liz's wits seemed to be returning. Paul, more afraid than he cared to admit, tried to jolly her out of whatever state she was in.

"I never knew you were religious. It must be the vicarage bringing it out."

Liz was calming down. Paul reached out for her and held her close. Her tremblings ceased. Gently he stroked her hair. Poor Liz. What was happening to her? He could feel her tension, feel the tautness of her muscles as he held her. She didn't even feel like his Liz any more. Lovingly he kissed the top of her head.

"We'll talk about this in the morning. Let's get some sleep," he muttered. Maybe he would suggest that Liz should see a doctor. At the thought he smiled grimly to himself. When he had suggested this to Liz a few days earlier her only response had been, "A priest would be better than a doctor. A priest, complete with bell, book and candle." Paul was still pondering the problem when he fell asleep holding Liz closely in his protective embrace.

CHAPTER SIX

Bright spring sunshine flooded into the bedroom. During the night Sally had resumed her proper position on the beanbag. Paul and Liz lay cradled together in a cocoon of warmth, each lost deep inside their own thoughts.

Paul was puzzled. Liz seemed to have changed, physically changed, since she had left work. He could understand a slight change in muscle tone or in the shape of her body, but, he found it hard to describe exactly what it was that felt so different about his wife. He was as familiar with Liz's body as he was with his own, but as they had made love a short time ago, he had felt that he was holding someone else, a stranger. Her body was charged, fired by an energy Paul had found difficult to match so early in the morning. She had writhed and responded to him in an entirely new way. He found the new Lizzie exhilarating and exciting. Smiling to himself he hugged Liz closer to his chest.

After a few moments Liz spoke, her voice muffled by his closeness.

"Paul, about last night."

"Let's not talk about that Liz, let's forget all about it."

Liz stiffened in his arms. "You don't believe me do you? You don't think that there was anything here at all?"

"I'm not saying that Liz." But his mind was working on the theory frequently advanced to explain poltergeists and other seemingly inexplicable events. Perhaps it was all down to Lizzie's new found energy brimming over. He didn't think that Liz was imagining it exactly, more a case of being the unwitting cause of things.

Liz pulled away from him, the intimate mood broken by her hostility. "I didn't imagine it all you know. And anyway, what about Sally? She must have been imagining things too!"

Paul thought for a moment. He didn't want to upset her but he was sure that Liz, isolated in the brooding atmosphere of the old house, was creating problems where none existed. She needed something positive to do. He had an idea.

"What about that book Simon suggested? Thought any more about it?"

"Actually, I didn't get round to telling you yesterday but I've booked a place in the County Records Office for next Monday. Roger ... "

At the mention of Roger's name Paul's face clouded but Liz ignored the fact.

"Roger is going to assemble some material for me to work on."

"Good old Roger! Why can't you make a start before next week?"

Liz explained about the booking system and Paul frowned unhappily. He had hoped that Liz could get going on something straight away.

"In the meantime though I have arranged to go and interview one of the old men in the village. He remembers a lot about the area and even remembers the last vicar!"

"Were you thinking that we'd go today? I could do with using this day off to get a few jobs done round the place."

"Actually, I'd planned to go by myself. I don't know how he'd take to two of us. He may be a bit overwhelmed."

"May resent a man going along you mean. I suppose you intend to wring every ounce of information out of the poor old sod by turning on the famous charm. I'd just be in the way, queer your pitch!"

Liz was about to protest indignantly when she saw the mischievous sparkle in Paul's eye. She picked up a pillow and threw it at him.

"The famous charm as you call it, demands a cup of tea, in bed, and a request to let your dog out."

"My dog! My dog!" and he threw the pillow back. In a moment they were locked in a playful tussle the earlier animosity forgotten.

* * * * * * *

It took Liz only a short time to get herself ready and walk down to the village. The Jenkinses lived at the far end, beyond the shop and just the other side of the 'pub. In the 1940s the local council had built a small crescent of houses intended for agricultural workers. It was a time when few people wished to live in small villages, when the young folk went off to the towns to live and to work in the industries that sprang up after the war. Old Mr. Shipton had brought up his family in Brabage. Most of his children had married and moved away, but one granddaughter, Eileen, had married a local man, Tom Jenkins. When they had been unable to find a house that they could afford Eileen had made the sensible suggestion that she and her husband should move in with the old man, by now widowed. In caring for him they would have a home of their own. The arrangement seemed to suit all concerned and now the house echoed once more with children's voices as Eileen and Tom reared their own family.

Liz unhooked the gate and walked up the path. The front garden was neat and well-tended. Small shrubs were pruned into conformity; roses had been planted with military precision. It was a garden that would not be out of place in an urban

avenue. To Liz it was a source of great amusement that country people never appeared to keep the cottage gardens which town folks made great efforts to cultivate in the mistaken idea that they were emulating village life! She reached the front door. The brass door knocker had been worn smooth by years of conscientious polishing. Liz took the pixie in her hand and knocked.

"Come in! Come in Mrs. Graham. I'm glad to see you. Granpa's through in the back room. I'll take you in and introduce you, then I'll leave you to it. I've got a million and one things to do I can tell you!"

Eileen bustled on down the hall leaving Liz to follow. Looking around the spotless room Liz could not imagine any of the 'million and one things' Eileen Jenkins found it necessary to do.

Eileen led the way into a room dominated by a large window looking out onto the rear garden which seemed to be given over entirely to vegetables. An old man sat in a chair next to the window, sucking contentedly on an empty pipe.

"Granpa!" said Eileen, quite loudly. When there was no response she yelled out, "GRANPA!" Still the old man didn't stir. Eileen reached out and touched his shoulder. He jumped and opened his eyes.

"Granpa, this is Mrs. Graham."

"Liz, please!" interjected Liz.

"Granpa, this is Liz. She's come to talk to you about the old days. You talk to 'er and I'll go and put the kettle on for a nice cuppa!"

"Sit down! Sit down!" The old voice was surprisingly strong. "You'm 'er from the vicarage an't you?"

"That's right Mr. Shipton!" bawled Liz, following Eileen's example on volume.

"No need ter shout Missus. I'm a bit deaf right enough, but if I look at yer, I can 'ear alright! An' call me Granpa, everyone else does."

"Sorry! Is it OK with you - Granpa, if I record our talk?" Liz indicated the small tape recorder she had brought with her.

"Don't mind. Let's have a look at 'im." Grandpa Shipton reached out and took hold of the recorder, examining it closely. Liz prepared to explain its workings in the 'heap big magic' mode but was fortunately stopped by Grandpa's comment:- "Aye, I thought so. Your'ns the same as mine!"

He got up and went over to a cupboard. Opening the doors he took out a machine of the same make and model as Liz's. "Use this a lot I do. Tape things fer our Luke ter take ter school. Part of 'is 'istory he tells me. D'y'know that I'm the oldest person in Brabage." He grinned proudly at Liz. "Remember two

world wars I do, an' rationin' an' electric comin' - an' the first buses. Now, Missus, what d'you want ter interview me about - an is it goin' on local radio?"

* * * * * * *

Paul waved Liz off on her visit to Grandpa Shipton. He closed the door and leaned back against it for a moment, thinking of the work he would like to do. First though he should really take Sally out. As if reading his mind Sally appeared from the kitchen, new ball in her mouth. She padded over to Paul and dropped the ball invitingly at his feet.

"OK then," he laughed," one short game. Come on!" and he opened the door and stepped out.

A quarter of an hour was spent in throwing the ball for Sally to retrieve. It wasn't as good exercise as a long walk would have been, but he really wanted to get on with some jobs in the house.

Paul came around the side of the house and glanced upwards, examining the facade and the guttering, noting the work still to be done. He sighed. It seemed never-ending. Still it would all be worth it - eventually!

He was examining the guttering above the old attics when he was sure that he detected a movement behind the glass of the central window. He stared hard. Nothing. It must have been a reflection - or his imagination! He was getting as bad as Liz. All that business last night! What on earth could he do about it? He was still pondering the problem when he saw what appeared to be a candle flame, dancing in the gloom behind the glass of the window. He closed his eyes for a moment; he opened them. It had gone. 'Christ! Liz is even beginning to spook me now!' he thought to himself. But as he looked upwards he was sure that he could see the hint of a figure, the pale smudge of a white face staring out.

'I'm not having this!' Paul thought. 'What I think I'm seeing must be something inside the attic, some old furniture or a scrap of curtain.' He decided that if he could satisfy himself about the optical illusion, he could then demonstrate to Liz when she returned from the village that the weird things that she was experiencing were more than likely self-generated. He called to Sally and raced inside.

His smug certainty didn't prevent a shiver of apprehension running its cold fingers down his spine as he mounted the bare wooden stairs to the top storey. Outside the centre attic door he listened carefully. Nothing to be heard but Sally's padding along the landing, intent on joining in this new game. He reached out for

the doorhandle, gripped it and began to turn it slowly. As he did so he became aware of a dull thudding, like a heartbeat. He paused for a moment. Then he realised that the sound was indeed a heartbeat. His own! It seemed to be thundering in his ears. Shrugging off his agitation he opened the door and strode in.

The room he entered was bare and lifeless. There were some boxes not yet unpacked, bundles of books, a couple of old suitcases. Odd pieces of furniture stood about and Paul knew that some of the junk had been there before they had moved in. As they renovated the house they had put anything that may prove useful at a later date up in the attic. Everything was covered in dust. Paul looked across at the window. It was bare of curtains and there was no furniture near to it.

Carefully Paul picked his way between obstacles towards the window. As he did so his eye was caught by a movement away to his right. He whirled around, and laughed in relief as he realised that what he had seen was his own reflection in a spotted mirror propped up on the cast-iron mantle of the old fireplace. His relief was short-lived, for as he stared into the mirror he became aware of a smell of candlewax. Between him and the mirror he could discern the faintest wisps of smoke, as though a wick had been hastily extinguished. He went over and picked up the stub of a candle, stuck by its own wax, to the mantelshelf. He examined it closely. It was unlike anything he had seen. It was creamy-white and felt much waxier than the candles he and Liz kept under the sink in case of a power failure.

He was still turning the candle over in his hands, feeling the warm soft wax near the wick that proved its recent quenching when he heard laughter coming from the garden below.

Hastily he pushed the piece of candle into his pocket and ran to the window. Reaching it just in time to see the tail end of a figure, disappearing into the dense shrubbery. 'Jesus! That's all I need. Village kids messing about in the garden. I'd better go and find them and throw them out!'

As he ran down the stairs and out of the door Paul was mentally recalling the plans he had seen of the vicarage. Somewhere in the middle of that wild part of the garden, a part that he and Liz had not yet got round to clearing, there was a pool and some sort of a summerhouse. The shrubbery had been too dense and too overgrown to allow them to yet reach it, but it looked as though Paul was going exploring now whether he liked it or not. If there was an accident, if anything were to happen to any of the kids he and Liz would be to blame.

As he ran across the lawn he called out to Sally to follow. She stayed, stubbornly refusing to leave the terrace. He shrugged his shoulders and ran on.

As Paul reached the edge of the jungle of shrubs he heard the laughter again, tinkling merriment, just out of reach. He pushed his way through the branches and shouted.

"Hey! You! Come out of there!" He waited. Nothing. Then there was movement and laughter, a strangely enticing laughter, just out of sight. He called again, trying to make his voice sound authoritative. His only answer was more laughter. Paul felt an overwhelming compulsion to follow.

He forced his way on, thrusting his body through snatching vegetation. His feet were mired and heavy, twigs were stuck in his hair, down his jumper. The ancient rhododendron branches were thicker than his arm, and really hurt as they sprang back and hit him in the chest and legs. He was sweating now; his face and hands were grimy. As he heard the laughter ring out once more out of his reach he determined to give the children a roasting - when he caught them!

Suddenly he was out, clear of the tangle. The undergrowth closed behind him and he saw that he was on the banks of a small pool, weed-choked and green with algae. A few yards from where he had emerged lay the rotting summerhouse. There was no sign of any children; no sound of laughter now. Everywhere was eerily silent. The only noise was his own ragged breathing. Then he heard it, coming from the other side of the summerhouse: A low moan.

"I knew they'd get into trouble!" Paul muttered to himself. "This place is dangerous!" Carefully he made his way across the rotting verandah of the summerhouse, determined to vent his spleen on the trespassers - as soon as he managed to lay his hands on them!

He stepped off the other side of the verandah. There was nothing. They must have slipped away again! He turned back. Crossing the verandah for the second time he turned to look inside the summerhouse. He pushed on the doors, rattled the handle. Locked! Of course they were locked. What else had he expected? Shading his eyes with his hand to avoid reflection he tried to look through the grimy glass. He stepped back, rubbed a small circle clean and peered inside.

The interior was a sorry sight: Dilapidated chintz curtains were mildewed and torn; a rickety old table sat in the middle of the floor with equally rickety chairs around it. Shelves on the wall had collapsed at one end, their books strewn about, lying where they had fallen. Paul wanted to get inside, to root about; after all this was a part of his property that he had not yet seen! He tried the handle once again. Perhaps the doors were merely jammed? He pushed them, hard. Their rotten appearance belied their strength. They remained firmly closed against him.

He was just considering landing a well-aimed kick in the region of the lock when he heard the laughter again. The sound brought him sharply to attention. He had almost forgotten why he was here! This time the voice came from behind the summerhouse, near the boundary wall. It was almost as though whoever was there was luring Paul onwards, leading him somewhere. Paul forced his body around the side. There was a gap of only a few feet between the rotting wood of the summerhouse and the stone wall. The trunk of a large silver birch filled this space, the crown of the tree towering almost twenty feet above. Paul heard footsteps in the lane on the other side of the wall. He scrambled up the tree and topped the wall ready to confront the trespassers who had played ducks and drakes with him and clearly escaped from the grounds only moments before.

"Hi! What are you doing up there?" It was Liz, standing below, staring up at a dishevelled Paul.

"Oh, I was just doing a little exploring and I thought that I heard kids messing about down here. Did anyone pass you?"

"I haven't seen a soul since leaving the village!" Liz stared at him, puzzled. Paul tried to shrug off his anxiety. He didn't want Liz worried any more than she was already.

"They must have run off in the other direction." Now was not the time to let Liz think that he was imagining things. Imagining things? His hand strayed to the small stump of candle in his pocket. That was certainly not imagination. Liz was talking to him. He hadn't heard what she was saying.

"Sorry, what did you say?"

"I said, you're not the only one to have climbed up there!" Paul looked at her eagerly, thinking that she had seen their trespassers after all.

"Look at the tree trunk, beside you," Liz went on. Paul turned and examined the tree. There was a mass of carving scarring the living bark: Hearts; initials; names and dates. Paul's fingers traced the names of Sarah, Ellen, at least two Williams and several Johns. The carvers were doubtlessly long since dead. He turned back to Liz.

"Maybe I should carve us up here!" he laughed.

"Don't you dare - you vandal," replied Liz, "and if you've nothing better to do ..."

"Cheek! I've found the summerhouse!"

"What's it like?"

"Rotten! Wait 'til you see it though. There's a small pool in front of it. It must have been lovely once. It's all locked up. We must check to see if we have a key.

I'll meet you at the front of the house. I won't get down your side - too high! I'll go back the way I came." His head disappeared behind the wall.

As he slid down the trunk he caught his hand on a rough patch and felt the warm blood flow. He put the hand to his mouth at the same time looking to see what had caught his flesh. His blood was smeared across the silver bark of the birch, crimson over a carved heart. As he read "John and Lizzie 1917" an unaccountable wave of horror washed over him. He heard screams, sobbing, a fierce wind rushing past his ears. He turned and fought his way blindly out, not heeding the barbs and branches that snatched at him hungrily. The overwhelming suffocation of blinding panic was all his consciousness.

Out on the lawn he stopped, panting, not understanding the terror that had possessed him. He looked up. Liz was at that moment coming through the gate. She saw his evident distress and broke into a run. Paul only blacked out when he saw that dark, shadowy figure keeping pace with her, matching her, stride for stride; rushing forward to engulf him in its horror.

CHAPTER SEVEN

Paul was glad to sit quietly at the kitchen table as Liz cleaned and bandaged his hand. She teased him unmercifully about fainting; his preference for going off exploring rather that getting down to any real work; his fuss over what was, after all, a very minor injury.

As she chaffed, Paul's uninjured hand fingered the candle stump in his pocket. How much of what had happened to him since Liz went out could be put down to imagination, even a sort of hysteria induced by his exertions through the undergrowth? On the other hand, perhaps Liz was right and there really was something haunting the vicarage.? Quickly he closed his mind against that possibility. The idea was nonsense and to pursue it, even within the privacy of his own mind, was madness. Let Liz have her fancies if she liked, let her follow her whim and investigate the history of the vicarage, but he would have none of it.

His traitorous mind asked where the candle stump had come from, still warm from recent burning; what had been the nature of the figure he had seen at the window; who he had been following through the shrubbery to the summerhouse. He refused to listen to the insidious questions, instead he asked Liz how she had got on with Grandpa Shipton.

"Splendidly! What a character! He remembers so much about the early part of the century in Brabage. He was only a young lad when the First World War broke out."

"So, I suppose that's what you ended up talking about?" Paul smiled, acknowledging Liz's interest in the period. In fact she had spent many years at Marshall's as their expert on the years leading up to the First World War, its duration and aftermath.

"Not only that. He had lots to say about the vicarage and its occupants. It would appear that he was 'a bit of a lad' and that the vicar was intent on beating it out of him!"

Paul was going to continue asking questions but Liz got up and fetched the tape recorder.

"Here, listen for yourself," and she plugged in the machine.

Grandpa Shipton's strong old voice filled the kitchen. Paul leaned forward, listening intently. Liz took out a pad and began to jot down notes.

Grandpa Shipton started by introducing himself, proudly stating his age. Well practised in the medium he went on to reminisce about his younger days in the

village. He told of the thriving shops (three at one time, including the Post Office), the other 'pub - now converted into a house, and the school which he had attended until the age of fourteen. That too was now a house.

Guided by a skilful Liz he began to talk about some of the characters he remembered. He coughed and spluttered with laughter when relating the tale of the greengrocer who, every morning, set out his wares on the pavement in front of his shop only to have his apples and pears pilfered by the village boys. He mounted sporadic attacks on them but usually came off worst, for while chasing one culprit across the village green, a compatriot would be liberating the odd apple behind the pursuing back of the shopkeeper.

Knowing that Liz had wanted only to talk of the vicarage and its inhabitants Paul admired the tact and patience she displayed in leading the old man to her goal. Prompting him about his schooldays she managed to bring Grandpa to the subject of the vicar.

"Eileen told me that you didn't get on with the vicar, Grandpa"

"No-one got on with 'im! 'E wus a bastard! Aubrey 'e wus called, Reverend Aubrey. 'E wus wicked to us scholars I can tell yer!"

"But surely his own family got on with him?" came in Liz's voice, fishing for details, but, once started on his subject, the old man refused to be diverted.

He continued, talking over Liz's voice, "Part way through the war - the Great War I mean - 'e came into school ter teach us kids. I spect the government made 'im, parsons only workin' on a Sunday! 'E'd bin bad enough wi' us on Sundays, beatin' us if we didn' know us scripture, mekkin us stand in the church porch if we wus naughty in Sunday school! Any road, he come in to teach us, so did his daughter, Miss Elizabeth.

Liz seized immediately on this piece of information. "Elizabeth? Was she his only daughter? Did he have any sons? What about his wife?"

Grandpa stoically ignored her interruption.

"Now Elizabeth (Lizzie we called 'er behind 'er back) wus lovely. Us lads wus all in love with 'er. She must've bin about twenty or so when she taught in school. Every day we used ter compete wi' each other ter see who could bring 'er something nice inter school. Some days we pinched apples or pears, others we picked 'er some flowers. Eh, one mornin' I remember, we 'adn't bin able ter pinch any o' Hughes's fruit an' I were desperate ter get Miss Lizzie somethin'. As we wus walkin' down the street, what should I see but some beautiful yeller flowers, daffodils. Us village folk never grew many flowers then, we 'ad ter give all us efforts over ter growin' veg. Food were short in the war yer know!"

Liz tried to interject, to tell Grandpa that she knew all about the rationing, shortages and panic buying during the Great War, but the old man ploughed on.

"The flowers wus in a winderbox, Missus Marner's. She wus rich compared to the rest of us an' she grew flowers where we grew cabbages! Any roads, I sin these flowers an' I thought them wus just the thing fer Miss Lizzie. So, I picked the buggers!" The old man wheezed with laughter at the memory.

"I'd just got a fair bunch of 'em when I 'eard a noise behind me. Who should be comin' out o' Mrs. Marner's but the vicar, ol' Aubrey 'imself! 'Hey, you boy, what do you think you're doing?' 'e shouted in 'is posh voice. Well. I didn't wait ter tell 'im. I scarpered! Course, an' ol' man like that never 'ad a chance o' catchin' me, an' I got clean away - at least I thought I 'ad!"

"Miss Lizzie made a great fuss over the flowers. I wus proud as a peacock, struttin' in front o' all the other lads. We'd jus' settled down ter lessons when the door opened an' in come the 'eadmaster wi' the vicar in tow. They jus' stood there, the pair of 'em, lookin' at all the class. Next thing the Reverend lifted 'is arm an' points straight ter me. 'That's him, headmaster, that's the boy!' 'e says, actin' like God on Judgement Day. 'Come out here Shipton!' said the 'eadmaster. 'Vicar tells me he saw you stealing flowers. What have you got to say for yourself?' Course, I pipes up, 'Vicar tells us in Sunday school that all the flowers belong ter God, an' that they're there fer us all t' enjoy.' (I wus a cheeky little sod in them days!). 'Quiet boy! And don't be insolent!' yells the 'eadmaster. Then 'e looks across at Miss Lizzie's desk, an' there, bright an' sunny, is the daffodils. I thought 'e wus goin' ter bust. Poor Miss Aubrey jus' went as red as a beetroot! 'Bend over boy!' 'Eadmaster says. I did, an' 'e whacked me. Give me two gooduns an'all. I wus jus' straightenin' up when 'e says, 'That was for stealing. Now you are going to get another beating for being cheeky to the vicar.' An' I did. Through it all the vicar stood there, smilin'. When it wus over - an' I wus cryin', I don't mind tellin' yer - Reverend Aubrey says 'Let that be a lesson to you boys. The wages of sin are never worthwhile!' An' 'e took the flowers off Miss Lizzie's desk an' walked out!"

Neither Paul nor Liz had noticed the growing chill in the kitchen as the anecdote unfolded on the tape recorder. Nor had they seen that Sally had silently crept from her bed by the stove and along into the living room.

On the tape Liz managed quite easily to encourage Grandpa to talk about the Reverend Aubrey and his family. As his voice rattled on the temperature in the kitchen dropped even lower and the air began to darken.

Grandpa told of the Aubrey family: the Reverend, his wife and two daughters

had all lived in the vicarage. Reverend Aubrey had been a stickler for punctuality and had frequently halted a service or Sunday school in order to scold the latecomer - even if it was his own wife or daughters. He ruled strictly with the rod in the Sunday school, and later in the day school, and it was Grandpa's opinion that even Lizzie and her sister Mary were afraid of their father. He had expected them to marry well but rarely permitted them to mix socially.

The Aubrey daughters had taught in the Sunday school, Elizabeth also undertaking teaching duties in the day school. The two girls were always about the village, parish visiting, and although Grandpa had liked both girls, it was for Elizabeth he had felt most affection. She had always seemed the kindest and most tender-hearted of the two. She had particularly loved the children and had taken special interest in those in her care.

Liz was interested to hear Grandpa talk about the rumours of Elizabeth Aubrey's pacifism during the war, but Reverend Aubrey had taken great care to "brush that well under the mat. A sly one was the old Reverend, no mistake!" Grandpa had added.

Grandpa had gone on to tell Liz of the merger of the parishes of Brabage and Framley. The Vicar had moved to Framley and the vicarage sold. The church had stayed open until more recent times, but now that too had been disposed of.

Liz asked Grandpa if he knew about the vicar who had lived in the vicarage before the Aubreys, but Grandpa couldn't remember. Asked about what had since become of the Aubreys the old man thought for a moment and then told Liz that he believed that the vicar's wife had died during the 'flu epidemic in 1918.

He thought for a moment or two longer and then added, "Now I think about it, the two daughters died as well. Reverend moved to Framley all on 'is own. Aye, I remember now. Miss Lizzie wus goin' ter get married to a soldier."

Even when pressed Grandpa was unable to remember names or dates, but volunteered the information that, "'Er sweetheart probably married someone else. Men wus in short supply after the war yer know! 'E might be alive yet, a grandfather, possibly a great-grandfather!"

Hardly had these words been spoken when the tape recorder was snatched up by an unseen hand and hurled against the wall. The single word 'NO' was shouted, over and over again, until it filled their heads, the room, the house. It tailed off into a howl of anguish which in turn became a sobbing, whirling around the room and finally sweeping out through the door. There was the sound of invisible footsteps hammering up the stairs. A temporary pause on the first

landing was succeeded by the rattling of the attic stairs and the sound of a door being slammed.

Liz and Paul were stupefied. They stared at each other in amazement. Before they could collect their wits there was a loud and insistent knocking on the front door.

* * * * * * *

Like a man in a trance Paul rose slowly to his feet and went out into the hall to answer the summons. He reappeared, moments later, followed by a whirlwind of a very different nature.

"Liz dahling! How are you?" and a blonde hurricane swept across the room and embraced Liz, loudly kissing the air next to her cheek.

"Lucy! What are you doing here?" spluttered an amazed Liz.

"Charming greeting! I'll go away again if you like!" pouted Lucy Thomas, Liz's former colleague.

"Sorry Lucy! What I mean is that I'm so surprised. It's really lovely to see you, but ..." Liz was lost for words.

Paul jumped in gallantly, rescuing Liz from her awkward situation. "...So unexpected. But then the nicest things usually are!" He winked at Liz and smiled disarmingly at Lucy. Lucy positively purred as she warmed to Paul.

"You do look well, both of you! I was so sorry to miss your party!" She looked, doe-eyed, at Paul. "And when I found that I had to see a client over here, I thought to myself, 'I wonder how those two darlings are? I haven't seen Liz since she left work, and I haven't seen Paul for ages' So, I thought I'd just drop in and visit. Paul," she turned to him and smiled, "Paul, could you be an absolute angel and get my bag from the car?"

"Bag?" questioned Liz, already losing patience with Lucy's 'little girl' affectations, "you've got your bag over your shoulder!"

"Not this bag silly, I mean my overnight bag. I thought that it would be so much nicer if I stayed."

"And cheaper!" thought Liz rather unkindly, never for one moment doubting that Lucy would be claiming extravagant over-night expenses.

"*Lovely!*" said Paul, managing to convey the idea that he really meant it. "I'll go and get your things!" and turning so that only Liz could see him, he raised his eyes heavenwards and went out.

As soon as Paul had gone Lucy sat down and looked critically around the

room. "I must say, Liz darling, this is lovely, straight out of the colour supplements! Large kitchen table; warm yellow walls; rush-seated chairs. You are lucky to have... Oh dear! What happened to your tape recorder?" She went and gathered together the fragments of machinery lying against the wall. "Don't think that will go again! Whatever happened? Did you throw it at Paul?" Lucy chuckled, relishing the thought of other people's rows.

"Of course I didn't!" snapped Liz, more sharply than she had intended. "I dropped it!"

"Dropped it!" exclaimed Lucy sceptically, indicating the deep indent in the wall. "Well, it hit the wall rather a bang on the way down didn't it?"

Liz was about to reply but thought it safer to change the subject altogether. "Tell me Lucy, how is everyone at Marshall's?" Unable to resist the temptation to gossip Lucy took a deep breath.

"You remember that horribly vulgar little Timkins man? Well ..." and Lucy launched into an orgy of character assassination and gossip of a mostly malicious nature.

At the end of forty minutes Liz was uncomfortable and restless. She no longer belonged to the world Lucy spoke of, and even when she had she had refused to join in the office gossip. Here she was trapped in her own kitchen, listening to things which held no interest for her. When she could stand it no longer she broke into Lucy's monologue, "Where on earth can Paul have got to? He only went out for your bag! I'd better go and see what's happened to him." Liz got up. Lucy immediately leapt to her feet.

"Let me come too. You can show me over the house. I'm absolutely dying to see it! Then it should be time for a little drinkies!" Lucy giggled in what she fondly imagined was and engaging manner.

Liz took some time, and a great deal of trouble, to show Lucy around. There was no sign of Paul and Liz felt a little resentful at having been left to entertain Lucy by herself. Lucy 'ooh'd' and 'aah'd' in all the appropriate places but was clearly more interested in finding Paul than in hearing the intricacies of the renovation work. As they emerged from one of the uncompleted bedrooms they heard noises from the attic. There were footsteps followed by the rattling of a door-handle. Lucy looked upwards to the top storey.

"Don't tell me Liz, let me guess. You've got a ghost! Or is it poor, mad Mrs. Rochester incarcerated in the attic?"

Liz laughed uneasily. The very last thing she wished to talk to Lucy about was the recent strange events.

"Er ... no ... I think that it's just wind in the chimney. All these attics have chimneys you know. The servants slept up there in the old days. Paul and I haven't got round to doing anything on that floor yet. Paul was going to make a start earlier today but -" Liz broke off abruptly, aware that she was babbling. Lucy stood back, amused at her confusion. 'Dammit! She can still make me feel like the village idiot -in spite of the fact that I've got more brains in my little finger than she has space for!' thought Liz. Just then Paul's voice came from the other side of the door to the central attic.

"Liz! Liz! Is that you? This rotten door's jammed on me!"

Liz's relief was almost palpable. She went up the narrow staircase. The door was tightly closed - with the key on the outside! Liz reached out and turned the handle. It was locked! Hoping that Lucy didn't see her actions, Liz quickly turned the key and opened the door.

"What on earth are you doing up here?" she snapped at Paul. Seeing Lucy's smug expression at the loss of her equanimity, she softened her tone quickly. "I thought that you had gone for Lucy's bag? That was ages ago."

"I know, but once I had put the bag in Lucy's room I ... I ... I remembered something that I'd left up here earlier. I thought that I may as well pop up and fetch it ..." Paul's not very convincing excuse tailed off weakly. Lucy's snigger prompted him on. "I'd just got inside the door when a draught slammed it closed."
"But it was locked Paul darling, on the outside!" commented Lucy.

Hating to see Paul at Lucy's mercy, Liz jumped in with, "Oh that's just one of the many things we need to fix. The old lock on this door is so worn that every time it slams with any degree of force, the lock slips." Paul stared at Liz in admiration at her glib excuse.

Knowing Paul as well as she did, Liz was convinced that he had come up to the attic to see if there was any evidence of the ghostly presence which had fled from the kitchen earlier. Paul read her unspoken question and shook his head.

"Come on then you two," said Paul, sounding more cheerful than he looked, "now I've been let out of my prison let's go and get a drink!"

"And I suppose that I'd better sort out something for dinner," put in Liz.

An eloquent glance from Lucy immediately made Liz feel like the tame, country, domestic little wife. "Or we could go down to the pub," she added on a defiant note.

* * * * * * *

The evening proved to be an excruciating embarrassment. Lucy, in overloud tones, described everything as 'quaint', clearly conveying the message that 'The Swan' was not up to her standards of decor. She insisted on greeting everyone present, speaking slowly and distinctly to 'the natives' as she referred to them. Liz and Paul finally managed to install her at a table in the corner. But the embarrassment wasn't over: just as Lucy was confiding in a stage whisper that the best food they could probably expect was likely to be beefburgers, greasy chips and mushy peas, Paul looked up to see the landlord, George Travers, appear from behind a pillar. With a solemn expression on his usually smiling face he handed out the menus, commenting to Lucy, "I think we can do a little better than that madam!"

Their meal was splendid, as befitted the gourmet reputation George had acquired. Even Lucy had grudgingly admitted that she hadn't eaten such a good meal for a long time.

Evidently Lucy felt it her duty as guest to drink as much as possible and she spent the evening growing progressively more drunk. As she slipped into insobriety so she cast increasingly more adoring eyes in Paul's direction, hanging on his every word and introducing highly suggestive 'double entendres' as frequently as she could. Eventually Paul could bear her behaviour no longer and, on the pretence of paying for the meal, he stood chatting at the bar.

Liz grew anxious about their ability to get Lucy back to the vicarage and was relieved when George at last rang the bell to signal 'time'.

With Paul taking one arm and Liz the other, Lucy was propelled homewards. Constant reminders for her to 'sshh!' seemed to make her worse.

Finally they turned in between the vicarage gateposts. Lucy was now silent and leaning heavily on both Paul and Liz. In the stillness of the country night they heard the deep, mournful howl of a dog.

"Sally!" said Liz, anxiously, and tried to quicken her pace.

"The Hound of the Baskervilles!" giggled Lucy, almost collapsing. Liz gripped Lucy's arm - hard - and propelled her forward.

Walking up the drive Liz's eyes were drawn upwards. The centre attic window was aglow with the glimmer of candle-light.

"Paul!" she gasped. "Look!"

Paul followed her gaze and then looked away quickly before Liz could see his alarm; his fear. The pretence of helping a stumbling Lucy up the steps removed the necessity to comment. Liz glanced at Lucy, hoping that she had not seen the illuminated window, mentally preparing an excuse if she had done.

She needn't have worried. Lucy was too inebriated to see as far as the top storey of the house, 'even supposing she was wearing the necessary specs!' thought Liz spitefully.

Paul pushed the door open; Sally hurtled out, licking; barking; crying; relieved to have human company at last. Leaving Liz to deal with Lucy (who was by now howling in imitation of Sally and giggling by turns) Paul raced up the stairs to the attic, taking them two at a time in his anxiety.

* * * * * * *

The door crashed back against the wall. Silence. Darkness. Once more Paul felt that movement had only just ceased. Again he could smell a hastily extinguished candle.

He snapped on the lights.

Instantly the objects in the room jumped into stark relief. Everything was just as it should be. No, not quite. Another candle, similar to that which Paul had retrieved earlier, was stuck to the same place on the mantle. Paul stepped into the room.

As he crossed the floor his foot sent something spinning. Paul bent to examine it. It was an old-fashioned fountain pen of a type Paul had seen only in antique shops. He turned it gingerly over with his foot and as he did so became aware of a sensation akin to pins and needles in his toes. Impatiently he snatched up the pen, determined to have a close look, only to drop it immediately, stung by the electric shock that seared through his hand and arm. The pen rolled away and disappeared into a gap in the floorboards next to the old hearth.

It was as Paul tried to retrieve the pen that he became aware of an eerie stillness, a feeling of being watched. He swung around. Nothing! Just the black, blank, reflecting windows. The stillness grew and the air was full of menace. The hairs on the back of his neck bristled; sweat stood out on his forehead and ran in icy beads down his face. He could feel the room repelling him; could sense the alien atmosphere. He did not belong; he was not the one wanted here.

Slowly he rose to his feet. Without turning he inched in the direction of the door, resisting the temptation to glance behind, to confront those watching eyes.

Relief flooded through him as he slammed the door, locked it and removed the key, placing it safely in his pocket.

* * * * * * *

Liz had finally succeeded in getting Lucy into bed and gained sweet revenge for the trials of the day by roughly scrubbing a face-cloth over her guest's heavily made-up face. She accompanied her action with the solicitous words, "Must get this off. I know that you'd simply hate to wake up in the morning still in your make-up - *dahling*!" As he passed the door Paul was just in time to catch the comment. He smiled to himself.

When Paul and Liz at last fell into bed, exhausted by the events of the day, both were glad of the reassuring presence of Sally in their room.

Paul held Liz in his arms, aware once more of the new, strange Liz. Her body was tense, bursting with suppressed vitality. He had never known her like this.

Liz tried to talk about the strange events of the day, but Paul kissed away her words. "Tomorrow Liz, we'll talk about it tomorrow," he mumbled, burying his face in her neck. As he ran his hands over her body he was aware only of his overpowering desire for Liz. Even after all these years he never ceased to be excited by her.

Later, when Liz lay asleep in his protective embrace, Paul lay wakeful. There was no reasonable explanation for all that was happening; for the candle stumps; for the pen. He didn't mind admitting to himself that he found the attic frightening. Not that he would ever admit that to Liz. He watched her, sleeping peacefully. Whatever was in the attic had not wanted him. The fear, wrenching at his gut, was that it was Liz who it wanted

They would have to do something - but what? Still pondering the problem, Paul fell asleep.

CHAPTER EIGHT.

Paul and Liz had a quiet, restful night's sleep, not so Lucy who appeared in the morning irritable, eyes shadowed, skin a little reddened on chin and cheekbones where Liz had applied her special make-up removal technique. Over breakfast Lucy complained long and hard about her uncomfortable night. She had tossed and turned for hours; been awakened by the quilt constantly falling off her and finally, rudely woken by falling out of bed and landing with a hard bump on the floor.

Liz had been unable to prevent her laughter from bubbling out and had got up to fill the kettle, hoping that Lucy had not seen her amusement. Paul had sympathised and commented that he too usually had a restless night when he'd drunk too much. Lucy scowled and insisted volubly that she had not over indulged the previous night, and that even if she had it would have made her sleep more heavily than usual. She added indignantly that she hadn't fallen out of bed since she'd been a child.

"It must be your house. It doesn't like me!" she concluded. They all laughed at the notion, but Paul and Liz exchanged significant glances.

Lucy's mood improved over the orange-juice, coffee and toast. It was as she was raising a piece of generously buttered and marmaladed toast to her mouth that she stopped, looked hard at Liz and Paul and said, "You two couldn't have had a very good night either. I kept hearing you, one of you anyway, shuffling along the landing."

They both looked embarrassed.

"That was me!" Liz jumped in to say, "I had to go along to the bathroom. That's the problem with drinking late."

"They say that you should ease off on the booze as you get older," Lucy sniped.

Liz desperately wanted to retort with 'You should know!' but instead said only, "I hope that I didn't disturb you too much?"

Lucy answered her waspishly, "I was disturbed already and when I did manage to get off to sleep I had the oddest dreams. I can't quite remember the thread of the story, but there was a woman wandering about, wringing her hands and weeping. That wasn't you as well was it Liz?"

Liz laughed self-consciously. Whatever it was in the vicarage she didn't want to discuss it with Lucy. Before she knew it Lucy would be spreading all sorts of

rumours around Marshall's. Liz suspected that it had been Lucy's malicious tongue that had circulated so much gossip about her and Paul's lack of children. So if Lucy were to get even the merest sniff that Simon had suggested a book then there'd be no holding her. She'd be muscling in, making up to Simon, visiting the vicarage - and Paul - every weekend on the pretence of 'researching'. She'd ...

"More coffee anyone?" smiled Paul, "or haven't you time?" He looked pointedly at the clock. Lucy looked up.

"Jeez! I'd better get a move on, it's after seven. No doubt I'll get caught in that awful traffic. How you kept this up for a year Liz I'll never know!"

Lucy paused on the way to her car. "Goodbye darlings. I'll be sure to come down again soonest. Perhaps you'd like to come up to town and stay a night or so with me - experience the bright city lights again?"

Although the invitation was issued to both, it was on Paul that she turned her baby-blue eyes, opening them wide and fluttering her lashes demurely in appeal. Liz felt like kicking her.

"We'd love to Lucy," replied Paul, his eyes twinkling mischievously. "We must get this place finished, then we'll all come up. I wonder what old Sally will think of the big city? What d'you say Sal," he asked, turning to the dog, "fancy a holiday at Auntie Lucy's?"

Horrified, Lucy responded quickly, "Oh, I don't think that's a good idea at all. Sally's a country dog; she wouldn't like the town!" Her expression showed that she was remembering the boisterous way Sally had romped around last night, fetching Lucy soggy, chewed dog toys to play with, trying to sit next to her on the settee. In fending her off, Lucy's clothes had become liberally coated in dog hairs. She probably also gave a thought to her collection of delicate china figurines scattered around the flat on coffee tables that were just about tail-sweeping level.

Paul's reply did however succeed in its aim, for Lucy got into her car and slammed the door quickly.

As the car disappeared through the gateway Paul and Liz could contain their amusement no longer and collapsed into helpless laughter.

"Oh Paul! I really thought you meant that about visiting her," spluttered Liz.

"Oh, I know that I tease Lucy, but she does deserve it all! What a ridiculous person! And as for last night, words fail me! We'll have to get down to the pub pretty soon, do a bit of apologising."

"I don't think George - or any of them for that matter, would have taken Lucy seriously. In fact I rather think that they sympathised with us! But all that aside,"

Liz was suddenly serious, "Lucy obviously heard something last night."

"Or thought that she did. Personally I'm more inclined to think that it was the after effects of all the alcohol she downed. I bet she wouldn't have drunk half so much if I hadn't been paying!"

"Paul! I never thought of you as being mean!"

"I'm not. I'm just a little fed up with freeloaders like Lucy." He was going to add that he was glad that she had fallen out of bed, but having successfully deflected Liz from the subject of the strange happenings, he didn't want to give her the opportunity to return to it.

* * * * * * *

"But Paul, you must admit that there is something, call it a presence, an unquiet spirit, a ghost, whatever -there is definitely something in this house." Liz paused for breath.

"Well, I don't know Liz. Lots of strange things happen."

"Come on Paul, for God's sake. You were here yesterday when the tape recorder flew through the air. You heard the noises. You were the one locked in the attic!"

"I know Liz, I know, but there has to be a perfectly logical explanation for it." Guiltily Paul fingered the candle stub still in his pocket. There had to be a perfectly logical explanation - didn't there? Meanwhile, there was that feeling that he'd had in the attic last night, the conviction that whatever it was was seeking Liz. He would have to try to keep her out of the house for a few days. He didn't like the idea of her being here alone all day.

"Well, what about a little investigating? See what you can dig up at the Records Office?" He suggested, trying to be positive.

"I told you that I couldn't get a booking until Monday."

"Oh, yes I forgot." Paul paused and concentrated on fastening his tie. They were in the bedroom. He was almost ready to set off for work but he was reluctant to leave Liz alone. He'd have to think of something.

"Why don't you get out and about a bit. The weather is really good and you could do with some fresh air."

Liz brightened. She too had been rather unnerved by recent events and hadn't been exactly relishing a day alone. "Good idea. Tell you what, why don't I make a start on clearing a way to the old summerhouse?" Paul might have guessed that things couldn't be that easy. If he couldn't yet bring himself to tell Liz about the

candles and the pen, how the hell would he start telling her about the summerhouse?

He spent some time in persuading Liz not to pursue that plan. Excuses such as wanting to get the heavy work done by someone from the village; the ground being too boggy; perhaps even needing to hire some specialist equipment to clear away the worst of the undergrowth, eventually succeeded.

"OK, you win! What I will do though is go down to the church, have a good root around. I may even be able to uncover some information about previous vicars! Hey, I could explore the graveyard!" Liz enthused.

This had not been exactly what Paul had in mind, but at least it would get Liz out of the vicarage for a good part of the day.

In spite of the certainty that Liz would be away from the house, Paul drove out of the gates and set off for Nantwich with a heavy heart.

* * * * * * *

Clipping Sally's lead on to the collar, Liz set out to walk to the church. The dog sniffed excitedly at the new smells and soon Liz felt confident enough to let her run free. Sally zig-zagged from one side of the road to the other, pushing her nose deep into the undergrowth of the verges, occasionally pouncing on scuttling movements. Once she put up an unwary rabbit which hurtled off, chased (but not caught) by an enthusiastic Sally.

The new growth testified to the onward march of spring. Lords and Ladies were at least six inches high now, flaunting their lusciousness. Blackthorn flowers were beginning to brown and fade, their delicate beauty giving way to the new, young, acid-green leaves now starting to burst out along the dark twigs. Spring was truly one of the most wonderful miracles of nature. Apparently lifeless branches became, quite suddenly, alive with vigorous growth. So pre-occupied was Liz in the beauty of the season that she was surprised to find herself so soon at her destination.

She stood for some moments in the shelter of the picturesque lych-gate looking up at the church. The building was a typical 18th Century edifice, built of grey stone. Once the bells would have rung out from the fine, square tower, summoning the people of the parish to worship: now it was empty and lifeless. The windows of the church were large and high. Modestly, they were of clear, leaded glass. Today the small squares glittered as their different planes caught and reflected the light from the dull, grey sky. Liz thought that on a sunny day the building would shine almost as though it was on fire.

Since the church had been de-sanctified it had been tastefully converted into what amounted to a craft workshop. All types of furniture restoration was undertaken by the small team of artisans who had moved out from the city centre in search of a better quality of life. Ironically they had found that most of their work still came from the city, for there is nothing that city dwellers like so much as confidentially informing friends that they intend to have their bureau, chair or table lovingly restored by a gifted craftsman they just happen to know who lives 'in the back of beyond'. It was all part of that glamorous image of the countryside portrayed in colour supplements; the game of status that had civil servants behind the wheels of off-road vehicles never driven further than suburbia; mortgage brokers arriving at the office in stained wax jackets in which they had trekked all the way from the station!

Liz walked around the exterior of the church, pausing to look at what was clearly a more recent extension and admiring the fine standard of stone-masonry that made it difficult to distinguish the new from the original. Set high in the wall was the only coloured window of the church. Its massive expanse of stained glass boasted a martial theme and Liz had an inkling that the angels there depicted were probably taken from contemporary accounts of the Angels of Mons. Set in the wall, directly beneath the window, was the plaque of dedication.

This window was given to the church by
MRS. LOUISE FARQUHARSON
In loving memory of her husband
COLONEL HAROLD FARQUHARSON
And all the men of Brabage who fell in
THE GREAT WAR FOR CIVILISATION
1914 - 1918

Glory be to God.

'War for civilisation indeed!' thought Liz. The recent work she had done for Marshall's had given her the opportunity to research the period of the Great War. The sacrifice, the waste, the pig-headed behaviour of the commanders had all made Liz form the opinion that it was a period of history for which we should feel shame, not pride. As in every war it was the ordinary people who had ultimately paid the price. No doubt the village of Brabage had lost its share of young men. Husbands, sons, fathers, lovers, all had gone to feed the greedy and ever-demanding maw of futile conflict.

Liz tried to shrug off the familiar feelings of depression but she remained melancholy as she searched among the gravestones for information about her forerunners at the vicarage.

For such a small village the graveyard was really quite extensive. Most of the gravestones were quite old and some had fallen over. Others had been taken up and placed at the side of the newly-widened pathway. The churchyard was rather overgrown, but in spite of the general air of neglect Liz could see that some of the graves were well-tended, for here and there were bright bunches of flowers on neatly trimmed islands in the sea of long grass.

At the end of an hour, Liz decided to give up her search. She had found the graves of various generations of Shiptons, Jenkinses and Allinsons. She had recognised many of the names of local families, but she could find no trace of the graves of any local clergy or their kin. As she called Sally to her Liz looked up at the sky and shivered. The grey cloud had given way to black and, if she didn't get home quickly she would be caught in rain.

She was scurrying along the road, the perimeter wall of the vicarage on her right, head bent into the cold wind that had sprung up from nowhere, when she noticed that Sally was no longer by her side. She turned. Sally was twenty yards behind and seemed to be cowering.

"Come on girl!" Liz called, but the dog refused to move. Liz walked back, calling encouragingly to the dog. Still Sally refused to come on. Liz reached her and took hold of her collar. By coaxing and cajoling in turns the dog reluctantly walked along, taking great care to keep Liz between herself and the wall of the vicarage. All at once Sally stood still. Stroking her, Liz was surprised to find that the dog was quivering.

"What's the matter Sal?" Liz asked bending over to comfort the frightened dog. All at once she became infected with the dog's fear. She was aware of a feeling of oppression, a brooding presence. She straightened up slowly; cautiously looked behind. Nothing. There was nothing. She listened but there was only silence. Suddenly Liz was alarmed. There should be noises, birdsong, the rustling of the wind in the trees, but all was silence. She could sense a watching, waiting presence. She held her breath. Her anxiety increased to become fear. She looked around helplessly.

She realised that she was standing in the spot where she had seen Paul yesterday. The old summerhouse must be just the other side of the wall. Unaccountably the scent of violets stole into her nostrils. Stupid! she told herself, how could she be smelling violets here?

The wall seemed to draw her forward, draw her into itself. She reached out a hand towards the lichen encrusted stone. A great sense of calm spread through her. Somewhere here was the answer, something was about to happen. She could almost visualise another hand, an ethereal, disembodied hand, reaching out of the wall to take her own pale hand in its grasp. She was close - she knew that she was very close, to the presence in the house. She became entranced, mesmerised, staring so fixedly that her eyes must surely penetrate the wall.

"Hi there!" boomed a voice at her shoulder, startling Liz out of her daze. She spun around. George Travers stood there a puzzled expression on his face.

"Oh, er, hi George."

"Are you OK Liz?"

"Er ... of course I am George. I was just taking Sally for a walk."

"I was just taking Satan for his stroll!" and he indicated the large Alsatian at his side. "You sure you're OK?"

"Course I am. Why shouldn't I be?"

"Well, when I came up you seemed to be in some sort of dream, just staring at the wall." Liz thought rapidly. "I was staring at the wall. I think we need to do a bit of repair work. The mortar is crumbling." George looked at her and then at the wall. His sceptical expression betrayed the fact that he could plainly see that at this particular place the wall was in fairly good condition.

Liz turned quickly. Sally was still trembling.

"I think Sally's a bit nervous of Satan. I'd better put her on the lead."

Her action diverted George who immediately attached a short lead to his own dog's collar.

They walked on together, chatting companionably. Liz took the opportunity to apologise for Lucy's appalling behaviour of the previous evening. George shrugged it off.

They parted at the vicarage gates. If Liz had glanced back as she went up the gravel drive she would have seen George looking after her, his expression a mixture of puzzlement and scepticism.

* * * * * * *

From the attic window she watched Liz and the dog. So near. She had been so near. She had felt Liz's fear. That displeased her. She didn't want to frighten Liz, but she must make contact. She needed her.

She would be patient, take things slowly. She knew Liz, could feel her sympathy. It was only a matter of time.

CHAPTER NINE

Paul sighed with relief as he pulled his car out of the vicarage gates and onto the road. It was Monday, and he admitted to a certain degree of relief in the prospect of returning to work. Not that anything further had happened. In fact things since Lucy's visit things had been very quiet - apart from the row on Friday night of course.

As Paul turned onto the Nantwich road he wondered about that row. What exactly was it that had made him react so aggressively towards Liz last Friday?

He had come home to find the ground floor of the house deserted. A familiar fear clutched at his stomach. Nervously he called out to Liz, just as she appeared, smiling, at the top of the stairs. What he saw there made him panic. Liz was dressed in a faded black calf-length dress; not one of her own. Her slim figure looked even thinner and the glow about her face made her look ethereal. She didn't look like his Liz. However that hadn't been the reason for his explosive reaction. Somewhere at the back of his mind he recognised that dress, recognised it and associated it with the unearthly presence in the house.

"Where did you get that from?" he demanded imperatively. Liz's smile didn't falter, her assurance didn't waver.

"Don't you like it? I think it's very elegant. Just what the well-bred young lady should wear to welcome her husband back from work!" and she laughed, a strange, girlish laugh.

"Take it off Liz, please," his voice quavered. "I don't like it. It's too black for your pale complexion. Where did it come from anyway?"

Slowly and dreamily Liz floated down the stairs towards him. She didn't even walk like the Liz he knew. As she approached he became aware that the dress smelt very strongly of violets. It was so overpowering that he felt almost suffocated.

"Where did it come from?" he shouted angrily.

His sharp tone seemed to penetrate Liz's self-absorption. Her face clouded for a moment.

"I was clearing some of the attics, going through those old boxes that were here when we moved in."

Paul's stomach lurched. Had Liz spent the day up in that centre attic? If so, God knew what had happened to her. He would probably have to tell her all about the candle and the pen, perhaps even about the summerhouse. With Liz in this strange state the last thing he wanted to do was bring up his own weird

experiences. His mind worked frantically in an attempt to think up reasonable explanations.

Liz was still talking. "Most of the stuff was junk, but there were one or two boxes of old clothes. This was in one of them. I particularly liked the look of it; it has a rather faded elegance. I would guess that it was a 'best' dress somewhere around the time of the First World War. When I tried it on it fitted me perfectly - almost as if it had been made for me."

"Get it off!" he shouted, a wild, red fury filling his mind. "It's horrible, old and faded. I hate you in it!"

Taken aback by Paul's aggression Liz stammered, "There's no need to be like that. I'm only having a bit of fun!"

"Fun like that I can do without!" and he was surprised to find that he was truly angry, not just afraid. Why was he shouting like this, and at Liz of all people? The mood of the house, the tension, must be getting to him!

Liz stood, head bowed, and he was ashamed of his temper.

"I'm sorry Liz, you just startled me, that's all."

Liz turned up her face for a kiss and in a moment her arms were around his neck. As he sank into her embrace Paul felt that he was drowning in a deep pool of darkness. How could Liz stand this dress, the smell was almost taking away his breath. Liz's hands were moving frenetically up and down his back. Her movements were filled with a sense of urgency which were soon matched by Paul's own passion. He kissed her and submitted himself to the velvet blackness that was Liz.

Now, driving to work on a dull Monday morning, Paul shook his head in wonder. Liz had been so very different. Their lovemaking was always a joy to him, but on Friday evening ...! He couldn't even begin to describe the deep emotions, the passion that had possessed them both. Liz had never been dominant, but on Friday it had almost been as though he was a callow youth being led along by an experienced woman.

The peculiar mood had remained with Liz all weekend. She was dreamy, walking about the house in a partial daze, an odd smile playing about her lips. She did not seem to notice the brooding atmosphere of the house, the growing air of menace that made Paul tense and rather irritable, made him jump at shadows and strange noises. He had been surprised that Liz had made no attempt to talk about all that had happened. At least that meant that he had not been forced to disclose his own experiences.

As he pulled into his parking place in the centre of Nantwich, Paul decided that

on the whole he was glad that Liz was to spend today at the Records Office, for, by unearthing information, facts about the vicarage and its former inhabitants, she could perhaps make a start on the book she had half promised Simon. If she was busy with that she would have no time for flights of fancy!

****

Liz's desire to be at the County Records Office bright and early meant that she was caught up in heavy commuter traffic. Chester's traffic problems were notorious and, dodging and weaving from lane to lane, Liz wondered yet again how she had managed to travel daily to Manchester. By the time she arrived at her destination and finally found a place to park, her nerves were frazzled. The silence of the records office came as a welcome relief.

Roger had clearly been waiting, for he greeted her eagerly, showing her the material he had already assembled. Liz felt rather awkward: she felt peculiarly possessive about the research on the vicarage and its past inhabitants and here was Roger trying to intrude! That thought made her pull herself up sharply. Roger was only trying to help. She was getting paranoid about anything to do with the vicarage! Quickly she smiled and prepared to tell the helpful Roger, diplomatically of course, that she would prefer to spend the morning 'digging around' on her own.

She was just about to speak when Roger said, "I'll leave you to it then. If you need any help, give me a shout. I'd love to stay and help but you can see how busy we are!" He waved an arm to indicate the rapidly filling room. He paused for a moment and then grinned, "So, what about lunch then? You can bring me up to date on everything then."

Liz would have agreed to almost anything, so eager was she to get on with her work.

In the event Roger returned to her shortly after 11 a.m. She had been having problems loading one of the files and he had come to help. As he eased the film-strip through the machine, Roger glanced at the material on her desk.

"You have got on well! But then Simon warned me that you were a quick worker!" He picked up her summary sheet with the comment, "Built in 1839. I knew that of course. That makes it only just Victorian. While I was amassing this material it struck me as odd that a vicarage built at that time should be empty less than a hundred years later. I seem to recall that Brabage merged with Framley in 1918 or 1919."

"I suppose that the population of Brabage was depleted by the war. That made Framley, always the most important of the two parishes, the obvious place from which to run the joint parish."

"Have you looked at the census records yet Liz? I don't think Brabage lost such a great number of people."

"Not in the war, no, but lots moved to towns to take up factory work. Crewe, Manchester, Liverpool, even Birmingham."

"Oh, yes, I'd forgotten. This is your period isn't it? I expect that you know a lot more about the day to day detail than I do!" Roger laughed.

Unsure of whether Roger was being sarcastic or making a genuine observation, Liz changed the subject rapidly.

"I've found out quite a lot about the various vicars. The first incumbent moved into the vicarage as soon as it was completed in 1839. Thomas Croaker. Thomas Carlyle Croaker actually! He sounds as though he has stepped straight from the pages of Dickens." Liz laughed.

Roger smiled, content to let Liz tell him what she had discovered in her morning's work.

"He had a wife, a maid, a cook-housekeeper and a stableman cum gardener. What's more he had ten children, although only seven of them survived infancy. Looking around the vicarage today I can't help but wonder where they all slept!"

"You must remember Liz, people didn't expect a room of their own, even a bed of their own, in those days. Besides," he added, a mischievous twinkle in his eye, "houses were much colder then and I expect it was far more desirable to live at close quarters!"

Liz refused to go down the path of innuendo and continued her account resolutely. "The Croaker family moved out in 1877. They went to Stannage. Quite a move!"

"And quite a step up. Stannage was a prosperous parish. I would expect that the Reverend Croaker must have had some sort of influence in the church to achieve that position!"

"Out with the Croakers and in with the Durbridges! They were only at Brabage for eight years, until 1885. Still, they managed to have five children in that time."

"Again, normal for the time."

Liz was sure that Roger was about to add a risqué comment and so she moved on rapidly.

"I came across these photos."

"Oh, yes, I got out quite a number for you. Did you find the ones of the Croakers?"

"Yes thanks. They were all lined up in front of the vicarage, staff as well, posing stiffly for the camera. These pictures of the Durbridges are quite different. Firstly, they all seemed to have individual portraits taken. Look at this one of Mrs. Durbridge. Her dress is beautiful."

"Yes, silk do you notice. I expect she caused quite a stir in the modest parish of Brabage! But then the Durbridges were society people," commented Roger.

"I can well believe it. Take a look at this." Liz responded passing over a sepia portrait of a rather foppish looking man in clerical garb. His curling golden locks were worn longer than was fashionable for the time. He held a book in his right hand; his left rested on a doric column.

"Ah yes, Reverend Durbridge. The artist. Had a volume of poetry published. Seemed to spend a lot of his time writing. If you're interested Liz I think the library holds a copy of his verse."

"Maybe sometime in the future. Thanks Roger. The Durbridges moved on to Framley in 1885."

"Again, promotion for him. I expect that they were happier in Framley. Far more prestigious than the modest Brabage. I guess that the move gave them the opportunity to spread their social wings."

"And now we come to the last vicar of Brabage. That sounds very Trollope!" Liz laughed. When Roger didn't join in she added quickly, "I mean Anthony, not Joanna!" As Roger still didn't manage so much as a smile, Liz made a mental note not to make literary jokes and continued, "Lewis Aubrey and his wife Sarah moved into the vicarage in 1885. Here's his photo. Looks a bit of a tartar doesn't he?"

Liz passed over a copy of an old photograph. A tall, dark man, sombrely dressed, stood next to a chair on which was seated a thin woman modestly attired. Behind the chair stood two young women. Both were dark and pretty, dressed quite plainly and appeared to be in their late teens or early twenties. None of the figures was smiling.

"Bit of a martinet I would say, going by the expressions worn by the ladies!" said Roger.

"Elizabeth and Mary, his daughters. Judging by their clothes the Reverend either wasn't paid very well or he was mean with the money!" responded Liz.

"Probably the latter. I don't think that any of the vicars of Brabage were too badly off, not judging from the church records. This was the vicar responsible for

the extension to the church, and to the graveyard. It was largely due to him that the magnificent 'War Window' was installed."

Roger had begun to ramble on, and Liz judged that this was not quite the moment to enlighten him on her opinions regarding the church window.

With relief Liz noticed that someone at a desk near the door was struggling with a viewer.

"I think that someone over there needs a bit of help," she interrupted. Roger turned quickly.

"Right. Yes. Well, we'll finish this conversation over lunch." And he was gone, leaving Liz to continue her work in peace.

* * * * * * *

In the event Roger seemed disinclined to talk about Brabage over lunch. He had chosen to take Liz to a small bistro of the type which are so prolific in the city. Over a splendid meal he entertained her with tales of the county. It wasn't until they were returning to the office that Roger turned back to the subject of most interest to Liz.

"So, Liz, do you think that you'll get together enough material for a book?"

"I don't know Roger. So far it all seems to be facts and figures. Very dull stuff!"

"Surely, though, you can fill it out with some of the detail from the parish diary? There's so much of the minutiae of everyday life there I was sure that you would have no problem."

"The parish diary?" echoed Liz stupidly. "I haven't come across that yet."

"Then I'll get it out for you as soon as we get back," promised Roger.

While Roger fetched the volume from the shelves Liz glanced idly through the Aubrey photographs once again. Suddenly she stopped, transfixed by what she saw. When Roger returned she was pale and trembling, holding a photocopied photograph in her hand.

"Where did this come from?" she asked. Roger looked over her shoulder.

The picture was of a soldier in the uniform of the First World War. He was standing, holding the back of a chair on which was seated a young woman in ankle-length skirts. In contrast to the other pictures of the Aubrey era, both were beaming at the camera.

"Just in the file I expect. It's one of those pictures everyone had taken during the Great War, the soldier and his sweetheart!"

To Roger, the photograph was nothing out of the ordinary, but Liz had recognised the picture that had appeared on their walls and then disappeared so inexplicably. She asked Roger for a copy. Left alone she had to fight the almost uncontrollable urge to pursue investigations concerning the photograph. That could wait until later. Liz felt that she must study the material which she couldn't photocopy and take away. Resignedly she turned to the parish diary. As she began to read the old book, leather bound and rather tattered, her excitement mounted.

CHAPTER TEN

Paul and Liz were finally sitting in front of their crackling log fire. After Liz had returned from Chester, laden with photocopied material and a sheaf of her own notes they had taken Sally for a walk, in an attempt to compensate for her long day of confinement. While they ate a hasty meal, Liz had told Paul most of what she had discovered. Now they sat in front of the coffee table which was stacked with papers. Paul was idly leafing through the photographs. Liz was watching him closely, almost greedily, waiting for him to come across the copy of the picture that they had so mysteriously discovered after the party. When Paul picked up the portrait of Mrs. Durbridge he whistled.

"Now, she really is something. Much too good-looking to be the wife of a vicar! If you're serious about this ghost Liz, I wouldn't mind being haunted by her!" So preoccupied was Liz with anxiety that she failed to respond. Not a flicker of laughter crossed her face. Paul shrugged; just another example of the way in which Liz had changed. She seemed to live in a world of her own these days, hardly noticing him for much of the time. He continued his perusal making only the occasional comment.

If Liz hadn't been waiting, hadn't been watching, she could have missed the momentary stiffening of Paul's face, the grimace that followed, and the determined movement that pushed the photograph hastily underneath some others. Liz reached out and snatched it from his hand.

"What about this then? Recognise it?" Paul pretended nonchalance.

"It's like a lot of those you see of the period; nothing special!" He tried to place it on the table.

"Nothing special! Nothing special! I don't believe this Paul! Can't you see what it is?"

Paul pretended to examine the picture closely.

Liz's patience ran out. She shouted, "It's that photograph, the one of the soldier and his sweetheart; the one that faded almost before our eyes! And, I know who she is. She is Elizabeth Aubrey, daughter of the last vicar of the parish."

Liz picked up a photograph of the Reverend Lewis Aubrey and held it close to Paul's face. "And, do you know what Paul? I agree with Grandpa Shipton. He was a bastard!" Paul shifted uncomfortably in his seat. Liz was becoming almost hysterical. He had to stop her, try to calm her down. But Liz was continuing to shout, her agitation and anxiety making her tone aggressive.

"Wait 'til you see this little lot then!" and she turned and picked up a notepad and a few photocopied pages. "Roger showed me the parish diary. It was incredible. It was musty and dusty and bound in tattered leather. The sides of the pages were marbled, you know those lovely, old, faded colours. The Reverend Croaker started the diary, used it to record parish matters. Reverend Durbridge continued the practice; though I must admit that his entries are of rather a lighter nature - mainly social. Reverend Aubrey took over the diary with the parish and, given what I've told you about him, as you would expect, his entries were dry and formal, giving only the briefest outline of events.

Paul shrugged his shoulders non-committally, "It was a parish diary, Liz, destined to become a public document. You can't expect the good Reverend to record his innermost thoughts and feelings!"

"Yes, I know, I know, but look at this!" and with an air of triumph Liz waved three photocopied pages under Paul's nose. "Roger copied these for me. I don't think he was supposed to, but that's where it's worth having a bit of influence!"

Paul was too intrigued by what he saw to take the opportunity to tease Liz .

The three pages were copies of entries made during the final few months of the existence of Brabage as an independent parish. Dated 4th November 1917, Lewis Aubrey had written,

> *Today I conducted the funeral of my younger daughter, Mary. The poor child was a victim of the influenza epidemic that is sweeping the country.*

Only five days later another entry read,

> *My loyal wife Sarah was laid to rest today in the same grave as my daughter Mary. Another casualty of influenza. May she rest in peace*

Paul shook his head sadly, "Only to be expected. Grandpa Shipton did tell you that Aubrey lost his family in the 'flu epidemic. I don't see anything special about the entries. Very formal I know, but ..."

"But look at this!" interrupted Liz as she passed a second sheet to Paul. He read it in silence.

The entry was dated November 25th. 1918. It stated,

Funeral of Elizabeth Alice Aubrey.
Interred: Brabage Churchyard

Before Paul had the opportunity to comment Liz handed him the third and final sheet with the air of a gambler producing the ace. Again the copy showed a diary entry.

This time the entry had been made and then heavily scored out.

Friday, January 24th 1919. Elizabeth Aubrey to marry John Fraser

"And if that lot isn't a recipe for an unquiet spirit then I don't know what is!" crowed Liz. "Reverend Aubrey clearly disliked his elder daughter, that's why such a cold, heartless entry in the diary. She was supposed to marry; she died; hence her ghost haunting the vicarage! What do you think?"

"I think that you're jumping the gun Liz. Firstly, the only evidence you have for saying that Lewis Aubrey hated his daughter is the diary entry. Maybe he was himself sickening for the 'flu, maybe he was just getting over it. We might be able to find out. Also, remember that he had just lost a wife and one daughter. You can hardly expect the poor man to be on top of his work!"

"Why should you defend him. Can't you see the sort of man he must have been?" retorted Liz, angry that her theory had been rejected so casually. "And then there's the marriage. We could trace John Fraser or his descendants, find out what really happened. But I'm sure that I'm right. It all fits so well. Elizabeth Aubrey is the woman in the photograph. She is the key to everything. She is haunting the vicarage Paul, I'd lay money on it."

"If she is, and I only say 'if' you notice, for I'm still not convinced that recent happenings don't have a perfectly logical explanation, then it's one thing to identify her, but quite another to do something about it. And I'm still not convinced about your theory on Aubrey. He may have been alright!"

As they argued back and forth, Liz in support of her hypothesis, Paul defending Lewis Aubrey, they became aware that someone - or something - had walked into their sitting room.

* * * * * * *

She watched them sitting closely together on the sofa in front of the fire. Memories flooded her mind. Her heart lurched and a sob rose to her throat. Quickly she stifled it. There must be no noise; she had promised herself that she would proceed gently. Only by a soft approach would she attain her goal. The dog lifted up its nose and sniffed warily at the air. In a moment it was alert, sitting up, hackles rising, fur bristling. A low growl escaped from bared teeth. It looked around the room, spotted her and stared. Slowly it lifted its nose until it pointed at the ceiling and uttered a long, mournful howl.

The two people were transfixed, staring at the dog. Cautiously she glided forward. She knew what was on the table. If only she could help, could show them, hurry things along a little. She could feel that their minds were closed

against her. With the woman there was a slight chance, but the man remained stubborn, unwilling, or perhaps unable, to communicate. Rage welled up inside her in a black torrent. She felt herself losing control.

* * * * * * *

Liz and Paul stared at Sally. If Paul had doubted their unearthly visitor, he had his proof now. As Sally howled, Liz began to tremble. Paul placed a protective arm around her shoulders and pulled her close to his side. He reached out a hand to comfort Sally. The miserable creature skulked towards the sofa, belly dragging along the carpet. She jumped up behind Liz and Paul, shrinking into the cushions and moaning softly.

Paul rocked Liz gently in his arms. In spite of the fire the air was chill, almost icy. Liz's teeth were chattering. There was a noise, a sharp intake of breath, released as a sigh. On the edge of the sigh was a hint of sobbing, stifled instantly almost as though a lip had been caught between grinding teeth.

"It's OK Liz. There's nothing to be afraid of. Whatever it is it can't harm us; it's not physical. Hold me. Close your eyes. Don't look: Don't listen."

"I'm not afraid Paul, I'm just so sad. Can't you feel it - the grief; the sadness; the horror? I just want to shut it out!"

Liz put her hands over her ears and closed her eyes. Slowly her sadness turned to fear. This was something against which she was unable to close her mind. Her terror began to mount, driving out her earlier sympathy. She felt that she was being invaded, driven along a road that she was afraid to follow. She wailed loudly into the cold air.

"Go away! I can do nothing for you! Leave me alone!"

Her words rose steadily, reaching a final, deafening crescendo. At that moment Paul saw - or thought that he saw - a wisp of black smoke. Before he had time to comprehend there was a shriek of anguish. A howling blast of wind ripped through the room; a flash of liquid fire seemed to tear the air apart. The atmosphere swirled around them. It seemed that all the devils in Hell had been released and were on the rampage through this room. Liz buried her head against Paul's chest. Paul held her tightly. The tornado picked up the papers from the table and swept them round and round like confetti in the wind. Paul watched them, mesmerised by their turning. He felt like a man lost in a blizzard. He peered through them but could see only blackness.

* * * * * * *

Hours later Paul and Liz regained their wits. The clock on the mantelpiece showed 2 a.m. The fire had burned out and the room was now cold with the natural chill of night, not the eerie, supernatural iciness of earlier. Paul unclamped his frozen fingers from Liz's shoulder. She appeared to be waking from a deep slumber.

Before them, on the table, the neat piles of paper were no more. The Reverend Durbridge had come to rest alongside a picture of the housekeeper and staff from Reverend Croaker's time. Of the beautiful Mrs. Durbridge there was no sign. Paul could see that, although the papers were in a mess, they were all still on the table. He was puzzled. He knew that they had snowstormed about him. One pile, however, remained intact. Everything associated with the Aubreys remained undisturbed. They stared at the table, unwilling to touch anything. Paul stretched out a tentative hand. Liz clutched at his arm.

"Hang on a minute. Look at that!"

The entire stack of Aubrey papers had been singed around the edges. Gingerly Paul lifted the top sheet. It was, or rather it had been, a copy of a photograph of Lewis Aubrey. As Paul held it, it crumbled away to dust between his fingers; a greasy grey ash falling onto the table.

"Don't disturb anything else yet. I won't be a minute," Paul instructed and left the room. He returned, moments later, with a fish-slice with which he proceeded to separate the sheets of paper with extreme care. His caution proved unnecessary, for each leaf was intact, only the edges being charred. As he lifted leaf after leaf and set them aside, Liz watched. Suddenly she pounced.

"Wait a minute. Let me look at that!"

The page that Paul had just manoeuvred onto the spatula was the copy of the diary page scheduling the marriage between Elizabeth Aubrey and John Fraser. Both had seen it; both had scrutinised it closely in order to read the words beneath the heavy, black scoring deletion. But when they had examined it there had not been that small painted violet on the page.

Liz began to cry.

CHAPTER ELEVEN.

Paul covered the last mile to the vicarage in just over a minute. He hoped that by leaving work early he had managed to reach home before Liz. The events of last night had certainly frightened him. He hadn't wanted to go to the office today, but had had no choice. At least now he had a couple of days holiday ahead; it would give them an opportunity to sort out their problem.

He had managed to persuade Liz to spend the day away from Brabage. She had shopped in Northwich and then met him for lunch in Nantwich. Liz had insisted on bringing Sally with her, not wishing to leave her alone all day in the house. The poor dog had been terrified by the events of the previous evening.

As he drove towards the vicarage Paul's brow furrowed. It was all very well to have a few days off, but how were they going to tackle what lay ahead? That there was something wrong at the house was undeniable; but a ghost? You simply did not have ghosts these days. All rubbish belonging to the superstitious past,' Paul thought. 'But there was something; a presence; a disturbance.'

The first thing to do would be to clear out all the junk in the attics. With that gone Liz's imagination would have less to feed on. But what about his experience? Did he think that what had happened to him in the attic; the day when he had pursued the ethereal voice to the summerhouse; the shadowy figure he had seen on more than one occasion, did he think that was all in *his* imagination?

"Oh, I don't know!" he said aloud in exasperation. Whatever the nature of the apparition it would have to be faced, even if that meant going along to the vicar and arranging a service of exorcism. Paul smiled to himself as he recalled Liz's words, ages ago. What had she said, 'Bell, book and candle'? Well, it might come to that yet.

As he turned into the gates of the vicarage Paul saw Liz's parked car. She had got home before him after all. Locking his own car, Paul resolved that they would spend the evening out, go down to 'The Swan'. They were most certainly not going to risk another evening like the last. Time enough to face the inexplicable tomorrow - in daylight!

Paul closed the front door behind him. Unusually Sally did not run to meet him. The sitting room door was half open; he could hear the television. That was strange. It was not like Liz to be watching TV so early in the evening. He crossed the hall and put his head round the door. What he saw made him rush forward, take hold of Liz, drag her to her feet and start shaking her.

The heavy curtains were drawn darkening the room. A fire was lit but the only other source of illumination came from the television screen.

Liz was sitting in an armchair. She was dressed in the dusty black dress which she had found in the attic and which had so unnerved Paul that he had told her to throw it away: the dress that was identical to the one worn by Elizabeth Aubrey in the photograph he had seen.

A video was playing on the television. It was one of Liz's; a favourite of hers which she had purchased in the course of her publishing work: 'Oh What A Lovely War!'

Liz seemed to be entranced, staring blankly at the screen. Paul gripped her, hard, sure that he must be hurting her. She didn't respond. She was a rag doll in his arms.

"Liz! Liz!" he shouted, shaking her gently. When there was still no response he shook her harder.

"Liz! For God's sake Liz!" Liz stared blankly over his shoulder. Suddenly her mouth started to move and her strangled voice sang with the soldier on the screen,

"When this bloody war is over,"

came the words of the soldier's song, sung to the old hymn tune.

"Liz! Liz!" Paul shook her harder, but she sang on,

"No more soldiering for me.
I will kiss the Sergeant-Major,
Oh, how happy I will be."

"Liz! Stop it. For God's sake stop it!" but still she went on. Her voice was that of the soldier on the screen.

"... No more Church Parade on Sundays, No more ..."

The sound swept over Paul, trying to imprison him within itself. He released his grip on Liz, letting her fall back into the chair. He ran to the TV and snapped it off.

This was insane! The switch was off, yet the video was still playing; Liz and the soldier continued to sing. A red rage swept over Paul. He would not give in. This thing would not dominate him! Angrily he pulled the plug from the mains and as he did so everything went black.

In a moment his eyes had adjusted to the fireglow which illuminated the room. Liz had slumped back in her chair, quiet now. He sat down beside her and took her in his arms. In the old dress she felt like an alien thing. Gently he rocked her to and fro. Almost noiselessly she began to sob. He stroked her hair, speaking softly, trying to calm her. She lay her head on his shoulder. As he soothed her

Paul became aware of something else in the room. A darker pool of blackness showed itself against the deep velvet of the air. As he turned it swirled, almost like smoke; moving; twisting; writhing; churning. Paul heard once more the strains of the song, hummed this time. He closed his eyes and shook his head. Imagination! It must be. This couldn't be happening.

When he opened his eyes again he saw that the amorphous black shadow had become clearer. It was most definitely a figure. The humming grew louder. Liz lay in his arms. She had curled into the foetal position. Eyes tightly closed, she seemed unaware of everything.

The figure drew closer to Paul. Madness. Paul knew that he could not cope with this, his mind could not accept what was happening. Gently he released his hold on Liz, laying her carefully on the sofa. At his movement the figure paused, leaned forward and appeared to be listening intently. The humming had ceased and Paul could hear nothing save for his own heartbeat and the sound of his blood thumping through his ears.

After a moment the figure straightened and began to hum once more. Again the soldier's tune filled the room. The figure grew more distinct and Paul, his eyes locked on it in a hypnotic spell, noted that it was a young woman, a young woman whom he recognised. This figure was Elizabeth Aubrey!

Logic told him that what he was seeing could not be so. Elizabeth Aubrey was dead; it was impossible that she could be here in the vicarage. Whatever his mind argued, Paul's senses recognised that dark hair, upswept and pinned behind, the pale skin, the dress that she had worn in the old photograph; the dress that Liz was wearing at this moment.

Paul tried to move but his feet felt like lead weights. The figure turned its face in his direction and its eyes were dark pools in white snow. The eyes fixed on him ,and Paul felt himself being drawn, inwards and downwards. The dark eyes filled with tears which began to brim over and snake in glistening, crystal trails down those pale, wasted cheeks. It began to weep and the sobs touched a chord that reverberated about the room.

All at once the figure flung itself away from Paul and the shock of his release made him groan aloud. He sank to the floor, his legs numb from the knees down. The figure continued to weep, gliding up and down the room in a frenzy of agitation. The atmosphere was charged with misery; with grief. As it paced, the figure continually glanced down at a leaf of paper it held in its hand. Each time it read from the page a new spasm of weeping shook its ethereal frame, making it quiver and shimmer.

Paul watched helplessly from his position on the floor as the figure halted above Liz. It loomed over her, a black carrion crow. Paul shouted but knew that neither the figure nor Liz had heard the sound. The shade of Elizabeth Aubrey reached down an imploring hand to touch Liz. It extended its arms to take her in its other-worldly embrace. All at once Paul knew with a dreadful certainty that if he allowed the ghostly shadow to enfold Liz he would lose her for ever.

He staggered to his feet. It seemed as though the floor itself grew grasping claws that clutched at him as he lurched towards the sofa. The figure turned in alarm. It seemed that the strangled wails of "No! No!" came from a long way away. He was determined to reach Liz, to save her from this abomination.

When Paul was a mere two feet away from Elizabeth Aubrey the shade reached once more for Liz. Paul yelled and launched himself at the figure. As he sank into the cold, black oblivion that was Elizabeth Aubrey his hand clutched the only solid thing it touched. His grip closed on the letter that Elizabeth was reading. He held fast as he sank, deeper and yet deeper into a bottomless, black chasm.

* * * * * * *

Paul could see nothing. He rubbed his eyes. There was blackness all around him. He knew that he must still be in the sitting room at Brabage Vicarage but the atmosphere told him that he was outside. He struggled to his feet.

Great clouds of smoke began to billow across his field of vision. A stinging, acrid smell assaulted his nostrils. He coughed. Out of the smoke he could hear others choking. Whistles were blowing. A voice shouted "Gas!" and illogically Paul's hand went down to clutch at the gasmask he knew was not there.

Through the dark clouds he could see shadows, figures moving. He had to reach them, to keep up with them. He pushed himself forward and slithered in the clinging Flanders' mud.

With the mud sucking around his feet Paul staggered forward. There were screams of agony, groans from the dying, coming from every direction. All at once Paul's world was lit by a fierce, blinding flare that hung in the sky. Immediately the horror was illuminated. Soldiers were pushing forward, stopping now and again to crouch and launch grenades. From all sides came the rattle of machine gun fire. Men were yelling, stampeding their way forward through barbed wire.

A shell fell to his left. The explosion shook the ground. All at once the air was full of the unspeakable. Men were being blown apart, their blood staining the

useless ground for which they fought. The force of the blast knocked Paul over, face down in the stinking mire. When he turned his head the slowly sinking flare illuminated only clouds of smoke which mercifully shielded from his vision the worst of the horror. He let his face fall forward in the madness of despair.

Into his insanity came the sound of weeping. Paul lifted his face. All was dark, but through the blackness he could just discern the glowing of a fire. Defying the clinging mud he fought his way to his feet. He stumbled forward. He could see more now, two figures, both dark. Somewhere deep inside was the insistent memory that he had to reach them, there was something he had to do. He waded on through the glutinous soup of nightmare.

There was a whistle, a high-pitched whine, a heavy thud and then Paul's world was filled with scarlet. As he fell forward he realised, with horror, that he was falling onto another body, another casualty. Mercifully, before he landed, consciousness fled.

* * * * * * *

Paul was woken by the soft wetness of a warm tongue. He opened his eyes. Sally was standing over him, licking his face. Dazed, he looked about him.

The sitting-room was in darkness, the fire long died out. Liz lay slumped on the sofa, exactly as he had left her. He was lying where he had fallen, hand extended towards Liz. Paul shook his head as the unwelcome memories flooded his mind. It was impossible; it couldn't have happened.

Bemused, he stared around the room, the mud of Flanders as real to him now as it had been in the depth of the pit of horror he had so recently inhabited. He must have been dreaming. Yes, that was it, he had been having a nightmare. He had been watching 'Oh What A Lovely War!' and had fallen asleep. Liz too. She must have slept.

One look at her curled body told him that Liz's was no natural sleep. He reached out to shake her and as he did so a scrap of paper fell from his hand. He retrieved it and smoothed out its creases. An old piece of paper; faded ink.

'My darling Lizzie' he read. The chill of fear that engulfed him brought beads of icy perspiration onto his brow. He felt helpless, swept along by whatever was in this house. He sat down beside Liz and wept.

* * * * * * *

Later, as he lay in bed, Liz held tightly in his arms. Paul reached a decision.

He had finally managed to rouse Liz who claimed to remember nothing. By the time he had got her into bed and joined her it was well after midnight. Paul calculated that his 'experience' had lasted more than five hours. Five hours of his life lost! He could not explain what had happened to him.

Liz was so dreamy, so lost inside her own mind that he had not attempted any account of what had happened. He accepted Liz's opinion that they had both dozed off in front of the television. But they hadn't. Paul had the scrap of paper to prove that something unnatural had occurred. The scrap of paper and something else: Liz was acting strangely, almost like an actress performing a role. She was self-absorbed and did not seem to hear anything he said. She moved as though in a trance

Now, lying wakeful in bed, Paul planned his actions. First thing in the morning he would persuade Liz to see a doctor. He was not happy at the way she was behaving. There could possibly be a physical reason for that; a doctor could tell. And when they had been to the doctor, Paul would go to a priest. This thing, whatever it was, had to be dealt with.

CHAPTER TWELVE

Liz was having a nightmare. She was swimming in the pool by the old summerhouse. Her legs were entangled in weeds. She was struggling, twisting and turning; writhing about. In her attempt to free herself her arms too had become hopelessly ensnared.

Suddenly she was awake. She stared around the room, wildly for a moment, and then relaxed as she realised that her near-drowning had been a bad dream. She was tangled in the duvet and her nightdress had become twisted around her body. That explained a lot. Sleepily she looked at the clock. 3 a.m.

Liz was lying quite still, trying to remember how they had spent the previous evening (for her mind was curiously blank) when she saw the shadow in the doorway. Anxiously she looked around for Sally but the dog was nowhere to be seen. She extended her hand under the quilt and nudged urgently at Paul's leg. There was no response; he was sleeping soundly. Her disquiet mounting she turned back with dread to the shadow.

It had thickened, darkened and taken on the distinct form of a human figure. As Liz watched it grew in density until she could no longer see the doorframe through it. Fear clutched at her stomach as she acknowledged that the figure was that of Elizabeth Aubrey. Almost against her will Liz found that her gaze was drawn to the eyes of the creature.

Elizabeth Aubrey's eyes were deep violet and they burned into Liz's with a compelling intensity. Hardly knowing what she was doing Liz threw back the covers and got out of bed. Elizabeth Aubrey beckoned; Liz followed.

As she trailed up the attic staircase in the wake of the ghostly figure, Liz knew nothing except for the unspoken command to follow. As Elizabeth Aubrey reached the centre attic she passed through the open door and crossed to the window. There she raised an imperious hand, summoning Liz to her side.

The attic, like the bedroom downstairs, was filled with moonlight. Liz crossed the rough wooden boards, her bare feet not heeding the splinters. She stood alongside the figure and, as one, they turned and looked down into the garden.

The gravel drive was silver in the moonlight; the lawns almost blue. Liz caught the flicker of movement over towards the far side. Two figures were emerging from the path through the shrubbery which led from the summerhouse. One of the figures was Elizabeth Aubrey, the other a soldier, the officer from the photograph. He had his arm around Elizabeth's shoulder but moved it, guiltily,

as they emerged. They began to cross the lawn and Liz craned forward to peer over the edge of the roof so that she could watch their approach to the house. As she did so the figure next to her placed a ghostly hand on her shoulder. A convulsive sob filled the air and the spectre cried out, "The happiest day of my life! All gone! All wasted!"

Liz turned quickly, but the figure was no longer beside her. Elizabeth Aubrey stood by the fireplace, wringing her hands in anguish and weeping. Still in a deep reverie, Liz could feel no fear, only the desire to ease the suffering of this poor creature. As she watched the figure opened its arms in a welcoming embrace. Liz stepped forward into the encircling arms; into oblivion.

* * * * * * *

Something awakened Paul. Sally was howling. He reached out towards Liz to stop her getting out of bed, to tell her that he would go down and attend to the dog. The bed was empty. The quilt on Liz's side had been thrown back and the hollow where she had slept was cold. Fear gripped Paul. He leapt out of bed. The door was open and he ran onto the landing, not knowing why a feeling of blind panic had overtaken him.

Anxiously he called out, "Liz! Lizzie! Where are you?"

"Upstairs," came the reply. And icy fingers of dread crept into Paul's mind when he heard; for it was not Liz's voice.

He took the stairs to the attic two at a time. Outside the closed door of the centre room he paused for a moment. Taking his courage in both hands he stretched out a shaking hand and turned the handle. As the door fell open he gasped, almost choking on the overpowering perfume that emanated from the room. The scent of violets filled the air.

Liz stood near the window and Paul almost screamed as he saw that she was wearing the dusty black dress. She turned to face him and the face she wore was distorted with anger, with hatred. He could not believe that this was Liz, his wife. He stepped towards her but came to an abrupt halt when Liz screamed, "Get out! Get out!" her voice was hysterical with rage. "This is my room. You do not belong here!"

"Liz, come on! It's me, Paul!" he pleaded, at the same time taking a cautious step in her direction.

"Stop there!" she cried. "You have no right to come in here, to follow me about!"

"I came upstairs to check that you were OK I was worried about you, frightened for you when I woke up and found you gone." He spoke cajolingly, gradually inching forward. He had to reach her, to help her. Perhaps if he could only touch her it would bring Liz back to herself.

It was clear that Liz had not heard him. She was speaking to some unseen person, responding to an argument that she alone could hear.

"I am a child no longer Father! I will not do as you command me. I am a woman. I have a right to my privacy!" Liz paused. Paul watched in fascination as she appeared to listen before responding, "Yes Father, I have continued to keep my diary, but it is for my own eyes. No-one, especially not you who have blighted my life, has any prerogative to it!"

While Liz paused, intent on hearing the response of her unseen interrogator, Paul took a rapid step forward and grasped her firmly by the wrists. Her strength surprised him and she bucked and twisted away, an untamed horse.

"Get off! Let go of me, you monster!" she screamed.

Paul looked into her eyes and beheld her madness, flickering, dancing; alive with consuming fire. And as he held her he became aware of a seething black shadow surrounding her; almost an aura of darkness.

In a moment there was a searing pain in his wrist. Liz had bitten him! He looked down. A slow trickle of blood was creeping from the wound. The insane creature that was Liz took advantage of his moment's diversion and jerked free from Paul's imprisoning grasp.

Her wildness frightened Paul and he stepped away. Abruptly his back was up against the old fireplace. This seemed to increase Liz's passion.

"Get away from there!" she spat at him.

Paul didn't move.

Liz's eyes scanned the room in a frenzy. All at once she lurched forward and seized a heavy hammer, lying where it had been left by a workman. Triumphantly she raised it above her head and began to swing it, slowly, rhythmically, menacingly.

"Get away from there Father or I will throw this at your head!" Her crazy eyes showed that she meant it.

Paul was mesmerised by the moving hammer. The moonlight caught it as it swung, round and round. He watched Liz but could do nothing. A great calmness swept over him and inside, unbidden, came the certain knowledge that this had to be; this was the way things had to happen.

Trance-like, Paul turned his back on Liz. He was facing the fireplace and

in the dusty speckled mirror propped up against the chimney-breast he could still see the hammer, swinging, swinging. He saw Liz's mouth open in a scarlet scream and heard the ragged, shouted single word, "NO!"

In a moment there was a rushing sound as the hammer passed his left ear, missing him by a whisker. The mirror exploded in shards of light which flew everywhere. Instinctively Paul raised his arms to protect his head, at the same time sinking to his knees.

Liz flew across the room, a thing possessed. She pushed Paul aside and scrabbled manic fingers through the rubble in the hearth, through the soot and debris dislodged by the hammer's impact. Sobbing she raked, her fingers not heeding the sharp fragments of stone. With a cry of triumph she uncovered a black metal box, seized it and clutched it to her. At the same moment Paul heard a sigh, a sob of relief. In an instant the charged atmosphere of the attic was gone. Liz crumpled forward enclosing and protecting her treasure: a puppet whose strings had been severed.

* * * * * * *

They sat at the kitchen table. They were dressed, Liz now in her own clothes. Each had a strong drink at their elbow. In the centre of the table sat the black metal strongbox. Paul and Liz regarded it warily.

After Liz's collapse Paul had carried her downstairs and laid her gently on their bed. She had never relaxed her grip on the grimy box. He had gone back to close the attic door, as though by shutting it he was excluding all behind it from their lives. He returned to Liz expecting to need to call a doctor. He placed a gentle hand on her forehead.

Liz opened her eyes and smiled up at him. Paul's heart leapt within him, for the lunacy was gone; the smile pure Liz.

"I guess it's all over. I guess that I have at last found what she has been driving me to?"

"Yes Liz," Paul sighed with relief. "It's all over."

In spite of the early hour both had showered and dressed, and now, here they were contemplating the firmly locked box.

"There's no option but to break it open," decided Paul, and he went to the drawer to fetch a knife. He handed it to Liz. "Here, you do it. I don't think Miss Aubrey would take kindly to my interference!" and although he laughed the chill of fear rippled down his spine. Events were all too recent to joke about.

Liz inserted the knife under the lip. With a sharp twist the lid snapped open. The air sighed around them as they looked inside.

On top of a stack of papers and books lay the ruin of a pressed posy. As Liz already knew, it was violets, friable and faded with age. Gently she removed them and placed them carefully on the table.

Next, Liz removed a bundle of letters, tied with ribbon. The top one was torn and, wonderingly, Paul withdrew the scrap of paper still in his pocket from the previous evening. He held it out to Liz. She took it and read 'My darling Lizzie'. She laid it on the bundle. It was clear that it had been torn from the uppermost letter. How? Neither could guess.

The letters put aside for future examination they turned their attention once more to the box. The pen which Liz removed next made Paul gasp, for it was identical to that which he had seen in the attic. Liz ignored his surprise. Indeed, Liz seemed unsurprised by anything, almost as though she already knew what she would find.

Liz lifted out three books: Diaries. The top one was handsomely bound in black leather, gold-tooled down the spine. She opened the front cover. Inside was inscribed,

To my own dear Lizzie, With Love, John Fraser January 1918

There was another, similar volume, again a gift from John Fraser, for the year 1917. The third and last book was a nondescript cardboard backed diary. Inside, a bold, firm hand had written,

The diary of Elizabeth Alice Aubrey 1916.

"This is it, Paul, this is the key to all that has been happening here. I told you that it was Lizzie Aubrey haunting this place. Now we can find out why: We can lay her spirit to rest.

The atmosphere around them was electric as Liz opened the first diary and began to read.

PART TWO

LIZZIE AUBREY'S DIARIES

NOTE: There follows relevant extracts from the diaries of Elizabeth Alice Aubrey. These extracts have been selected and presented by Liz Graham and are taken from three volumes discovered in Brabage Vicarage. The diaries cover a period from June 1916 to November 1918. Elizabeth (Lizzie) was aged twenty to twenty-two during this period of her life.

June 19th 1916 - Monday

Father is furious. Mother says that we must go to the social evening at the Farquharsons' - Father does not want us to attend. Mother says that it is positively our patriotic duty to go; Father does not think it desirable for us to mix with all those uniforms! It's all quite exciting. I have never seen Mother stand up to Father before as she is now doing. Father says that he is master in this house and that we must abide by his decision. Mother was tight-lipped and said nothing in reply. However, later in the day (this afternoon) Colonel Farquharson himself called on Father and asked if he would be so kind as to allow "his charming daughters, Elizabeth and Mary, to attend a small gathering of local gentlefolk and army officers".

The officers are all from his own regiment and very soon will be off to the Front. The Colonel thought that it was the very least we could do before "the brave chaps face the Boche", we must give them a good send off. Of course Father could only assent, for to refuse would have been churlish. Also Father would not wish to offend the Farquharsons - or indeed any of their class.

Mother came and told us - Mary and me - that we were to go and she could not fail to hide her own excitement at the prospect of chaperoning us. Poor Mother! I'm sure that beneath that sober exterior is the heart and soul of a fun-loving girl.

June 22nd 1916 - Thursday

I am so excited that I can barely sit still to write my diary. Tonight we are to go to the Farquharsons' and we are to stay out until three in the morning! Father has done nothing but mutter and grumble and dismiss all the 'silly nonsense'! Mary and I have chosen our dresses and spent hours trimming them and smartening them up - another cause for complaint from Father who said that the time would be better spent on church business or parish matters. Mr. Carstairs is to let us have some of the choicest blooms from the conservatory to make our corsages. I'm sure that if Father knew of this he would tut-tut and comment on the profligate waste of God's gifts of nature!

I cannot spare the time to write more. Mother is coming upstairs to help dress my hair. Think of it, my first proper dance - at twenty years of age!

June 25th 1916 - Sunday

I have been in such a spin that I have been unable to discipline my thoughts to write my diary. It is Sunday afternoon and I have claimed 'indisposition' preventing me from taking Sunday School and attending Evensong. I do not know how Father has reacted as I have remained in my own room since returning from morning service. I am truly indisposed. My insides feel like water, my hands tremble and my heart is a-flutter.

The social evening was wonderful. I could hardly believe that there were so many cheerful and charming young men in the whole world, let alone in one regiment! Mary and I danced until I was sure that our shoes must be quite worn out! Even Mother was pestered with requests to dance. She refused of course and spent the evening sitting with the other parish matrons "watching the young people enjoy themselves". Naturally they indulged in a good gossip, something which Mother seldom manages. They were mainly dressed in black and made me think of nothing more than rooks gathering in their parliament and chattering over the day's business.

In the excitement of the evening, in the whirling and swaying of the dance, it was easy to put out of mind the fate of these noble young officers. They are all so brave, so manly! Mary and I had decided that it was our patriotic duty to dance with as many of them as we could. We set about our duty with enthusiasm! I did my part commendably until Lieutenant John Fraser asked me to dance. I heard a polite, low voice from slightly behind my left shoulder,

"Excuse me Miss Aubrey..."

I turned and our eyes met. I felt a spark leap between us. I stood, stretching

out my hand towards him before he had even finished his request! He held me as one would handle a marvellously fragile piece of delicate porcelain. As we danced he chatted politely with me but we were both aware of the undercurrents flowing between us.

Within the space of two or three dances I felt that I had known him all my life. By good chance, as the music died away after the third dance we had shared, we were on the other side of the room from Mother and Mary. The Colonel mounted the small orchestra dais and requested everyone to proceed to supper. Nothing could have been more natural than for Lieutenant Fraser - John - to escort me to the supper table. Mother had neither time nor opportunity to object for Colonel Farquharson and some of his fellow senior officers descended on the "rooks' parliament" and escorted those ladies to supper in the most charming manner.

I danced every remaining dance with him. My feet were dancing on air. I am in love! He is to come and see Father just as soon as he can in order to ask permission to correspond with me from the Front. There is no reason for my dread, for John is of good family. Indeed, his people are, if anything, above us socially. But I know that Father will not approve. I think that he has already determined that Elizabeth Alice Aubrey will remain "Spinster of this Parish". Well. I will not! I have more to offer than sick visiting, Sunday School, day school and parish duties, and of course helping Mother with the housekeeping accounts. John has ignited a spark in me which is rapidly fanning to a flame. I don't care what Father says, I will write to him!

June 27th 1916 - Tuesday

The storm is come! We were sitting in the morning room, the whole family. Mary, Mother and I were sewing some small clothes for the Bates' baby. The family are in such poverty that the poor mite has arrived in this world with no clothes to be dressed in. Father was lecturing us to have a care that we were not too generous else the next babe born in the village may also be without clothes when it is seen how easily they are got!

There was a timorous tap at the door, and on Father's instruction in came Hester to announce a visitor. Of course it was Lieutenant Fraser! He greeted us all most politely, not able to refrain from squeezing my hand and so making me blush uncontrollably! He asked Father if he might have a private interview with him. Father rose and led John to the study. On their leaving the room Mother and Mary turned immediately to me, sure of the reason for my blushes. I babbled on about the work in hand, the visiting rota, anything to keep our talk away from John.

After what seemed like an age Father sent for me. In the study John was standing before Father's desk. Father was seated. Father told me that Lieutenant Fraser had made a formal request that he may correspond with me when he returned to France. Did I wish that to be? Trying to disguise my eagerness, but blushing furiously, I said that I did.

Father stood, and then rose to his full and dignified height, "Then you may correspond with each other, with one stipulation."

We both stared at him, rabbits hypnotised by the snake.

"And that is that I see each and every letter that is sent and received!"

I looked down at the floor, ashamed that John would see how Father kept us all so firmly under his control.

After momentary faltering John replied, "Of course Sir! Thank you Sir! May Elizabeth accompany me to the gate Sir?"

Father, who hates to give anything away, paused before consenting. John reached out to shake Father's hand but he had already turned and was looking out of the window. I knew that his unspoken words were a caution to me to beware; from this window he could see the entire length of the drive. We would be under his gimlet eye as we walked together!

After taking his leave of Mother and Mary we left the house together. As we stepped outside John snatched one brief kiss as we stood under the verandah - momentarily outside of Father's field of vision. John then produced a posy of the most beautiful hothouse violets. They were a little crushed as he had kept them inside his jacket, but magnificent. I intend to press them and keep them for ever! We walked demurely, side by side, to the gates. A nonchalant look back at the house showed Father at his study window, watching us intently.

John is expecting to have a few days embarkation leave and after that to be sent to France. How my heart trembles at the thought of him fighting over there. We have decided that we will think of a way to outwit Father and evade his spying. When we meet again next week we will lay our plans! The large buddleia bush by the gate allowed us to escape Father's vigilance and indulge in a last kiss, which has only left me hungry for more of his lips! How sinful it seems for a young lady to write down such thoughts! Is true love sinful? I know that whatever happens between us the love that John and I share is too beautiful, too pure, to be sinful!

July 6th 1916 - Thursday

He is gone and I am so cast down that I see no point in living! I think that I must have experienced the happiest three days of my life. John has been spending his embarkation leave at home, the other side of Framley, but we have been together every day. Father has not been well pleased that my parish work has suffered, but I will have plenty of time to make amends for that, whereas John is now on his way to Hell! (How Father would disapprove if he was to see my use of that word.)

We have walked and talked every day. Mary had been instructed to accompany us but has been so discreet in her behaviour that we may almost have been alone. We are all in all to each other. We have decided that we are to write two levels of correspondence. The superficial correspondence will be carried on in the regular way to the vicarage. Father will have the opportunity to open John's letters to me and my replies to him. There will however be a second, secret correspondence carried on between us. John will send letters to be passed to me by his valet's young brother, Arthur Mayfield. Arthur will bring these letters, as soon as he is able, and leave them in the secret place we have discovered in the summerhouse. I will then collect them. I will write my reply to these letters and send it in the usual way, making sure that Father does not suspect anything. Perhaps what we are doing could be perceived as wrong but I consider it wrong for Father to wish to intrude on our own private thoughts and feelings for each other.

I have confided the secret to Mary. She is afraid and thinks it most terribly modern of me to be so headstrong where Father is concerned. Modern! Who could be modern with Father as a parent?

I am to have a portrait taken and send it to John. He has already given me his. I keep it in my tin box with my diary. Pressed here, between the pages, are the violets which John brought me as his first tribute. I treasure them, and as I inhale their scent I see him standing there in his uniform, so strong and tall. I feel his arms around me yet, and feel his lips pressed to mine. Oh John! Why must this terrible war take you away from me?

I sit writing my diary up in the attic. It is one of the few places in the house that I can be certain to remain undisturbed. As I look out of the window, over the sunlit grounds, I cannot but remember the days we have just spent together. The weather was glorious and we walked each day in the 'wilderness' (as we called it). The small lake is buried in the midst of the plantation, and next to the lake is the summerhouse which John and I have, in these past few days, made our own.

Mary has been so good. She would walk with us to the trees, no doubt closely observed by Father! Once inside the wilderness she stayed a discreet distance in front of us, never turning; never interrupting. At the lake she spent her time on the shore, sketching or sewing, while John and I have been free to enjoy the pleasure of each other's company in the privacy and freedom afforded by the summerhouse. I feel that I have grown up at last! For the first time in my life I know that I have the strength to stand against Father. John is my destiny. I will stay true to him and when this horrible war is over at last we will marry and set up home for ourselves. When the children come along (for children will surely come into such a loving home) they will know only happiness and freedom and joy. They will not be reproved or told off to do their duty as we have been.

John has promised that when he is back next I will be asked to meet his mother (his father being long since dead). How I quail at the thought. And yet how I long for his return!

Today I have once again taken up my parish duties -much to the satisfaction of Father. Even though I am busy the time passes so slowly! I feel that while John is away there is a part of myself missing. Several people in the village have had cause to comment on my abstracted air. Mrs. Silcock made me blush when she said, before a great group of people, that I must be in love! I hastily covered my embarrassment. Father would be so angry if he thought that I was being gossiped about. Who knows what form his reaction would take?

As I reach to snuff out my candle my last thoughts are of John. Please God, keep him safe.

July 14th 1916 - Friday

Today I had my first (formal) letter from John. Father has made a point of telling Hester that all letters received at the house must be placed in his study. He alone will be responsible for their delivery. At breakfast time he entered the room and handed over a letter which he had opened and clearly read since he commented on it over breakfast. John has described his journey to the Front and the settling in of his company. In spite of finding the trenches in rather a mess and having to start their period of duty in cleaning and organising their living quarters, they are in good spirits.

John's letter is full of energy and bursting with patriotism. He says that one of the most important roles of the new arrivals is to breathe new life and enthusiasm through the jaded atmosphere of the trenches. There is nothing wrong with the letter - indeed it is very interesting - but it is so distant; so cold and formal.

I cannot believe that such is written by the same man who has spent his time with me. I am very much afraid that I am going to find it an onerous task to answer this letter. John tells me to be certain, should I see his batman's younger brother Arthur - who has cause to come frequently to Brabage in order to see an aged relative - to tell him that his brother Thomas is well and will write to the family very soon.

Whist I know that Father is displeased that I should be the vehicle of conveying a message to a servant he will allow me to do so, as in the war we must all play our part. I am sure that this message to John is a warning for me to expect a secret letter from him soon; that I must pay a visit to the summerhouse.

July 25th 1916 - Tuesday

At last it has come! I have been to the summerhouse every day and looked in our secret place. Until today there has been nothing. I began to believe that John regretted our love and that the cold, formal, 'Dear Elizabeth' letters would be all that I would receive. I hold his letter next to my heart. 'Dear Lizzie' it starts. Such outpourings of his love bring a blush to my cheek. He says that until he met me, to do his patriotic duty was the ultimate aim of his life. Now he wants the war over and to be back here at Framley where we can be together. I do not think that his patriotism is diminished, it is rather that his love for me overrides it. Oh John! I wish that you could be with me. He says that they all get very little sleep. There are raids every night, and even when they are not on duty the noise of the guns, the whistles that signal gas alerts, the screaming of overhead shells and trench mortars, the constant state of alertness, do not permit rest. The officers are more fortunate that the men in that they are at liberty to withdraw behind the lines when not on duty. The men have no choice but to remain. John does not say it, but I feel certain that he does not approve of such division.

This letter was written on the same date as that which went through Father's hands, and John says that this should be our pattern. We should write both the official and the secret letters on the same day, for then I will know when to go to the summerhouse. He waits anxiously for my reply and urges me to enclose my portrait in order that he may feel closer to me.

Oh John! I love you so much!

YOUR FACE IN THE FLAG

Not cattle but men spill from the train.
They gather their kit, form up into line;
They march away singing, off to the Front,
Like hounds on the scent, they're eager to hunt.

Their eyes shine with ardour,
Their breasts swell with valour,
They march ever forward.
He each has his story,
His own private glory
Driving him onward.

Not for their country, nor yet for their King
It is rather for love that these men sing;
Love for their comrades, their kith and their kin
Makes them so brave, so determined to win.

Their eyes shine with ardour,
Their breasts swell with valour,
They march ever forward.
He each has his story,
His own private glory
Driving him onward.

So what spurs me on? What vision is mine
Through the horror of trenches, the hell of the line?
You keep me safe, it's you that I see,
Your face in the flag, love, proud to be free.

Our eyes shine with ardour,
Our breasts swell with valour,
We march ever forward.
We each have our story,
Our own private glory
Driving us onward.

John Fraser 1916

August 9th 1916 - Wednesday

When I went to take my regular lesson at the day school today I found the children buzzing with such sad news. Two of the young men of the village have been killed in France. Young Jamie Shipton, a relative of one of them, was kept away from school as a mark of respect. (Father did not approve of that and told the headmaster so!) The other young man is Peter Thomas's son and was only conscripted a short time ago. They both perished in the Battle of the Somme. It is such a great battle and they say that the roar of the guns can be heard even in England! How such news makes me fear for John's safety. Father merely pooh-poohs my anxiety and says to remember that Lieutenant Fraser is an officer. While it is in the nature of things for the ordinary ranks to be killed, the officers usually remain safe. How little he knows the character of my John! Father has instructed me to visit the bereaved families and, with much bad grace, has decided that he cannot avoid mentioning these deaths in his sermon on Sunday, although, he says, neither the Shiptons nor the Thomases are exactly part of the backbone of the church! For a man of God, Father can be most uncharitable.

August 25th 1916 - Friday

Great excitement! Mary and I have received an invitation to visit Mrs. Fraser (John's mother) at Park House, Framley. She writes to ask if we would care to take tea with her. Father is to allow us to go! John must have suggested the invitation to his mother. This probably means that he does not expect leave for some time. I look forward to meeting Mrs. Fraser, though my excitement is tinged with trepidation!

August 30th 1916 - Wednesday

Yesterday Mary and I took tea with Mrs. Fraser. She is charming! She is very correct and yet she manages to be warm and friendly. Mary says that it must be the Scottish blood, for I believe that the family came originally from Scotland. She talked about many topics which were of interest to Mary and me. However, she spoke mainly about John, whom she obviously adores. While wanting him, indeed urging him to take up a commission and do his duty, she has a mother's natural reluctance to have her son exposed to the dangers of war. Mrs. Fraser is a widow and has two sons. Her other son, Charles, is only sixteen years old and is away at school. She lives a lonely life during term time since John has been away. She hopes fervently that the war will be over before Charles leaves school, for in her eyes he is still a baby! To think that when this war began we were all

told that it would be over in such a short time (by Christmas they said at the time). Now I think that we all feel that it could go on for ever!

Mrs. Fraser expressed her joy that John and I were such good friends and hopes that Mary and I will be permitted to visit regularly in the future. She was not specific but I am sure that she knows how things lie between John and me.

Of course, when we got home Father was extremely scathing. He made much of the parish duties we had missed and supposed that we had found it more spiritually uplifting to be visiting the gentry in Framley rather than the poor homes in Brabage. I felt so angry when I thought about how he had regarded those same families when their sons had been killed in France. I was about to speak but Mary, seeing the expression on my face and knowing my feelings exactly, pinched me hard. I bit back my words but felt them nevertheless. I am sure that Mary and I do our parish duty fully and that even we may be allowed some time to do as we please. Mother was standing near and heard Father rebuking us, but she tightened her lips and said not a word. Her loyalty is so great that she would never speak to me against Father, but I am sure that she feels his injustice.

When I next write to John I will tell him how well his mother liked me and how we are to be great friends. I am anxiously awaiting a letter from John. The Battle of the Somme still rages and so many have been killed or wounded. While I pray to God to keep John safe I question the very existence of a God who can let such useless battle rage and so many young and innocent men lose their lives. I attempted some discussion with Father on the subject some days ago but he refused to discuss theology with a woman! I try to counter by using Mrs. Pankhurst's arguments. I told Father that if women can work in factories making the shells that are fired from the guns, then surely we have a right to discuss the war that these guns are used in! Father glowers and wonders where I have got hold of such outrageous ideas. He adds that Mrs. Pankhurst should learn her place as a dutiful wife instead of filling women's heads with such nonsense. I am thankful that John is a little more enlightened and applauds the efforts of Mrs. Pankhurst and others like her. He believes that women are to be regarded as equals by men. What a wonderful marriage we shall have!

August 31st 1916 - Thursday

Almost the worst has happened. A letter arrived this morning from John and Father was more than usually grave when he handed it over - opened as usual. John is wounded! He has been sent back from the Front to a field hospital from where he writes. He has a bullet wound to the left shoulder and carries his arm

in a sling. He reassures us all that it is no mortal wound, but I felt my face whiten and my head spin when I read the dreadful news. I know that it is a silly idea but I felt that our love would protect him from all harm - now that protection is shattered. I want to go to France. I could nurse; I could do anything just to be close to him. If I did such a thing it would have to be undertaken in secret, for I ventured to suggest the idea to Father and he regarded me coldly and said,

"What use would you be in France? You are totally without training and I would not have you scrubbing floors and doing menial tasks. You are of more use to me here in the parish!"

Father really lives in the last century. It is as though all that Florence Nightingale has done has gone unheeded by him! I am now up in the attic. There has been no letter in the summerhouse, but I know that the two letters, though despatched together, may at times be separated by some days. The grounds are in darkness and only the lights from the house windows illuminate the lawns. Everywhere I look in the gardens I think of John, of our happiness during those few short days together. I seem to see him everywhere, hear once more our laughter as we walk through the shrubbery or around the walled rose garden.

Father is in his study; Mother and Mary sit sewing in the drawing room. I pleaded a sick headache in order to enable me to come upstairs, just to be alone and write my diary. I have made this attic my own, a place where I can be myself. I write to my diary as the only trusted confidante I have. I hope and pray that soon there will be a letter from John.

September 5th 1916 - Tuesday

It has taken until today for John's letter to reach me. I would walk to the summerhouse in spite of Father's protestations regarding the weather. It has been wet; an unpredictable wind blowing squally showers around the house. I have been to the summerhouse every day since John's 'official' letter arrived. Father expressed surprise that I would venture out today in such weather. I told him that I must take my daily exercise, however inclement the day may be! Furthermore the weather is hardly worse than the poor weather of the summer. People have said that it is the dust and smoke from France that has spoiled our summer. My insistence was rewarded for there was indeed a letter from John under the window seat in the usual place. Now that I have read his own words reassuring me of the minor nature of his wound I am much comforted. I almost wish that his wound was more severe, in order that he would be sent home - but that is a wicked thought!

He has received my letter and my portrait. How he writes about my portrait! He tells me that some of his fellow officers have begun to tease him when he receives two letters together, both in my hand. They wonder about the identity of the lady who writes these letters, two by two. Perhaps, they wonder, would she also care to write to them as she seems to greatly enjoy the occupation of writing? John replies in kind! While not disclosing my identity he tells them that I love him far too much for all the love to be contained in one small envelope! He got his wound in a small skirmish when he and some of his men were caught out in 'No Man's Land'. How dreadful that sounds! They all got back and only he and one other were wounded. They are both expecting to be back at the Front very soon. Please God, preserve him!

September 8th 1916 - Friday

Mrs. Fraser visited us at the vicarage today. She was so anxious about John's wound that she needed to come and talk to us, seeking mutual reassurance. She looked quite ill - for no doubt the anxiety has taken its toll. She got on famously with Mother. (Father was absent as it was one of his days for teaching in the village day school.) She has asked that we all go and visit her soon. As she left she squeezed my hand and kissed my cheek so fondly, whispering, "God will protect him my dear!" I know, by the look in her eye, that she knows all and will prove a friend and ally to us both. I hope that she may charm Father as she has succeeded in charming Mother!

October 6th 1916 - Friday

Today we all (Father, Mother, Mary and me) went to visit Mrs. Fraser. It was the first time Father had met her. She was her loving, charming self towards me and she made Mother and Mary most welcome. However it was to Father that she paid most attention. She cajoled and flattered him until he fairly shone. Mother could see the game that was afoot and stood back, enjoying the fisherman (Mrs. Fraser) playing the trout! She hooked and landed him and Father has come away with the notion that there is not a finer lady in the parish than Mrs. Fraser. How easily Father is won over by flattery! Mrs. Fraser's anxieties continue. In spite of the fact that John has recovered fully and returned to the Front, her fears will not be quieted. I, on the other hand, have become peculiarly fatalistic. I believe that whatever fate has in store for us, so we will receive it accordingly; there is nothing we can do to avoid it. Father would no doubt perceive that as a pagan belief - well, pagan I may very well be (although try as

I might I cannot see myself dancing naked around the Maypole come the proper season!).

I had a private talk with Mrs. Fraser. Her anxiety is not limited to John alone. She is worried on a second count; about her other son, Charles. She has received reports from school that are not good. Charles is unsettled and talks of joining his brother at the Front, though he is underage. When I write my next private letter to John I will make space to voice his mother's fears and ask that he write to dissuade Charles from his intention. I believe that such was Mrs. Fraser's intention in mentioning the subject to me. What a fine, discreet woman she is!

Once more it is after dark when I write my journal. I have come to feel more at home here in the attic with my pen and candle than I am downstairs. I take care to hide my diary, together with John's letters (quite a collection by now) up here in the attic. The 'official' letters I leave in my room; after all if Father has read them why should I not leave them open to the world? Perhaps I may consider publishing them in the 'Framley Gazette'! I must not be jocular.

As always, my closing thoughts are with you John. God bless you and keep you safe my darling.

October 18th 1916 - Wednesday

Today Father almost caught me out in our double correspondence! I am sure that his suspicions are still not allayed. Father was reading his newspaper, Mother was making up some household accounts. Mary and I were organising our day's visiting in the village. (Mrs. Shipton is ill and needs some medicine and Joan Wycherley has taken to her bed and rants that the end of the world is nigh!) Father put aside his newspaper in order to correct some small item with which Mother was struggling and my eye was taken by the large headline. The losses continue to mount at the Somme. I took up the newspaper, anxiously scanning the columns for any item pertinent to my own John. There is a deal of criticism of Marshal Haig concerning the lack of progress in the war. Of course, most of the criticism is implied as it cannot be allowed that the morale of the nation should decline! Father turned back as I was reading the account and commented that such was not suitable reading matter for a woman! Naturally the usual disagreement followed and we went on arguing about the progress (or rather, the lack of it) of the war. Among many things that I said I commented that our troops were not as well trained as those of the Germans. Furthermore, the Germans kept their own men more informed and provided them with better equipment than did our own government. Father denied the truth of my assertion. I countered by

telling him that John had said that in the trenches, which they had fought so hard to win, they had found the evidence of German superiority. Father started to bluster and then suddenly stopped, mid-sentence.

"When did John write this, Elizabeth? It is in no letter that I have read!"

I coloured and stammered, realising too late that I was betraying information from our private correspondence. Eventually I managed to stammer out that Mrs. Fraser had told me of it; that it had been in a letter that she had received. Although Father did not counter, he gave me suspicious looks as he took up his paper, scorning further discussion. I must be careful to keep a tighter rein on this impulsive tongue of mine!

It has been a dreary, wet October day and my heart goes out to all those of our soldiers floundering in the mud. There have been more men lost in these last few months than were lost in the whole of Ypres. Please God be with them all - but most especially with John!

October 21st 1916 - Sunday

Today I have taught Sunday School as usual, but very interesting it has proved to be. Jamie Shipton started it all by asking me about white feathers. He is a cheeky young monkey and really very quick and intelligent. He asked why it was that in the Bible we are told not to fight back, to turn the other cheek, but yet we had hundreds upon thousands of men fighting in France. Did this mean that the government disobeyed the word of God? I was puzzled for a moment until I hit upon a way out of the matter. I explained the fact that the events of the Bible took place almost two thousand years ago when the world was a different place. He did not listen to my answer but merely continued his theme, asking how it was that 'Parson' (meaning Father) thrashed him but two days ago for fighting in the playground with Daniel Evans and preached at him to turn the other cheek. Young Hannah Wright answered him sharply that,

"War be different. Them as is fightin' is sojers - it be their job to fight!"

Before I could intervene the class began to discuss the merits of being a soldier or flying in the Royal Flying Corps. A heated debate followed about whether it was better to be flying high above the guns, dropping bombs, or to be on the ground receiving them. Some maintained that it was better to be on the ground, firing at the easy target the aeroplanes make against the sky. Hannah again stepped in and lisping slightly, giving me shy, sidelong glances, she capped all the arguments by saying,

"Miss 'Lizabeth's young man be a sojer, so it must be better !"

I hastily changed the subject back to the lesson!

Such words make me fear that if John is widely perceived as my 'young man' Father may come to hear of it and put a stop to our correspondence to avoid any sort of gossip!

November 8th 1916 - Wednesday

Mother, Mary and I went today to Park House in order to visit Mrs. Fraser. We found her very weak and pale. She told us that she had suffered before with this type of ailment and that a week or two, resting in bed, would cure her. She forbade me absolutely to tell John that she is unwell. She asked Mother if I might be permitted to stay with her for a few days. Mother was in a quandary. While wanting to please Mrs. Fraser (she does genuinely hold a deep affection for her) it is a decision that she dare not make without consulting Father. Needless to say, no-one consulted me! I am twenty years old and yet my wishes are as insignificant as if I were two! Mother feared that Father would object to my neglect of parish duties. I was reluctant for another reason. I would have to contact Thomas's brother in order to alter the arrangements for the letter delivery. I would not wish John's private letters to me to lie unopened in the summerhouse until my return. I did not know where he lived or how I could make the necessary enquiries. While I wished wholeheartedly to stay with Mrs. Fraser I was afraid that I would miss our correspondence. Seeing my consternation, Mrs. Fraser managed to whisper that she would 'arrange things with Arthur'. So I was correct in assuming that she knows about our secret letters!

Mother decided that we should all return home and that, if Father agreed, I should return to Park House tomorrow. While Father was not pleased at the thought that I would be out of his control and absent from my duties, he does so wish to impress Mrs. Fraser, he knows that she is an important person in Framley, her influence even extending to the church! While Father claims that he is not a worldly man, he does have ambitions and I think that he likes to be well thought of socially. Mrs. Fraser's good opinion of him may further both his social aspirations and his ambitions for advancement in the church! Whatever his reasons for so deciding, I am to go!

I have had to arrange things very hastily and have hidden John's letters in a tin box in the chimney of the attic. My diary will go with me. I have packed sufficient to stay some weeks with Mrs. Fraser, but cannot imagine that Father will let me stay away for so long.

I look forward to spending time with Mrs. Fraser, I like her so much. I am sure

to find out much more about John than I already know! It will be wonderful to spend time in the relaxing atmosphere of Park House, to live for a time in the house John has known all his life and where we shall live together after our marriage.

November 12th 1916 - Sunday

This morning I went to Framley church. Mrs. Fraser was much too ill to accompany me and so I went along to face the interested stares of the villagers. Whether it is because I am a stranger or whether they already know of my relationship with John I cannot say, but their constant interest kept my face glowing throughout the service.

How different that service was to those conducted in Brabage. The form of the service was, of course, the same, but the Reverend Spencer has such a happy, open face and clearly enjoys his vocation. The sermon was not all gloom and despondency. I must confess that I almost felt that religion could be enjoyed and indulged in with some pleasure. (What a heretical concept that would be to Father!) At the end of the service the Reverend Spencer asked us to join in a few minutes silence to allow thought for those who have died, and those who are still fighting, in the mud of Flanders.

After the service was concluded the Reverend Spencer make a great point of coming to meet me, asking kindly after Mrs. Fraser and asking me to convey the message that he would call on her. He introduced me to some members of the parish who made pleasant conversation, all sending their good wishes to Mrs. Fraser for a speedy recovery.

I walked back to Park House along dank, wet lanes, the November chills striking though my heavy winter coat and the cloying mud caking my shoes. I could not help but think of John and the mud in which he and his men must be suffering. I wondered if they broke off from battle to have church services. There is so much that I do not know about his everyday life!

I spend the afternoon reading to Mrs. Fraser, who dozed gently from time to time. I think that at last she looks a little improved. She has been so very ill. I am writing my diary in my bedroom after tea, while Mrs. Fraser lies down. I find that the leisure hours I enjoy here are hard to accustom myself to. I value the time greatly and know that when I return to Brabage I will miss it most dreadfully.

Mrs. Fraser and I are firm friends and I find that she holds very liberal and up-to-date opinions on the role of women. She is sure that now women have moved into industry enfranchisement must surely come. She anticipates with glee the

time when women will not only be able to vote but may also take up seats in Parliament! I fear that such an event is a long time away. In our debates together I have come to value my own opinions: I feel that the ideas I hold are valid and worthwhile. I can present a sound argument and hope that when I return I will have the opportunity, and indeed the strength, to stand up to Father. We discussed the progress of the war and, like many people, Mrs. Fraser abhors the losses on both sides. It is rather a dilemma to oppose the whole idea of war and yet to feel patriotic towards 'our' soldiers. We are all war-weary and just want our people back.

* * * * * * *

I write again some hours later. After dinner Mrs. Fraser and I played cards for some time (on a Sunday!). She is far from strong and tires easily. She called Alice, her maid, and retired early, leaving me to my own devices. I was far too energetic to sleep and thinking that reading would relax me a little, I walked along to the library to select a book. How grand that sounds! The library is not a large room, being somewhat the size of Father's study. There are hundreds of books there, a huge family Bible and several rather good paintings. The family Bible is always kept on the desk and I opened it, curious about John's background. Recorded there were the births, marriages and deaths of the Fraser family stretching back over many generations. I feel a warmth in my heart when I realise that <u>our</u> marriage will be recorded there one day! I closed the Bible and selected a novel by Trollope. Father would <u>never</u> approve of me reading for pleasure on the Sabbath. I turned out the lights and left the room. As I turned the corner of the passage my attention was caught by a figure sitting in the bay window. It was a soldier, sitting in the gloomy shadow. His face was blackened and his uniform smeared with mud. On looking more closely I saw that the tunic was besmirched by more than mud; there was blood pouring from a huge, gaping wound in the thigh. I stepped forward. His head had, until that moment, been bent forward. He looked up and there was a deep, soul-searching plea in his silent and tormented face. It was John!

I must have fainted for my next memory is of returning to consciousness with Alice chafing my hands and cheeks. She fussed and fretted me into bed, alarmed that I may be seriously ill. I make no attempt to explain how I came to be collapsed on the hall floor, preferring to give the whole matter some thought. I told Alice that I thought I may have a chill coming on, a slight feverishness, after my soaking when returning from church that morning. After busying about, bringing me a

hot drink and ensuring that I was warm and comfortable, Alice left me alone. As she closed the door she muttered that if I were no better by morning Dr. Armstrong would be summoned!

I thought over what had happened to me. What did it mean? It may be merely that we have talked so much of war today, and I have been thinking constantly of John and, of course, I was much mud smeared this morning, that it has all played on my mind. I am in John's house and actively imagine him here with me. Have I conjured his image out of my fertile imagination? Please God let it be no more than that. I have heard of cases where loved ones have been seen at the time ... I cannot even bring myself to write the words! God keep you safe, my darling, and pray that I receive a letter from you soon.

November 14th 1916 - Tuesday

A letter from John this morning! My relief was such that Mrs. Fraser's curiosity was aroused. Of course, I told her nothing of my experience on Sunday.

My relief was, however, short-lived when I found that the letter was dated more than a week ago! As I opened the letter (my own private letter) a folded paper fell out. On opening it I found that it contained three pressed poppies. In his letter John explained that he picked the flowers when he first returned to the Front after our meeting. He pressed them between the leaves of a book, intending to send them to me. He said that during the summer Flanders fields were red with poppies; now, he says, the fields are red with the blood of the fallen.

He is battle weary and makes great efforts to spur on his men. They are all so tired of the Somme. They all keep feeling that the battle is coming to an end but fear that it may be more desire than reality!

He writes of his love (of course) and of his urgent desire to see me again soon. He does not look forward to the prospect of Christmas in the trenches. Poor John! How can any of us celebrate the joyous festival of Christmas with the war raging?

It is such a short letter, he was very tired when he wrote it, but wanted to send me the flowers before the next big push in their sector. He asked if I had seen his mother as he is anxious, not having heard from her for some time. I told Mrs. Fraser of the letter and, now that her health is improving somewhat, she has agreed that I may tell John that I have been staying at Park House. I am to tell him that she has been ill but has now recovered. I intend to write my letter tomorrow as I am uncomfortable at secrets lying between us.

I pray that my letter finds John safe and know that I will have no peace until I hear from him once more.

November 17th 1916 - Friday

Tomorrow I am to return to Brabage. Father sent Mother here to enquire about Mrs. Fraser's health and to ask if I could possibly be spared to return to my parish duties. I could have guessed that Father would not let me stay away for very long. Of course, Mrs. Fraser is much improved. She has said that if I return now, Father may permit me to come again soon as he will be quite easy in his mind that I will not stay away too long. I am sorrowful for I am so very worried about John and I would prefer to stay here, in his own home, until I receive news from him. After my vision on Sunday night (if such it was) I think constantly of John's safety. However, as I am to return I must see Arthur in order to reinstate the summerhouse arrangement.

November 18th 1916 - Saturday

Father is impossible! After returning home before noon today I asked if I could see the newspapers he has had in the past week. I must scan the casualty lists, I am so worried about John. Father made a great show of going to his study in order to fetch them, but did not return. When I sought him out later he was most evasive and wanted to know exactly why I wished to see the newspapers. I was embarrassed by his question, sure that even Father would have been sensitive enough to realise my purpose. He tut-tutted at my discomfort and said that he was sure the papers had been burned. I was forced to tell him plainly why I desired them. He told me that a young lady such as I should not be reading the casualty lists - it was vulgar curiosity. It also demonstrated an unwholesome interest in war.

Of course a furious argument ensued. I cannot believe that Father is so old-fashioned, he gives me such responsibility in the running of the parish yet cannot allow that women should hold any responsible position within society. Our argument has quite spoilt my return home, poor Mother and Mary! Perhaps I should hold my tongue and allow everything to remain quiet and peaceful, but when I think of this the red demon inside me raises his head and will make me speak my mind!

I worry so about John and I cannot think of any way to find out about him - for of course I did not get the newspapers (who can ever win against Father?). Good night and God bless, my darling. My dealings with Father only serve to make me love you more.

November 22nd 1916 - Wednesday

There is still no news from France. Today I was so anxious that after a fruitless visit to the summerhouse I asked Father if I may visit Mrs. Fraser. To my surprise he consented, suggesting only that I take Mary with me. He then instructed me to re-schedule today's parish business to tomorrow. What an onerous task it is to be a parson's daughter!

Mrs. Fraser had no more news. She looked pale and drawn and so I did not dwell on the subject. She is brightened by the prospect that John must be due some leave soon and may be able to cross the Channel and come home. Charles will be home from school in a few weeks and Mrs. Fraser is full of schemes to entertain him. She hopes that I may spend some time here at Framley with them during December.

The news from France is not good. Our losses continue to be extremely heavy. Father will not discuss the war with me, but Mother, Mary and I talk of little else. Mother has collected a great quantity of socks, knitted by the ladies of Brabage. They are to be sent away to France, as she has heard that the puttees the soldiers wear do not protect their feet from the cold and wet of the trenches. How distant the war seems from our small Cheshire village!

December 5th 1916 - Tuesday

At last the news is come! Mrs. Fraser drove over today to tell us that John has been badly injured in his right leg and is to be invalided home. I knew that something was wrong. She does not know the whole story but she has John's own letter. His writing is a little shaky but it is most reassuring to read his own hand. On the night of November 12th (Sunday), John's company took heavy bombardment. John was injured and has been lying in a field hospital until well enough to travel. His leg is broken and the wound quite severe. He is only now able to travel and will be with us in a few days. Mrs. Fraser saw how I paled at the news and embraced me most affectionately. She is to go to London to meet John and to bring him back home. She is to ask Father if I may accompany her. I think that it is most unlikely that Father will give his consent.

December 7th 1916 - Thursday

Mrs. Fraser must be an enchantress indeed! She has persuaded Father to allow me to go with her to London. She used the excuse of her own delicate health and pleads my company as I have cared for her previously. We are to go next Monday, stay the night and return with John on Tuesday. My sorrow is almost taken away at the prospect of going to the capital and returning with

the person dearest in all the world to me. Mother makes as much fuss as if I were going to China! She insists on doing my packing and is as excited as if she was going herself.

December 10th 1916 - Sunday

I am so excited I can hardly write. Tomorrow we are to go to London. I have been so busy getting my parish affairs ordered and passing over my duties to Mary. I am to stay at Park House on my return and may be absent for more than a week. I am sure I will be unable to sleep tonight in the excitement and anticipation of seeing John so soon. I am so grateful for the love and understanding of Mrs. Fraser.

December 11th 1916 - Monday

I write my diary very briefly before I retire for the night. Our journey to town was very tiring and Mrs. Fraser had need of my assistance on several occasions. She remains quite frail after her illness. London is full of soldiers and one hardly sees any man who is not in khaki. While the theatres and music halls continue with their programmes it is evident that a war is in progress. The men here on leave seem to throw themselves into enjoyment with a sort of desperation.

The waiter apologised at dinner for the sparseness of the hotel menu. To me, however, who has never been in such a place, the menu seemed grand indeed. Mrs. Fraser ate a small meal and I am afraid that my own excitement is such that I was unable to eat as well as the grand food merited. After dinner Mrs. Fraser retired early and, after seeing her safely to bed, I sat for an hour in the lounge. I can hardly believe there are so many smart people in the world. They are dressed beautifully and make me feel quite dowdy in my country fashion.

People chattered and were happy - and not a soul was engaged in knitting socks for soldiers! I was asked if I would care to join a game of cards but declined and decided to retire.

My room is most luxurious. I note everything carefully in order that I may give an account to Mother and Mary. However, while I delight in my surroundings I cannot enjoy the luxury. Somewhere John is jolting his painful way towards us. Please God, bring him safe home!

December 12th 1916 - Tuesday

He is here! We are home at Framley! I am too exhausted to write more tonight. My poor John! How I cried!

STAND TO !

"Stand to!" and weary, out we gaze
Across the wasted land.
My keen eyes pierce the swirling haze
My gun clasped tight in hand.

My seeking eyes can almost find
The rolling Cheshire Plain.
A trick of light, a sleight of mind
Can take me home again.

At dawn we hunted, cold grey chill;
Flushed pheasants from the wood.
Now different quarry we must kill
For King and Country's good.

That life's now gone, all swept away
By war and death and slaughter.
Honour and glory now hold sway
Where one ruled light and laughter.

No sweeping vales, no distant spire,
No peaceful mere or river.
Instead it's mud and cruel barbed wire
That fill my view for ever.

Cold hard duty makes me ponder
On life, on love, on you.
At times like this I often wonder
Is this my last 'Stand to!'?

For Death waits eager in the wings
To ambush, gas and blast.
But peace is all this full day brings,
"Stand Down" is called at last.

John Fraser 1916

December 13th 1916 - Wednesday

I can now make amends for my brevity of yesterday. We met John and accompanied him back to Framley. He is so changed that I scarcely recognised him!

His hair has not turned grey; he is not disfigured or anything so dramatic, but he looks so worn. When I saw him last he was a youthful twenty-four; now, when I look into his eyes, I see the burden of war and he looks almost ancient! Still, he is at home and his mother and I will nurse him back to health. Perhaps he will never have to return to the Front, for the war may be over before he is completely well. How my mind jumps about! I must try to write a coherent account of the last two days.

On Tuesday morning Mrs. Fraser and I went to the station to meet John. When the troop train came in I did not know quite what to do. Everywhere there were injured men and their attendants. They were on stretchers, on crutches, in chairs. Some of their wounds were most horrible to behold. Each time I saw a lieutenant I looked apprehensively into his face to see if he were my own John, so changed that I could not recognise him. Nurses were solicitously ushering their charges away and the platform was becoming quite deserted. I had almost given up hope when Mrs. Fraser, who was so much more capable in so many ways than I was, let up a cry. "John! John! We're here!" He was one of the last off the train and came haltingly towards us using a pair of crutches quite clumsily. Fussing around and trying his utmost to be of help and only succeeding in hindering, was Thomas. Mrs. Fraser and I discovered later just how a young lieutenant had wielded enough influence to have his batman on leave at the same time. John kissed his mother and then, much to my own surprise, he put his arm around me and pulled me to him. He kissed me! Thomas looked away discreetly but Mrs. Fraser watched the warm welcome, beaming her pleasure at our reunion.

After much fussing over luggage (our own as well as Thomas's and John's) we were at last on our way to Framley. There was no conversation to be made in the train as John subsided into a corner and slept. He only woke when Thomas came along the train to rouse him for our arrival at Crewe. I was most distressed to see how pale and drawn John's face was, even in sleep. At the first touch of Thomas's hand on his shoulder he was instantly alert and made to leap to his feet. He remembered too late the injury to his leg and sank back into his seat stifling a groan. We all tried not to notice his distress, and soon all our attention was taken up with alighting from the train. After an uncomfortable and jolting ride, we were back at Park House.

Later, when we had rested and had our bags unpacked, John and I were able to enjoy our first proper talk together. How wonderful Mrs. Fraser is, for much as she must wish to spend time with her son, she leaves him to me! Our first conversation was all about John's mother. He had noticed that she looked much thinner and paler. I told him of her recent illness (for he had never received my last letter). At this he looked most concerned and explained that some years ago, shortly after his father's death, his mother had suffered a similar malaise. At the time the doctors feared that she would not survive. When she did recover they warned that she must take great care of her health as a repetition could well prove fatal. I have promised John that I will do what I am able to look after her.

I then asked John about his life since he saw me last. I told him that I had heard what hell it was out in the trenches. He was determined to make light of it and dismissed the conditions by saying that it was rather like being away at school! On pressing him for more information I have eventually been able to put together some idea of what life is like at the Front.

Firstly, I was wrong in assuming that once there the company remains at the Front. It would appear that they live in 'billets' some way behind the front lines. The companies take turns in doing their tour of duty at the Front, generally staying there for about six days. During that whole time they must keep the utmost vigilance, the officers and their own platoons take turns in guarding the front line - usually in shifts of four hours. During that time, if it is day, they watch over 'No Man's Land' with the aid of periscopes (it is far too dangerous to put one's head above the parapet). Should their duty be at night then the officer in charge fires Very lights at intervals. These flares serve to illuminate the whole of 'No Man's Land' and allow the soldiers to see that no attack is being made.

The trenches are hemmed in by barbed wire in order to interfere with any enemy attack. Occasionally wiring parties are sent out to renew the wire defences, and sometimes to cut the wire in preparation for an attack by our side. There are quite frequent raids made on German lines. Sometimes a prisoner is brought back in order that information may be gained.

Each morning, just before dawn, the company have 'Stand To'. Every man must step up to the front trenches, guns ready, bayonets fixed. This is the time when the enemy is most likely to make an attack so everyone has to be at the ready. After two hours, when the day is fully come and no attack with it, they are allowed to 'Stand Down' and all except the men whose turn at duty it is, fall back and go to wash and breakfast. Then they get on with their daily chores such as cleaning equipment and so on.

Up until this point John had told his story in such an enthusiastic manner that I was moved to say wryly that things sounded very exciting, and that I was almost sorry that I had wasted so much of my time worrying about him when he was obviously enjoying himself immensely! John's eyes clouded and he said that I must not imagine that life was always as he had described. There was a lot of sitting about, just waiting for things to happen. There was also the mud and the dreadful cold. When at the Front one had to sleep the entire six days with one's kit on - including boots! This was to be in readiness for immediate action. There was the constant roar of the guns and the sky lit at night by the flares. Rest was impossible. It is a measure of what John has undergone that he did not recognise my poor joke. I folded him in my arms and told him that I had merely been teasing. He was sorry; he found it so difficult to react in a normal way. It would take some time for him to readjust.

Our embrace was interrupted by the arrival of John's mother heralding tea. Alice brought the tea things through and Mrs. Fraser did her best to enliven the silence that had fallen between us. Noticing how John enjoyed his cake she asked about the quality of the food at the Front. John replied that in billets things weren't too bad but at the Front one had to get used to monotony; little food, poorly cooked; picking insects out of everything. Mrs. Fraser commented that it all sounded rather similar to complaints she received from Charles about school food. This made us laugh and lifted the mood of sadness that had descended.

After tea, while both John and his mother rested, I took the opportunity to walk in the grounds. Park House has admirable gardens and, even with so much space given over to vegetable production (as it is everywhere in the war) they are still most impressive. While walking in the rose garden - at this time of year a melancholy place - I rounded the corner and came upon Thomas having a quiet smoke. He hastily discarded his cigarette and fastened his collar studs, standing up straight and apologising to me. I told him that I did not mind him smoking, nor taking his relaxation in the rose garden! I talked to him for some time. I was determined to find out from him the circumstances of John's injury, for John will not talk about the incident at all. I was also curious to find out how he had managed to get leave at the same time as his master. Thomas told me that he was due for leave but that when John spoke up for him before the Colonel he was allowed to leave immediately. John's injury was sustained under the most heroic and harrowing circumstances. Such was his triumph that the Colonel was ready to grant him almost any request. I am unable

tonight to write about the awful events Thomas told me of and must put it off until tomorrow.

We passed a quiet evening, Mrs. Fraser and John being tired and I thinking over what Thomas had told me. We retired early but it is now past one in the morning. I must go to bed or I will be unable to be happy and cheerful tomorrow for my darling John.

December 14th 1916 - Thursday

It is seven o'clock in the morning and I must write what I had no time (or spirit) for last night. I have been awake for some time, being unable to close out of my mind the story I heard from Thomas. I will write it here in my diary in the hope that it will help me.

It was Sunday 12th November. There had been Church Parade as usual (most of the men detest it but all must attend except those on duty at the time). After the service most of the men who were not on duty were sitting about smoking or writing letters home. Some were sleeping. It was wet; drizzle that soaked through and left a body colder than ice. The meagre Sunday dinner rations were just being served up. Thomas had helped in the cooking of the officers' food, as he did each day. He carried it through to the officers' dugout and set it on the table. John was lying on his bed, sleeping, for he had been on duty for most of the night. Lieutenant Henderson was fiddling about with his bed, trying to cover the chicken wire with more layers of brown paper, in a vain attempt to make it more comfortable. Lieutenant Johnson pulled up the boxes that served as chairs and called to Henderson to take his lunch. He then told Thomas to wake Lieutenant Fraser. He called through to the other dugout to summon Lieutenant Dedderington, who had been sitting censoring a pile of letters written by men in his platoon. He was putting blue pencil through anything which the men had written which, if falling into enemy hands, could give away important military information. He would also score out anything which may lead to a lessening of morale back home. Captain Spencer was on duty and would eat when he came down. Just as John sat at the table a coloured flare went up and whistles started to blow. It was an attack at one of the least expected times. The officers slung their gasmasks around their necks, unholstered their guns and went up.

All was chaos! The enemy had loosed some smoke and clouds of it were blowing across No Man's Land. The cry of 'gas' went up and all donned their masks. Thomas declared that it was like a scene from hell. No-one could see very far. Shells were bursting all around them. Sandbags were being dislodged from

the parapet by the blasts, to be hastily snatched up and replaced. Men were running along the trenches to take up their stations - buckling on kit as they went. There were shouts, whistles, large shells exploding and grenades falling all around them. Suddenly, out of the mist, sprang a group of German soldiers.

They had breached the barbed wire under the cover of smoke and fire from their own lines and were overrunning a gun emplacement. The soldiers on the Lewis gun hadn't a chance but were killed instantly by the German attack. At that moment Captain Spencer raced in only to be felled immediately by a blow to the back of his neck, beneath his helmet. John and his platoon arrived in time to see the Germans retreating carrying the limp body of the officer. They were obviously making back to their own lines with the prisoner. Apparently this sort of thing is common practice and is one of the ways in which both sides gain their information. John did no more than lead his small group of four men over the parapet into No Man's Land in the wake of the raiding party.

They could not fire as they went for fear of hitting their own Captain. The mud was terrible. In addition there was smoke, noise and gas. Inside his gasmask Thomas's breathing was laboured and his vision was limited. He saw John slither to a halt in the shelter of a shell hole. Thomas watched as John took careful aim and fired. He hit one of the soldiers which made the others re-double their efforts. The lines were only eighty yards apart at this point so by this time they were nearer the enemy lines than their own. John remained unruffled. His calmness made the four men with him keep their heads. All took up position, took careful aim through the smoke and fired. The three German soldiers were felled and the body of Captain Spencer tumbled down with them. It slipped towards a shell hole and began to slide into the dank, stagnant water which was flooding the crater to a depth of about six feet.

Thomas saw John start crawling towards his Captain. A shell landed in front of them and the other three men and Thomas could see nothing. Shells were by now exploding all around them and bullets were whistling overhead. Just for a moment the smoke cleared and Thomas saw that John had reached the crater where Captain Spencer lay, still unconscious. They watched in silent agony as John reached out to grasp the arm of the Captain. He could not quite reach. He inched forward. Immediately there was a rush of machine gun fire. The smoke clouds closed once more over the scene. The only consolation for Thomas and the others was the fact that if they were unable to see the shell hole then the chances were that the Germans could not either. They lay in the oozing mud for what felt to them like hours. The guns began to quieten.

A voice came from behind them - a whispered command from Lieutenant Dedderington. "You men make your way back slowly and carefully. We'll try to give you cover."

Thomas turned and shouted as loud as he dare (for he did not wish to betray their position),

"Sir, Lieutenant Fraser and Captain Spencer are out there. If you fire you may hit them!"

"The devil they are!" came the reply. "Right-o, we'll try to give you smoke!"

In a few moments smoke was once more blowing around them. The fact that this time it was from their own lines made it no less difficult to penetrate. Wearily the four crawled, slithered on their bellies, back to their own lines. Thomas was last in, hoping against hope to hear or see John close behind him. As he neared the parapet willing hands reached up to help him over, he heard a groan some yards behind. Within seconds his feet were firmly on the duckboards at the trench bottom and he was turning to give what help he could to those behind. He could see that in the trench in which he was standing all was confusion. Stretcher bearers were carrying away wounded, others were lying on the floor, patiently awaiting their turn. Two or three he saw who would no longer be requiring the services of doctors. Just as well as they were so shot to pieces that they would not have wished to live.

Thomas looked over the parapet. To his amazement he saw John, inching his way forward, dragging the inert body of Captain Spencer. The Germans too had spotted them and bullets were hitting the parapet all around them. As Thomas ducked he heard Lieutenant Dedderington call out for more smoke. The kindly clouds enabled John to push the still living Captain Spencer through a gap in the sandbags to land in a heap on the duckboards. Numerous hands reached out to haul John in and as he was pulled over the edge it was clear that he had been injured.

So, John had gone out to rescue Captain Spencer and had succeeded in bringing him back. None of his party was wounded. The Captain sustained concussion and would be left with rather a headache for a few days but was otherwise unhurt. John had sustained a broken leg and a deep flesh wound. By his action he had prevented a very valuable prisoner falling into enemy hands.

Thomas told me proudly that for his actions John was to receive a recommendation for the MC. And the rumour was that he would be promoted to Captain!

Now, my darling, I know how you were injured. I know the horrific situation

you were in and how bravely you responded. Is it your natural modesty that prevents you telling us all of circumstances or can you not bear to go back over it all once more?

I must finish my diary now and go down to breakfast. I will note here that the very day I saw John's image outside the library was the day on which he was injured!

* * * * * * *

It is now evening. We have spent a very quiet day. Mrs. Fraser does not seem very well and John clearly requires rest. I forbore to mention anything of what Thomas had told me. John does not wish to talk about the war and I would not upset his mother. Instead John asks me all about how I spend my days. I fear that I will bore him with stories of endless sewing circles (we make the lint circles which are inserted into gas masks), bandage rolling sessions, muffler and sock knitting as well as my normal parish duties. I may be able to offer more entertainment by telling him about the children in Sunday School and in the village day school. Teaching is one part of my duties that I find enjoyable. John is curious about Father and his attitude to our correspondence. He knows that I may only remain at Framley for a short time and says that he will come and visit us all at Brabage as soon as he is able. He expressed a wish to talk to Father, but confesses that he is rather in awe of him. I do not find it at all odd that there should be a flicker of fear in his eye when he speaks of Father. I do believe that he would prefer to face the full wrath of hostile German fire than beard the Vicar of Brabage in his den!

The weather has been dreary - grey and drizzly. In spite of this John asked me if I would walk with him in the grounds. When I explained my anxiety about him catching a chill he laughed and reminded me that in France the weather is far worse; and of course we would not have to beware snipers' bullets in the garden! At this reminder of war he became quiet and thoughtful, but his mood was soon lifted by our walk together. He leans heavily on me for his leg is very weak and, I would guess, rather painful. I welcome the burden.

I wish that I could stay here forever but know that I must shortly return home. While it is dreadful that John has been hurt, it is wonderful to have him here with me.

December 15th 1916 - Friday.

Mary, Mother and Father paid a call today. Although Father was most polite and courteous (I even discerned a glitter in his eye which may have been a tear as he looked at my poor injured darling) I feel that he is here in order to hurry me home. It is so near Christmas that I feel that I must return to Brabage and yet I yearn to stay here with John. However, I have agreed that I will return home tomorrow. It is a great pity that I cannot stay long enough to meet Charles who is not yet home from school in Shrewsbury. John is so very fond of him and Mrs. Fraser is looking forward so much to having her younger son home with her.

It is agreed that John will accompany his mother and Charles to visit us at Brabage next week - before the Christmas festival. I have a plan to ask Mother it she will approach Father with a request for John to stay with us for the New Year (and so be with me on my birthday!). If I ask Father he is sure to refuse. I will suggest to Mother that she hints to Father that John, as an injured hero, may inspire our small parish to keep on with its war efforts. Father is sure to bask in the reflected glory and so he may just consent. How ever it is to be worked I am determined that John will come!

December 17th 1916 - Sunday

I have been home less than two days and already I am exasperated by Father. He regaled me with a long list of duties which must be performed before Christmas and when I dared to suggest that some may be kept until after Christmas Day he launched into a torrent of reasons why I must make up for my period of leisure before enjoying the festival of Christ's birth.

Today I have taught my usual class at Sunday School. However these things happen the news has reached the village that John has returned injured and there are some rumours of the manner in which he sustained those injuries. Young Jamie Shipton was, as usual, the most forward of my pupils and I came up quietly behind him as he was giving a most graphic account of trench warfare. I was concerned as the way in which he described it glorified and romanticised war, when I know from Thomas's account of the real squalor, misery and danger that is the Front! I began to tell the children some of the awful, sad things about war, even daring to suggest that the German soldiers were only like our own men and did as they were ordered by a commander who remained some way behind the lines in safety! The boys looked very doubtful at this and Jamie spoke for them all when he voiced his determination to go to the Front and fight the 'Boche'. He only hopes that the war lasts long enough for him to be able to enlist! Hannah

was, as usual, my ally, and I felt a small, timid hand slip into mine as, with the intuition and insight of childhood she said,

"Doan you worry Miss, war may be over afore your young man 'as ter go back!"

Out of the mouths of babes and sucklings ... For that is indeed what I hope for.

Sunday has passed in its customary dreary fashion and I miss John more knowing that he is only a few miles away than I did when he was in France!

December 19th 1916 - Tuesday.

Today I was summoned into Father's study. It would appear that some of the children have told their parents what I said on Sunday. Those parents have told others and now it is (to quote Father on the matter), "All around the village, that Elizabeth Aubrey, the vicar's daughter, is a German sympathiser and, some would have it, a pacifist to boot."

I tried to explain to Father what I had intended. It is not right that those young minds should be filled with ideas of heroism only to have them blotted out in the unforgiving and relentless mud and thunder of war. I went on to tell him that I could not understand the waste of so many young lives - on both sides.

Father, of course, responded with the thing most guaranteed to inflame me - that as a woman I could not expect to understand such things! I held my temper admirably, though it took a great deal of accomplishing, and told him coldly that as women breed the sons who are called on to feed the guns then we should understand something of the nature of war! Father turned a livid white and, as two spots reddened on his cheeks, told me harshly that he hoped that my correspondent did not hear me speaking in such a traitorous manner. What I said belittled the heroism he had so recently demonstrated on the battlefield. He forbade me to talk of such topics outside the house and added that he would very much prefer me to refrain from the topic inside it too! I was then summarily dismissed.

Oh John! I do not wish to belittle your heroism. I am so confused. I understand that you wish to show valour, to be an example to your men, to do your best. My heart responds to such sentiments. But when I think of you lying there wounded, and in pain, all your platoon anxious for your safety, I cannot but think of the futility of war. Perhaps if I talk to you about it you can help my confusion? I wish that I was with you. Goodnight my darling!

December 21st 1916 - Thursday

I have had such a wonderful day. Mrs. Fraser came to visit bringing with her John and Charles. I was so delighted to see John. It is with mixed feelings that I notice that his leg is improving. What a dilemma! I want him to get better but I do not want him to go back to France.

It is the first time that I have met Charles and he is a charming young man. He obviously adores his older brother and out of his company cannot refrain from talking of John's heroic deeds. When in John's presence if he so much as broaches the subject of war, or talks about the guns, shells and so on (he knows all the soldiers' slang terms for these things) John soon stops him. It is in a way rather frightening to see such a young boy so fired with enthusiasm about things martial! He is quite determined to enlist just as soon as he is able. Mrs. Fraser maintains that the war will be over before Charles is of an age to fight - but I noticc the worried expression on her face that tells me that she doubts that assertion!. John tells Charles that he is best here at home for a few years yet - the war is not for boys. Charles retorted that Thomas had told him that the war makes men out of boys! John was dismissive of this comment but I was angry and could not help adding,

"Yes, and it makes old men out of young!"

Everyone regarded me silently and I blushed profusely, glad that Father was not present. Mrs. Fraser - as always the diplomatist - changed the subject to the forthcoming festive season. Although general chatter resumed I was conscious of John regarding me curiously.

Later, encouraged by Mrs. Fraser, John and I went for a walk. The day was cold and the ground frozen. John can now get about quite ably on his crutches and we were able to get as far as the summerhouse - our summerhouse. The pool is frozen over and John used the end of one of his crutches to break the ice so that birds may drink and ducks may swim. How thoughtful he is - sensitive to all living creatures. Father would never think of the welfare of any wild things! Hoar frost still clung to some branches and twigs making a delicate tracework of cold, white lace. The summerhouse is all closed up but I always keep the key in my pocket. It was far too cold to stay long but we valued our private time together - however brief. When I am in John's arms nothing else in the world matters to me.

All too soon it was time to return. I didn't feel the cold at all, kept warm as I was by love! Father had been out of the house, down at the village school, and would be sure to be back very soon. We did not want him to know that we had been out alone for some time. As we walked back to the house John asked me

what I truly felt about the war. I told him of my doubts and uncertainties. He stopped and turned to face me. He tried to explain his own views. While he neither sought war nor enjoyed it, when his country called on him to do his duty, he must respond. He asked how I would feel if he was a coward who refused to fight? I tried to explain my feelings to him. I asked why young men, who were really no more than boys, should fight and die because the politicians did not agree. Why did they have to go on and on when it was clear that there was stalemate? Would there ever be an end to all this? Perhaps the end would only come when there were no more men left to die! John dropped his crutches and grabbed hold of me, hugging me close.

"Lizzie, I'm sorry. When you are not out there, when you are not a part of it all, it is so difficult to understand. Yes, war is dreadful, but it gives one such a great feeling to be a part of the army. The men are splendid and, yes, I do believe that they would stand and fight until there was no-one else left, but that only adds to the feelings of loyalty and patriotism, it does not diminish the fervour in any way at all. To stand in a trench, shoulder to shoulder, knowing that the man next to you would risk everything for you, is a truly wonderful feeling!" As John said these words I could see that his eyes were shining. I could stand no more of it and burst into tears. I was sobbing so much that I was unable to put together a coherent argument. John held me tightly as I sobbed out,

"I just don't want you to die!"

"I won't die my darling Lizzie, not with you to love me!" He dried my tears and we set off across the lawn to the house. As we reached the gravel drive Father came through the gates.

"Good," said John, "I'm glad he's back, for I would like to speak to your father, Lizzie. I am going to ask him if I may marry you!"

I was too shocked to respond, but merely stared at him, my mouth open, until Father came up with us.

When we returned to the dining room it was to discover that Mother, independent of consulting Father, had invited Mrs. Fraser and her sons to stay with us for a few days after Christmas. Mrs. Fraser accepted gladly, only requesting that Thomas may also come as John had such need of him.

John asked Father if he may speak with him and they went off to the study. I was summoned there shortly afterwards and Father told me that John had asked for my hand in marriage. Father added that he did not consider that we knew each other well enough to embark on such a step. (How could he know how well we knew each other, being unaware of our 'real' correspondence?) He would

however not rule out the request. We could not be officially engaged, but he would sanction a closer friendship. Apart from anything else the times were too uncertain for such a commitment. I hated him for these words for what he meant was that John may be killed! He would reconsider his opinion when the war ended. He conceded that when the war was over we may be permitted to marry. This was only a small step forward, but such a victory!

We all spent a most pleasant evening. I am sure that John told his mother of the interview with Father as she was kinder to me than ever! After our guests had departed and we retired for the night, I took Mary into my room and told her all about John and me. She is so pleased about it all. To her the uniform is so romantic and she thinks John so wonderful, dashing and handsome! She was sure, she told me, right from the first time she saw us together, that we would be married.

Just as I was going to sleep there was a tap at the door and Mother entered. Father had only then thought to tell her the news. She had got straight out of bed and come to me. She embraced me lovingly. She too, I feel, is half in love with John!

So, a wonderful day! While Father is not entirely won over, I think that I am on the road to having John as my husband! For the first time in my life I wish Christmas over in order that we may arrive at the time for the Frasers' visit! Goodnight my love, my husband to be - eventually!

December 27th 1916 - Wednesday

Our visitors arrived today - my real Christmas present! John's leg has improved considerably. The shame of it is that the sooner he is fit then the sooner he will return to the Front! Although the battle for the Somme is finally over, the war still rages and swallows up an increasing number of our men. Father became quite excited when he talked to John about the war. He has heard of the new weapon which was used - tanks - and is sure that these things will win the war for us. John is not so certain. He says that the design needs modifying and only then will tanks be useful in France. Am I alone in thinking that Father, a man of God, is wrong to relish the subject of war? He is immersed in it all, quoting facts and figures (gleaned only from his newspaper) that prove the British to be winning. I am sure that all that is in the newspapers is blatant propaganda. Even Mr. Rudyard Kipling now writes regularly in favour of the war - and this in spite of losing his only son in action just last year! I do not know how he can write in such a way. Perhaps to a writer all war, however appalling, is the same to them as the adventure stories they write.

John looks inestimably sad when the talk turns to the war. For all his fine words to me, I know that he must hate and dread it all. Charles, on the other hand, is as enthusiastic as Father and they sit for ages discussing all aspects of battles, weapons and such like. Charles's great fear at the moment is that the tanks will finish the war before he joins it!

John and I did not have much time to ourselves but managed a short walk this afternoon. He is confident that Father will allow us to marry. To assuage my doubts and convince me of our eventual union he reminded me that I will be twenty-one years old in a few days, and that as soon as the war is over we will be married, whatever Father says! He thinks it ridiculous that in this day and age Father behaves as he does. I say nothing, for I know that I am a coward where Father is concerned. I am only too grateful that we are permitted this time together.

We passed a very gay evening, all being still full of Christmas spirit. Mother and Mrs. Fraser are quite like old friends. I feel sure that Charles is mooning about over Mary, but I know that she feels that as he is yet at school he is only a child. She will give him no encouragement whatsoever! How glad I am that I am not seventeen again!

December 29th 1916 - Friday

What a commotion there has been today! John and I were taking our customary afternoon stroll in the grounds when, from behind the walls of the kitchen garden we heard a hymn being sung. John blushed to the roots of his hair and, when I listened to the words, I understood the reason. Instead of the sacred words of the hymn there had been substituted other, rather vulgar words. Although John asked me to remain where I was while he went to investigate I could not. Curiosity got the better of me and I followed him towards the arched gateway in the wall. The song changed to another hymn, 'What a Friend We Have in Jesus', but once more the words were altered. As far as I can remember them the words were :-

"When this b .... y war is over,
No more soldiering for me,
When I get my civvy clothes on,
Oh! How happy I will be."

The song went on to celebrate the fact that there would be no more Church Parades to be attended and said something also about kissing the Sergeant-Major. I am unable to recall the exact words. I thought the song rather melancholy. The

singing was replaced by the sound of a mouth organ being played. This stopped abruptly when John went through the gateway. I followed to find John giving Thomas a dressing down while Charles stood by rather shamefacedly. It appears that Thomas has been entertaining Charles with his 'Tales From The Trenches' and teaching him some of the soldiers' songs.

After the dressing down was complete and Charles had been sent off to his room, John turned once more to Thomas. His tone became kindlier and more gentle. He explained to Thomas that he did not want Charles to be enchanted by the glamour of war; in fact he wanted to keep Charles away from the subject altogether as his interest was becoming obsessive. He instructed Thomas to cease this type of association with Charles and sent him off to the kitchen. We resumed our walk. John apologised for the incident and hoped that I was not too much offended. I actually thought that some of the songs were quite entertaining and shall never again stand in church and hear 'What a Friend...' without thinking of the soldiers' version! John explained to me that he is extremely anxious about Charles. He can talk of nothing but war and yearns to be out there. John and his mother agree that Charles must go through his officer training in the normal manner before 'going out'. At least officer training gives some chance for survival, for the ordinary recruits are so 'green' that many are killed soon after arriving. He allowed himself to be carried away with emotion and spoke with great feeling about the obscene loss of young life. Even now, when Mr. Lloyd George has taken over from Mr. Asquith, young boys not out of their teens are falling in their hundreds. The whole thing was a mess.

John suddenly stopped his tirade, looking rather shocked. He apologised to me for getting carried away and explained that it was only because of Charles. He did not want his young brother to go to war! He looked rather shamefaced as we continued along the gravel walk.

I was so glad! Thank God! I realise that in his heart John's opinion of the war is closer to mine than I had believed. Under the surface of the man who must be a 'good chap' and 'do his duty' is the man I love who considers war an abomination. Please God let this really be 'the war to end wars' as the politicians tell us it is.

The remainder of the day was passed quietly and happily in the company of the family. John said nothing of Charles's behaviour as he is determined not to worry his mother, who I think looks rather frail.

December 31st 1916 - Sunday

My birthday! Today I am twenty-one and I am a woman. What a year it has been. I have met the man who will make me happy for the rest of my life; I have learned to trust my own opinions and stand up to Father a little more than formerly; I have been through sorrow, anger, joy - I have really grown up!

We are to welcome the New Year and have a small celebration for my birthday. Father will not permit us to celebrate overmuch as it is the Sabbath!

I have received some beautiful gifts - a writing case from Mrs. Fraser, a scarf from Charles (his mother's choice I think!). Mother and Father have given me a Bible and a gold cross on a gold chain to go around my neck. Mary gave me a very pretty brooch. John though gave me a new diary which I shall start tomorrow, and a ring. He gave me the diary in public and the ring in private. He says that it is to be a token of our engagement and, while I cannot wear it openly, it will please him to think that I keep it about my person, close to my heart.

I am ready to go down to dinner. I am not vain (I think!) but the love that is in me makes me shine. Indeed it makes me look almost pretty!

On this last day of the old year I pray to God that the new year, 1917, will bring a better world. Please God let the war end; let us all resume our lives and let those who suffer regain their health.

Farewell 1916 - Welcome 1917.

Wednesday 3rd January 1917

John and his family returned to Framley today and I am quite desolate without him. The Frasers have considerably enlivened the past week and I think that we have all had our spirits lifted by their visit. Mother and Mrs. Fraser spent hours together discussing I know not what! Charles has pursued Mary relentlessly, though she will have none of it. John and I have spent hours together and alone! I cannot bear to think of the next - how long? - without him. Father has been absent from home for considerable lengths of time - something that we all welcome! He is in pursuit of various church officials in order to arrange the matter of the extension to the churchyard. His business seems to entail trips as far away as Nantwich and Chester, and even Knutsford on one occasion! It would appear that too many people in this village are dying and there is not space in the present churchyard to inter them all.

When Father returned today he rebuked me for walking about with a long face. He cannot understand what I feel. I wonder was he ever in love with Mother? It is hard to imagine Father inflamed with any passion other than anger!

As the Frasers went away Mrs. Fraser whispered to me to be sure to visit her soon, and I will, no matter how Father may criticise me! I wear John's ring around my neck always. Mary is so curious to know what precious item I have on the ribbon which she catches a glimpse of occasionally.

Tuesday 9th January 1917

Today Mother and Father received a charming letter of thanks from Mrs. Fraser. She goes to some lengths to stress how she and the family enjoyed their visit to us and hopes that very soon we may be able to go and stay at Park House. She writes that she understands Father's difficulty in leaving the parish, and indeed Mother's in leaving the household. With that in mind she proposes that Mary and I should go over and stay for a few weeks with her. Father looked very glum, but it was so charmingly put that even he will have difficulty in refusing.

We are in any case to go over on Thursday. My heart aches for that day to come. I miss you so much my darling. How will I feel when you have to return to the war? I will not write of such a terrible event, instead I will look forward to Thursday. There is one small cloud on my horizon, and that is that Father intends to accompany us. However, who cares about clouds when I will be seeing my own John! Goodnight my darling, and God bless.

Thursday 11th January 1917

I am so weary that I can hardly find the energy to write my diary. I am tired and yet so strangely excited, and I notice that the pen shakes as I write. I am in the attic once more. Earlier I attempted to write my diary in my room, only to have Father knock loudly on the door and complain that I was out of bed too late and creating ruin in Mother's household accounts by using an inordinate number of candles. It was on the very tip of my tongue to retort that I would in future purchase my own candles when I bit back my words. I am too happy tonight to start squabbling with Father. Besides, he is in a dreadful mood and I would be sure to come off the worst in any battle! Instead I called out my compliance and blew out my candle. When the house was quiet I crept up to the attic - my sanctuary! In future I will attempt to write my diary nowhere but up here. Also, from this room I can look out of the windows over the gardens. On such a clear, starry night as this I can give myself over to my dreams.

Today, as planned, we visited Park House. By a singular stroke of good fortune Father was detained at the last moment by a clerk from the Bishop's

office. He had come to inspect the churchyard and Father was forced to remain with him in order to discuss his proposals. Mother too remained, as she had to entertain the visitor, and so Mary and I went to Framley alone.

While Mrs. Fraser was sorry not to see Mother, she was unable to conceal the relief, indeed the pleasure which she felt at Father's absence. Charles was especially happy to see Mary as he returns to school on Monday next. I know that he spent a long time imploring Mary for a lock of her hair or a portrait of herself to take with him. She ignored all his pleas. I think that in her heart she is very fond of Charles but her pride will not allow her to show it. Mrs. Fraser was very jolly and made much of Charles. She told us that he has learned to play the mouth organ and she asked him to play some tunes for our entertainment. Of course he has learned the skill from Thomas and the tunes he plays are the soldiers' songs. Mrs. Fraser was proud of Charles as he played to us but was sensitive enough to notice that this reminder of the war cast gloom over John. Rather than see him brood on the trenches she suggested that John and I go out for a walk. The weather was damp, but not so much as to discourage us.

We walked together for almost two hours. I know John so well that I feel that he is a part of myself. His leg is so much better that he no longer needs to lean so heavily on me, though he did so for all of that! We walked towards Framley and through some narrow country lanes which were muddy, but not too bad. We were able to gain some spectacular views of Beeston Castle, standing as it does on its lonely hilltop high above the surrounding Cheshire countryside.

John told me that silhouetted as the castle was against a tumbling sky made him recall a ruined church that he had seen in Flanders. The Company was billeted in that place for some time and each night he would look out at the church, black against the paler evening sky, and think of home, of his family, but most especially of me.

Talking of war made him turn to the subject of Charles and John told me how worried he is for the boy. While Charles is loth to go back to school he relishes the return so that he can re-commence the officer cadet training which they do there. Charles is too eager, John says, for the war; it will come to him soon enough.

Another anxiety which John suffers is for his mother. Some days she is quite weak and delicate. However in spite of these worries John and I spent most of the time talking about ourselves and our future together. John placed an arm comfortingly about me when he told me that he must soon return to France. I could not repress a shudder. He held me more tightly and urged me not to worry, for

he had the best incentive of all to stay alive - an 'almost wife' waiting for him. How I thrilled to hear his words. He turned me around to face him and then kissed me so long and so passionately that I felt that my knees must surely give way. His hands were everywhere; my neck, my shoulders, up and down my spine (which made me shiver with pleasure). Finally they came to rest on my breast. (Oh Heavens! Father must never find these diaries. To think that he would read this!)

Suddenly John pulled away quickly and reddened at his trespass on my person. He apologised and muttered in a most embarrassed way that he had been carried away by the moment. Apologised! Modesty would not permit me to tell him how I felt. My head was spinning; my face burned. I was lost in a world of passion inspired by John. I would have done anything for him at that moment!

We walked on in embarrassed silence. I know that I acted immodestly when after a time (during which we had walked at least a foot apart) I reached out my hand and grasped his fingers. He responded immediately, holding my hand and pulling me close to him. How I thrilled at the closeness of his body! We laughed at our awkwardness and by the time we had reached the gates of Park House it was beginning to grow dusk - and we understood each other completely.

Mrs. Fraser met us, anxious that we had been out for so long. Mary and I had to start immediately for home. It cost me such pain to leave my darling.

Father was, of course, extremely cross that we had stayed so late, but Mother managed to smooth things over. Father's mood was especially angry as the Bishop's clerk had seemed to welcome the plans for the churchyard but had stated that he was sure that the Bishop would stipulate that the necessary funds for the land purchase must come from within our own parish. Father muttered and grumbled and spent the entire evening after dinner in his study - examining finances he said!

As I have written this account of my day I have felt my heart quicken once again at the recollection of John's caresses. I love you, I love you, I love you. I cannot bear to be apart from you. Goodnight my darling. Speed the day when we no longer need be separated.

Wednesday 17th January 1917

The clouds gather! John visited the vicarage today with the most unwelcome news that he is soon to have a medical examination and expects to be back in France within a short time. I scrutinised his face when he told us this news, but he seemed sincere in his desire to return to the Front. We had all lingered in the breakfast room and it was there that we received John. I was rather embarrassed

at our first meeting since the intimacy of yesterday, but John seemed to be his normal self. Mother and Mary were cast down at John's news but Father was quite buoyed up by the prospect of John's return to war. He said that there was nothing for him, quite as good as reading the news from the Front 'fresh from the horse's mouth'. It was with revulsion that I realised that Father was speaking of John and my own 'open' correspondence, which of course he received and scrutinised before passing it on to me. Until this moment I had felt that he undertook this task as a duty; now I know that he takes a certain pleasure in 'snooping'. I looked towards my darling and his expression was clear for me to read - he too was repulsed by Father's actions. I sent him a look which conveyed that I would like to speak to him alone.

My abhorrence of Father gave me the strength to turn and say (in an ordinary, matter of fact way),

"Perhaps you would care to take a walk in the gardens John?" Father almost swallowed his newspaper whole (he had been reading it at the time) and Mother's eyes widened in amazement. John assented readily and I went and put on my outdoor things. During our walk John told me that Father had taken the opportunity of my absence to warn him to be sure to keep within view of the house at all times. Oh! How I have come to detest that man!

The weather was too inclement to permit our walking to the summerhouse - else I would have been bold enough to defy Father's instruction. Once outside we had to content ourselves to keeping to the gravel paths. We talked of John's forthcoming return and of course I cried. John steered me into the shelter of the friendly kitchen garden wall where he comforted me. We dared not linger too long, for Father was certain to be watching. John is to have his examination before the end of this week and hopes to be back in France by the beginning of February. He tried to cheer me by reminding me that the battle for the Somme (surely the worst battle in our history) was over and the war was certain to end soon. I responded bitterly with the statistics I had read recently in Father's newspaper. The battle for the Somme had cost one million casualties in order to gain just ten miles of ground. If the war progressed at such a rate there would soon be no young men left in Britain, and still all the enemy territory would not be captured. John laughed a little at my reasoning (but not in the patronising, mocking way which Father has). He asked if I would care to go back to Park House with him in order to visit his mother. There we would have more opportunity to be in each other's company. I looked doubtful, which made John immediately suspect that my reasons for hesitation concerned his behaviour of

last week. I hastily reassured him that I was thinking of my parish visits. If I missed them I would be sure to anger Father. He immediately volunteered to accompany me around the village if I would then go with him to Park House.

I have neither the space nor the energy to describe the wonderful welcome the people of Brabage gave to my wounded soldier. Everywhere there was respect and honour for the hero! John began to get quite self-conscious about it all. Such are John's finer feelings that he took time to visit two families not on my duty rosta - both families having lost sons in the war. He spoke to the bereaved parents with sympathy and respect, bringing tears to my own eyes. I think he is such a wonderful man!

We then spent a quiet afternoon at Park House. Mrs. Fraser stayed some time in our company, but during the latter part of the afternoon she went to her room to rest. John accompanied me home and unexpectedly was greeted warmly by Father who insisted that he stay to dine. It was only after John had left later in the evening that I discovered from Mary that the change in Father's attitude was due to the fact that he had been out in the parish in the afternoon. He had found that basking in a hero's reflected glory was most pleasant. The people of Brabage had spoken highly of John and congratulated Father for having such a man in his circle. It makes me love the people of Brabage more for their generous opinions and yet Father falls in my respect! I begin to think that he is shallow and vain as well as strict and stern!

In our time alone together John and I allowed our intimacy to grow! As we sat side by side in the drawing room I know that he was as aware as I of the warmth and closeness we shared. Such was our proximity that I could almost hear his heart beating through his clothes.

All too soon it was time for him to go and leave me. I became half of a whole being! Good night my love.

Friday January 26th 1917

I am to spend the week-end here at Park House. It much upsets Father that I have been here for almost a week and am to remain longer. He should not complain for, as agreed, John has accompanied me to Brabage each day in order that I may carry out my parish duties. I have missed nothing - not even the bandage-rolling sessions! As we travel about together I can almost feel that we are an old married couple - such is the intimacy with which we share our lives. We are only apart at night when we sleep. I look forward to the day when we are married and need not separate at all!

There is however a hateful reason for the extension of my stay. John is returning to duty on Monday. I cannot believe that in a few short days this happy period of my life will be brought to an end. John has been passed fit enough to fight - so much for my hopes that he would be able to stay safe in some office behind the lines. He is torn, for while wishing to return to his comrades and do his duty for his country, he does not want to leave me. We must enjoy the few days that lie ahead of us for the Lord only knows when we will see each other once more. We are to resume the old method of correspondence for we are sure that Father will continue to read his 'bulletins from the Front'!

I have been so happy here. Each night I lay down my pen and diary knowing that the person who I value most in the whole world lies just a few rooms away from me. I almost dread my return to Brabage.

Monday 29th January 1917

Today I lost half of myself on Crewe Station! I saw John safely on to the train and bid him a tearful farewell. There were many others on the platform for of course Thomas returns with John and his family came to say their goodbyes. None dare to let their eyes meet lest the unspoken thoughts are voiced. So many young men have been seen off from this station; so many of them never to return, their poor, broken bodies lying in a foreign country, leaving loved ones without even a grave over which to mourn.

Mrs. Fraser was unable to accompany us to the station; she still remains so fragile! When I returned to Park House I packed my things and came home. Mrs. Fraser was most sorry to see me go and hopes that I will be able to return very soon. So, here I am, back at Brabage Vicarage.

Home! How can anywhere without John be considered by me as home! As time goes on I love him more and more, and it becomes harder than ever to be apart. Mother and Mary were very pleased to see me. I think that when I am here my argumentativeness deflects some of Father's wrath from them. Father greeted me in his usual cold manner, as expected commenting that now my duties would receive my full attention and so be performed properly!

As I lay my head down tonight I am further from John than I have been for some months. Please God, keep him safe for me. Good night my darling, wherever you are.

Friday 2nd February 1917

Poor Mother! While Mary and I sat with the sewing circle Mother was fretting away in her own room. Eventually she came to us and I could tell by her manner that she was upset. She was flushed and very agitated. Mother asked if I would accompany her back to her little room (it is an ante-room to the bedroom she shares with Father). I hurried along after her, fearful to find out the cause of her anxiety. In her room her small desk was littered with papers. She turned to me and raised her hands in a helpless gesture, tears running slowly down her cheeks.

"Oh Lizzie!" she said, "I am in such a mess. I am unable to balance my household accounts for last month and your father has already reminded me that they are a day overdue for his examination. What am I to do?"

I was myself upset to think that Father could be such a hard taskmaster to his own wife. A small knot of certainty was warm inside me - the knowledge that John would never behave in such a manner towards me.

We sat together and after almost an hour I had found Mother's problem - a bill left from Christmastime which she had overlooked. Mother's gratitude was touching and she put her arms around me and murmured her thanks. She added that she did not know how she would manage without me, but she would have to learn to do so for it was clear that as soon as the war was over, John and I would be married. I was embarrassed at Mother's words, for I think that it is the first time there has been such open acknowledgement of our relationship. Mother kissed me and told me that our love was obvious. Furthermore she had entered into a conspiracy with Mrs. Fraser that whenever John was home on leave they would contrive to allow us to spend the most possible time together. She added that Father must not know. She was like an excited child as she told me this; I believe that her small rebellion against Father quite stimulates her!

The maxim is that all the world loves a lover. Most of my small world seem intent on helping us to reach our happiness. I look forward to your return my darling.

Wednesday 21st February 1917

How my dislike of Father grows! He was hateful this morning. He came into the drawing room carrying some letters. One was from France - from John. As Father handed it over to me he could not refrain from disclosing its main news:-

"Here, Elizabeth," he said, "a letter from Captain Fraser"

I looked up at his use of the title 'Captain' and he explained, "Yes, Captain

Fraser! He is promoted. Furthermore he is to receive the MC for his gallantry during the Battle of the Somme!"

While I was so pleased to receive this letter from John, I was annoyed that Father had read it first and passed on the news in such a public way. Mother regarded me steadily, her expression telling me that she understood exactly how I felt. I closed my lips tightly, preventing the complaint that I would have made against Father, but as truly as I know myself, I know that the words will be spoken!

John's letter was in his usual, formal manner and described his return to France, his greeting of old comrades, and a little about his first duty at the Front. That is the point at which he disclosed that he is promoted and led his first company as Captain. He went on to write that his promotion was due to "that business when I was injured". At the same time he modestly added that he was to receive the MC. He asked kindly after the family and went on to write that when I next saw his mother I was to be sure to write and tell him of the exact state of her health - for he is sure that she does not tell him all the facts in her own letters.

However formal, it is a letter from John. I know that his 'real' letter will arrive at any time. I hope that the weather remains fine so that I may go to the summerhouse without arousing Father's suspicions or attracting his criticism.

While I am pleased that John is made Captain, I know that it will not keep him out of danger. Indeed, knowing him as I do, I realise that he will be more at risk for he is a man who will lead his company from the front. He would never expect a subordinate to do what he would not risk himself. Oh. My love, please be careful!.

Friday 23rd February 1917

Today my letter arrived, delivered safely by Arthur Mayfield. I get such a wonderful feeling opening the letter and knowing that mine are the first - indeed the only eyes - to read it since it left John's hands. The letters from the Front are supposed to be censored. It is one of the duties of an officer to read the letters written by members of his platoon, putting a blue line through anything that may be considered 'sensitive'. However, although the rules dictate that an officer should have his letters censored by his immediate superior, it is a rule which is never enforced. John told me that it would be considered 'bad form'; that it is to be expected that officers are intelligent and astute enough to operate a self-

restraint on information. However it is, I know that I am the first to read the words since he wrote them.

The letter is so very different from the 'official' communication. I detect an undercurrent of unease. The morale of both officers and men would appear to be on the decline and much time and effort is spent in attempts to boost the flagging spirits. After all the efforts made and lives cost for the Somme the impasse would appear to be total. Much time is spent sitting about in dugouts and it takes all the officers' time and effort to keep the men alert and ready for any action. John tells me that some of the officers, and some of the men, have begun to write poetry. While some consider it a thing to be hidden, many respect the poets for their words. John considers that things may be written in poetry which could not be said elsewhere.

John only touches briefly on his promotion and mentions his medal not at all (how very typical of him!) He does say how dreadfully he is missing me and writes fondly of our recent days together.

The letter is quite short, for I believe that once he has written his 'official' letter there must remain little time and energy to write a second. I am determined to speak to Father.

After I had read the letter I sat for some time in the summerhouse. The day was bright and cold, and watching the ducks paddle in and out of the reeds reminded me of the day we came here and John broke the ice that they may swim. What a compassionate man he is - and how I love him!

Wednesday 28th February 1917

I have been trying all week to speak to Father and have only today succeeded. I wish that I had not troubled so! I tried to be diplomatic with him, starting by reminding him that I am now twenty-one years old and am really a woman. Thus I consider that I should enjoy some rights and privileges.

Father interrupted and most belligerently reminded me that Mrs. Pankhurst and her 'regiment' had not yet succeeded in securing the vote for women. Women must still allow that a man is master in his own house; that a man is naturally the master - and so on and so on with much more tosh!

After he had given me this lecture he asked me what I wished to see him about. I suggested that I may be permitted to receive John's letters unopened and unexamined. Father replied that while he respects John immensely (I really think that he likes John more as a Captain with an MC - the pompous, worldly, vain man!) it was his duty as my father to protect me from anything distressing which

may appear in John's letters. Also, he added, that as my father he has a moral obligation to know what passes between us.

I tried to argue, but Father was obdurate. In my heart I know that the real reason for Father's behaviour is simple nosiness. I know that he may have my welfare at heart but his behaviour of last Wednesday shows how greatly he relishes his task.

Father ended our interview by telling me that he was considering putting me in charge of the Sunday School as his own duties at the day school and church business take an increasing portion of his time. He would, of course, have to ensure that I behaved responsibly in my conduct towards both the teachers and the children (he was referring to the business last year when I was labelled 'Pacifist'). If I could behave in a responsible manner and he felt that he could trust me without reservation, then he would be prepared to re-consider my request.

I left his study like a small child, touchingly grateful to have been given a sweet. How I hate myself for behaving like a pathetic puppy dog! I am so frustrated to be treated in such a way by Father; I feel completely in his thrall. I always intend to say so much to him, even planning the precise words that I will use, but Father turns all my argument in his aggressive, authoritarian way. Oh John, how I long to talk to you - you to whom I am an equal. Meanwhile we must continue to correspond secretly, and that at least makes me feel that I have the advantage over Father.

I submitted my 'official' letter to him for inspection with a very bad grace. I know that Father dislikes me for my attitude towards him, but why is he so unable to show us any love. Why must he always be so cold and hard? I have written my secret letter and will post it when I go to the village to take my lesson at Brabage School tomorrow. I am defying Father and I do not care! My loyalty is now all to John who merits my love and respect.

Monday 12th March 1917

I am to go to Park House again! While I am delighted that I am to stay with Mrs. Fraser and so be out of Father's control, I am unhappy at the reason for it. Mrs. Fraser is ill once more and the message we received today requesting my presence had quite a morose effect on us all - even Father. I do believe that Father is genuinely fond of Mrs. Fraser and her illness saddens him. Father would normally be reluctant to let me go, but the shortage of food and the difficulties we have in obtaining our supplies convince him that I am better at Park House eating their food than staying at home!

Father's newspaper tells us that the German submarines continue to harass our supply ships. Many foodstuffs are extremely scarce and a number of things are totally unobtainable. America tries her best to get ships through but the evil submarines seem able to conquer everything. Father said that the Americans will probably come into the war. Anything to shorten the war would be most welcome!

I am glad that I will be at Park House for I can write to John and receive his letters in freedom and privacy. Father thinks that Mrs. Fraser reads John's letters, performing the same duty as he does here, but that sensitive lady declines the intrusion! I wonder whether I should tell John of his mother's illness? I will have patience and see what awaits me tomorrow. Meanwhile I must hide away my diaries, for I do not know how long I will be absent from home. Mother and Mary are to accompany me but will return to Brabage in the evening. Mother has been busy putting together many little delicacies which she thinks may tempt Mrs. Fraser to eat. I do not need to add that she does so without Father's knowledge. Father is unable to accompany us tomorrow as he has a busy day teaching at the school and made a great point of telling me how he has re-arranged my parish duties in order that I may go to Framley! I place a curb on my tongue for, when Father complains like this I wish to remind him that he is far better off than even the most favoured soldiers at the Front who have much more serious matters to concern them!

I wonder where John is now? I do not even know if he is in billets or at the Front. Tomorrow I will sleep at his home, in a house that will one day be our own home!

Tuesday 13th March 1917

Things are worse than I had feared. We arrived today and found that Mrs. Fraser is seriously ill. She is confined to her bed and has been so for the past week. It is the same old problem. The doctor has told her that her chest will never be strong and that she must take great care to avoid chills and other infections. He added that worry and anxiety will exacerbate her condition.

She is pale and has gone very thin. She was most grateful for our attention and thanked Mother very sincerely for the food she brought. She could eat none of it however for at present she is limited to an invalid diet.

We passed a quiet afternoon and after tea Mother and Mary returned to Brabage. I went back upstairs to see Mrs. Fraser but found her soundly asleep after the exertion of receiving visitors. I did not wake her but sat by her bed

writing a letter to John. Much as I am loth to worry him I decided that his mother's condition was grave enough for me to inform him of her illness.

Mrs. Fraser awoke before I had finished my letter. I told her that I had written to John, and what I had said about her. She consented to my action.

That fact alone tells me that she herself knows how serious is her condition. I read to her until she fell asleep and then slipped quietly from the room. I went along to my own room where I finished my letter to John.

I must confess to some trepidation as, later in the evening, I went along to the library to select a book to read. I could only think of the last time I had walked along that corridor and what I had seen in the alcove. My fears were groundless and I passed a quiet evening, retiring early. I looked in on Mrs. Fraser before going to my own room and found that she was still sleeping. I do not think that my duties here will be onerous, for Mrs. Fraser is hardly a demanding patient.

Wednesday 14th March 1917

Today I was able to speak to Mrs. Fraser's doctor - Dr. Armstrong. He is glad that I have come to look after Mrs. Fraser and gave his opinion that she is a mite better since I came, relaxing and enjoying a little company. Dr. Armstrong told me that Mrs. Fraser's condition is made worse by anxiety and added that while he acknowledges that she is concerned for John's safety, her chief worry is about Charles. He is convinced that fretting about Charles's determination to 'join up' has brought on this latest attack. Charles wants to go off to the army immediately - nevermind that he is under age! He does not wish to complete his training as an officer. While Mrs. Fraser does not object to him following John to the Front (once he is old enough of course!) she does not wish him to go as a private. She has assured Dr. Armstrong (for it was he who told me of this matter) that this is not for reasons of class; she holds her opinion for practical reasons. She has pointed out to the Doctor how much more likely Charles is to be injured or killed as a private than as an officer. I cannot but agree with her, for the casualty lists show time and again that it is the youngest soldiers, lowest in rank and latest gone to the Front, who are in most danger.

I asked Dr. Armstrong if he thought it would help if I was to speak to Charles during his forthcoming holiday but the doctor told me that Charles is not coming home from school this term. Instead he is going to a special training camp, organised by the school, and due to Mrs. Fraser's illness, once that is over will spend the remainder of the holiday with family friends (the Donalds at Shrewsbury). I will not see him at all, but I think that I shall write to Charles.

In the meantime I must try to allay the fears of Mrs. Fraser. She is such a good, kind lady she does not deserve to undergo such worry. Many people have called at the house to ask about her health and to each I can only report that she is making a slow recovery.

We spent a quiet day together, Mrs. Fraser slipping in and out of sleep as I sat with her. Mr. Thomas (the old gardener) came in with some beautiful early spring flowers to brighten up the sickroom. Mrs. Fraser's face lit up when she saw them and she exclaimed that spring was at last here. She added that God willing she would soon be well enough to see the flowers in their beds, not they in hers!

Mrs. Fraser was well enough in the afternoon to write a short note to John in order to reassure him that she was beginning to recover. I took the opportunity to add a few words and we sent the letter off in the late afternoon.

I find that the only problem with my quiet life here is that I have time to think and to worry about John. Everything around me makes me think of him and I wonder all day what he is doing at the particular moment that I think of him; where he is; what he is thinking. I pray nightly that the war will end and we may be together but the stalemate would appear to be absolute with both sides content to sit in their trenches and fight it out. What madness!

Monday 26th March 1917

I went today to teach my class at Brabage School. Mrs. Fraser is recovered sufficiently to be left for a few hours and I found that I was really looking forward to seeing the children again after my absence. The children had been told that I would come today and their warm welcome quite touched me. However one dreadful thing did happen.

After being greeted by the headmaster and collecting my materials together I went along to the class. Once the children had welcomed me they settled down to their lesson. Ten minutes later young Jamie Shipton arrived (very late). I was going to chide him for his poor punctuality when he pulled out from behind his back a beautiful bunch of yellow daffodils. He stammered out some words welcoming me back and presented me with the flowers he held clutched in his grubby little hands. Of course I was completely disarmed and could only say that he must not make himself late for school by scrambling through the countryside in order to pick flowers for me. He blushed at this but took his place quietly. I put the flowers in water and placed them on my desk where all could see them.

Some time later the door opened and in stepped the headmaster accompanied by Father and Miss Marner from the village. Father took one look at the flowers

in their place on the desk and his face went almost purple. To make my account short it would seem that young Jamie had not scrambled through the woods to gather the flowers but had plucked them from Miss Marner's garden. Jamie was ordered out to the front of the class. He made the mistake of attempting to defend and justify his actions. This only earned him two thrashings - one for the offence and the other for impertinence. Poor Jamie returned to his place, stiff and chastened. When the door had closed behind the visitors I heard him mutter in a loud stage whisper to his fellow pupils

"Parson said t'other week that flowers were God's gift to us. If that be true then how comes it that they belong to Miss Marner?"

While young Jamie spent the rest of the morning standing in his place (he was too sore to sit) I attempted to explain the concept of private property.

When I returned to Park House and gave an account to Mrs. Fraser, she was greatly amused. She was rather concerned for poor Jamie Shipton and resolved that when she was recovered the children of Brabage School should be provided with some sort of treat. She refrained from adding what we both knew to be true - that a small kindness may go a long way to alleviate the tyranny of Father!

While at Brabage I managed to spend a little time with Mother and Mary and both are to call tomorrow. Mrs. Fraser is now so very much improved that I feel that I will be home again in a few weeks.

We have not heard from John for three weeks and we are both unwilling to voice our fears. Please God, keep him safe - for both our sakes.

Wednesday 28th March 1917

Today, at last, we received news from John. He is most upset to hear that his mother is ill but is more sorry that he is most unlikely to be able to come home on leave for some time to come. The officers have been hard pressed to get more than two days together away from billets and he could not possibly manage to cross the channel and come home in so short a time.

His letter is as loving as ever but I detect some difference in him. He writes little about the war except to say that his company have suffered several periods of severe bombardment (how I shudder at that news). He goes on to say that his new rank of Captain brings with it many more responsibilities, and that while he feels no different from Lieutenant Fraser, he is sensible of a change in attitude of some of his fellow officers. I cannot be specific about the alteration in John but it is as though some of the fire, some of his enthusiasm, has gone. Oh, how I wish that we could talk, face to face. Letters are so artificial. I dream that I will be

permitted to go to France, for I hear that several of the field hospitals are short of staff. I know that Father will not hear of it and is most unlikely to sanction such an action, but I think that I could find the courage to defy Father and go anyway. When I reply to John I will ask his opinion.

The talk is all of the possibility of America coming into the war. John too writes that the ranks are buzzing with rumour and counter rumour, but then that is nothing out of the ordinary! He relates an amusing incident that happened a few weeks ago. John was required to go to Headquarters and who should he meet but Colonel Farquharson. (Although he is a colonel in John's regiment the men at the Front see little of him.) John saluted in the customary manner but, despite feeling a little awkward, felt that he should have some conversation with the Colonel, as his father and the Colonel had been such close friends. He asked the Colonel how Mrs. Farquharson was. The Colonel replied that she was fine. He went on,

"And how are your parents my boy?"

"Mother is rather unwell at present Sir, and as you know Father died some years ago," answered John, trying to keep the amusement from his face. The Colonel looked a little embarrassed but struggled on, still not having recognised his good friend's eldest son. They made pleasant conversation about Framley and Brabage and the Colonel finished by saying,

"Must hurry, got such a lot to do. Bye the bye, if you happen to see that other young chap from Framley - Fraser - do tell him that I send my congratulations. Got the MC you know, and promotion! Must try to get along to see him; very fond of the boy; Father was a very good friend of mine y'know!" John was so nonplussed that he could only gape at the retreating back of the Colonel who, in spite of his claim to 'never forget a face' had clearly forgotten the face of John Fraser whom he had seen less that six months before! John went on to write that the rumours are obviously true - war does change one! He hopes that I will not walk past him at Crewe station when he does eventually get home on leave. As if I could! Oh, how I long to see you again. Good night John, and may God keep you safe and grant that I see you soon.

Wednesday 11th April 1917

A terrible thing has happened. This morning we received an urgent message from Mrs. Fraser asking us (Father in particular) to go over to Park House immediately. There were no details and I was intrigued to find out what Mrs. Fraser's business could be - to ask for Father in such a special way. In spite of

grumbling Father sent a message to cancel his lessons at school and we all went off to Framley. As I have noted before I believe that he really does like and respect Mrs. Fraser, as well as desiring to impress her.

When we arrived at Park House we were taken directly to Mrs. Fraser who looks more ill than when I left her a week ago. She was pale and nervous. She waited until we were seated and then she herself got up and began pacing the room in an agitated manner. I saw that she was leaning heavily on her stick and, remembering what Dr. Armstrong had said about keeping her calm, I rose to let her lean on me. She soon came to a halt and once more seated herself.

The story came out all of a rush. It would appear that she has been worried about Charles for several days, not having received his expected letter. However she is familiar with the nature of young boys and knew also that Charles was busy with training camp and then his visit to the Donalds. However, yesterday afternoon (Tuesday) a Mr. Smithson, who is a master at Charles's school, made a special journey to discuss a serious matter with Mrs. Fraser. It transpired that Charles had not returned to school after the holiday. On enquiring of the Donalds the headmaster was informed that Charles had left them some days before in order to be able to visit his mother at Framley before his return to school. The headmaster of Wellfield School, Dr. Jenkinson, knew the delicate state of Mrs. Fraser's health and so contacted Dr. Armstrong in order to ascertain whether Charles had indeed returned to Park House. On receiving a negative answer they had instituted an investigation in order to determine Charles's whereabouts. Only that morning they had discovered that Charles had taken off to a recruiting station in London and had attempted to enlist. Fortunately the Recruiting Sergeant had had doubts about Charles's age and, while seeming to process the application, had actually delayed matters while investigations were made.

By that time Mr. Blenkinsop, a teacher at Wellfield, acting on Dr. Jenkinson's instructions, had succeeded in finding Charles and was accompanying him back to school. Charles's housemaster, Mr. Smithson, had come to Park House in order to discuss with Mrs. Fraser what was to be done. They had decided that even with Mrs. Fraser's delicate state of health Charles should be sent home for a few days. Dr. Jenkinson had hoped that Charles's older brother John may be able to make him regret his silly escapade. If Charles remained in school then Mr. Smithson was sure that he would become a hero to the other boys and his actions would be celebrated rather than be considered disgraceful. To be sent home from school would be disgrace enough. Mrs. Fraser had explained to Mr. Smithson that John was unable to take leave at present, but that she would arrange for

someone suitable to 'give Charles a good talking to'. Of course that someone was Father who was noted locally for his strictness and severity in all matters of discipline. While Mrs. Fraser was uncomfortable asking Father to do this thing she knew that it was likely to be the only way to prevent Charles from repeating his foolhardy actions.

Father readily undertook to discipline Charles on the matter and it was decided that I should stay a few days more with Mrs. Fraser as this latest shock had set her recovery back several stages. Mother, Mary and I returned to Brabage where I packed my things together. I returned to Framley and found that Charles had arrived home and Father was closeted with him in the library. I went to Mrs. Fraser and offered what comfort I could. We decided that we would each write to John, tell him what had happened and urge him to use whatever influence he could bring to bear on Charles.

Father came to us later and told us of his interview with Charles. He was sure that the boy would not attempt such a thing again and assured Mrs. Fraser that her son was full of remorse for the pain and sorrow that he had caused. Father had spent some time (I discovered later that it was two hours) lecturing Charles on the error of his ways and then sent him up to his room. Father returned home and left us together.

Charles came down later in the evening and was most contrite. He acted very lovingly towards Mrs. Fraser but could not refrain from talking about John and the war, and all the bold deeds he will do when he eventually 'joins up'. I regret that Father does not appear to have had much influence with the boy, who still seems determined to rush headlong into the fray just as soon as he can lawfully do so! We can only hope that a letter from John and the influence of the masters at school will influence him and guide him into a more sensible path.

Tuesday 17th April 1917

Today I returned to Brabage.

Charles went back to school yesterday and Mrs. Fraser is quite well again. Father is more pompous than ever, reminding us all frequently of his 'widely acknowledged influence with the young'. As I was leaving Park House this morning I received a letter from John. He is most concerned to hear of Charles's exploits and has written to him in the strongest terms. He tells me that he has made little of it to his mother, describing it as 'a typically boyish escapade which will soon be forgotten'. To me he writes more seriously and urges me to talk to Charles, stressing the delicacy of Mrs. Fraser's health.

In all other matters he is the same. The war continues in its unchanged, tedious and grinding way and the men are tired of it. They are more cheerful now that the weather has improved and they have spent more time resting in billets. John hopes for leave soon. Now that America is in the war they all hope that it will soon come to an end. Please God!

Friday 27th April 1917

Today I have written a letter to Charles. I have used all my powers of persuasion to attempt to make him settle down. I have told him that soon he will have the opportunity to go to war legitimately, and as an officer. I have reiterated John's opinions, that as an officer he may have more power over his movements and so it might be possible for him to serve with John. I have even told him of the precarious state of his mother's health and urged him, if only for her sake, to be patient. The war has gone on for almost three years now (it feels more like three decades !) and is sure to continue long enough for him to join it. I do not know what influence my letter will have, but it is the best that I can do. After teaching for some time both in the Sunday School and the day school and seeing what influence Father's discipline has on the boys of the village, I fear that the 'stern talking to' will have little lasting effect on Charles's behaviour. Only time will tell.

I feel that the regular visits I am now paying to Park House are helping both Mrs. Fraser and myself, she in her health and both of us in our loneliness and yearning for John's company. Father seems to be far more amenable towards my relationship with John. He still resents my many absences from home but is unable to offer substantial criticism as I faithfully fulfil all my duties within the parish. I try not to let these duties depress me but it is in their very nature so to do. Today is the day on which we hold our sewing and knitting circle. We have finished our current issue of filters for gasmasks and have gone on to knitting socks and mufflers. I was most despondent and voiced the fear that knitting such items tacitly expressed our expectation and acceptance that the war will continue into another winter. Mrs. Jameson could not prevent a significant glance at Mrs. Farquharson who sniffed and commented that the men who were defending our liberty deserved our best efforts. They were doing their duty to the utmost, and if the war did continue then the very least we could do was to supply them with a few small comforts. I did not respond for I do not wish to enter into discussion with Mrs. Farquharson in such a public place. She already dislikes me and believes the gossip of last year that branded me a pacifist. Mrs. Jameson would

carry my every word to Father and as he is currently well disposed towards me I do not wish to antagonise him and upset the equilibrium.

In my heart I do believe that the war will continue for some time to come. America's involvement has not yet had an effect (we are still short of all manner of imported goods). When John writes he seems almost despondent, resigned to the war and doggedly doing his duty. How heartily sick they all are of it! He writes that all that keeps him going on is the thought of me and our love. On cold nights, in the middle of his watch, he is kept warm by the promises we have made and the expectation of our marriage. Oh John, I love you so much that I can hardly bear our separation. How can the world be so cruel? I hope that soon we may be together, even if only for a few short days. If absence truly does make the heart grow fonder, then mine is about to burst with love! Goodnight John, my love.

Tuesday 1st May 1917

Today I had a letter from John and I also went to Park House to visit Mrs. Fraser.

Father appeared at breakfast with my already examined 'official' letter. He made little comment except to say that the progress of the war was 'steady' and that he hoped the Americans did not come along in their loud and vulgar way and claim all the victories when our loyal troops had laid all the foundations for those victories. I was unwise enough to retaliate with the opinion that anything which shortened the war would be wonderful and most welcome, no matter whose head was crowned with laurels. Father responded that young Charles would not agree to a curtailment of action, and he added that John was worried about him. All this time he held on to my letter and I could not help but betray my eagerness to read it. Father looked at me curiously. I think that at last he is beginning to wonder how John and I have grown so close on the evidence of the 'formal' letters.

After breakfast was over I declared that before going to Park House I would take a walk in the garden, ostensibly to check on our vegetables, which are beginning to thrive. Mr. Carstairs does not approve of his flower beds being put to such a use but is glad enough to share in their produce. Father passed an opinion that the weather was a little too wet to walk about for too long, but knowing that there was a possibility of a letter from John in the summerhouse I dismissed his objections.

I was rewarded with a letter in the usual place. I sat for some time in the summerhouse reading John's words over and over again. He sounds so very tired. He hopes to be home during July and looks forward to it. Everyone, he says, is

heartily sick of war, he is so kind and loving and gentle. I cannot prevent a wave of excitement and love washing over me as I read his letter. July seems an impossibly long time away!

I fell into a reverie, building castles in the air for our hoped for re-union, when I was disturbed by Mary's voice calling to me from the edge of the trees. As I looked out of the window my stomach lurched, for I saw with dismay that Mary was accompanied by Father! Mary, the good soul, knows my secret and was obviously calling from a distance to give me warning of Father's presence. I leapt up and began to look busy. Father was very disgruntled and complained of my long absence. He was not pleased that in coming to find me he had got his shoes all over mud! I excused myself on the grounds that I was checking the summerhouse after the winter, for now that May was here we would surely wish to make some use of it. Father looked suspicious and I was glad that my regular visits to the summerhouse have made it look cared for. Father told me that Mrs. Fraser's pony and trap was already at the door, waiting for me, and that I must hurry. I was reluctant to leave him at the summerhouse lest he become curious and pry and poke about. I had great difficulty in engineering our departure together but it was managed eventually.

Mrs. Fraser's condition is stable, if not entirely well. I passed a happy few hours with her and we talked mostly of John. She is content to accept his assurance that Charles is unlikely to abscond again. At the moment his time is all taken up with examinations so he would not have the opportunity to lay plans. Also, Charles has been selected for the school cricket team, which pleases him greatly. Perhaps that will help him to fulfil some of his desire for glory! I wish that I believed that!

All too soon it was time for me to come back to Brabage and I expected a frosty welcome from Father. On the contrary, he was charming. It turned out that when Albert had driven over the pony and trap earlier he had delivered a letter to Father from Mrs. Fraser. She has promised Father the funds to enable him to extend the churchyard and Father is delighted. Peace and happiness reign in the house tonight and the name of Fraser is blessed by more than just me! How dreadful it is that the happiness of an entire household is dependent on the moods and whims of one man. Oh to escape! When John and I are married how happy our household will be!

Thursday 10th May 1917

What a horrible day! I have once again been summoned into the presence of Father to be told off like a recalcitrant child. What incenses me the most is that I take it all so meekly and walk out suitably chastened. One of these days, Father, the worm will turn!

It transpires that Father has heard (has been informed by Mrs. Jameson is more likely) of my disagreement with Mrs. Farquharson on Tuesday. In his usual mule-headed way Father did not ask for my side of the incident. He contented himself in railing against me for criticising officers who are doing a fine job (a fine job! With so many killed?) leading our soldiers. He told me that I had upset Mrs. Farquharson greatly and that he had managed to smooth things over with the promise that I would make a full, public apology to her. Well, I will not. What I said to Mrs. Farquharson two days ago at the sewing and knitting circle was justified, for it was nothing but the truth. I tried to explain to Father that when Mrs. Farquharson had mentioned that the Colonel would be home on leave by the end of the week I had merely observed that it must be wonderful to be of such elevated rank that one managed so much more leave than the more inferior of the troops. Father blustered in with,

"Don't try that Elizabeth, I am quite familiar with your 'merely observed'! You have a way of intonation accompanied by a certain expression of features that makes your meaning clear and is offensive! How dare you suggest that the Colonel has more leave than the other troops?"

"But Father," I responded, "the Colonel has been home twice this year already and John has had his leave cancelled on every occasion!"

"John, John, John! I expect you mean Captain Fraser?"

I reddened at his angry tone but attempted, once again, to justify my comment. Father would not let me speak. He said that if indeed circumstances had forced the cancellation of Captain Fraser's leave then that was most unfortunate. That the Colonel's leave had occurred when the progress of the war allowed it was just how things fell out. Also I must always bear in mind that someone with as many responsibilities as a Colonel must be permitted more respite or he would collapse under the pressure of duty. I wanted to retaliate, to tell Father of the pressures in the lower ranks, in particular of the constant bombardment, the poor food, the lack of morale. Just in time I realised that were I to tell Father of these things he would wonder about the source of my information, for such details were not to be found in the formal correspondence carried on between John and myself. I bit back my words, having to be satisfied with the rather weak comment that such

a state of affairs was not fair. Father laughed at this, contemptuous of my innocence.

"Elizabeth my dear, life is not fair. There must be inequality for society to function efficiently. To talk otherwise is - well it's almost Bolshevik my dear!" He then dismissed me with the instruction to consider my apology to Mrs. Farquharson. As I will not see her until next Tuesday's sewing circle, then I have plenty of time to decide how I will not apologise to her!

Mother and Mary were most kind towards me for the rest of the day, both being very conscious of Father's towering rages having experienced them personally on numerous occasions. I tried to explain to Mother but she hardly listened and just commented rather vaguely that Mrs. Farquharson was very important and influential locally and that her favour is important to Father. Mary merely changed the subject each time I broached the topic. We are all so very afraid of Father - what a tyrant he is! I am thankful that I can pour out all my thoughts and feelings into my diary - that most uncritical listener! Once written I feel almost that I actually spoke my defiance to Father. Imagine how angry he would be if he was to read my diary. That will never happen.

Meanwhile I end the day feeling injured. I know that I was right to speak out as I did and I will not apologise!

Monday 28th May 1917

Today has been a black day for us all. Mrs. Fraser sent Albert in the trap this morning with an urgent request for my presence. Although Father did not like it, he is sensible of his obligation to Mrs. Fraser and allowed me to go.

When I arrived at Park House all was confusion. Charles has once more disappeared from school and there is no trace of him at all. It appears that last Wednesday he took his cadet training as usual and after supper went to bed early. It was not until he made no appearance at breakfast next morning that the alarm was raised. On going to his room it was discovered that he had placed pillows in his bed to look like himself, sleeping. He was nowhere to be seen. He had taken a number of personal items with him. It was decided not to alert Mrs. Fraser but rather to institute a search on the lines of the last occasion. However, the search has been fruitless and nothing has yet come to light to show how he even got out of the area. Dr. Jenkinson came himself today to lay the whole matter before Mrs. Fraser.

Mrs. Fraser has taken the news very badly and is prostrated. I stayed long enough to calm her and put her to bed. Dr. Armstrong had to be sent for and gave

Mrs. Fraser a sedative. She could not settle, however, until I promised to return tomorrow to be with her.

Father was dismayed when I told him of the matter. I may be a little uncharitable when I say that it is injured pride that concerns him rather than any thought for Charles's welfare. He is to come to Park House with me tomorrow.

Tuesday 29th May 1917

Another hateful day. I am glad that the evening is here at last. As agreed Father and I went to Park House this morning. Father's blustering manner, his intentions to exonerate himself with Mrs. Fraser all came to nothing when he saw how pale and drawn she was. There had been no news whatsoever concerning Charles.

We were in the small downstairs room which Mrs. Fraser uses when she is ill. She was sitting in a chair and Father and I were standing. We were discussing whether we should straightaway inform John or wait until Dr. Jenkinson reported back to us, when our attention was drawn to the gateway. A young boy was wheeling his bicycle down the path, clutching a telegram envelope in one hand. The conversation stopped in mid-flow and all our attention was riveted on the boy. We watched as he made his seemingly agonisingly slow way to the front door. I felt horror in the pit of my stomach; I could hear my own heart beating and the rush of blood in my ears. I could not quieten my breathing and I felt as though I was gasping for breath. The edge of the table I reached out to clutch in order to steady myself felt like cotton wool; the room began to pulsate around me. In that half dream world I heard the peal of the bell through the house and Alice's quick steps hastening to answer. We heard voices, the door closing and then Alice's light tap on the door of Mrs. Fraser's room. It was only Father who had voice enough to call, 'Come in'. She entered.

"Telegram Madam," she said, walking towards Mrs. Fraser, her own face was white, her eyes showing fear and alarm. Mrs. Fraser had half risen from her chair to receive the envelope when, with a small stifled cry, she fainted. Father immediately turned to her aid and I was left to hold out my hand and take the telegram from Alice's shaking hand.

The envelope felt smooth and thin in my hand. I was beyond doubt that it contained the news of the death of my own John. My hand trembled. Father and Alice had placed Mrs.= Fraser in a chair and Alice was making good use of the smelling salts. Father looked towards me and snapped out,

"Well, open it Elizabeth!"

I was recalled to reality and my trembling fingers opened the envelope. The message slip inside was bald and to the point:-

MOTHER STOP HAVE GONE OFF TO ENLIST IN ANOTHER NAME STOP DO NOT TRY TO TRACE ME STOP THIS IS SOMETHING I MUST DO STOP WILL WRITE LATER STOP DO NOT WORRY STOP MUCH LOVE STOP CHARLES.

The tears were trickling freely down my face as I crumpled the slip in my hand. Angrily Father got to his feet and took the ball of paper from me. He read it.

"The young idiot!" he ejaculated.

When Mrs. Fraser came round we acquainted her with the contents of the telegram. In the face of her concern for Charles I felt guilty at my relief that the telegram was not about John.

Once Mrs. Fraser had recovered we decided that it was not worth continuing the pursuit of Charles. If he was determined to enlist under a false name then the best efforts at tracing him would be thwarted. All that we could do was to wait for a letter to come. In the meantime Father promised to inform Dr. Jenkinson at Wellfield and I was to remain the day with Mrs. Fraser.

I came home late this evening after I had seen Mrs. Fraser settled for the night. We have decided that I shall write a private letter to John and tell him all that has happened. Perhaps he may be able to institute some enquiries in France. This is the very thing we all feared. Charles is so foolhardy; such a young hothead. Wherever you are tonight, Charles, may God bless you and keep you safe.

Sunday 2nd June 1917

The news of Charles's enlistment has filtered back to Brabage. Today in Sunday School the talk was all of what a brave young man he is. Jamie Shipton loudly voiced his intention of following Charles's example. Hannah brought him down to earth with a bang when she told him that they would never believe him to be old enough - he would have to start shaving first! Poor Jamie blushed to the roots of his hair. I had no care whether or not I angered Father but gave the entire Sunday School, teachers as well, a lecture on the evil of such foolhardy behaviour.

There has still been no news from Charles. I have written to John and told him all that we know. Mrs. Fraser is not yet up to writing. Visiting her daily as I have done it is difficult to distance oneself and any improvement may go undetected. However she is very weak and while she attempts to be cheerful her eyes, and the many lines around them, betray her deep worry.

I was surprised when, after dinner, Mary proposed that we should go for a short walk. It was a beautiful evening and still quite light. I could see that she wished to talk confidentially to me and so I readily consented.

Poor Mary! No sooner were we out of sight of the house than she broke down sobbing. It transpires that since Tuesday last she has been out of her mind with worry and guilt about Charles. She told me that Charles had written to her a number of times from school. She blushed at my knowing look at her admission and hastened to assure me that it was purely out of friendship. Knowing what great store Charles set by Mary I feel that there may have been more than friendship involved - certainly on his side. However, in his letters Charles had hinted that he may take this course of action. Mary's response had been to scorn him and tell him that not only was it a silly, immature thing to do, but that his age and identity would be sure to be discovered and he would be sent home in disgrace. (How like Hannah she sounded!) She now feels guilty as she thinks that Charles may have gone off in order to prove his point, almost as a dare; an act of bravado. I reassured her and told her that I thought that Charles would have gone whatever she had said; it was just as likely that a fellow pupil had said the same sort of thing to him. Mary dried her eyes and cheered up a little. I promised that she can come to Park House with me tomorrow. She was delighted for I feel that she is as much oppressed by Father as I am!

The remainder of the evening was passed quietly and we all retired early. Each night when I come up to the attic I take out John's letters and read them over. How I love and long for him. The yearning I feel is almost a physical pain inside me. I had not realised how painful love can be. As always I pray for his safe, and soon, return to me.

Wednesday 13th June 1917

Today I received two letters from John. It seems that my letter only reached him last Friday and he has replied immediately.

In his 'official' letter, which I received from Father after breakfast, he expresses his regret at Charles's behaviour. He asks me to thank Father, Mother and Mary for all the help and support they give to his mother. I made a great point of thanking Father, just as if he had not seen the letter already; I will make the charade obvious and ridiculous! John goes on to write that he will endeavour to discover Charles's whereabouts, although, he reminds me, Charles is unlikely to have embarked as yet and is doubtless still in some training camp somewhere. The remainder of the letter is taken up with general chit-chat about his comrades.

He is likely to have leave soon and hopes to get home to Framley. Meanwhile he would be grateful if we will continue our efforts with Mrs. Fraser.

In his own letter to me, which I recovered from the summerhouse and read while sitting by the lake, he expresses his true emotions. He is devastated that Charles has done such a thing and intends to contact everyone possible in order to discover him. John goes on to rail against the recruiting officers, the government, the war and even God for letting the war continue. It is as though Charles's action has unstoppered his emotions. It is as well that his letters to me go uncensored else I fear that he would face some charge for his words! He tells me that the new recruits, even when of the right age, are so thin and undernourished that they look more like boys of twelve than young men of eighteen. After the war, should there be any young men left, John is of the opinion that the government must act in relation to the health of the nation. Until now he had not realised what poor physical specimens the poverty and ill-health endemic in our towns and cities breeds. I have not read such deepfelt anger and emotion from him before. His rage about Charles makes him scathing on many aspects of the war.

He begs me to give him a true report of his mother's health and says that he is determined to be home on leave soon. I must not, however, mention the possibility to Mrs. Fraser for fear that things may go awry and disappointment take further toll on her.

As far as the war goes things are a little quieter for his company. This he sees as a mixed blessing for it provides the men with the opportunity to sit about and talk of every topic imaginable - from the progress of the war and politics to women working in men's jobs. All are desperate to get home, even if only for a few short days. John writes that he keeps my portrait always about his person and that his last action every night is to kiss the photograph. A poor substitute in his opinion for the real thing! I have determined that I am going to be brave enough to ask Mrs. Fraser for a small picture of John that will fit inside my locket. I think she is aware of how matters lie between us and as she is such a kind, understanding woman, I am sure that she will comply with my request. She is wearing herself out in waiting for the promised letter from Charles. Each time I visit she asks if there is any news and I must reply in the negative. We all put our trust in John and hope that he may uncover a trace of Charles. My faith and love for John tell me that if there is anything that can be accomplished then he will accomplish it.

Tuesday 19th June 1917

How Mrs. Farquharson exasperates me! I have seen very little of her since our earlier contretemps, and when I have been forced into her company I have managed to avoid the subject of leave for soldiers. I have still not apologised and I am determined that I will not - for I do not feel that I have anything for which to apologise. Mrs. Jameson seems intent on making mischief and always manages a provocative question or two - 'Captain Fraser has not been able to come home yet Elizabeth dear?' or, 'How is poor Mrs. Fraser, she must feel quite bereft since both sons have now left her - and Charles so very young!" and so on.

Today at our knitting and sewing circle Mrs. Farquharson began to question me about Charles. She has only just heard the news from Mrs. Jameson and is aghast. She seems particularly upset that Charles is more than likely serving as a common soldier. She seems unconcerned that he is a raw recruit, a child really, to be facing the perils of war. While she considers that what Charles has done may be ascribed to youthful high spirits, she is at pains to remind me that 'people of our class do not do such things!' I could stand no more and, gathering up my things, I expressed the opinion that enemy shells did not appear to discriminate on the grounds of class but were just as deadly to all. I made what I hope was a dignified exit but I could feel Mrs. Farquharson's hostile glare boring into my back. As I closed the door behind me I heard Mrs. Jameson begin to twitter in her inane way. I can, I suppose, expect trouble from Father.

I spent two hours this evening with Mrs. Fraser. The anxiety about Charles is undermining her delicate health. We still have no news and can only wait. She has dictated a letter to Mr. Lloyd George informing him of the disturbing fact that underage boys are joining the army as men. She has as yet had no reply. I find her naivety touching and have so far refrained from pointing out that so greedy are the recruiting stations for numbers to swell the ranks to supply fodder for enemy guns that no-one looks closely at either documents or men! I am of the opinion that hundreds of underage boys have joined up this year alone. I wonder how many still survive?

I expected to be greeted with hostility when I returned home, but Father was quite pleasant to me and asked kindly after Mrs. Fraser. (He is seeking the opportunity to remind her of her promise of money to enable him to purchase the land for the churchyard extension. I am grateful that even Father is not heartless-enough to ask her at this time.) He has clearly not yet heard from Mrs. Jameson! No doubt the storm will break in its own time.

Thursday 21st June 1917

At last some news! When I visited Park House this morning Mrs. Fraser was beside herself with a conflict of fear, anger and relief. Charles has written to her. He is currently on embarkation leave (how very soon these poor young men are sent into the arena of war!) and is spending it in Portsmouth. He gives no address but explains what he has done and why he has done it. As we were already aware he was desperate to join the war and was afraid that all would be over before he had the opportunity to play his part.

The first time he ran away from school and was returned there he became a hero. Far from being treated with contempt by his fellow pupils his actions were celebrated by his peers. One pupil, Roger Chaterham, took pains to explain where his plan had gone wrong. To make short work of the story, with Roger Chaterham's aid and assistance, Charles managed to obtain a false birth certificate and laid his plans for escaping from school. He went directly to Birmingham, which was the area where his birth certificate originated. No wonder there was no trace of him in London! He soon enlisted and says that no questions were raised about his age - no doubt as he looked so much bigger and stronger than others in the queue! He has only just finished basic training and as they have been closely supervised and he did not wish to give away his identity, it is the first opportunity he has had to write the promised letter. He is to embark within days and thinks that he is bound for France. (The men do not know their destination until they are aboard ship.) If he finds himself in France he will be sure to acquaint John with his whereabouts and hopes to meet him soon.

He has the grace to apologise for the anxiety he knows he will have caused but goes to great lengths to explain himself and begs understanding and forgiveness. He reminds us that as a private soldier his letters will be censored and that when he is in France (or wherever he lands) he will write to us using his new name, Alfred Simpson.

Mrs. Fraser set the letter aside and allowed the tears to flow freely down her cheeks. She could say nothing. I embraced her and we held tightly on to each other united in silent sympathy. After some time we discussed the letter and agreed that there was little that we could do. Portsmouth is so crowded with troops, and we have no idea of Charles's regiment, that we would be looking for the proverbial 'needle in a haystack' if we were to go there. Instead I will lay all before John and hope that he may achieve some success. We should soon receive Charles's letter which will supply details of his regiment. We can then decide on our future actions. Mrs. Fraser wants, above everything, the return of Charles

- at whatever cost to his pride. I, on the other hand, would prefer to wait for John's opinion. We are cushioned here in rural England and cannot comprehend how war alters and effects the individual.

I returned to Brabage with my news and all were relieved that the waiting is over at last. Mary is particularly happy and has told me that, as soon as we know Charles's whereabouts, she intends to take up correspondence with Private Alfred Simpson!

I have written to John and told him all that we know. At last he will be able to search constructively for, until now, he has spent all his spare time in a fruitless search for an anonymous brother. I pray that his efforts will be successful.

Friday 29th June 1917

Today I received a very excited letter from John. At last he had a few days leave and after receiving my letter he went down to the base camp at Le Havre to check on new arrivals. It is a mammoth task for apparently hundreds and hundreds of men arrive at one time and sleep in tents at the base camp until they are sent off to their own part of the war. Fortunately John is not without influence and he was not put to going from tent to tent looking for his young brother. He is good friends with Captain Benthall who is a part of the administration at Base Camp. While not explaining the circumstances John told him that he wished to make contact with Private Alfred Simpson, but that he did not know his regiment. He went on to say that Private Simpson had arrived in France in the past few days (although that was a pure guess!). Captain Benthall told him that things may take a little time, and indicated the huge piles of records. However he went on to assure John that if Private Simpson had arrived during this past week then in a day or two he would be able to pass on to John details of his regiment, company, number - and location.

John was so pleased that he was tempted to tell Benthall the whole story, but as he had expressed no curiosity and was obviously extremely busy, John refrained from doing so. He writes that he intends to meet Charles and talk things over with him before any action is decided upon.

John asked me to pass on the news to his mother as he is so short of time that he has barely managed the letter to me. I will go to Park House tomorrow but must beware of raising false hopes - for all we know Charles may not have been sent to France but may be in some other part of the world altogether!

Thursday 5th July 1917

While I was at Park House today a telegram arrived. While I was unable to suppress a deep fear I was sure that it did not contain bad news. Mrs. Fraser's hands were trembling too much to open it so at her direction I unsealed it and read the contents:-

DEAR MOTHER STOP CHARLES FOUND STOP I WILL SEE HIM ON TUESDAY STOP LOVE JOHN.

We both-cried with happiness and felt that we had received the best present in the world! Soon however we started discussing the situation and speculating over the outcome. Our guessing was interrupted by Mother, Father and Mary who came to Park House in order to collect me. They were as delighted as we at the news and Mary actually cried! I do believe that she is fond of Charles after all!

Father took the opportunity presented by Mrs. Fraser's delight to broach the subject of the purchase of the land for the churchyard. Mrs. Fraser clapped her hand to her mouth and exclaimed,

"Oh, I am so sorry. I quite forgot all about it with all this trouble about Charles. Now that it is untangling itself I must see my lawyer and get things organised!"

Father was as pleased as a dog with two bones and even on the way home in the trap could not help driving past the churchyard and explaining his plans in detail - for the hundredth time!

I wrote to John expressing my delight and describing how his mother had received the news. My only complaint was at the brevity of the telegram and I told him that I looked forward, with excitement, to hearing the whole story. I know that my poor darling gets little opportunity to write, but, oh how I wish that I could hear more.

I sent my love - and my admonition - to Charles and asked John to find out from him if he wishes Mary to write. (I can guess what the answer will be!) The remainder of my letter was all love to my darling. I am so happy, and so relieved tonight that I am sure that I will not sleep!

Friday 13th July 1917

There can be no God. I cannot believe in an Almighty who is so cruel. Charles is dead. I cannot write more today.

Tuesday 17th July 1917

I have been unable to face writing my diary since we received the fatal news. So much has happened. John has been home and has returned to the Front, leaving his mother so very ill that a nurse has had to be employed to care for her - my services are not sufficient for the constant care needed. I have spent all my time since last Friday at Park House and I am still here. I am likely to remain for some time to come. I can still make no sense of the catastrophic news. I think that perhaps if I write everything down as it occurred, I may find it easier.

On Thursday evening when I wrote my diary I was excited that we should soon have news of Charles. John was to see him last Tuesday and Mrs. Fraser and I both expected a letter to arrive by the end of the week. I was with her each day, and each day we were disappointed by the non-arrival of news. We talked excitedly together of what we would have to say to Charles, whether he would be home immediately, what John would have to say about it all. When I went to Framley on Friday morning I was quite confident that news would arrive that day. Little did I dream what that news would be!

The post had been delivered and still had brought no letter from John or from Charles. Mrs. Fraser and I were sitting discussing, of all mundane matters, the outing she had recently provided for the Brabage School children. She was regaling me with Alice's account of the children's various escapades when I, who could see over her shoulder and out of the window, was transfixed by the sight of Miller's pony and trap coming through the gates. I know that Miller's trap is usually kept at the station and hired out as and when necessary. I could see that sitting beside the driver was a tall, military man. Something in my fixed expression conveyed agitation to Mrs. Fraser who turned around to see what I was watching so intently. As she turned she exclaimed, "John!" and the instant she said it I knew him. He is so thin and gaunt that I had for a moment not recognised him! I can only imagine the turmoil in Mrs. Fraser's mind by that which was churning inside myself. In moments several different and conflicting explanations for John's appearance here presented themselves to me. In such a flurry I ran from the room to meet my darling as he entered the hallway. I flung myself into his arms and he held me so tightly that I felt all the air crushed from my body and my ribs being almost certainly bruised. From his intense stillness and iron grip I knew that he brought bad news.

Mrs. Fraser had risen and, with the aid of her stick, had reached the doorway to the sitting room. One look at John's face told all and she uttered a whispered question, "Charles?"

John was instantly at her side and held her as he had held me. He said only, "I'm sorry Mother, I was too late!"

I do not know how long we stood there. I was aware of Alice coming along and, brushing away tears in her own eyes, leading Mrs. Fraser to the divan. She sat down heavily, placing her head in her hands and weeping so profoundly that I thought that she would never stop. I sat beside her and put my arms around her. John stood behind, his arm on his mother's shoulder. The other arm he placed around me. In a low monotone he told his tale.

After his latest duty at the Front John had returned to billets with his company. Usually the time there is taken up by inspections, parades, drill - all the day to day business of the soldier. As all is routine and usually runs like clockwork, John had received special permission to go along the lines to seek out Alfred Simpson. He knew which sector he should be in and hoped to meet up with him before the company was sent to the Front.

It took John two and a half hours to make his way to the place he had been told 'B' Company was. He had begged lifts on all manner of vehicles and finally walked into the small inn yard where he expected to find the Company commanders. He had been aware since starting out of the increased mutter and grumble of the enemy guns and had several times heard the vicious rattle of machine gun fire at close range. It looked as though the Germans were stepping up the action in that sector and he hastened his step.

In the inn yard silence reigned supreme. John called out loudly but the only response came in French from behind closed shutters. He went and rattled the door and eventually his summons was answered by a short, round man who, in happier times would have been a genial 'mine host'. Over the innkeeper's shoulder John could see that all was chaos and confusion. The inn stood less than three miles from enemy lines and it would seem that during the previous night a sudden, surprise assault on the Allied trenches had allowed the Germans to break through. While the innkeeper was confident that the British would drive the Germans back again (indeed all the young soldiers billeted in his inn had been hastily despatched to deal with the attack) he was taking no chances. He had decided to remove his wife and two daughters, together with their portable valuables, to safety until the danger had passed. He did not wish to find himself and his family in German hands.

As he listened to the news John knew that he had arrived too late and that young Charles (or Alfred Simpson as he must now call him) was on his way to the front line, if not actually in it. John hurried from the inn yard and was lucky

enough to catch a lift on one of the old London omnibuses used for transport behind the lines. It was rumbling along the road towards the Front, the boarded up lower deck and open upper deck crammed with young soldiers.

After jolting along for a couple of miles the omnibus came to a halt. The road ahead was blocked. An earlier transport vehicle had suffered a direct hit from an enemy shell and its shattered remains (and those of its occupants) had been scattered across the road. The wreckage was slowly being cleared and the devastated remains of the young soldiers were being placed on one side. The carnage was such that none could be easily recognised. John refrained from giving me a graphic description but my own imagination more than fully supplies the awful details he omitted.

The driver of the omnibus was directed around the wreck and as the vehicle slowed to bump across the fields John jumped down. Making his way towards the wreckage he knew in his heart that his search had ended and that he had found his young brother.

The officer in charge was frantically shouting directions to his men, aware that the sooner the road was clear, the more successful would be the retaliation against the enemy and the more likely would the British be to regain lost ground. John greeted him and asked for permission to identify the dead. The Captain was relieved that one small part of his duty could be delegated and readily gave the required permission. He also detailed a private to assist John.

John told us little of what must have been a gruesome search. Efficiently he identified each body by its belongings and the private dutifully listed the names of the dead. At last John opened the pocketbook on one body to find the name 'Alfred Simpson'. He could not recognise Charles. John held the ruin of a body close to him, cradling what had once been a head in his arms. The private looked on curiously, for so hardened had he become to the horrors of the war that the raw emotion displayed by John caused him great embarrassment and no little surprise. Eventually John laid the body aside and, his task completed, got to his feet and walked away, there was nothing further he could do for his brother.

To the Captain he merely explained that one of the soldiers was a close relative and therefore he would be grateful for permission to remove some effects. The permission was readily granted and, with Charles's ring on his finger, his watch in his pocket and his pocketbook next to his own breast, John made his painful, weary journey back to his own company. Charles would be buried in France, in a war grave, under the name of Alfred Simpson. A casualty in a war in which he had not fired a single shot.

Mrs. Fraser and I listened to John's story in total silence. When he had finished his mother wordlessly held out her hands. John placed in them Charles's meagre belongings. She clasped them to her tightly and sobbed quietly.

We three held each other close, all lost in our own thoughts, our own sorrow.

After some time John prevailed on Mrs. Fraser to put down Charles's things. The ring she immediately placed on her own finger; the other things lay in her lap.

I find it difficult to remember how the rest of the day passed. Someone must have sent word to my father, for he and my mother appeared to comfort Mrs. Fraser. Of Mary there was no sign and I dread to think how the poor girl has taken the news for I have not seen her since. While Mother consoled Mrs. Fraser, Father approached John, hand outstretched. He shook John's hand, muttering,

"So sorry my boy, so sorry! The comfort is that he died a soldier's death!"

John looked down contemptuously at Father and for one moment I thought that he was going to voice our now common opinion - that Charles had never even had the opportunity to be a soldier; that his death was a profligate waste of a young and promising life; that he was but a boy. Before Father had caught the look of contempt John had lowered his own eyes and muttered his acceptance of Father's condolences. I suppose that anger would achieve nothing, only making the loss of Charles worse by surrounding us with contention and acrimony.

That I was to stay at Park House was taken for granted and that evening I did what I could for Mrs. Fraser. She has taken to her bed and hardly speaks. She cries continually, sobbing out occasionally words such as,

"He was only a boy. What right has anyone to kill a boy?"

Since that day she has deteriorated. I found her yesterday with Charles's picture - a photograph that had been taken of him in cricket whites. His face is open and friendly, proud of his sporting success. Mrs. Fraser clutched the photograph to herself, rocking backwards and forwards, sobbing deeply. The doctor has, of course, attended but can do nothing. It is clear that her heart is broken. She will not eat - but none of us has any appetite for the food which is placed before us and taken away untouched. A nurse arrived this morning and it is hoped that her brisk manner will prevail where my gentleness has failed and that Mrs. Fraser will eat.

John was allowed home only in order to break the news to his mother and returned to France yesterday. His own commander knows the entire story but John has advised that it would not be worth bringing out the truth for there would be nothing to gain. I am of the same opinion but Mrs. Fraser flung herself

at John and shouted her misery that Charles was not even to be buried under his own name.

That the search for, and the discovery of, Charles has taken its toll, on John is obvious. On the three nights he stayed here (Friday, Saturday and Sunday) I was awoken by his shouts. I ran immediately to his room - for there can be no false modesty in such a matter - to discover that he was still sleeping but dreaming a nightmare. Each night I reached out and stroked his brow and whispered gentle, comforting words, Each time he has quietened and eventually slept peacefully. I have not been able to tell him of this but now that he has returned I wonder how his fears will be stilled?

I know that I am wickedly selfish, but Charles's death has made me fear more for my own darling. That life can be so suddenly and so casually terminated is horrifying. John has returned to the Front, for such (he says) is the duty of all Englishmen - and with him goes my life. If anything were to happen to him, I know that I would not wish to live. There would be no point in life without him, for what is the sky without the sun?

Mrs. Fraser is so distracted that I do not think she is aware of John's return. John was fearful of leaving her in such precarious health, but that hateful word 'duty' arose once more.

We are all stunned by Charles's death and none of us, including the servants, can believe that he is dead. Perhaps it would be more real to us if we had a coffin; a grave; a funeral?

I am to remain here for as long as Mrs. Fraser needs me and Mother and Father are to visit again tomorrow. I do not know, I cannot guess, what the future holds. I only know that I am filled with dread as I look forward.

When I have the opportunity I would like to asks Father to explain to me how his loving and caring God can permit such things to happen. For in allowing the death of Charles He has surely destroyed Mrs. Fraser, and is just as certainly destroying John, and through him - me. What purpose is served by a boy's death? What good can come from it? None that I can see. It is with weary sadness, even despair, that I finish my diary tonight. I will not ask God's blessing on John, for God has surely cursed us all.

MY HUSBAND! MY SON!

Three hundred men he said we'd lost,
Killed in that last battle.
He hardly frowned when counting cost,
Men worth less than cattle.

But each man dead was someone's son,
Husband or a brother.
In him they've lost the only one,
Grief can heed no other.

Three hundred letters will be sent,
Three hundred families weep.
How many lives in mourning spent
Now life is bought so cheap?

No man stands in isolation
And countless tears will fall.
No brave words bring consolation
To those in mourning's thrall.

For every death's a stone that's cast
Into life's brooding calm.
Widening ripples for ever last
And all they touch they harm.

Three hundred lost: The number high,
But sorrow's not yet done,
At least three hundred still to cry,
'My husband!' or 'My son!'

John Fraser 1917

Friday July 20th 1917

Poor Mary! Today Mother came to Park House and brought Mary with her. My sister is so pale and thin, with such black shadows under her eyes that I hardly recognise her! It is as I expected, she is guilt-ridden over the death of Charles. To comfort her I found myself uttering platitudes and consoling words that I cannot myself believe. When she railed against God, what could I say, I who cannot reconcile a belief in a loving Father with the events that have happened? I opened my mouth and poured forth the conventional wisdom. Mary hardly listened but was clearly in a trance, a dream-world of her own. At last I grasped her shoulders and gave her a sharp shake, at the same time snapping,

"Don't be such a silly girl Mary. You are not so important that you could have prevented Charles's death. I believe that you are acting in this way in order to draw attention to yourself. Now come on and pull yourself together before I take you along to Mrs. Fraser's room. She is the one who has every right to grieve!"

I did not of course mean my sharp words but they served their intended purpose and called Mary to herself. She reddened and started to apologise. I hugged her to me and we comforted each other. When we were more composed we went along to Mrs. Fraser's room. Mother was already there and looked so sad that I was at first alarmed that something terrible had happened. However Mrs. Fraser was just the same. She was asleep and it was her whimpering aloud that had so touched Mother. We all long to bring Mrs. Fraser some comfort but are unable to do so. The only one, I believe, who could bring her solace is John, and the Lord only knows when he will next be allowed home!

Mrs. Fraser awoke and was able to hold a little conversation with us. Her talk is all of Charles and how she plans to have him buried under his own name and in his own country, even if she must journey to France herself in order to accomplish it. We were all anxious to change the subject, but however hard we tried she always returned to the same topic. At the end of an hour even Mother's patience was sorely tried and she said that she would have to return home.

Outside, Mother took the opportunity to speak privately to me. It would seem that Father is in a dreadful temper. He is angry that the agreement for the payment for the purchase of the land for the church was not drawn up before this latest trouble. He told Mother that she must ask me to come home, even if only for an hour, in order that he may instruct me how I should proceed on his behalf! I am learning that my father is a heartless monster. How could anyone seeing the condition of poor Mrs. Fraser be so concerned over a material matter - and such

a trivial one at that! In my present attitude to God I can only say that the servant fits the master!

However much I am inclined to ignore Father's request (demand) and say that Mrs. Fraser is too ill for me to leave her, I feel so sorry for Mother and Mary that I have said that I will go to Brabage on Sunday. That will also provide me with the opportunity to visit the Sunday School, for however much I am dissatisfied with God, I miss the children! Mother brightened considerably at my reply and went home with a lighter heart. I know how appalling life can be when Father is in such a mood!

During the evening I sat with Mrs. Fraser. She spent hours re-living the childhood lives of Charles and John. I know so much about John from her talk of the past few days that I feel that I have known him all my life!

When Mrs. Fraser had gone to sleep I came to my room and wrote a letter to John. I know that he is due to write to me but tonight I feel all alone in the world except for him. God has gone from my life; Mrs. Fraser is ill and confused; Mary is isolated in her deep grief and guilt; Father is immersed in his 'project' and Mother is so dominated by him that there is little space for anyone but him in her life. The only person who has room in his heart for me is so very far away and in such danger. In my letter I tried to be cheerful and constructive but I fear that my mood of isolation will be communicated. I am so angry with the politicians and generals who seem to delight in prolonging the conflict. I feel that I could almost imitate Mrs. Pankhurst's former tactics and chain myself to Parliament's railings, not for female emancipation but rather to demand an end to the war. When will it all end? I am so morose tonight that I must put down my pen and hope that a good sleep will improve my mood.

Sunday 22nd July 1917

I am thankful that my 'interview' with Father is over. It was just as bad as I had expected it to be. All his persuasion, his domineering attitude, has merely served to make me more determined to go my own way.

I was deliberately late in arriving at Brabage Vicarage. Father was on the point of leaving to prepare for the service when I arrived and he greeted me with the curt announcement that there would be no time for our 'conference' before church and so he would see me after the service. That is all he had to say to a daughter whom he has not seen for more than a week!

Mother, Mary and I walked together to church and I sat through the service scarcely taking notice of anything. In fact I was meditating on the place that

religion had once held in my life. For as long as I can remember the church has been central to my whole existence. God's existence, indeed his munificence, went unquestioned. It was God who rewarded the just and devout; God who punished the unjust and godless. Was I, were John and Mrs. Fraser wicked and godless to be punished in such a way?

My straying thoughts were called to attention during Father's sermon. I became aware that he was leaning so far forward in his pulpit that he seemed about to fall over the front. He was lecturing the congregation quite heatedly on the subject of duty and obedience. I realised that he was looking straight into my own eyes. Hastily I did what at least three-quarters of the congregation had done already, and bowed my head. Father's words washed over me: Duty to God; duty to one's country; duty to one's lords and masters. Here (with careful emphasis) duty to one's parents. Duty! Duty! Duty! Obedience! Obedience! Obedience! To accept with quietude whatever life chooses to throw at you - that was the core of Father's sermon. I felt my temper begin to rise. Was it then a sin to have a will of one's own? Was everything directed by this God? What then of Charles? How did the death of such a child, a shining beacon in his mother's life, have a place in the great scheme of things? His death was not yet over, for the suffering would always be left behind.

By the end of the service I could feel that my nerves were raw and I was ready to tackle Father with some of the questions with which I had taxed myself. As the congregation left the church I noticed that Colonel and Mrs. Farquharson were present. They spent a long time talking to Father and so I took the opportunity to avoid them all!

Over lunch Father told us that the Colonel had passed his condolences to Mrs. Fraser. He had only just heard the news about Charles. I was about to pass an acid comment on the fact that the Colonel was once more on leave when I bit back my words, for I did not wish to remind Father of that old quarrel. Father must have picked up my thoughts, or my face betrayed me for he added, rather hastily, that Colonel Farquharson was not home on leave but had been attending an important conference in London. (Mr. Lloyd George runs the war in this way - always calling high ranking officers to meetings in Downing Street.) The Colonel had managed to 'slip down' to Brabage to see his family 'just for the day'. There was an awkward silence, for by reading John's 'official' letters Father is well aware how difficult John has found it to get enough leave to enable him to come home. Mother broke the silence with some inane chatter about the difficulty she has in getting servants. I had noticed that Hester was not there this morning, that

there was a new girl, Madge, but as in our house servants come and go with great rapidity I had not thought much about it. Mother prattled on about how the girls either go off, starry eyed, to nurse the wounded or go off to Crewe or Birmingham to work in the munitions factories or do some other job previously carried out by men. Very few wish to 'go into service'. We all avoided looking directly at each other, for while we acknowledge that there is a general difficulty in finding servants, each of us knows that no girl with any sense would stay in Brabage Vicarage given Father's abominable temper and tyrannical nature. I remember poor Hester in tears once for the way in which Father had shouted at her for committing the grievous sin of bringing his shaving water five minutes late!

My confrontation (for such it was sure to be) with Father was postponed once more as I had to attend Sunday School. I am afraid that I said some harsh words to some of the children when I heard that they had been unmercifully teasing and taunting the Farrington children. The family had recently arrived in the village. George Farrington, the father, is a Conscientious Objector and has moved to Brabage seeking peace from the barrage of animosity, hostility and outright hatred he and his family have faced in Nantwich. The children had made a great show of presenting the three Farrington children with white feathers when they appeared at Sunday School. The children turned and fled. I told the children and the teachers that sometimes it needs more courage to refuse to fight than it does to go along with the majority. The teachers regarded me sympathetically and whispered to each other - sure I suppose that my opinions have been temporarily swayed by the death of Charles. The children remained silent, and even Jamie Shipton had nothing to say for once! They all looked most uncomfortable.

My interview with Father could be put off no longer and I dutifully presented myself in his study at four o'clock. I do not wish to dwell on the acrimonious words that passed between us. Father explained that all was ready for the purchase of the land and only the sum of money from Mrs. Fraser was outstanding. He insisted that I inform her that the money is now required. When I reminded him of the grave state of her health he merely observed that such being the case it was more important than ever to act quickly. On seeing my reluctance he offered to write to John in order to discuss the matter with him. I could scarcely contain my contempt as I said that in his situation at the Front John would have more important things on his mind than the minor business of extending Brabage Churchyard!. From that point on our discussion deteriorated - Father calling in God on his side, for the land was wanted in order to serve the 'greater glory of God'. Inevitably my doubts about God surfaced and I was castigated as being,

'thankless, Godless and a most undutiful daughter'. Father considers that it is my absence at Framley which has caused me to 'stray from the path of duty'. I had no more to say and Father dismissed me with the warning that he would have to consider my continuing stay with Mrs. Fraser.

I need hardly add that my return to Framley came as a great relief, even though I found Mrs. Fraser worse than when I left her. Her mind is now wandering and I fear for her sanity. I am torn about whether to write the true state of things to John. I wish I had someone to advise me.

Wednesday 1st August 1917

A new month and with it some great news! Mrs. Fraser has received a letter from John in which he says that he will be home on Friday. I am so excited that I wish to rush up to London to meet him. I am not sure that Mrs. Fraser fully understands the news, for her mind wanders quite dreadfully often in the middle of a sentence and she has become very forgetful.

One black cloud has appeared on my horizon - Father! I went to Brabage to convey the news of John's home leave and Father has said that I must return home as it is 'not proper' for me to remain at Park House with Mrs. Fraser an invalid and John at home. I pleaded the necessity of my remaining with Mrs. Fraser and that in these modern times people do not think in that way. It was all to no avail and Father is to come to Framley on Friday. He will bring with him Mother and Mary and once John has been welcomed home we will return to Brabage. It will be like going into prison after the freedom I have enjoyed.

Friday 3rd August 1917

I am so dizzy with happiness for John is home at last! I was up early this morning in order to ensure that everything was ready to greet John. When everything was finished I went and sat with Mrs. Fraser.

"John will be home soon!" I said.

"That's nice dear. Will Charles be with him, do you think?"

I could not answer her and merely patted her hand. She is so confused that I do not know what is to be done. She soon fell into a light doze and I left her. The nurse tells me that she is like this more and more frequently, however her appetite has improved. All we can hope is that John's return helps her to regain her former mind.

Mother, Father and Mary arrived at two o'clock, and while I was pleased to see my mother and sister I could only greet Father coldly. Such is his insensitivity

that I do not think he even noticed my unfriendliness.

As the time drew near for John's arrival I could not sit still but walked restlessly from window to window hoping to catch first sight of him when Miller's trap arrived.

It was a beautiful, hot, sunny, summer's day and quite stifling inside the house. Mother suggested that we could perhaps go outside and wait for John under the verandah. This we did. Mary and I left Mother and Father and walked down towards the gate. We had barely got ten paces when the trap turned in at the gate and he was here!

John got down from the trap and accompanied Mary and me back to the house. With such great sadness I note that he has grown even thinner. His hair has begun to grey at the temples and there are so many lines about his eyes. He walks with a slight limp and on me referring to it was dismissive of it, saying that his old wound troubles him sometimes. John greeted Mother with warmth and Father with correctness. We went inside. John wished to go straight to his mother, but I persuaded him to take tea first, explaining that his mother was normally asleep at this time. Over tea it fell to me to break the news of his mother's sad condition. I went along to Mrs. Fraser's room to prepare her for John's arrival. She was asleep and I touched her shoulder gently.

"Mrs. Fraser," I whispered, "John is home." She awoke instantly.

"John, yes I was just dreaming of John, is he home from school then?" she said, confused.

John was the other side of the door, but he told me later that he had heard his mother quite distinctly. He pushed the door open and went to her, folding her in his arms. She put her arms around him and hugged and hugged.

"John my darling, you are home. Thank God! I knew that you would not desert me now that Charles is gone!"

She was in her right mind at last and I crept from the room, leaving them to each other.

Later, John came to join us in the drawing room. He was so cast down and morose that I wished that I could go to him and hold him. He asked numerous questions about his poor mother, finally determining on an early interview with Dr. Armstrong to discover the true state of affairs and the prognosis. Our conversation was stilted and artificial and I know that my darling was experiencing the same difficulty that I was. Our 'official' correspondence is so very correct and distant that our behaviour towards each other must be just as correct and distant lest Father's suspicions are aroused. When I looked into his eyes I could

see my own longing mirrored there. Father told John that he would like a private interview with him and I saw John look hopefully at me and then at Father. I gave the merest shake of the head to indicate that the subject of the interview was nothing to do with me. Father went on to tell John that it was a business matter and so I know that it is about that wretched land!

All too soon the time came for our departure and how sad I was to be packing my things into the trap to go back to Brabage. John managed to whisper to me that he will see me soon. It cannot be too soon for me; how I ache for him.

After a quiet evening I retired early in order to write my diary. When the house was quiet I came up to the attic to continue it here, It is now almost two o'clock in the morning and I must put my candle out and my diary away or I will not be sufficiently awake to greet John when he comes.

So, in spite of all the grief of the past weeks, I am happy. John is home - even though it is only for a short time. Mrs. Fraser is restored to her right mind and I feel that I have something to look forward to. Perhaps John's presence will restore Mrs. Fraser to health. I am excited that I will see him soon, and frequently!

Saturday 4th August 1917

As I expected John visited Brabage today. He had been to see Dr. Armstrong and was grave regarding his mother. The doctor has explained that grief has brought on an exacerbation of her old complaint. In addition her mind is very much disturbed. Some days she is better than others and it is this very variability which makes her difficult to treat. The doctor hopes that with good care she will recover. Of course John will do all that he can while he is here, and already reports an improvement in her condition.

Mary, John and I walked in the grounds after tea and John praised our kitchen garden generously. I told him that it was all Carstairs' doing as Father will not allow us to do any work of that kind - it is not ladylike! Of course John knows that at Park House I have been helping with the gardening and is impressed with the improvements. He laughs at Father's old fashioned ideas of 'ladylike'.

Somehow in our wanderings we left Mary behind and quite naturally found ourselves at the summerhouse. It was so pleasant to sit in the shade by the lake and just be alone together. John began to play about and to score our initials in the sandy shore of the lake. I laughed and took him to the rear of the summerhouse and showed him the great silver birch on the bark of which local lovers carve their names. John at once took out his pocketknife and, turning to me, his eyes alight and his troubles momentarily forgotten, he said,

"Let's pretend that we are just two village sweethearts and there is no-one to hide our love from."

He climbed some way up the tree and carved out our names - 'John and Lizzie' - and the date - 1917. Climbing down he took me in his arms and kissed me so passionately that I felt that I had entered another world. My love for John is so great that it feels like a huge living beast, throbbing inside me. I know that it is considered immodest for a young girl to think such things (no doubt Father would consider it a sin!) but I am not as ignorant as many suppose. I know what happens physically between a man and a woman, and I say, here in my diary, I would give myself to John in that way if he wished it so. There! I have written it and I mean it.

We roused ourselves from our passion and, hand in hand, came round to the front of the summerhouse. There we found Mary and I do not know who was the more embarrassed! We spent a pleasant half hour on the lake in the small boat but soon had to come ashore and return to the house. Father made a great show of consulting his watch and saying what a time we had been, but we were too happy to take much notice.

John returned to Framley but for the remainder of the evening my thoughts kept returning to the idyllic afternoon I had spent and more than once Mother had to speak sharply to me in order to recall me to the present. It was fortunate that Father was hard at work in his study preparing tomorrow's sermon and so I escaped his harsh criticism!

I would that this happy time could continue for ever. I go to sleep tonight warm and secure in the love of the best man in the world.

Sunday 5th August 1917

Today has been so very long and tedious that I am glad that it is over. I have not yet had the courage to face Father with my doubts about the existence of God and so quite naturally am expected to attend church and resume my duties at Sunday School. With such a heavy heart I have gone through the day.

I was even more downcast at Sunday School when I heard the latest village news. When I asked why the Farrington children were not present the children shifted about uneasily on their seats. At last Jamie Shipton had the courage to speak for them all. Evidently it was not only the children who were being taunted for their father's lack of khaki, but life was made miserable here in Brabage for the entire family. One by one the local shops refused to supply Mrs. Farrington and there was no work at all for her husband to do. Wherever he went to seek

employment he was turned away - though God knows how the farmers in the area are desperate for good strong men. At last no-one in the village would speak to them and they quietly put their things together and went from Brabage. They had to walk as there was no-one willing enough to even hire them transport. Rumour has it they have gone towards Liverpool, I suppose that they will be easier lost in such a large choke of people

I was not only upset but disgusted by the attitude of the whole village and so, caring not for their opinion, I told all present in no uncertain terms that if they were true Christians they would have welcomed the family, whatever their beliefs. There followed a lesson centred on the parable of the Good Samaritan and, though no longer considering myself a believer, I returned to the vicarage feeling very much better!

When I asked at home about the Farringtons Mary had no idea what had become of them. Mother fidgeted about and was uncomfortable, looking sideways at Father. Father held his head up even higher than his stiff neck customarily keeps it and retorted,

"We don't want their sort in Brabage Elizabeth. The father should have been man enough to do his duty for King and country"

I looked at Father - a man totally innocent of any military association; a man who had never considered joining the army but had contented himself in sending others to the Front. My contempt was audible as I burst out,

"Yes, Father, we must all do our duty!" My meaning was clear and I did not stay for the wave of Father's anger to break but turned on my heel and left the room. Some time later I heard Maud (the latest of our long suffering maids) being shouted at for moving some papers in Father's study. I suppose that such a man must vent his tyrannical spleen on some poor creature!

Tomorrow I am to visit Park House. I will tell John about the Farringtons. Also I think that it is time to tell him of my doubts about religion.

Monday 6th August 1917

Tonight I am pleased to write in my diary that Mrs. Fraser is very much better. She is almost her old self, and while still retaining a residue of sadness for Charles she is able to talk about him to John and me in a rational way. She still tires easily and while she had a sleep in the afternoon John and I were able to have the long talk that we so needed. Mother and Mary had of course accompanied me to Park House but the ever faithful Alice had offered to show them both over the house which they had not seen to any great extent before.

John and I walked in the grounds and, being overtaken by a sudden thunderstorm, took shelter in a small summerhouse. (How we seem drawn to summerhouses!) I was so alarmed to see that the deep rumble of the thunder and the brilliant flash of lightning brought on a great trembling in John which took me some time to calm. Eventually he was able to speak of his fear, telling me how the violent storm was like the shadow of war, the dark finger of which dominated his entire life. We talked about his life at the Front - something he has not been inclined to do before. He told me that in his experience all the men are afraid of war, except for the stupid ones who are afraid of nothing. He, and many of his brother officers, feel so wretched ordering their men out sometimes to certain death. Though they rage and rail against it, all feel helpless, caught up in the great administrative machine which demands their very selves. Many of the new soldiers are so young that, experiencing war for the first time, they freeze in the trenches like terrified rabbits with the fox outside the burrow. It is the hardest thing (John says) to encourage such a man out of his hole and into the fray, particularly so when everything seems so pointless. Each time John looks at such a young soldier, the bright shining face of Charles appears before him and he realises anew that he will never see Charles again, that the flame of his young life has been snuffed out, and like a candle, has left a pool of darkness behind.

I had become aware that John was disillusioned with the war but had not realised that such discontent is widespread among both officers and men. They dare not voice their feelings or all would be lost; instead they continue, day after day, month after month, carrying out what appear to be such useless orders.

I told John about the Farringtons, he was quiet for a moment or two and then said,

"You know Lizzie, one has to be more of a hero to stick to one's convictions in the face of adversity than to take the easy route and go along with the majority."

I told him that I had said very much the same to the Sunday School children. I did not think that John had heard me for his eyes were glazed and he was obviously thinking of something else. I recalled his attention and he apologised. I asked what he had been thinking about. He was reluctant to tell me but finally I forced him to it! I wish that I had not for those thoughts will haunt me for ever. He was thinking of the numbers of deserters who had been shot and how much better it would have been if they had never been forced to go to war. Surely shooting one's own men must be the most hideous thing of all, especially if their only crime is to display that most natural of feelings: fear! John told me that it is rumoured that a large camp of deserters is set up somewhere near Le Havre and

that the men (of all nationalities) thrive there. Such intelligence is squashed wherever it is heard for fear that discontent will spread.

I walked to the window and looked out over the lawn. The rain was still coming down hard. John came up behind me and put his hands on my shoulders.

In the quiet of the summerhouse I found the courage to tell him that I thought that I had turned away from God. He was silent, merely gripping my shoulders more tightly. I thought that he was displeased but when he spoke he said,

"I am not surprised Lizzie. All that we have experienced in the past few months makes it hard to believe."

I asked if he still believed in a loving God. He hesitated before replying,

"What I have undergone in the last few years has rocked the very foundations of my belief until all lies in ruins about my feet!"

We were silent. I turned to him and we held each other in close embrace. The rain finally ceased and we left the summerhouse. Neither of us were willing to talk further on the subject, for I believe that facing our unbelief so candidly had shaken us to the core. It is sufficient to know that we both share the same doubts.

On taking our leave I noticed that Mother was rather agitated. She clearly had something on her mind. As we stepped up into the trap she started, as though she had just remembered something.

"Oh dear! I almost forgot," she said to John, "Reverend Aubrey asked if you could come to Brabage this week as he has business to discuss with you."

Relieved that her message was delivered, she awaited the answer.

"I'll come on Wednesday," John replied, "for my leave is up on Friday." Until then there had been no mention of the end of his leave. Friday! I had not realised that it would be over so soon!

Back at Brabage we discovered that Maud had left without giving notice. Gentle probing of Father by Mother has shown that he had complained to her for some trivial (he says) matter today and she put down the tea tray and walked out of the study. That was the last he saw of her. Mother is in quite a state and does not know where to look next for a maid. How Father makes life difficult!

The evening passed uneventfully, except that cook had to serve dinner herself there being no maid. She muttered under her breath but Father merely ignored her. I suppose that we will all have to turn to and help out until another poor girl is found!

INNOCENT EARTH

Howitzers tear the innocent earth,
Bomb craters scar her face,
Though never bringing this war to birth
She suffers man's disgrace.

With what She has She fights the battle;
She thunders, rages, rains.
Men wade through mud, are mired like cattle,
Ensnared in Nature's chains.

At last it passes, on men blunder,
They'll not by mud be foiled.
She's wounded, damaged, torn asunder,
Her innocence despoiled.

Will ever this broken earth be whole,
Will flowers bloom once more
Where humanity did lose its soul
And sank in bloody war?

Yet in other times, in other wars
The earth has borne this stain.
She's grown lush, grown green, She's covered scars.
Pray God she will again.

John Fraser 1917

Wednesday 8th August 1917

Today has been quite eventful. First of all our new maid started work. She is Hannah Wright's sister, Edna. She is as dull-witted as Hannah is bright. She is slow and a little clumsy but at least too dim to be hurt by Father's scathing comments. She has held several positions in the past year, even working in a factory in Northwich at one time. However, for one reason or another, she could not keep her situations, so, here she is, landed up with us. We will have to see

how she goes on. I hope that her skin is as thick as her skull appears to be! Mother is pleased at finding a replacement for Maud so quickly and cook is delighted to be relieved from her extra duties. Edna is in some way related to Carstairs - I think that she is his niece. Perhaps that will help her to keep her place here as Carstairs well knows how foul Father's temper can be and will have been sure to have warned the girl!

Of course the most important news of the day is that John came to Brabage. When he arrived I was away in the village but returned as he emerged from Father's study having been closeted with him for more than an hour. Father was in a moderately good mood and asked John to stay to lunch.

After lunch Father suggested that we should all walk over to the site of the proposed churchyard extension. Mother declined, adding that to go out in such fierce sun would make her headache worse. I regarded her quizzically for until then she had made no mention of a headache. She looked down, refusing to meet my eyes and I realised that her aim was to avoid Father's company as much as possible. Father, Mary, John and I went out.

Father was all puffed up with the importance of yet another project. He says that as soon as the churchyard extension is complete he will concentrate his efforts on adding to the church. I muttered to John,

"For the glory of God or the glory of man - a man?"

John said nothing. Luckily, as we were about to walk home, Mr. Taylor, the verger, came out of the church and asked Father to step inside as there was something that required his attention. Father instructed the three of us to walk back to the vicarage. We stepped along with such a light tread; we were like children newly out of school.

As we passed the long wall that bounds the vicarage grounds I could not but pause a moment behind the spot where I know the summerhouse to be. Mary walked on a short way and I tried to see on the birch the place where John had carved our names. It faced inwards however and so I was unable to see it. How warm I feel inside when I think of our names carved there. Our love will grow and be as strong and tall as the tree itself. John must have thought the same for he pulled me into the shelter of the wall and kissed me long and hard. I heard Mary turn back and, flustered, I pretended that we were looking for something I had dropped in the verge. We all searched for the 'lost' clip, and of course it was me who found it (having just that moment contrived to drop it from my hand!) How very underhand love has made me! We resumed our walk. Mary's looks and behaviour tell me that she knows all and approves. What a good sister she is!

John told me that he has agreed with Father that now that Mrs. Fraser is so much better he will ask her to arrange to have the money paid over for the land.

We are all to visit Park House tomorrow morning.

John returned to Framley and left us to a dull evening at home. Father's brightness at the success of his plans cast a gloom on us all - I cannot say why but there is something so very depressing about a smug, self-satisfied air.

Thursday 9th August 1917

I feel so sad tonight for today I said goodbye to John as he returns to duty first thing tomorrow morning. It is a relief that Mrs. Fraser is so much better that he is able to return with a lighter heart - but how heavy is my heart when I know how much he hates and fears the war. He hopes for another home leave before Christmas, but when he told me this my eyes filled with tears, for how far away Christmas seems to be! We had only a short time alone. John took the opportunity to tell me not to write anything about what we were discussing in the summerhouse when I next send a letter. While his post is not examined who knows what could happen to a letter and, while he does not mind our love becoming public knowledge, (indeed he would be proud to boast it from the rooftops!), he does not want his doubts and misgivings about the war to become known. It would be construed as 'unpatriotic' and we know where that would end!

Father, John and Mrs. Fraser spent some time together and composed a letter that is to go to Mrs. Fraser's lawyers instructing payment for the churchyard land. While I am so cast down to lose John, Father is elated, delighted that his plans are coming to fruition at last. I went to say my farewell to Mrs. Fraser and, while I acknowledge that she is very much better, I noticed that she was tired out after her talk with Father - but then who would not be!

Too soon it was time to say goodbye to John and as we drove through the gate I turned and saw him standing alone on the steps of Park House. What a forlorn figure he was! I could not help but to cry a little at the thought of our separation. I had thought that I had managed to hide my tears, however, Father snapped at me to control myself, it was unbecoming to display such emotion. He is such a hard man!

Mary was a great support and comfort to me. She knows how things stand between John and me and seems willing to further the course of our love in any way that she can. Mother had said a fond farewell to John and told me on the way home that she is glad that she only has daughters for it would break her heart to send sons off to war.

When John goes from my life it is as if the sun were blotted out. I have no heart to do anything and find it impossible to contemplate the months until Christmas. I suppose that I must continue with all my usual duties, but have no enthusiasm for anything. I came early to my room and sorted through my 'treasure chest'. There are all my real (not official) letters from John as well as the pressed violets that were his first gift to me. I must find somewhere safe to keep them all as I do not dare to imagine Father's reaction if he were to find them! I feel too that I must lock away my diary for, looking back over the entries I have made, I see how truthfully I write in my journal. I would not like any eyes but mine to read those words.

Friday 17th August 1917

Another furious row with Father but this time Mary too was involved. This morning Father had followed his usual practice and gone to teach at the school. It was a fine day and so Mary and I went into the garden. While Father is away from home we give Carstairs all the help we can as the garden is too much for such an old man, especially now that so much is given over to vegetables. We had been picking raspberries and wished to know what Carstairs would have us do next but he was nowhere to be found. Eventually we found him in one of the empty stables with a bucket of water and a basket of mewling kittens. He would have drowned them but with shrieks of outrage Mary and I descended upon him. Suki, the poor mother cat, was walking to and fro in such a distressed manner and was so pleased when we restored her babes to her. When we tackled Carstairs he disclosed, shamefacedly, that he was carrying out the instructions of 'the Reverend' and that this was normal practice when the cat had a litter of kittens. The kittens were not normally so well grown for Suki had hidden these last ones and Father had found them only this morning when he went into the stable to get the trap. He called Carstairs and, after berating him soundly for his neglect in not having found the kittens sooner, instructed that they were to be drowned immediately. Thus spake the man of God! Mary and I collected Suki and family and took them safely away. Carstairs looked rather nervous that he was not carrying out Father's instructions and so I hastened to reassure him that I would speak to Father on the matter and inform him of what had occurred. At this Carstairs looked very relieved and went off about his duties.

We took Suki and her four babes into the house and showed them to Mother who was delighted with them. The kittens played happily in the sunshine that flooded Mother's small sitting room. Suki was rather nervous and quickly

collected any of the litter which strayed too far. We soon heard Father's return and Mother gathered up mother cat and kittens and said that she would take them down to the kitchen, for cook or Edna were sure to be able to tell her what was to be done with them.

Mary and I took our courage in our hands and went to meet Father as he entered the house. We immediately told him what we had done and his rage was terrible to behold. He was inclined to blame Carstairs for not carrying out what is an everyday procedure but I told him that I was the one who had countered his instructions. By now Father was icily calm and lectured me on the duties of a daughter. He told me that I was becoming wayward and was also leading Mary astray. He went on to say that he was the master in this house and we would do as we were told. He alone was responsible for what went on in the house and how the servants were ordered. Who did we think we were to countermand his instructions?

I protested about the sanctity of life and asked what harm would be done if the kittens were allowed to live out their lives. Father responded that I was ignorant of life, for controls are needed else we would be overrun with cats. I retorted that to be overrun with cats was preferable to being overrun with rats and mice, which were certainly present in the attics as well as in the stables. (This was, of course, not true, but I had to stop Father's tirade!) Just then Mother came through the door leading from the kitchen. Father turned and snapped out,

"Sarah, Elizabeth claims that we are overrun with rats and mice. Is this true? Have you any awareness of such vermin about the house?"

Mother turned pale at being addressed in such a confrontational manner, but I admired the courage with which she responded,

"Well, Lewis, I did hear rather a lot of scuttling about in the attic the other evening." (My heart quailed at that for it was I up there, writing my diary and finding a place to hide my treasure chest!) "I said to Edna to put Suki up there for a day or two to see if there were any mice."

Father looked rather taken aback that the evidence seemed to be conspiring against him. He thought for a moment or two and then said,

"Very well, you may keep this litter provided that they earn their living and catch vermin, but never interfere with my instructions again Elizabeth. Also, if I see any of those kittens about the house I will drown them with my own hands!"

The expression on his face was positively evil as he uttered these words and he turned on his heel and strode off angrily to his study.

Our celebration at our minor victory exacted its price however, for throughout

the remainder of the day and evening Father was in an abominable temper and never ceased complaining about one thing or another. Mary and I though congratulated ourselves on our action and have determined to remain watchful so that when the time comes again for Suki to have kittens we will be able to thwart Father's cruel practice once more.

Whether it is because I grow older or because I grow confident in John's love, I do not fear Father's rages in the same way as of former days. The sad aspect of these last few months is that I have grown to despise Father. I cannot say that Father has ever shown any of his family the love and affection one expects from a parent, however I do consider that at one time he did command my respect. By his own actions he is diminishing in my estimation, and I see that Mother and Mary also regard him as a tyrant.

When I am married to John, Mary shall come and live with us, and if she so wishes she shall have a whole houseful of kittens. Poor Mother though, for when we leave home she will be left all alone with Father. What a dreadful prospect!

Wednesday 22nd August 1917

Today I went alone to visit Mrs. Fraser. I have some misgivings about her supposed recovery. She tries to appear bright and cheerful but is much weaker than I have ever seen her. Alice is constantly at her side. I asked what the doctor had said and Alice told me that his opinion was that Mrs. Fraser is unlikely to ever make a full recovery but that she is stable and will probably remain in this condition for several years to come.

For the first time Mrs. Fraser talked openly of my relationship with John and expressed it as her dearest wish that we will marry - and soon. I coloured at this frank talk and she added gently that she was aware that my father would likely prove a stumbling block but that she would take it upon herself to talk to him of the matter. She would present the subject in such a way that Father would think that he had thought of the plan himself. She asked me to invite Father to visit her next week, ostensibly to discuss the church extension. Now that Father has acquired the land to extend the churchyard he is full of plans to extend the church. He is convinced that Mrs. Fraser will be happy to contribute financially to his cause! With an ally as strong and determined as Mrs. Fraser I begin to have some hopes for an early marriage!

I had taken Mrs. Fraser some raspberries from the garden, which brought to mind the episode of the kittens. I related the story to her. Her face clouded but she was careful as she commented,

"I suppose that animals do need controlling Lizzie dear, but there is no need for such brutality in that control!"

I knew then how she felt about Father's actions and we did not talk of the subject again.

The day being so fine we had sat on the verandah and our conversation was interrupted by the postboy coming around the side of the house with a letter. It was from John and Mrs. Fraser took in my greedy expression as I saw her receive the letter.

"Elizabeth my dear, I am so tired. Perhaps you would be kind enough to read this letter to me?"

What a kind and understanding lady she is!

John had little news except to say that he had settled back into the routine of war almost as if he had not been away. He notices the noise most of all, having become accustomed to the quiet of Framley. He passes on news of some of the men in the locality and jokes that several of the young men are so rooted in France (and attached to the local female population) that they will likely settle there when the war is over. There was little more, but it was sufficient satisfaction to me to be holding a letter from his own hand!

After I had read to Mrs. Fraser I was anxious to return home knowing that it was likely that a letter (or even two) would be waiting for me. She understood my impatience and said that she would like to go and rest for a while so I took my leave.

There was no letter at the vicarage on my return and so I went to the summerhouse in the hope that Arthur may have delivered something there. I was rewarded, for in the secret place was a letter from John. I sat for almost an hour reading and re-reading his words.

At tea I almost gave the game away. Mother was asking about Mrs. Fraser and her talk led naturally to John. I started to talk of him and began to talk of the various tidings in his letter. Father watched me and then said, suspiciously,

"Elizabeth, how can you know these things? I have your letter from John in my study. I have read it but have forgotten to pass it on as yet!"

I coloured instantly but had the presence of mind to tell Father that I had read Mrs. Fraser's letter of that afternoon aloud to her. Reluctantly (or so it appeared to me) Father accepted my explanation but continued his tea in a thoughtful manner.

I spent the next half hour racking my brains to ensure that the information I had related was indeed in Mrs. Fraser's letter, for I would not put it above Father to ask her if he might see the letter! Oh well! That is a bridge that may well have to be crossed in time.

Mary and I spent the evening helping Mother to finish some sewing and put together a basket of baby clothes for there is yet another addition to the Bates' household. We dare not tell Father for he considers that family to be feckless in the extreme and has warned us before that by being generous we serve only to encourage their lack of responsibility. How, though, can we let a baby suffer deprivation due to the lack of prudent parental housekeeping? Mary and I will deliver the basket tomorrow - Father will doubtless deliver the sermon on Sunday!

As I look back over my diary for today there is one further thing that strikes me - Father had kept back my letter from John. I wonder, without my slip, how long he would have kept it? It is bad enough of Father to read my letters, but how much worse it is of him to delay them! I think that if I did not have my 'real' correspondence I would go mad!

Tuesday 28th August 1917

Today we all visited Park House but found Mrs. Fraser a little unwell. We therefore did not stay long. Father was so frustrated as he wished to discuss the church extension. I too was unhappy, for Mrs. Fraser was to have talked to Father about marriage! I had a few quiet words with Mrs. Fraser and she hastened to assure me that it was but a slight indisposition that kept her in bed. She especially asked that I would not tell John, for she will be well again before he even receives news of her illness. We talked about Charles and while she is so very sad, she has now accepted his death and has deferred her plans for his reburial at Framley. She says that although she misses him now she will see him in Heaven. I sat and listened to this with aching heart for, as well as disliking her talk of death, I find that I cannot concur with her idea of Heaven. If I have ceased to believe in God then I have also ceased to believe in his Kingdom.

All the way home Father talked of his anxiety over Mrs. Fraser's health. He is sure that she is merely weak and needs 'building up'. He exacted a promise from Mother (gladly and freely given) to visit Park House three or four times a week, taking with her the best of delicacies. That indeed is generous of Father who is so careful to oversee the most stringent of household economies. Is it mean spirited of me to feel that it is neither his Christian faith nor his human compassion that moves him so, but solely the desire for the fulfilment of his ambitious 'project'?

Our visit to Park House being thus curtailed we had some unexpected hours at our disposal. Mary and I took the opportunity to do some parish visiting and were saddened to enter the home of the Bardell family and find them mourning

their eldest son, James. He has, like so many, been reported missing presumed dead, in action in France. I am doubly cast down by such a death. Firstly he was in the same company as John and his death shows that they must recently have been in action. I will not relax until I hear again from John. Secondly, James Bardell was one of the young soldiers whom John particularly mentioned, when he was home on leave, as being terrified of war but who went 'over the top' white faced and shaking, to 'do his duty' . I say "Damn duty!" I aver once more that this war will never end until every young man in Britain is killed!

Mother told Father of James Bardell's death and he merely shook his head gravely and said that no doubt he had died honourably in the course of duty. He promised to make mention of the event in Sunday's sermon - much good may that do the Bardells. How cynical I have become! I feel so frustrated sitting here in the Cheshire countryside, unable to influence the course of war one way or another. Perhaps if I could join with others who think in the same way we could have some effect?

Mary and I spent a quiet evening walking by the lake. Mother joined us later and talked quite nostalgically of her youth. She too regrets the war - for she says that it has taken away our youth, (meaning mine and Mary's) as well as destroying so many of our generation. As the dusk began to creep over the water and there was no sound except for the rustle of the wind among the reeds, she said, quite sadly, that after this Great War things will never be the same again.

Wednesday 5th September 1917

At least I now know that John is safe. I received his letter today and my anxiety about him was relieved. He does not write much about the battles except to say that his company have been kept quite lively and seen a lot of action. He says that several local men have been lost over the last few weeks and sends his condolences to the families. He asks me for true news of his mother for, he says, in her letters she is unerringly cheerful and he cannot see behind the words to know truly what her condition is.

The rest of his letter is all love for me and yearning to be back home again. How wonderful it is to feel so utterly needed and wanted by another person.

Mrs. Farquharson came to the vicarage this morning. She was coldly polite to me and asked, most correctly, after Mrs. Fraser. I showed her to Father's study and he was so effusive in his greeting that I felt nauseated and was glad to close the door on them. I could not imagine what Mrs. Farquharson wanted with Father but I was sure that of late I had neither insulted nor upset her.

Later in the day Father told us all that Mrs. Farquharson had come to see him in order to discuss the church extension. I think that if anything she seems more enthusiastic than Father about it all. Of course she can see great glory for herself and her husband in such a work for she has told Father that she and the Colonel intend to bestow a window upon the church - a large stained glass window in the new extension. Given the Colonel's career she feels that it would be fitting to portray a military theme. She has been discussing her ideas with Father. Of course there will be a prominently displayed plaque proclaiming the fact that the window was dedicated to the church by Colonel and Mrs. Farquharson. When Father told us all this in the evening I could not prevent myself from commenting that a military theme seemed rather inappropriate for a sleepy country church. Father criticised me for my ungrateful and uncharitable attitude and told me that if people had not fought in the name of God for hundreds of years then I would not be sitting so comfortably in Brabage! I did not respond, not being ready for the debate, so I merely bent my head diligently over my work.

I have not been to Park House for almost a week but feel that I must go to see Mrs. Fraser before I write a reply to John. I will arrange with Mother and Mary that we may go on Friday.

The wind has got up this evening and as I hear its lonely howling around these attic tiles I fancy that I can hear the wind in 'No Man's Land' and the mournful sound of shells. What a sad thought with which to end the day!

THE BLACKBIRD'S SONG

In dawn's 'Stand To!'
A blackbird flew
And perched on a tangle of wire.
He showed no fear,
His joy sounded clear
In a lull in the midst of fire.

I heard his song.
It made me long
For the hillsides and fields of home.
For soft grey dawn,
For sunlit morn
And for valleys and woods to roam.

His song was fair.
He had no care
But to answer sweet nature's law.
For this is spring
And he must sing
In spite of this folly of war.

He ceased his call,
Let silence fall.
No roar of machine-gun or shell.
No man fired
On either side.
No-one broke blackbird's magic spell.

A peace profound,
None made a sound
But each thought of those we hold dear.
A lonely life,
This war and strife.
How I wished that my love was near.

My love's an ache,
A thirst to slake,
A longing I cannot fulfil.
I need you here
To calm my fear.
Life alone is a bitter pill.

Fluttering wings.
The female sings.
She's flown down to be with her mate.
If I called to you,
Would you come too
To be with me here, share my fate?

John Fraser 1917

Tuesday 11th September 1917

What a dreadful, awful, terrible day! I cannot imagine that we can suffer any more bad news this year. I sit and write my diary very late after writing to my own dear John. Father has at least had the decency to tell me that due to the delicate nature of my communication and its urgency, he would not delay the letter by 'examining it! And what is the 'delicacy' and the 'urgency' of my letter. Mrs. Fraser has died! It is such a great shock for it is less than a week ago that I was writing to John to tell him how much his mother's health had improved. That she needed tender care we all acknowledged, but none of us imagined that she was so close to the end.

We were sitting at breakfast this morning and Father was instructing me on how I should conduct myself towards Mrs. Farquharson during today's sewing circle (now that she is to be such a generous benefactress) when we were disturbed by an urgent ringing at the doorbell. Edna is so sluggish and such was the imperiousness of the summons that I ran out myself to open the door. There stood Edward Mawdsley, the gardener's boy from Park House. Alice had sent him to summon us immediately as Mrs. Fraser had taken seriously ill during the night and now lay on what would appear to be her deathbed. We lost no time in getting to Framley.

At Park House the door was opened by Alice herself, and by her grave demeanour I knew that the tidings were not good. We entered the hall just as Dr. Armstrong was closing the door to Mrs. Fraser's downstairs room. He shook his head sadly and came towards us. He spoke to Father. There was no hope; she was sinking rapidly. There was nothing further that he could do.

Alice went quickly to Mrs. Fraser's door and, over her shoulder, asked that I would accompany her inside as Mrs. Fraser had most especially requested that I be sent for. I went in. The curtains were drawn and the room darkened. I scarcely recognised the figure in the bed, so much had she aged in such a short time. As I sat down next to the bed her eyes flickered open and she whispered something. I could not hear and so bent over to put my ear next to her mouth. In a weak voice she told me that she knew that she was dying and was prepared for it - indeed she almost welcomed it for she would see her beloved Charles once more. She knew that John would have me to console him and asked me to remove the ring from her finger. (She always wore this plain gold ring on her smallest finger.) Every word cost her so much effort but she would speak. The ring had been in her family for many generations and it was her dearest wish that it should be used by John for his bride. She was, therefore, giving it to me. She asked that

I would give Charles's ring to Mary (what great insight the woman had). There was no-one else left now in her family except for John, and me. It was up to us to carry her memory forward. She asked me to think of her as 'Mother' for that is what she would be to me.

I was so choked with emotion that I was unable to speak. Mrs. Fraser was breathing raggedly and Alice stepped forward to ease her. Alice told me to take the rings, she knew all about it. I did so but it was with heavy heart that I placed her gold ring on my own finger. When it was done she held my hand, lightly touching the ring. She was too weak by this stage to speak but merely held fast to my hand with one of hers and to Alice's with the other.

Some time later she fell into a peaceful sleep, yet still her fingers did not release their grip. Dr. Armstrong came in quietly and went out again almost immediately. My father came in and stood behind me. Mrs. Fraser opened her eyes and she must have confused Father with another for she looked in his direction and said quietly,

"There you are Charles. I am coming now."

They were the last words she ever spoke for she lapsed into an unconsciousness from which she never awoke. She died at two-thirty this afternoon.

There was little to do, for John is her only close relative. Alice asked me if I would write to him rather than have the news conveyed by the lawyers. I undertook the difficult task and wrote briefly, informing John of the events of the day and asking if it were possible for him to return home at once. I have complained often enough that I want John back home, but God forbid that my wish should be granted in such circumstances.

There is nothing more to do now until John arrives and the time hangs heavily on us all. Mother has felt the loss most for she visited Mrs. Fraser very often and had become a great friend over the past year. Nothing that any of us can say or do can lift the sadness that engulfs us all.

This evening I gave Charles's ring to Mary, repeating the words of Mrs. Fraser. Mary could not speak but took the ring from me and held it close to her heart. There are no words to ease the sadness of the loss. Oh that I could call on God to aid me and give me comfort, but I know that there is no God!

All that I can do now is to sit in the midst of this desolation and wait for John. I turn Mrs. Fraser's ring on my finger and its touch brings me some comfort. Truly I have lost a great friend, a second mother. A great void is left in my life.

Monday 17th September 1917

What a sad greeting I gave John when he arrived here today. He looked tired and worn. He is only able to stay a few days as his sector is under great pressure and all leave has been cancelled. The funeral is on Wednesday and John must return to France that same day. John arrived during the morning when Father was out on parish business (he has gone off to see the Bishop again - there is some fuss about the church extension. As the Bishop is a great friend of the Farquharsons, I can see that any small difficulty will soon be smoothed over!) Mary was in Brabage on her visiting rounds and so Mother and I were quite alone. Edna showed John into the drawing room and he went directly to Mother, who held out her arms in tenderness. She was choked with emotion and could not speak, but her deep grief and sympathy were written plainly on her face. John then turned to me and, totally oblivious of who might be present, embraced me, crushing me close to his chest. I immediately began to sob and could tell from John's breathing that he was making a great effort to control his own emotions. I became aware that the buttons of John's uniform were pressing hard into my face and I pulled slightly away from him. He led me to a seat and it was only then that I noticed that Mother had quietly left the room. We were alone in each other's company.

When my sobs had subsided and he had kissed away my tears, I was able to tell him of his mother's last hours. When I had finished he sat so still and silent that I began to think that he was in some sort of trance. I reached out my hand and clasped his. He turned to me and was not ashamed to show me that his eyes were full of unshed tears. Tenderly he fingered his mother's ring, now worn on my own finger.

"I remember that she wore this always," he said sadly, "it is right and proper that it comes to you."

He asked if Father had objected to my wearing of the ring and I explained that I had told him that it was a gift, a final gift, from Mrs. Fraser. I had not explained the significance of the ring to him.

We sat quietly, talking sadly of Mrs. Fraser and Charles. John was not as shocked by his mother's sudden death as we had been, for he had suspected for some time that her health was worse than she disclosed. His mother's affairs were quite in order and, as John is the only surviving close relative, quite uncomplicated. Alice is to stay at Park House until after the funeral when she will leave in order to live with her sister in Knutsford. John is confident that Mrs. Fraser will have made generous provision for her but if not he will himself ensure her future

security. Alice has been in the Fraser household since she was a young girl and in addition to tending to Mrs. Fraser had acted as nursemaid to John and Charles. Poor Alice is so very shocked and upset that John is sure that she has not taken in all at has happened. I feel guilty that I have not seen Alice since the day Mrs. Fraser died. How selfish my grief has been.

There was a gentle tap at the door and Mother entered. John stood but when Mother was seated he resumed his place next to me and once again took possession of my hand. Mother was quite unsurprised. We talked together for some time until we heard Mary enter the house. She came directly to the drawing room and, as soon as she saw John, broke down into mournful weeping. John went to her and comforted her. What a gentle man he is!

Mother asked John to stay and share our midday meal. John replied that he would be glad to as he wished to talk to Father on his return.

The afternoon was too wet to allow us to walk outside and so we sat in the conservatory. It has been rather neglected since we have had to put all our efforts into producing food for the table. Carstairs expends his time and energy mostly in the kitchen garden and has no regular boy to help him, for as soon as they are old enough off they go to join the war! Mother and Mary left us alone and we spent some hours sitting together amongst the palms in perfect accord. Just before tea Mother came in and sat down. Father arrived home a very short time later and Mother's conversation led him to believe that we had all spent the afternoon in the conservatory together!

John went off with Father to the study for he wished to ask him to help in conducting the funeral service. He has already spoken to the Rector at Framley who will welcome Father's assistance. John also suggested that we should all come to Park House on the day of the funeral as we could keep Alice company at home while the service was taking place. (Our backward country ways still do not like to see women at a funeral service. It is a practice that grieves me greatly for I would wish to be present to say a last farewell.)

After his interview, John still remained with us. He was reluctant to return to the loneliness at Framley for Alice is in her bed and there is no-one else to keep him company so it was late when he went from us. In the darkness of the porch he snatched a kiss from me and, grieved as we were, I could feel that his excitement matched my own.

Wednesday 19th September 1917

I am glad that today is over - even though I had to say goodbye to John. It has been a great strain on us all, except for Father who seems to have thrived in the glory of the solemnity of the occasion. The weather has also gone into mourning for it rained heavily, making our journey to Framley even more miserable.

We arrived early at Park House and Alice greeted us kindly. She looks so much older and more careworn than when I saw her last. When John and Father had gone to the service and we were left alone the time passed very slowly. Alice spoke about her sister and her new home in Knutsford. Her sister is a widow and has lived alone for several years, it has always been understood that Alice would go and live with her should she ever leave the Frasers.

We all avoided talking of the subject most in our hearts and minds - Mrs. Fraser. We talked about every other subject under the sun and I confess that I was relieved when the guests returned to Park House for I felt that I could think of nothing more to say on any matter!

The formalities were soon over and Mrs. Fraser's lawyer called Alice and John into the study to hear the will read. Mrs. Fraser had (as expected) provided generously for Alice and made several small bequests to other servants. Later we had a quiet time to sit and talk together - just my own family, John and Alice. John stressed that Alice must stay at Park House for as long as she wished to do so and must not think that she had to rush away immediately. Alice thanked him tearfully but said that she would prefer to go soon, for all around her was tinged with memories and served only to remind her of her sad loss.

John plans to close the house up until the war is over. The gardener will continue to manage the gardens and his wife will supply all the care that is required in the empty house. Father asked John where he would stay on his future home leave and Mother immediately said,

"Of course, John will stay with us at the vicarage!" Father stared at her, amazed that she had suggested such a thing without prior consultation. I was delighted and found it difficult to hide my pleasure. John stammered his thanks for I do believe that he had not thought of the future at all.

Too soon the time came around for us to take our leave of John who was returning immediately to France. He has promised to write as soon as he is able - I know that will not be soon enough for me!

We returned to the vicarage and spent a very gloomy evening. The rain has persisted all day and darkness came early. We were all thankful to retire.

Friday 5th October 1917

I have only today received John's first letter since his return to the Front. I have been beside myself with worry but the only thing that has sustained me is that his name has not been listed in Father's newspaper as being among the killed or missing in action. The war continues as fierce as ever and the sector in which John is placed (Ypres) is seeing the worst of all action. The mud has been terrible, the newspapers say, and the men in miserable conditions. Mrs. Farquharson has used the gloomy tidings to urge us on to greater exertions in the knitting circle, telling us that the Colonel has mentioned to her how much the men appreciate the warm socks and mufflers so thoughtfully supplied.

John makes little complaint about the war, the whole tone of his letter is of loneliness. More than once he tells me that I am the only person he has left in the world. I will write in my reply that although I have my family around me he is the only one I care for! He has not yet had the opportunity to absorb his grief and so many demands are placed on him in action that I fear that it will be some time before he steadies. There is a touch of cynicism in his letter when he urges me not to worry about his safety, for, if he was a betting man, he would put money on his life: two of his family already having died in such a short time the odds are in favour of the third (himself) surviving! My poor darling.

He has met Colonel Farquharson since his return and - wonders! - the Colonel recognised him and offered his sympathy for the death of Mrs. Fraser. It is the first anyone has spoken of it to John and he writes, 'I am not a coward in admitting my weakness for, Lizzie, when the Colonel spoke of Mother I could not prevent the tears coming into my eyes. I obviously embarrassed the Colonel, who coughed and spluttered, clapped me on the back, urged me to 'bear up' and strode off rapidly!'

I had received my letter as usual in the summerhouse and as I was reading it for at least the fiftieth time I was startled by Mary's appearance through the trees. She had come to fetch me for Father was looking for me.

When I returned to the house Father complained petulantly that I am never there when he needs me. He wished to remind me that I had promised this week to help him to rearrange his books in his study. (In her first week poor Edna made the grave mistake of 'tidying up' in the study and Father claims that he has been unable to find anything since. She has been banished from the room.) As it was now Friday did I not think that I ought to fulfil my promise instead of idling away the day as I was sure to have been doing?

I do not wish to dwell on what happened during the next hour. In moving some

books I found several of John's 'official' letters. I held them out towards Father,

"What are these?" I asked (although of course I knew exactly what they were!

"Oh," he replied nonchalantly, "let me see." He took them off me and pretended to examine them - for all the world as though he did not know what it was that I had found! "I believe that I must have forgotten to pass these letters of John's over to you Elizabeth." He raised the open flap of each. "Yes, I have checked them and everything is in order. Here you are." Without a word I took the proffered letters, turned on my heel and went to my room.

There were four letters in all. The fact that none of them contains information that I do not know already is not the point. They were written mainly during the time of the trouble with Charles, when he ran away for the first time. I now understand the references John made in his 'private' letters to strategies which he had suggested. At the time I thought that he was confused, suffering from the pressures of war, for I could make no sense of those references. The worst part of all is that Father did not even have the grace to look ashamed of his actions or to apologise to me. I cannot find it in my heart to forgive him. I will not speak to him any more than is absolutely necessary in future.

I have been in my room for the remainder of the day, pleading the excuse of a sick headache. Mother was sympathetic and sent Edna to me with a light meal. It is fortunate that Edna is not very bright or she may have questioned how someone with such a severe headache could sit and write letters (for I was writing to John when she came). I have not informed John of Father's conduct, for I do not wish to remind him what a tyrant Father is!

Wednesday 24th October 1917

Today I received a letter in an unfamiliar hand. Father looked very suspicious as he passed it to me and watched my face carefully as I read it. I was alarmed at the contents. It was written by Thomas, John's valet (I believe that he is called a 'batman' in the army). John had dictated the letter to Thomas, for he is ill and suffers badly with his chest. At first he thought that it was merely that he had received 'a whiff of gas'. The Germans use gas in that sector more than in any other and many of the men suffer badly from its effects. However John's cough got worse rather than better and eventually he was persuaded to see the doctor. The doctor has placed him in hospital until the infection in his chest clears up. He is himself too weak to write, but he has had Thomas write so that I may not be anxious at the lack of news. The letter was very short and when I had read it I put it down solemnly.

"What is it Elizabeth? You have gone very pale," said Mother. "Who is the letter from?"

Without another word I passed the letter over to Mother for her to read. I could see that my action angered Father, but I have not yet forgiven him for his behaviour earlier this month. Mother began to read but was stopped by the imperious summons,

"Sarah, pass that letter to me please!" Mother acquiesced without comment. Father read the letter and passed it back.

"Nothing much to worry about there I think. Do not behave in such a silly, emotional way Elizabeth. The army will look after him. Now, I must get off to school!"

I am glad that Father has to teach so much in school, for I know that he hates it! The government has decreed that preachers and parsons, working but one day a week, must take the place of teachers in the schools so that they (the teachers) may be released for 'war duty'.

When he had gone Mother read the letter aloud to Mary. Both were distressed at the contents and immediately began to plan the contents of a parcel to be sent to John; things guaranteed to improve his health. It is most generous of Mother for as I am aware of how closely Father supervises the household budget I know that it will only be managed with difficulty.

As we left the breakfast table to go about our daily duties Mary squeezed my hand and whispered,

"Cheer up Elizabeth, for remember that while he is in the hospital he is not in the line of fire!"

What a comfort she is!

I carried out my tasks mechanically today, hurrying through them in order to set aside some time to write to John. I was careful in what I wrote for if he is too ill to write, he may need to have another read my letter to him. I am sure that my letter sounded as though written by his mother, checking on his care, his food and his comfort - and yet I do not care, for John's welfare is all that I am concerned about.

Tuesday 6th November 1917

Father came home this evening after being out since early morning at the Farquharsons'. Now that the churchyard extension is complete he is ready to start on the church. No doubt he will have ample time to consult with the Colonel as I note that he manages to come home frequently!

After dinner Father went to his study to open his letters. They had arrived after his departure this morning. He had only been away a few minutes when he rejoined us, looking rather grave. I saw that the letter he was holding was on official army paper and I started from my seat. I must have gone deathly pale for Mother flew to my side and gripped my arm tightly. Father seemed unaware of our anxiety as he said solemnly',

"A letter from Captain Fraser's Commanding Officer."

I remembered no more, for I must have fainted away, convinced that my darling was dead and that there would be no happiness for me in this world. When I came to myself Father had returned to his study and Mother was bathing my temples with cologne. She lost no time in informing me that it was not bad news about John. I was immediately better and sat up to hear why John's Commanding Officer should write to Father. It appears that John's health has not improved, indeed it is rather worse than it was. He is not fit for duty and the doctors can do little more for him. It is their opinion that what is required is rest, care and convalescence. There lies the dilemma: Colonel Shaw knows that John has no close family remaining and that Park House is closed up. He knows that we are close friends and has written to Father on Colonel Farquharson's recommendation. Colonel Shaw writes to ask if Father would be willing for John to stay at Brabage Vicarage until he has recovered. The alternative is a convalescent home, but the Colonel feels that John needs a family about him at this time. I listened to all that Mother said and then asked,

"What is Father's opinion?"

"Well, Elizabeth, you know your father as well as any of us does. He is pleased to be asked to help but has warned me that the cost of John's keep must be absorbed within my household budget or, alternatively, contributed to by John himself."

How typical of Father! John is ill and in need of care and all that the good, Christian parson can think of is the cost! I wonder if the Good Samaritan was so very careful with his budget?

However, it is settled that John is to come here and Father is to write to Colonel Shaw to tell him. I went to Father's study and thanked him courteously, for I am grateful that we will have John here with us, however much Father may begrudge that hospitality. Father looked surprised at my thanks for I have spoken little to him since the incident with the letters earlier this month.

As I put away my diary tonight I know that in a very short time John will be home and I will be able to devote my time in caring for him.

Friday 16th November 1917

I can spend little time in writing my diary tonight for it is late and I am tired. All the plans of recent days were fulfilled today when I went with Father to Crewe station to mcct John. Thomas had been permitted to accompany him and after he had seen John settled here he went off to his own home to spend the night with his family. He must return to France early tomorrow. John looks as ill as I had expected, pale and thin and with a cough that racks his body. After the journey he was glad to get back into bed. The doctor has visited and is confident that John will improve rapidly with careful nursing. Father has left things very much to us (Mother, Mary and me) to arrange - he does not like his own routine disturbed.

Mother and Mary were very understanding and left me directing Edna as to the arrangements of the sickroom. I need not say that I lost no time in sending Edna on a trifling errand in order to leave me alone with John. Edna is so dull that she thinks no further than the task in hand and went off gladly without a moment's misgiving. I put my arms around John and caressed him gently. His breathing is so ragged and his cough so deep! He clasped my hands and reached his face towards mine and our kiss only ceased when John's cough forced it!

I am sorry that John is ill, yet I am so glad to have him here with me. He is away from the war; away from danger. I will nurse him, but not too carefully for I do not want him to recover and return to France too soon! Who knows that the war may yet be over before my darling is well.

The latest battle around Passchendale has gone on for so long since July - and so many men have perished. Surely it must all be decided soon, one way or another.

I must go to sleep for I intend to wake early and refreshed, for now there is a wonderful purpose in my days.

Wednesday 28th November 1917

We heard some sorry tidings today; Colonel Farquharson has been killed in France. It was Father who came back with the news, having heard it from the verger, Mr. Taylor. I had a lot of criticism to make about Colonel Farquharson, but now that he has been killed I am sorry for it.

I did not know whether I should tell John. So many men have been killed at Passchendale - they say almost three hundred thousand and seventeen thousand officers. How can the capture of such a small amount of territory be so costly? As John's condition has improved so much I decided that it would be best to tell him. He took the news quite badly for, as he so correctly points out, if Colonel Farquharson is killed then the losses in that sector - and in his own company - will

be high. I am so very thankful that he was not there! John expressed a desire to go and see Mrs. Farquharson and I promised to discuss the prospect with Father.

John managed to sit out of bed for a few hours today and Mary and I kept him company. I think that Mary has half fallen in love with him herself! However it is, the current diversion of caring for John has helped to lessen her sadness over Charles.

The weather has been dreadful today, misty and damp. Mother came back from her village visiting covered in mud. When we complained of it John brought us back to reality by saying that such a little mud is nothing compared to that in France. He has spoken little about his life there and I do not wish to bring the subject to his attention. He claims that it is the mud and the damp conditions which caused his bad chest. Many of the men succumb and several have died of pneumonia. I cannot imagine mud so deep that men wade in it! They have duckboards laid on the most used routes but frequently are forced to wade through flooded shell holes, holding their rifles and ammunition high to save them a wetting,. They skid and slide all about the place. It is dreadful to think of them trying to fight in those conditions. They cannot get dry anywhere as the walls of the trenches run with moisture. While they are on duty at the Front they may not even remove their boots for fear of sudden attack. It is nothing for men to have their boots on for three or four days at a time. No wonder they suffer infected feet and trench fever, for their boots and socks often rot in these circumstances. Their only relief comes when they are off duty and can spend some time behind the lines. Only then can they dry out and be a little more comfortable. The only consolation is that the enemy also suffer in the same way.

I knew that conditions were miserable but had no idea that they were quite so bad. The newspapers have told us about the mud but no-one here knows how awful things are. Perhaps if we did we would force our government to abandon this senseless conflict!

It was such an inclement day that darkness came early and we were glad to draw the curtains and sit around the fire. Father was absent for most of the evening, and we spent a pleasant time, Mother, Mary, John and I. How cosy our home life will be when we are married.

Friday November 30th 1917

Today Father and I went with John to pay a consolatory visit to Mrs. Farquharson - and how I wish that we had not bothered! For someone so recently and tragically bereaved she bears all extremely well. She speaks of the Colonel's

'noble sacrifice' and the need for those left behind to 'bear up and carry on the fight'. The charitable interpretation of her behaviour is that she is a brave widow, keeping her emotions in check. To think otherwise is to think that she could not have cared greatly for her husband! She ordered tea and chattered on to John as if we were making a pleasant social visit. I know that I could not behave so if John had been killed.

Father was odious! He flattered and crawled until my stomach was quite turned with his sycophancy. Mrs. Farquharson talks of the window in the new extension to the church being dedicated to the Colonel's memory. On the way home we discussed this matter. Father thinks it a splendid idea (no doubt because Mrs. Farquharson would spend more money than ever on the project!). John was very diplomatic and suggested that the window could perhaps be dedicated to all who had fallen. I kept trying to speak but was silenced by Father. I eventually managed to make my point that surely the church is to the greater glory of God. To glorify one individual was wrong. Father told me that I did not understand the window would not be 'glory' but 'remembrance'. I wished to reply but John flashed me a warning glance and the matter was dropped.

Later John told me that, while he agreed with me, I would never have got the better of Father in argument and indeed would only have caused more antagonism and made life uncomfortable for us all. He clearly considers Father to be a stubborn bigot but would not for worlds say so!

The outing (John's first) had quite tired my darling and he spent the remainder of the day in bed. Mary and I went parish visiting and I told her about Mrs. Farquharson. She shared my indignation.

A quiet evening when I bit my tongue and allowed Father to give Mother an uninterrupted account of Mrs. Farquharson's courage and fortitude. Mother's eyebrows were arched in clear disapproval at Father's evident admiration. How I look forward to marrying and leaving this home to make my own. I dread John's return to the war.

He has said that he intends to take his first proper walk outside in the next day or two and feels that he is firmly on the road to recovery. I only hope that the doctor will not pass him fit until things quieten a little in France - or at least until after Christmas. How much I would love to spend Christmas with John! I can but hope.

Saturday 1st December 1917

Thinking over the events of today I do not know whether I should be ashamed or excited. I confess that I am excited - exhilarated - by what has happened. To write it here in my diary enables me to relive it all!

As planned, John got out of bed this morning and appeared, a little unsteadily, at breakfast. He was quiet and Father tried to make conversation with him. The difficulty he encountered made me realise how little John and my father have in common - thank goodness! The only topic that they could both talk about at some length was the progress of the war. I could see that John was soon tired of this subject and wanted to avoid prolonged discussion about the supposed 'progress' on the Ypres Salient. Mother could see that talk of France was a strain to John and she was brave enough to turn the conversation to other matters. John voiced his intention of taking a short walk in the grounds. The day was fine and dry and Mother thought it a good idea. She warned John that he should not venture far and really should not go alone for he is still so very delicate. Mary has gone this morning to spend the weekend at Malpas with the Westons (Father encourages her friendship with Jane Weston as the family are so very rich and Mr. Weston will one day inherit a title. What an egalitarian Christian parson he is!). Mother and Father are to visit Mrs. Farquharson and so John and I will be alone, save for the servants. Father paid close attention to what Mother was saying and while he doubtless considers John too weak to pose a threat to my maidenly modesty (how wrong he was!) he insisted that Mr. Carstairs would accompany us on our walk. I was about to remind Father that Carstairs was himself absent today when Mother flashed me a silencing glance. She intended that John and I should have time alone. I closed my lips and was content to let Father go off with Mother, satisfied that propriety was being maintained at the vicarage.

I was so excited at the prospect of being alone with John until tea that it was all I could do not to race through my breakfast and bundle Mother and Father off on their visit. They were soon gone and we were alone, except of course for cook and Edna, but we would see little enough of them! Strangely we were both quite embarrassed and talked awkwardly for some time. John was so correct and well mannered that I felt like shouting out in my frustration. Anyone observing us could not believe that he was the author of the passionate letters of recent months! I suggested a short walk about the garden while the weather was dry, thinking that walking together might serve to put us both at ease.

We were soon walking about the gravel paths, John leaning heavily on my arm. We could go only slowly, pausing frequently in order that John could rest.

Considering that today is the first day of December the temperature was quite mild. We were soon relaxed and chatting familiarly. John introduced the subject of our marriage and resolved that before he returned to France he would ask Father once again for consent to our engagement. I was saddened by his reference to his return to duty but excited at the prospect of our formal engagement. If only Father would consent! We had been sitting on the stone seat in the kitchen garden and John's arm crept about my shoulder, he kissed me and whispered such loving words that I cannot bring myself to write them down. (The words that pass between lovers and inflame their desire for each other look silly and commonplace when recorded.) Mild as the weather was I was concerned that John should not get chilled and we resumed our walk.

Soon we passed out of the gates and walked for a time on the road. We encountered a group of village children whose voices stilled and eyes grew round when they saw John's uniform. They began to whisper together and eventually Jamie Shipton - the habitual spokesman - was thrust from their midst and he addressed John haltingly.

"General" (for he had seen John's ribbons and epaulettes and thought that he must be of exalted rank!), "tell us about the war. Are we goin' ter win it soon?"

John turned very solemnly to them and said quietly,

"I don't know, young man, I really don't know."

He saw that his answer had disappointed them and hastily made reparation.

"I don't know when the war will be over. We will win of course." (At this he saw their chests puff out and their eyes brighten.) "for we in Britain have the best army in the world. Also we are fighting for justice, so we cannot fail."

The children were pleased at this and began to boast to each other and to John about what they intended to do when they eventually got to war. Each tried to outdo the others' boasts and I saw John's expression as he realised what he had done: in his desire not to disappoint he had excited their patriotism and their yearning for excitement and adventure. He hastily attempted to make amends and assured them that the war would be over well before they could be part of such a conflict. Jamie Shipton again spoke up, saying that he intended to go and try to enlist, for he had heard that you could get in young if you had the nerve! I stepped forward for I had seen the deeply powerful and painful memories of Charles cross John's countenance. I held his arm tightly. The children too had seen the expression and were silent, for some of them had realised who John was. It was young Albert Bates who saved the day by pleading with John to tell them about the tanks and aeroplanes. So John was with the children for some time and

told them about France - the mud, the danger, the cold, the fatigue all calculated to make them realise that war was quite the reverse of glorious! They listened carefully but then asked questions about guns, medals, the 'Boche' - were they really monsters? They were not pleased with the answer John gave that the German soldiers were the same as our own men, just ordinary men carrying out their orders. I could see that whatever John said he would not destroy the glamour of war for them so I stepped forward,

"Come on now children, Captain Fraser has been ill and is very tired now. You run away and play."

They were clearly disappointed that the stories had come to an end but they turned and shuffled back towards the village. As they retreated I heard Hannah's voice raised in argument with Jamie Shipton, her customary sparring partner,

' 'T is so, 't is. John an Lizzie. He be Cap'n Fraser - John, an' 'er is Miss 'Lizbeth!"

I did not hear Jamie's reply but I knew that they must have been on the wall and seen the names carved on the tree. As I turned back to John my embarrassment was forgotten when I saw how drained he was. I helped him back to the house where we found that our lunch was ready.

Now that I have recorded the ordinary events of the morning I can, without embarrassment, write about the events of the afternoon.

After John had rested he proposed another outing. He wanted to go once more to the summerhouse. I was unsure as I did not want him to tire and ducking and weaving between the trees can be quite exacting. He was, however, determined to go. The summerhouse has become a symbol of our love. It is there, by the lake, that we can be our true selves.

It took some time to reach the lake and John was exhausted. He was leaning heavily on me and breathing hard. His pride would not let him give up, but when I suggested that we should go and sit for a while inside the summerhouse he could only nod his assent. As we reached the steps he collapsed. I did not know what to do for I was not strong enough to lift him. I ran forward and unlocked the door and made a comfortable place for him inside on the sofa. I ran back to where he lay. I tried to lift him but was unable to move his body. I was in a dilemma for if I ran back to the house to fetch cook and Edna to help me I would have to leave John alone on the cold ground for some time. What should I do? He was feverish and his eyelids were flickering. I ran to the lakeside and dipped my handkerchief in the water. I carefully sponged his forehead. John groaned and his eyes opened.

"I'm sorry Lizzie. What a pathetic thing to do. I think that I've overdone it a little!"

I was so relieved that he had returned to consciousness that tears sprang into my eyes.

"Help me up" he said, "I think I can stand."

I reached for his hands and it took all my strength to help him to his feet. As he stood he swayed and groaned. Afraid that he would fall once again I held him firmly. We staggered up the steps and into the summerhouse. I led him towards the sofa. Suddenly he stumbled and his weight was too much for me as I fell backwards onto the sofa. John fell on top of me. He lay still for some moments and I was afraid that he was again unconscious and that I was trapped. The tears came once more to my eyes and ran down my face. John stirred and kissed away my tears.

"Don't cry my darling Lizzie, I am not going to die!" He nestled comfortably against my neck and lay, regaining his strength. He began to nuzzle under my ears, to kiss my neck, my face. I was still lying half under him, trapped by his body and I rejoiced in my imprisonment. He kissed my lips hungrily, and through the mists of my ecstasy I slowly became aware that he was unbuttoning my blouse. I began to tremble - but with passion rather than apprehension. John could not manage to unclip my brooch, which fastened my blouse at the neck, and with an unmaidenly action I loosed it and let it fall. My blouse was being peeled from my body, he was kissing my neck, my shoulders, my breasts. Soon I was half naked and I did not care - I was not ashamed. Never have I experienced such feeling of passion, of desire.

"Oh, Lizzie, you are so beautiful, I cannot believe that you love me!" John gasped.

"Oh, I do John, I love you more than anything else in the world."

We were kissing and caressing so passionately that I hardly knew how the remainder of my clothes came off and I lay, naked, in his arms. He was so wonderfully loving and tender and I loved him so much that I knew that I would let him do what he would with my body. After some time, when I hardly knew what was happening to me except that I was borne up on a golden, glittering cloud and voices were singing exultantly in my ears and in my heart, he suddenly stopped.

"Oh, God, Lizzie! I'm sorry! I can't do this to you. It's not right. We are not even engaged. What would your parents say?"

I tried to persuade him that none of that mattered to me, that our love was the

most important thing, but the spell had been broken. Our passion had been killed by a moment of conscience. We lay quietly together and he held me, stroking my body and protesting his great love for me. I shivered and he sat up, ashamed that he was clothed and I was naked.

"Lizzie, my darling, you are cold!" and he pulled my clothes towards me and helped me to dress. By the time that I was fully clothed I was ashamed of my behaviour, thinking how low I must have sunk in his estimation. He held me close and gently stroked my hair. I was crying quietly.

"Lizzie, Lizzie, please don't cry." He kissed away my tears. He tried to explain that it was because he loved me so much that he had stopped himself. In my turn I attempted to explain that I was afraid that he would think me immodest. I would not dream of behaving in such a way, but I loved him so much. He held me close.

"Lizzie, we must be married, for you know that I cannot live without you and" (he paused for a moment) "and Lizzie, I cannot control myself indefinitely. I want to possess you, body and soul, and I want you to possess me!" We clung to each other, words being superfluous.

After some time I noticed that the day was becoming gloomy. I looked at my watch and was surprised to find that it was after three o'clock. Reluctantly we roused ourselves and walked slowly back to the house. Mother and Father had still not returned and John was relieved to take himself off to bed without having to face anyone. I was glad that he stayed there for the rest of the day as I am sure that our emotions are too near the surface to remain undiscovered by Mother or Father. I am not ashamed of what I feel, but it is a very private thing; something that I do not wish to share with anyone.

As I look back over the events of the day, particularly those of the afternoon, I know that we cannot be apart: we must be married and be together. I cannot bear to think of John returning to France. If Father will not consent to our marriage, then our love will not be denied and Father must take the consequences - whatever they may be!

Sunday 2nd December 1917

I confess that it was with great trepidation that I went down to breakfast this morning. I had not seen John at all since our walk to the summerhouse yesterday and feared what I would see when I looked into his eyes. What would be his opinion of me? Would I have fallen from the lofty pedestal on which he had placed me?

I should have entertained no doubts; I should have been sure that our love is so strong, and John is such a good, sincere man that he could do nothing but love me. He came to breakfast a few moments before Mother and Father and just had timc to squeeze my elbow lovingly and whisper,

"My darling Lizzie, how I love you!" before we had to take our places.

Throughout the meal he gazed into my eyes and was very pale (not all attributable to his illness I think). Several times father had to rouse him from his reverie and repeat his remark, for John was lost in some other world. Eventually he pulled himself together and said to Father,

"I am sorry sir for my abstraction. I was lost in thought, for today would have been Charles's birthday."

We were instantly all sympathy and I believe that John would have been granted anything he asked of Father at that moment.

Father went off over to church and John accompanied Mother and me sometime later. We are never very early for the service, having the shortest distance to travel. Indeed we are habitually the last to arrive. I looked around the church and found it somewhat empty; the people who have taken work in the factories in Crewe and Northwich deplete our already meagre congregation. I noted that Mrs. Farquharson was not present and was not unduly surprised as her loss is so recent.

Father had ascended to the pulpit and the service was about to commence when we heard an ugly grumble approaching the church. We knew what it would be for the Farquharsons are one of the very few privileged families in the area to possess a motor car. Father remained silent. The motor car was heard to stop at the church gate and we waited silently until the latecomers would enter. The door was thrown back with a flourish by Mrs. Farquharson's chauffeur who is also the gardener. In walked a vision! At first sight the figure, heavily veiled and in the deepest black, resembled nothing more than a ship under full sail. As she strode, majestic and alone, down the aisle and took her place, Mrs. Farquharson held her head high. She sat down amid a flurry of rustlings and raspings of new (and expensive) mourning clothes. Father was about to commence when Manders (the chauffeur) walked quietly down the side aisle and delivered Mrs. Farquharson her prayer book. Eventually Father started the service.

Later, when the service was over and the congregation leaving the church, Mrs. Farquharson beckoned to John to approach. She talked for some minutes to him and then rose and went out, stopping on the way to have some words with Father. Father could not have abased himself more had Mrs. Farquharson been

the queen that she was imitating so closely. I saw that Mother was angry to see Father behave so and made sure that we hurried away to the vicarage.

I asked John what Mrs. Farquharson had wanted but he was a little evasive and would only say that she had enquired when he would be returning to France. I can see that he feels guilt at his continued absence, for later he said that he must arrange a medical examination soon to see when he could return to duty. I do not know what Mrs. Farquharson said to him but feel sure that it was some barbed comment on him being away from the line of fire!

Later we discussed Mrs. Farquharson and Father could not help but exclaim what a magnificent, courageous woman he thought her. He went on at some length about the example she set other widows and how bravely she was bearing her great loss. Not one of us would contradict him but I am sure that we all shared the same thoughts - that Mrs. Farquharson was, on the contrary, not sincere; that she was more concerned with pomp and show than she was about the death of the Colonel. Why else would she arrive late and make such an entrance? I would also add that under her veil there was no sign of reddened, sleepless eyes. She looks well and rested, serene almost to the point of happiness. How easily Father is deceived by the vanities of women!

In the afternoon I took Sunday School as usual and John rested for a few hours. We went to the evening service but Mrs. Farquharson did not put in an appearance (after the morning any appearance would have been an anti-climax!).

Things passed off far less dramatically.

We passed a quiet hour before bed and John managed to be alone with me for two or three minutes. (Father was in his study and Mother was fetching her sewing from her small room.) John pulled me to him and held me hard. He kissed me firmly, but tenderly, on the lips.

"Lizzie, my love, I have arranged an interview with your Father tomorrow morning. You know what I am to ask. Is the answer still 'yes'?"

I started to reply, "Yes! Yes, yes, of course, yes!" when he kissed away my words. There was a noise at the door. Mother had, most tactfully, dropped her sewing and was noisily retrieving it. We sprang apart. When Mother entered we were separated by some yards and talking quietly, but I know that the fire in my cheeks and the sparkle in my eyes confirmed all that she already knew!

My last thoughts tonight as I close my diary are for tomorrow. My whole future, my entire happiness lies in that interview between John and Father. Surely love must prevail?

Monday 3rd December 1917

How happy I am as I write my diary tonight: Father has said 'yes'; he has consented to our engagement and I am still in a state of disbelief.

John went into Father's study straight after breakfast this morning and was in there for what felt like positively hours! While he was in with Father I told Mother what his intention was. Mother hoped for Father's approval but thought it unlikely. John emerged, almost an hour later, his beaming face broadcasting the good news. Of course Father had to then call me into his study to formalise his consent (how very typical). He has agreed that we may become engaged at Christmas and as the war will (hopefully) be over well before next summer, we may plan an August wedding! He suggested that in these austere times, when most families in the area have cause to mourn, that we hold a quiet, informal gathering to celebrate our engagement - perhaps some time between Christmas and New Year. John hopes that his return to the Front may be delayed until after the party but Father (generously) consented that, should he be recalled sooner, then our engagement may take place before his return. I cannot understand what has come over Father, he is so changed! Mother is of the opinion that Colonel Farquharson's death has had its effect and that it may be that genuine sympathy for Mrs. Farquharson and the awareness of the close proximity of ever threatening death have melted his heart! I do not know, but neither do I care, for all that matters to me is my forthcoming engagement - the first step along the road to a new life with John!

Of course John and I have talked all day, making plans, building castles in the air. If only this wretched war would end and allow us to get on with our lives.

When Mary returned from the Westons this afternoon I told her all about it and she was as amazed as I was at Father's 'volte-face'. Later, when we were alone, she told me how pleased she was for John, for now he will have a family once again! The old sadness for Charles still lingers with her.

John must face the medical board next week and I hope and pray that he will not be passed fit for duty. I want him to be here with me now - and forever.

I close my diary tonight happier that I ever dreamt that I could be!

Tuesday 11th December 1917

John went to Chester today and, I am delighted to say, was not passed fit enough for active service. The board has ordered him to appear again in another month. When John returned to Brabage with the news I threw my arms around him and hugged him - I did not care who would see! As it happened, Father was

visiting Mrs. Farquharson (again) and Mother had gone with Mary on the parish visits. So it is 'full steam ahead' with our plans! I am myself torn to see the dilemma which John suffers. One half of him is glad that he is not to return, but the other half feels that he is not doing his duty; that he is 'letting the side down' and other such nonsense. Talk to him how I might I am unable to dislodge the guilt.

When Father returned I told him the news. I have tried so hard to be more pleasant with Father since he gave his consent but he is so difficult. Today he has upset me by insisting that Mrs. Farquharson must be one of the guests at our engagement. Much as I railed and blustered against it Father was most insistent. I even tried to claim that Mrs. Farquharson would not wish to attend as she would still be mourning the Colonel but he dismissed my opinion. He insisted that Mrs. Farquharson would consider it a duty to attend, for she has known John since his early childhood. For what was intended to be a small, informal gathering, the numbers invited are snowballing rapidly. John and I feel that we have lost control and so have handed everything over to Mother who is glad to undertake the task.

Mary was most upset when she returned from her parish visiting. Before she went to the Westons Mary knew that Mrs. Bates was ill, but she has deteriorated alarmingly. Poor woman, she has been worn out by too much childbearing. She has had fourteen pregnancies in as many years. Nine of her children survive and only the eldest, Susan, has left home. She works in a factory in Northwich and lodges with an aunt there. What a burden the poor woman has to bear! Mary is at a loss to know how to proceed and I have promised that I will go with her tomorrow to see what can be done.

I do not know quite how these things are managed but I know that when John and I are married we will have our share of children, but I think that three or four will suffice!

Wednesday 12th December 1917

As I had promised, today I went with Mary to visit the Bates' house. It is some time since I have visited there and I was shocked to see the change that has occurred. The house is at the edge of the village. It is poorly built and the walls are damp. Thc windows are so small that they admit very little light. Inside, the ground floor is divided into two rooms. There is a kitchen with a dresser, a kitchen range, some chairs and a large, rickety table. The other room is called the 'parlour' and is not used very much as a rule. The upper storey consists entirely

of one room under the thatch which sleeps all the family. Because of this a bed has been made up for Mrs. Bates (Catherine) in the parlour. When I had last visited this room shone and sparkled. The few pretty things which Catherine Bates has managed to collect over the years are proudly displayed on the mantelshelf and on the poor sticks of furniture in the room. Since Catherine has been in her bed for some weeks now the room has not been cleaned and a thick layer of dust lies over everything. Catherine lay under some tattered blankets on a straw palliasse which had been placed on an extremely dirty floor. She looked so thin and ill that I hardly recognised the woman who had laughed as she dandled her latest baby on her knee some months ago.

I do not doubt that she is gravely ill. I asked what the doctor had said. She told me that she had not seen a doctor as Joe, her husband, had said that they could not afford it and that a few days in bed would soon set her right. I wondered, silently, how Joe Bates can afford his drink in the 'Swan' each day, but is unable to manage the doctor's fee when his wife is ill.

We made poor Catherine as comfortable as we could and induced her to eat a little of the food we had brought. She told us that the neighbours had been very kind and were helping by caring for the children. I asked where Joe was and Catherine avoided my eyes as she said quietly,

'He be out, lookin' fer work."

Joe is an agricultural worker and will sell his work on a casual basis to any who will employ him. Unfortunately, in December, extra hands are not needed and I was sure that if I cared to search I would find Joe lounging about somewhere with some of the other 'ne'er-do-wells' of Brabage

Before we left, Mary sent young Joss (who shares his Father's name but fortunately not his habits) to collect some wood. She instructed him to keep the fire in the parlour well made up for he must do his best to keep his mother warm. We made Catherine as comfortable as we could before leaving her to walk back to the vicarage. The sky had darkened and the first flakes of snow had begun to fall as we walked through the village. Mary asked if I thought that we should call the doctor and bear the expense ourselves. I told her that I did not think that a good idea. I truly believe that poor Catherine is beyond a doctor's help for I saw the stamp of death on that face as surely as if it were written in Indian ink on the forehead. I tried to prepare Mary for the blow that would inevitably fall. She remained hopeful however that Catherine, given care, would recover, responding with,

"She is after all, only thirty-four years old!"

I was shocked for I believed Catherine to be much older. Joe, I know is in his fifties and I had thought her to be in her late forties. How the years of childbearing have taken their toll! What a burden women must shoulder!

When we returned to the vicarage I could not find John anywhere. Eventually he was discovered in the conservatory, watching the snow fall. It had become much heavier and John was entranced, staring into the gloom with the white flakes dancing past. He had lit no light and as I entered he did not stir. The conservatory was cold and I was concerned that he would take a chill. I went to him and touched him gently on the shoulder. He turned to me, his eyes full of tears. He was remembering, he said, how excited he and Charles had been as children when the snow fell. They had a great sledge which was kept in the stable loft. When the snow was thick enough it would be brought out and the two boys would be content to play all the short winter's day.

"How carefree we had been. Little did we imagine the shadow of war which would end our happiness so completely and part us so finally!" I could say nothing, but merely stretched out my hands, which John grasped and used to pull me close to him. After some time I stirred from his embrace and said that we must go inside for the conservatory was cold. We went in silence, for neither had words to ease the sadness in which we were engulfed.

We passed a quiet evening. The snow continued to fall heavily and brought its own particular silence. More than once John spoke of his Company and expressed the hope that the snow was not falling in France, for trench life would be made even more intolerable. John's quiet sadness spread and pervaded us all and we were happy to go early to bed.

Saturday 15th December 1917

Today presented the first opportunity that Mary and I have had to go to the village. The snow has been so thick that no-one could venture out.

We made our difficult way to the Bates' house But when we arrived we found that poor Catherine had died early this morning. Mary was dreadfully upset for she had been sure that Mrs. Bates would recover. The poor woman was not to be permitted to rest quietly for controversy was raging in the kitchen while her sadly worn out body lay in the parlour. Joe Bates and Rachel Shipton (Catherine's sister) were arguing over what was to become of the family. Rachel was clearly upset and bitter at her sister's death, blaming Joe for what had happened. She could see no reason why Joe should not look after the children. There are five boys and three girls at home. Joss, the eldest boy, is thirteen and Ruth, the baby, only

a few months old. Rachel maintained that all the children could 'pitch in and help' and she herself could lend a hand on occasions.

"What about my work?" asked Joe, belligerently.

"What work be that then? Lounging about the village brings in no bread and if it weren't fer Susan, this family would've starved long ago!" (For many months Susan has been sending a large proportion of her wage home. I am loth to say it but I think that a good amount of that money was spent by Joe in the 'Swan'!)

Joe wanted Susan to come home to look after the children, maintaining over and over again that caring for a family is 'woman's work'.

"Aye!" said Rachel, "an' earnin' bread is man's. If Susan does your work then happen as 'ow you mun do 'ers!"

Each side appealed to Mary and to me. Mary would not get involved but I (incautious as ever) agreed with Rachel. It would be better to have the secure wage of Susan than the unreliable earnings of Joe, which were at best seasonal and at worst, nonexistent! Joe was most unhappy at my siding with Rachel and muttered darkly about 'That Pankhurst woman, settin' females above their station'. Susan was to come home for the funeral and the matter would be discussed then. I very much fear that Joe's prejudices will prevail over Rachel's common sense. Why must the man be so mulish, can he not see what would be best for the family? It is more than twelve years since the Women's Social and Political Union was formed and I fear that while women may make progress in some areas, in men's hearts and minds we will ever be inferior!

During the evening we discussed the plight of the Bates family and the predicament they were in. Father is adamant that a family needs a woman to care for it; Mother conceded the point as a general rule but in these circumstances needs must rule convention. Mary, John and myself were all of one mind - Susan should be allowed to continue in employment and the care of the family should devolve upon Joe. Father shook his head sadly,

"What a world we will have in years to come with people thinking like this. No woman will want to care for her family but will want to be off, doing man's work."

I commented that perhaps if men had to look after the children there may be fewer born and deaths such as Catherine's could be avoided! There was silence. Father and Mother both considered the mention of childbirth to be indelicate. Mother hastily changed the subject and we reverted to the plans for Christmas and, more importantly, the engagement party.

Now that we know that John is not to be recalled before Christmas the party is set for the twenty-eighth of December and Mother has been sending out

invitations. It is to be quite a gathering for, however we strive to trim numbers, there is always someone whose claim to an invitation is strong. At the last count we were to be thirty. I am sure that everyone who is invited will not accept for notice is short and people do tend to be rather busy at Christmas time. We will see. Meanwhile it pleases Mother to occupy herself with these plans and she plagues Father with questions about who should and who should not be invited; whether there should be music; if it is wise to prepare extra bedrooms in case the weather turns bad again and so on and so forth. Father is so bothered by Mother that he can spare little time to criticise me and supervise my time with John. We have spent a great deal of time in these past few days alone in each other's company. How impatient I am to be married to him - he is all that I could ever desire in any man.

Friday 21st December 1917

The day has been crisp, clear and cold. John and I spent much of the morning walking in the grounds. He maintains that as long as he is wearing warm clothes the fresh air, even though cold, helps his recovery. When I am in John's company the hours pass as though they are minutes. John spent a long time telling me what our life in Park House would be, trying to familiarise me with what would be my home. I think that John must not realise, or must have forgotten, how much of my time in the past year has been spent there. I do not stop him for I love to hear him talk of our future together.

The ground was frozen hard and we were able to make our way to the lake. The edges of the lake were frozen and the ground in the shadow of the trees was quite white with frost. The lake and summerhouse are our favourite place and as I looked at the forlorn windows the memory of that earlier visit flooded back. John's mind was obviously running on the same paths for he pulled me to him and kissed me passionately. As our kiss ended he whispered into my hair,

"Soon my darling, soon Lizzie, we will belong to each other totally!" It was too cold to stay for long or even consider going to sit in the summerhouse and so we made our way back to the house.

As we came from among the shrubs we heard the familiar sound of Mrs. Farquharson's motor car. The glance which passed between us showed that flight was uppermost in both our minds. However we were cold and had been out for some time and with a resigned shrug of his shoulders John pulled me forward saying,

"Come on Lizzie, let's go and face the music. I really think that I would rather face the Boche!"

Laughing, we made our way into the house.

Mrs. Farquharson was sitting with Mother in the drawing room and it was immediately clear that she did not approve of John and me being permitted to walk out alone. However John, who can charm the birds from the trees, set about winning her over. She was soon giving us the benefit of her experience and lecturing us on the essentials of a happy marriage. The lecture was interrupted by Mary's entrance who, after the formalities of greeting, could not suppress her indignation at what she had discovered. She has been in Brabage and has found out that Susan Bates has left the factory in Northwich and is to stay here in the village to care for the children. Bold Mary went along to see her and when asked, Susan had told Mary that she had had little choice in the matter, for her Father had made it clear that if she did not return in order to look after the family, then the family would not be cared for at all. He had his own work to do and the women must learn to do theirs! There was nothing that Mary could do and she left Susan hoping that when Joss left school he would be able to work and young Janey, who was now twelve, could look after the family. Susan would then be free to return to her well-paid work in the factory.

We had talked for some time about the problem when Mrs. Farquharson, who had overheard part of our discussion, interrupted and gave us her own opinion. Of course, she said, looking after a family was women's work. Men and women each had their appointed tasks and it was best if each carried out those tasks without forever fretting and wanting to do the other's work. One of the main reasons that she and the Colonel had been so happy together was that she knew a woman's place and was content to fill it!

I was about to respond when a warning look from Mother silenced me. An adept at her task, Mother led the conversation to other topics but I frothed and fumed internally and when Mrs. Farquharson had at last left I could not prevent my anger boiling over. Mother was so very philosophical, saying that Mrs. Farquharson was rather like Father and was so set in her ideas of what was right that all the arguments in the world would not persuade her from her belief. When Father returned he was angry to have missed Mrs. Farquharson's visit. She is a good friend of the Bishop and has promised to speak to him about the church extension.

During the evening John helped Mary, Mother and me pack small parcels for the village children. The whole population of the village is so tired of war and sad times and shortages that we are determined that each child shall at least receive a small Christmas gift. We have not told Father for he is sure to criticise

us for extravagance, though the parcels are modest, containing home made items such as peg dolls and knitted scarves. I saw the kindness of John for, sure that he was unobserved by us, he slipped a penny in each package going to the Bates family. I only hope that the children do not tell their Father of the money or he will take it all for drink!

Tuesday 25th December 1917

Christmas Day is meant to be one of the happiest of the year - how then do I often find myself thinking such sad thoughts?

After the service this morning Mary and I went through the village distributing our Christmas gifts. Everywhere they were accepted and opened with joy, laughter and the most touching gratitude. The Bates's cottage was the last on our list and we entered, rather apprehensive of what we would find. Poor Susan has tried so hard to take the place of her dead mother! She had the children assembled around the kitchen table and was about to serve a scrawny fowl for their festive treat. The children's eyes were as round as the pudding that was boiling away on the stove. Planks of wood had been laid across chairs to enable them all to sit at table, for there were not enough seats. (The family rarely dine together.) We did not wish to interrupt the festivities but merely handed over our gifts and made to leave. The older children had excitedly torn open their parcels and were happily examining the contents. Young Charlie, who is only two years old, immediately placed his penny in his mouth and it had to be hastily removed by Mary who had seen what had happened. Poor Susan could not prevent the tears coming to her eyes as she thanked us. When I asked where her father was she put a finger to her lips and urged us to silence. He was still sound asleep in the parlour. He had come home very late and exceedingly drunk, too drunk in fact to climb the stairs and Susan had thrown a blanket over him where he lay on the floor. The men of Brabage keep up the old custom of wassail and while Joe has not a great community spirit, it would be against his nature to refuse the opportunity of a free drink or two (or more!).

Our errands had made us late for our own Christmas dinner and we were criticised by Father for our unpunctuality. In the afternoon Mary and I put on an impromptu concert and even persuaded John to sing a song.

The evening was a sad time, for John spoke to us of his mother and Charles and the Christmases they had kept at Park House. He only retains vague memories of his father who died when Charles was only a few months old. My admiration for Mrs. Fraser increases as I hear more about her life. Though she

was urged over and over again to re-marry in order to provide the boys with a father, she refused, preferring her independence. She maintained that true love is experienced once in a lifetime and when that lover is gone, then there can be no second best. John said that he had never felt the lack of a father, and knowing what a sterling woman his mother was I do not doubt his assertion.

Before we went to bed John took me aside and pressed a small box into my hand. We had all exchanged gifts in the morning and so I could not imagine what this was. I opened it and found a small diamond brooch. It was set in a flower formation and the stones sparkled in the candlelight. It was beautiful!

As I lifted it from its nest of wadding John took it from me and pinned it to my dress.

"This was an engagement gift from my father to my mother. Although I know that on our marriage you will receive all of Mother's jewellery, I want you to have this now."

I could find no words in reply and could only cry as he kissed me.

Now, as I look at the exquisite piece of jewellery which lies alongside my diary, I can only make the fervent wish that I am able to live up to John's expectations of me: To fill Mrs. Fraser's shoes is an awesome task!

Friday 28th December 1917

John and I are engaged to be married and I am supremely happy!

Saturday 29th December 1917

It was so late and I was so tired and excited that I was unable to write my diary properly yesterday. Today I will remedy that omission and as I write I see John's ring, our engagement ring, on my finger.

The party was small and informal. We were, after all, only twenty six. Father proposed that we get the 'business' of the evening over early. When everyone had been greeted and served with a glass of wine Father called the room to attention. He signalled towards the door and Cook, Carstairs, Edna and her sister Hannah (who was present to help for the evening) filed in and stood along the wall. When all eyes were on Father he made a speech, acknowledging that we were all gathered to mark the betrothal of his elder daughter, Elizabeth Alice, to Captain John William Fraser. He went on to describe the fine qualities he had found in John and to express his confident hope that John found many desirable qualities in his future wife. He talked at some length of John's family and I wished that he had not for I saw John bow his head, remembering his recent losses.

Father explained why the gathering was small and informal - John's own circumstances and of course the stringencies of war. Once mentioned he was unable to resist talking at length about the war; sacrifice; duty. Mrs. Farquharson beamed at him and it was only when some began to get restless that he finished his speech with a toast.

John stood and responded beautifully (and mercifully, briefly). He said that it was an honour to be engaged to me and that he only wished that he was worthy of me. He made a great ceremony of placing the ring upon my finger and whispered quietly to me that soon he would be placing a wedding ring there! Of course I blushed to the roots of my hair. John then proposed a toast to me.

After the formalities were over we danced and dined and danced again. Naturally I danced with John all evening and occasionally I caught sight of Mrs. Farquharson as she sat with Mother, no doubt bestowing upon her the benefit of her expertise and experience in one field or another! Poor Mother sat stoically through it all and beamed radiantly at us each time we passed. (Mother told me this morning that Mrs. Farquharson was reminding her that John and I had met first at her house. She went on to say that it was only a few weeks ago that she had urged Father to allow us to become engaged. She truly believes that men fight better when they have loving ties at home! Thus is Father's 'volte-face' explained! Perhaps I should be a little grateful to Mrs. Farquharson after all.)

My happiness made the hours race by and it seemed hardly any time at all before people were beginning to leave. John and I stood at the door and bade each farewell. In their turn they wished us happiness, and several expressed the hope that it would not be long before they were dancing at our wedding.

Mary went off immediately to bed but Mother and Father sat with John and me for some time. We discussed the events of the evening, odd scraps of news, our own prospects; our topics were diverse. Mother stifled a yawn and Father sent her to bed. When she had wished us goodnight and left the room, Father turned to us and said,

"Now that you are officially engaged I have something to say to you. John, you will be going back to France soon and will doubtless resume your correspondence with Elizabeth. To date your correspondence has been most correct. As a mark of my trust in you I propose that you may write to Elizabeth and she may respond to you without me examining the letters. I trust that your future correspondence will be as correct as it has been up to now."

With that he wished us goodnight and left the room. I was so surprised that

I could only gape. What a blessing that Father has not seen my other letters; he would hardly think these 'correct' and 'proper'.

We had the time for only one brief kiss before going upstairs to bed. We were both aware that poor Edna was waiting to go to bed. She must be about again at six o'clock in the morning. Father will expect his water hot at six-thirty, late night or not!

Today the weather has been extremely inclement and John and I have been content to sit close together in the company of Mary and Mother. Now that we are officially engaged both of them strive to leave us alone more frequently. How happy and contented I am. I imagine that marriage can only bring a deeper, more fulfilling satisfaction. John has scarcely let go of my hand all day and when I get up to fetch an item of work or a book, his eyes follow me everywhere. I know that he too is supremely happy. There is only one dark cloud on the horizon and that is John's return to the war. How fervently I hope for an end to the hostilities. It is unlikely to happen soon however for both sides are firmly entrenched and the breakthrough in November to the Belgian ports has made little difference.

I vow that I will not think unhappy thoughts today, or any day, until my darling (my fiancé) returns to France. At this moment I have almost all that I could ever wish for!

Monday 31st December 1917

I am twenty-two years old today. After the excitement of the celebrations of the engagement we spent a quiet day with only a dinner, more special than usual, to mark the occasion of my birthday.

I received a most beautiful diary from John. Mother and Father gave me a needlework box and from Mary came the gift of a pen. I am well blessed that people are so kind to me.

The morning was wet and dreary and we spent it mostly indoors. John took great delight in reading to Mother, Mary and me as we sat with our sewing. He stopped when Father returned, knowing that Father would be unlikely to approve of the reading of a novel.

The afternoon brought with it drier weather and John persuaded Father to allow him to drive us out in the trap. Father did not accompany us on our excursion and I think that we were the happier for his absence! Mother, Mary, John and I were quite exhilarated by the sharp trot around the country lanes.

In spite of the season the Cheshire countryside displays its own magnificence. The patchwork of fields is a tribute to the Cheshire farmer. As we gazed over the

rolling farmland I watched John greedily drinking in his beloved homeland. I know that he must hate that other landscape far from here. How I grieve for him having to undergo the hell of war while we sit back safely at home.

More than once John turned the trap towards Framley but clearly thought better of it; afraid, I am sure, of his memories. Instead we turned towards Bunbury. Beeston Castle stood clear and proud, and beyond it were the dramatic mountains of Wales tipped now with snow. At last it was time to turn for our own home and I noted the reluctance with which John turned Prince's head.

Mrs. Farquharson called in the early evening and surprised me greatly by giving me a small birthday gift (a scarf). How that woman astonishes me! I must note that as she handed over her gift she made a great show to Father, saying how well she thought of me and how she could not fail to mark the occasion of my birthday.

We stayed downstairs long enough to welcome the New Year with a toast. Father was rather long-winded in his speech dismissing the old year (touching on sensitive ground which would have been better avoided) and in his welcoming of the new. We were all, I think, thankful to retire!

* * * * * * *

Tuesday 1st January 1918

Each year on this day I have wished for an end to the war. Today I write no such wish, for I feel that the hope is a vain one. The war seems to have gone on for ever and looks set to continue for as far as I can see into the future. In August 1914, at the beginning of the war, everyone said that it would all be over by Christmas. It is as well not to listen to popular opinion!

Today, John and I made a sad pilgrimage. We went to Framley Church to place some flowers on his mother's grave. I had thought yesterday that John's thoughts turned in that direction and so I was not surprised that he wished to make the journey. We drove over early, in the trap, for the weather looked rather threatening.

Before we went into the churchyard we went to the vicarage to call on the Reverend Spencer. He is so old that he seems to merge with the church architecture! John told me that the vicar will soon be eighty years old but as he is still so active and as strong in voice as ever he has not yet felt the need to retire.

The church and congregation at Framley are much larger than at Brabage and the churchyard is huge. The Reverend Spencer shook John's hand and then mine, congratulating us on our engagement.

"So heartwarming," he said, "to have young folk being sufficiently optimistic that they can plan for a future in spite of the turmoil and the wreckage of war."

He informed John that the mason had finished the requested inscriptions on the tombstone and trusted that we would find everything in order. He excused himself from accompanying us to the Fraser family grave as he had pressing duties. (I am sure that his duties were not so pressing but rather that he was sensitive to the fact that John would prefer solitude on this visit to his mother's grave-side.)

As we made our way through the churchyard I threaded my arm through John's. Everything is so very bleak at this gloomy time of the year and there were only occasional splashes of brightness where winter foliage and berries had been placed on some of the newer graves. The churchyard was well tended with even the oldest of the graves being kept trimmed.

We soon stopped at a rectangle of low railings. The white marble headstone distinguished it as the Fraser family grave. There were the names of John's grandfather and grandmother. Beneath them was the name of John's Father. At the bottom, newly inscribed, the edges of the letters sharp and clear, were two more names. I approached the stone and read the name of Mary Elizabeth Fraser (John's mother) and below, set on a line of its own I read,

Also to the memory of Charles George Fraser
Killed in Action in France 10th July 1917

I could say nothing. I stepped back to John and silently took his arm once more, gripping it more tightly. After some moments of silence John turned to me and said,

"I could not bring back Charles's body but I have put his name next to Mother's, for I believe that to have been her dearest wish."

Again we lapsed into silence, each thinking our own thoughts. I thought of Mrs. Fraser and of Charles; about how grim death claims us all, no matter how bright and shining our youth and our ambitions. Such ideas of mortality made me shudder and I could not repress the thought that this small plot in Framley Churchyard would doubtless be my own resting place, for I was to be a Fraser in the none too distant future.

Misinterpreting my shudder John pulled me close, apologising for keeping me out in the cold. The black cloud that had hung low all morning suddenly broke and the downpour silenced my protests of reassurance. John quickly grasped my hand and we ran for the church porch.

As we stood watching the great curtain of rain sweep across the churchyard and turn the gravel paths into chattering streams, John buried his mouth in my hair. Muttering indistinctly he told me that he must soon return to duty. He silenced my anguished protest with a kiss and went on to explain that he felt fit and able to return to the Front. Much as he would like to delay his return, to stay longer with me, the longer he delayed, the more difficult his return would be. If he stayed in Brabage for many more days he feared that he would never be able to face the war again. I asked,

"Is it so very dreadful in France?"

He replied, "Lizzie, it is hell on earth. I cannot bring myself to talk much about it. People like your father and Mrs. Farquharson see no further than the glory of war. Were they to stand for half a day next to a raw recruit, up to the knees in mud and paralysed with fear, or be with a young officer ordering his obedient men to certain death, then they would know that there can be no glory in war!" He spoke more than he had ever done; the constant fear; the awful conditions; the terrible rations. For the first time he told me that there was a growing feeling of anger in the ranks, anger against the higher officers. In John's hearing several men had muttered their resentment that 'the top brass' gave impossible orders costing hundreds of lives at one stroke, without ever having to risk their own safety.

"If the war doesn't end soon Lizzie, I don't know what will happen. I do not believe that revolution is part of the British character, but when these men come back after the war society will change drastically; it will be forced to!"

By this time the rain had passed and we made our way back to Brabage. On the journey we discussed the likely changes in society and agreed that many alterations and developments were both necessary and desirable. How I enjoyed our discussion, for it is so refreshing to be treated as an intellectual equal rather than, as Father treats me, like a child.

As we drove through Brabage we were able to collect Mary who was walking home after visiting the Bates's house. She has made quite a mission out of caring for that family. She had better take care that Father does not find out for he would be sure to censure her.

When we arrived at the vicarage all was chaos for today, being the first of the

month, is the collection day for parcels for France. Mother was sorting and wrapping a multitude of items and could scarcely be seen for brown paper and string. She was rather overwhelmed by the magnitude of her task but we all pitched in to help and the parcels were soon wrapped and stacked neatly in the hall.

We hosted a small gathering of friends in the evening, as is our custom on New Year's Day. I hardly left John's side as, after his words of today, I am aware that he will not be near to me for very much longer. The most enjoyable thing about the evening was that, now that we are engaged to be married, John and I are treated as a couple. How anxious we both are for our marriage when we can be together at all times. I noticed that a number of guests asked John when he would be returning to France and each time he responded,

"In a very short time."

How my heart sank to hear those words! I will not end my first diary entry of 1918 on a sad note, instead I will consider my blessings: I am young, with my entire life before me; I have the complete love of a wonderful man; we are to be married as soon as we can manage to do so. Mother and Mary are wonderful and if Father is horrible I am managing to keep out of his way. When I am forced to spend time with him I succeed in keeping my temper (most of the time!) and behaving impeccably.

Yes, this is going to be a good year!

Friday 11th January 1918

After all the flutter and fuss of the last few days it was only today that I sat down and realised the extent of my loss. John returned to duty early this morning, and what a vacuum has been left in my life! How easy it is to take people for granted when they are with one continually. Their value is not appreciated fully until they are gone!

I must reluctantly agree with the doctors who, earlier this week, passed John fit for service. I have not seen him look so well for almost a year. How cruel is fate that just as he has recovered and is enjoying his restored health he is snatched away from me! After spending all day every day in each other's company we will now have contact only through our letters. I suppose that at least they will be private to us and Father will not be reading them first!

Before Christmas I felt that engagement would not make me feel differently, but how very wrong I was. I almost feel part of John, and he of me. Over the last few weeks we have grown so close, physically and emotionally, that part of

myself has today departed for France! I will have to get on with life, pick up the threads I dropped so readily so long ago in order to look after John. Mary will doubtless be relieved as most of my duties have fallen on her to carry out.

When I had seen John off early this morning I went out visiting with Mary. Wherever I went all missed John, asking me where he was and sending their good wishes to him. In particular the young boys in the school think of him as a hero. The fact that he was home through illness and not a wound has in some way passed them by and all that they can talk about are his brave deeds and his medals. What a paradox, for I love to hear John talked of with such great respect but I detest the whole business of war. What complex creatures we humans are!

We called at the Bates's house and found poor Susan sadly overworked and tired out. I am sure that in the factory she never got so tired. Mr. Bates conducts himself as before and I can see no way out of Susan's drudgery. She behaved most oddly, very nervous and looking away when she spoke to us. I hope that there is nothing further amiss in that sad household.

Father made a great point of voicing his pleasure at my 'return to duty' as he put it, and gave me a long list (which he has been keeping for months) of parish business in need of my attention. How meticulous Father is!

The day passed so very slowly that I could not believe that John had left only this morning. We spent a quiet evening, Father reading aloud to Mother, Mary and me as we worked. Once or twice, when I let my attention wander and my expression become morose, Father recalled me, curtly reminding me that to sorrow as I appeared to be doing was both selfish and sinful. I was thankful when I could at last retire, pleading the excuse of my early rising. Once alone, up in my room, I could let my thoughts roam as they would, and be sad if I cared to, without attracting criticism. I have sat and recalled our time together over the past weeks. How I miss the warmth, the gentleness, the passion of John. The space next to me has felt so very cold and empty today that I do not know how I can bear our separation. I would give anything to have him here to touch, hold, to caress, to kiss. Tonight I go to sleep only half a person, hoping to dream about the other half of me. My only wish is for John to be safe and to be kept out of danger. I hope that I do not wish in vain.

THE TRAITOR 'BUS *

I watched them disembark: young boys.
All London lads I'm told.
Their faces show it should be toys,
Not rifles, that they hold.

They saw the 'buses, gave a shout,
Regarded them with glee.
"As kids these 'buses took us out
To seaside, zoo and tea!"

Such brave young men. A splendid sight!
Eager they climbed aboard.
Their former transport of delight
Carried them off to war.

A bright adventure lay before,
Or so they'd like to think.
Too young to realise that war
Is madness at Hell's brink.

I wondered, did they feel betrayed
When they got down the line?
When these young men are killed or maimed
Is glory then so fine?

**Old 'buses from The London General Omnibus Company were used behind the lines as troop transport.*

John Fraser 1918

Wednesday 23rd January 1918

My intuition was correct, for there is trouble at the Bates's house. This morning as I went about my visits I met Susan. She asked if she could walk some way with me and naturally I assented. I made conversation with her, chatting

about the children, asking about the baby and enquiring whether her Father yet had any work. I could see that she was not paying full attention to my chatter for more than once her replies were not forthcoming. When she did reply her answers were hardly related to the questions I had asked. Eventually I asked her what was wrong. She turned to me, her eyes full of fear,

"Oh, Miss Elizabeth, I don't know what to do! Things couldn't be worse."

She began to cry and I comforted her as best I could. We were close to the vicarage by this time and I prevailed upon Susan to come in. She refused saying that she was afraid that she would meet Father or Mary, and indeed I saw that her fear was real and not imagined. As a compromise she agreed to walk to the summerhouse where we could converse privately. I had the key with me for, not having yet heard from John, I had planned to take out and read some of his old letters, just to feel close to him.

The day was cold and wet and our feet got muddy on the path through the shrubbery. We carefully scraped our boots, wiped them and entered. The atmosphere was quite cold, but dry, and we sat down, Susan on the window seat and I on the chair. She had calmed considerably and I asked her if she was ready to talk to me. She bit her bottom lip hard, but nodded slowly. After a pause she took a deep breath and launched into her tale - and what a tale it turned out to be! I heard her in silence and afterwards we sat quietly together while I considered what could be done.

Susan is expecting a child. She thinks that it will be born in early July. (I looked critically at her figure and saw that her slender shape was indeed thickening. If it was not for the anxious expression she would look very well, rosy and plump.) When Susan had worked in Northwich she and the other girls from the factory went out with the soldiers who found themselves at home on leave in the town. Some time previously Susan had found herself especially attracted to one young man - Alfie Cooper - and since going out with him she had ceased keeping company with the other girls. Of course she was teased for it but she did not care, for she knew that she and Alfie were deeply in love.

"I can't explain Miss, the feeling inside. You just know that y'love 'im, that yer want ter be with 'im fer the rest of yer life. It's a sort o' warm feelin', safe an' excitin' all at the same time. Oh! I can't explain Miss, I ain't got the words!"

(No need to Susan, no need, for I know the feeling you describe, I know it so very well!)

Alfie had gone back to the war and had sent Susan several postcards from France. She had written back only twice for she found the letters difficult to

compose and was easily put off relaying anything of real import as she knew that the letters would be read by an officer. Alfie came home and came to see her. He went back to France. They were both broken hearted. Alfie came home again but was unable to get to Northwich in the limited time he had. Susan met him in London and they spent one precious day together. They were in love and the world was at their feet. Alfie was sure that the war would end soon and, on the strength of it, proposed to Susan. Without hesitation she accepted.

Back in Northwich she could only dream of Alfie. Alfie wrote and told her that he would like her to visit his family. He would be home again in early October and hoped that she would accompany him to his mother's house. She wrote and said that she would. Mrs. Cooper welcomed Susan most warmly, pleased to see Alfie settled with such a 'nice young girl'. Before Alfie returned to duty from that leave they had sealed their relationship in the most natural way. The result was that now Susan found herself expecting a baby.

I was silent. Susan took my silence for disapproval and her words came tumbling out - she hadn't meant to; they were carried away; they did not realise what they were doing; she loved Alfie so much and he was going back to that awful war with no comforts at all. This one bit of comfort couldn't do any harm. Anyway, they were to be married soon.

I roused myself for I saw that Susan had misinterpreted my silence. I asked why she and Alfie could not marry now and at this her eyes filled with tears.

"That's the trouble Miss, no-one ain't seen nor heard of Alfie since Christmas. His ma's at her wits' end. I can't tell 'er about the baby or she'd worry even more!"

I suggested that perhaps Mrs. Cooper could help out. Could Susan go to live with her?

"What about our own littl'uns Miss, who'd look after them if I was ter go. Father ain't fit!"

Whatever solution I proposed there were many strong reasons why it would not work. We were silent again. Susan was awkward in that silence.

"I tole you Miss," she said, twisting her hands together," 'cos I thought as 'ow Cap'n Fraser could look out fer Alfie, try ter find where he is. I daresn't tell Miss Mary. I know she'll feel as I 've let 'er down, after all she's done fer us. And as fer the Revcrend! You've 'eard 'im, same as me Miss 'Lizabeth, rantin' on of a Sunday 'gainst them that 'as sinned. I can't go through it Miss, I'll run away first. If Father finds out 'e'll beat me black an' blue."

I patted her hands, put my arm around her shoulders, jollied her along. I said

that I would think of something and that she must not worry. She dried her eyes and immediately looked better.

"I knew as you'd 'elp me Miss 'Lizabeth, I knew you'd be the one to'elp."

Her faith in me was touching. She went off from the summerhouse with a considerably brighter step than the one that had brought her there. She agreed that if she met Father or Mary she would say that she had been helping me to sort out some parcels.

When the door closed behind her and I watched her drab, grey, patched coat disappear along the path, I sat to think. I had been silent and thoughtful while she told her story for I could understand clearly how she felt. I knew that I could almost be in the same position, so deep and passionate were my feelings for John and his for me. Far from being critical of her actions I was full of sympathy and understanding.

I sat for almost an hour, turning the problem over in my mind. John's letters remained unread, safe in their hiding place. Something would have to be done, and quickly, for Susan's condition was starting to be noticeable. After dismissing several plans I started to think in a different way, ruling out the absolutely impossible and re-assembling the remaining possibilities (however slight) to try to find a way out.

Father must not know until her condition could no longer be concealed. Susan was correct in assuming that there would be no charity there, only harshness and censure. Likewise, Joe Bates must not know. Mary and Mother would probably help if only I could put the situation to them carefully. (How perceptive Susan had been in realising that Mary would be likely to feel 'let down'.) Mrs. Cooper may help, she liked Susan and perhaps the hope of the baby in the future would take her mind off her present anxiety for Alfie's safety. Then there was John. What mixed feelings I had there. I thought that to ask him to search for Alfie would bring back hurtful and damaging memories too soon. On the other hand he knew more about the army and its movements than we did. What a dilemma!

I went through the remainder of the day in a dream, forever lighting on a solution only to dismiss it a moment later as being impractical. Mother asked me more than once if I was quite well. Eventually I could bear it no longer and I spoke privately to Mary. I couched the story in such terms that her sympathy and natural kindness would be aroused - and indeed they were! She wanted a happy ending and was full of plans to write to the War Office and take up a personal crusade for the discovery of Private Alfie Cooper. I should have known that Mary's sterling qualities would shine through.

In the meantime I turned everything over and over in my mind. It was past midnight when I decided that writing my diary may help me order my thoughts. It has done so. As I sit in my attic, a small stub of candle on the edge of the table, I have made my resolve. I will tell the entire story to John, for he knows Susan and her family well. I will not ask him to do anything, but merely seek his guidance and ask his advice. I will write first thing tomorrow morning. Now that I have settled that I am sure that I will sleep well.

Thursday 31st January 1918

Today I received a letter from John. It felt so very odd for the letter that was delivered to the house to be the only letter. Several times I had to prevent myself planning a trip to the summerhouse, so hard is it to avoid falling into old habits.

He has not yet received my letter telling him about Susan Bates, but writes of his return to the Front. Strange that he almost welcomes the return, being among his own men again. It is an odd thing, he says, that when in France it feels like the real world and England and the old life merely make-believe. His company was pleased to see him back again. They are very sorely pressed along the front lines for the Germans seem to be gearing up for some sort of major offensive. John has led several raiding parties but they have only breached the wire twice. They did however manage, to bring back a single prisoner on each occasion. He tells me that if H.Q. have managed to extract any information from the prisoners, then it has not yet filtered back down the lines. Things just seem to drag on and on, and the men grow ever more despondent. John writes that some are so desperate to end it all that they become reckless during raids and attacks, risking their lives and not caring whether they are killed or merely sustain an injury severe enough to be invalided out of France. (They call it 'A Blighty One', 'Blighty' being the soldiers' name for England!)

I am relieved that John appears to be in better spirits than he has for some time. It makes me hopeful that my own letter to him will find a sympathetic reception.

I visited Susan once again today: Mary and I went together. She is in good spirits and is certain that Alfie is safe. However, she says that if the worst has happened and Alfie is dead then she will bear his baby with pride in his memory. I judged the time propitious to suggest that Susan contacted Mrs. Cooper. She was doubtful but promised to consider it.

Father does not approve of us spending so much of our visiting time in the Bates' house. The children attend Sunday School and Susan attends church almost every Sunday, but Father considers Mr. Bates beyond redemption and

would therefore prefer that we avoid the contamination of his house! I had the temerity to rebuke him and to point out that Jesus himself considered no-one beyond redemption. Christ spent most of his time amongst the sinners and outcasts. Was Father then putting his own judgement above that of his Lord's?

I was amazed at my own boldness, and fell quickly silent. Father did not reply but satisfied himself by glaring with hostility at me for the remainder of the evening. It may well prove that this feeble woman is finding the confidence to face up to the tyrant!

I wrote to John this evening, hoping that my letter arrives before he replies to mine of the twenty-fourth of January. What a mix we are in! I wrote to him of my stand against Father, and I am sure that he will approve of my courage!

Tuesday 12th February 1918

What a horrible day; Mary and I have been so upset by the events of today that we have quite worn ourselves out with crying!

We went out together this morning to carry out our parish duties. We left the Bates' cottage until last, as usual, for we like to spend a little longer with Susan than the normal parish visit.

We knocked at the door and there was no reply. Susan usually calls out for us to enter, but all was silence. We knocked several times and considered whether we should go in. Just then the door to the next cottage opened and Mrs. Edwards called out to us,

"Doan think she'll 'ear yer Miss, an' if she do she woan let yer in. They's bin such a row - terrible! It were shockin'. Joe Bates 'as stormed off early an' 'as not bin sin since!"

We thanked Mrs. Edwards for her information and quietly conferred over our course of action. We decided that with such an argument Susan would have more need of us than ever and so we lifted the latch and entered the cottage.

The ground floor was deserted and the fire out (almost unheard of, especially in these raw, cold, February days!). We called and listened but could hear nothing. We went tc the bottom of the stairs, opened the door and called up the narrow staircase. We heard a low sobbing.

I had never been upstairs in the Bates' house before and what I saw surprised me. While everything was fairly clean in the one room which was the upper floor, the furnishings were mean and ragged. Susan lay on a straw palliasse on the floor in the far corner. We made our way towards her, stepping over other mattresses which were tightly packed in the small space. Susan had to be coaxed to raise

her face. When she did so what I saw made me gasp,. Her face was badly bruised and her lip split in several places. The blood had dried on her face and tears had made white snail trails through the stains. She attempted to cover her face with her hands and I noticed that they too were bruised and bleeding, as if she had held them before her for protection.

Of course it was her father, Joe, who had inflicted this shameful treatment. I should have been more aware, known that someone who had lived with Catherine through her carrying of so many children, would be bound to notice the early stages in his own daughter.

Little by little Susan told us the story. Her father spent most of his time out with his cronies, down at the 'Swan', only occasionally doing odd jobs here and there. He arrived home late, when all the children were in bed and was usually so inebriated that he scarce had words for Susan. Each morning she would be busy and out and about her chores when Joe finally got out of bed and staggered from the house, making himself what breakfast he would. Consequently it was not until yesterday that he had sat for any time in the kitchen. He had no work to go to and sat, idly watching Susan as she went about her tasks.

Something about the way in which Susan held herself as she bent over the tub to lift out washing (for she takes in washing in order to earn a few shillings a week) struck a chord in Joe. He put down his pipe and spoke sharply to her. At first Susan denied his accusations but he became increasingly violent, accompanying each question with a savage blow. He eventually beat the whole truth out of her and stormed from the house. She staggered up to bed, knowing that she must lie down. The next thing she knew was that Mary and I arrived.

We carefully removed Susan's dress and bathed her poor wounds. Her shoulders and spine are black and blue. She told us that her father had used a walking stick on her and that is how her hands are so damaged for she had used them to cover her stomach to protect her unborn baby from her father's blows. Our actions calmed her and we were able to sit and discuss what would be done. Her father had cursed her for bringing shame on the family and told her .that she must go from the cottage, from Brabage, from the whole countryside around. But Susan would not leave the children no matter what her father said. She was almost glad that he knew, for now that her secret was out in the open she was no longer afraid. She was sure that in time her father would see the practicality of her remaining - for if she were to leave who would care for the children?

By this time Susan was feeling, and looking, a great deal better. We took our

leave, promising that we would call again tomorrow. All the way home Mary and I discussed Susan's plight. We agreed that our lot was preferable to poor Susan's, for while our father abused and assaulted us verbally he would never do so physically. I never thought that I would be thankful for my own father!

We were late for lunch and Father chided us for it. Of course we could not tell him the real reason but rather claimed a general delay on our visiting rounds due to the inclemency of the weather.

All the afternoon in the sewing circle I could not put Susan out of my mind. Mrs. Farquharson was 'holding court' and I know that several times she tried to provoke me by her comments on pacifism and socialism. She has much to say about the new 'Ministry of Information' which Mr. Lloyd George has set up. Lord Beaverbrook, with the aid of Lords Northcliffe and Rothermere and able writers such as Mr. Kipling are publishing long articles which are intended to undermine the German morale. She made a few barbed comments about "people here" doing little to bolster allied morale with their lack of enthusiasm for the war but I did not rise to her bait, my mind being too much occupied.

Mary taught in the school during the afternoon and I know that her mind too was active on the problem for we discussed Susan at length on our return to the house. We decided that we would wait to see what John would say on the matter. We would watch events carefully and if Susan made no move to contact Mrs. Cooper then we, one way or another, would do so ourselves. With that resolved we felt much better and planned what we might spare from the household to take to Susan tomorrow.

As I settle into my comfortable bed, between soft, white sheets, I am conscious of the difference in the Bates' cottage - no sheets and a straw mattress. I have my own room, they sleep, nine children and a drunken Father, all crowded together in a dark attic. Father is forever complaining about money but we always have enough to eat, warm fires and good, thick clothes. We do not have to endure the harsh life experienced by the Bates', and thousands of others like them. Is it true what Father says - that men are what they make themselves? He maintains that to be in such a state of poverty as the Bates's are is due to profligacy, laziness and general bad management. In a Christian nation I am puzzled at the class differences presented everywhere. Can God exist and allow such inconsistencies to continue?

I ease my conscience with the resolve that I will do all that I can over the coming months to make life a little more comfortable for Susan Bates.

Wednesday 13th February 1918

Today we found Susan much improved. Her father had come home late last night, hopelessly drunk. She is sure that in such a state he will have broadcast her condition loudly throughout the village - no doubt expecting sympathy for having such a shameless daughter. He had left the house early this morning, refusing to speak to Susan. She is convinced that he will 'come round' as she puts it, but knowing Joe Bates stubbornness and belligerence of old I cannot be so sure.

Susan was delighted with our basket. Besides some good, nourishing food we had placed in it some materials for her to make clothes for the coming baby. Mother had sent along several small garments that she had made and Mary has made a shawl. I have a confession to make in that I had taken a warm woollen blanket which I had been knitting to send to France and gave it to Susan. Furthermore I intend to collect more such items together for I argue that the needs of the Bateses, with such mean bedclothes, are as strong as the claims of our soldiers who do at least get issued with supplies from the government. Doubtless if Father knew he would counter my argument but as he is in ignorance I will proceed with my resolve!

We tried once more to persuade Susan to contact Alfie's mother but she would not. She asked anxiously if I had yet received a letter from John and I confessed that I had not.

We passed a very tedious afternoon for Father was entertaining the Bishop (accompanied of course by Mrs. Farquharson). He has come to see about the church extension. Building work has started. It is an irony that Joe Bates has got work from Father in labouring to build part of a church he never frequents. Father, I notice, has no qualms of conscience about employing such a man to build the church. I am, though, grateful, for the steady work will keep Joe busy during the day and away from home and so from Susan. Father had warned me not to speak of anything controversial before the Bishop and I have to report that I was the ideal daughter - a model of modesty, rectitude and obedience. What an effort it cost me!

Once the Bishop had departed our dinner, and indeed our entire evening, was dominated by Father discussing the day's events. He is certain that Mrs. Farquharson has used her influence with the Bishop to make him well disposed towards himself. He cannot hide his admiration for the 'splendid' Mrs. Farquharson and I saw the efforts poor Mother made to prevent herself from speaking. She does not share Father's admiration!

I hope that I receive a letter soon from John. Father's newspaper beats the

patriotic drum more loudly than ever but from experience I know that such is the case when all is not well. I have a great sense of unease about the near future. I hope that it is merely the natural anxiety I feel about Susan and about the war. I could not bear for anything to happen to John.

Monday 25th February 1918

At last I have John's letter! The anxiety I have felt is not lessened by its arrival, for I do not think that John is his usual self. He tells me that the men are under great pressure, that the Germans are beginning to push forward. He also hints that some men are starting to question orders - they are not as tractable as they once were. Too many of their comrades have been killed, destroyed for no obvious reason. All the officers are under orders to do their utmost to boost morale and to be vigilant in pursuing and punishing cases of disobedience (however slight). With all the problems that John has I was sure that Susan Bates and Alfie Cooper would be far from his mind, but towards the end of his letter he writes that he will try to make enquiries about Alfie. He is not hopeful for he says that over the past few months so many have been killed or injured, or lost in other ways. (I can only presume that he means that they have deserted) that it is difficult to locate anyone in particular. About Susan he writes,

'I feel sadness and sorrow for Susan, but having a baby is not the end of the world. Please assure her that I will do my best out here to help to find Alfie. I hope that she is both strong and brave enough to face the inevitable condemnation of her peers. Perhaps Mrs. Cooper could be persuaded to help?' He goes on to say that as a captain he receives many letters each week requesting information about specific soldiers. Susan's case is by no means unique. He will, however, do what he can.

I am pleased that John is of the same mind as myself and am now more determined than ever to persuade Susan to turn to Mrs. Cooper. I was surprised to find how common Susan's problem is. When one is in the midst of adversity one thinks that one is alone - that few, if any, can be in such a dilemma. To hear that such circumstances are commonplace makes me feel that we are not quite so alone and that a solution will be found.

I sat for some time pondering John's letter. I could not identify exactly what aroused my anxiety. There is a tension behind the words that I do not like. This wretched war!

In the afternoon Father asked me what news there was from John. I reddened, not because I am ashamed of anything that John has written, but rather because

it is so novel to relay news to Father instead of him knowing it first! I told him, briefly, of some of the things that John had written.

"Poor show!" he said, shaking his head, "can't have the men losing heart y'know. We British haven't lost a war for hundreds of years; they should be told that. Can't have them letting the side down!"

And with that he strode off back to his study. I think that it is all too easy to judge others when we cannot possibly imagine what it must be like to be in that situation (and I am not thinking solely of the war).

I did not manage to visit Susan Bates today but Mary had gone, alone, this morning. Mr. Bates is no different - still sulky and sullen towards Susan. I wish that I was brave enough to talk to him! I have made a plan to write to Mrs. Cooper. I will get her address from Susan on the pretence of requiring further information about Alfie.

I was unable to write in reply to John this evening for I feel that I need a day or two to re-read his letter carefully. I do not wish to convey my unease to him.

Wednesday 27th February 1918

Susan Bates was correct in assuming that her father would tell all and sundry of her plight. Her 'shame' is now common knowledge and is gossiped about through the whole of the village. She has so far managed to hold her head high - long may it continue. Thank goodness that Father does not yet know. I cannot imagine how I will face the inquisition that must follow his discovery.

I had a long argument with Mrs. Farquharson in the sewing circle this afternoon. She was (as always) discussing the 'progress' of the war. I said that the poor soldiers must be losing heart after so long a time, for I surely would. Mrs. Farquharson pulled me up for my faintheartedness and said that it was as well that our officers had more stamina than I. Of course I opened my mouth again and retorted that it was a pity that more officers were not in the front line facing the reality of war rather than safely in the rear, manoeuvring troops as if they were tin soldiers, not flesh and blood. Perhaps if more officers had led from the front rather than the rear the war would be over by this time! Mrs. Farquharson regarded me stonily.

"I hope," she said, that you are not passing any criticism on the late Colonel?"

With this she affected to wipe a tear from her eye. I could take the woman's sham grief no longer and merely retorted,

"I was speaking in general, Mrs. Farquharson. For such a war to drag on for such a time; for so many to lose their lives is, I consider, a cause for shame, not

pride!" With that I packed up my things and left. As I went out I heard Mrs. Jameson reminding Mrs. Farquharson that she had still not received an apology for my behaviour of last May.

I waited all evening for the expected summons from Father, but it never came. I suppose that it will come in time, however I will not give way, for I do believe the war to be wrong; the officers to be wrong; the government to be wrong.

Saturday 2nd March 1918

It has happened: Father has heard about Susan Bates. He came back from the church this morning in a raging temper. Mr. Taylor, the verger, had seen fit to enlighten Father on the 'sinful goings-on' in the village. Father immediately sent for me and asked me what I knew about it all.

Thinking of my resolve earlier in the week I stood firm and told him the facts of the case. He was furious. He said that it was only to be expected that the 'lower orders' would behave in such a manner but that I have concealed this information from him is unforgivable. Where, he asked, was my notion of duty, of obedience? I looked steadily back at him. I then asked him what he would have done if he had known.

"That," he said, "is not the point. The fact of the matter is that you, Elizabeth, have proved to be an undutiful daughter and I am disappointed in you. I expect you to uphold certain standards, not to condone such sinfulness." With that he dismissed me, promising to talk to me at greater length on another occasion. He told me that he was going to be busy, as he had a sermon to re-write for tomorrow, "For be sure, Elizabeth, Susan Bates will not escape the wrath of the church in punishment for her actions!"

I lost no time in putting on my outdoor things, intending to go to Brabage in order to warn Susan to stay away from church tomorrow. As I went through the front door Father heard me and called out. He asked where I was going. I told him the truth, that I was going to Brabage to see Susan Bates.

"Oh, no, Miss Aubrey, none of that. You will stay here for the day. I have much for you to do." He bade me take off my outdoor things and set me to sorting out his books and papers which were once again in a muddle.

It was early evening before I escaped Father's vigilance. I managed to write a short note to Susan, briefly explaining the circumstances and advising her to stay at home in the morning. I gave the note to Edna and she promised to do her best to deliver it for me. Just then Father came in and, seeing me with my writing things, asked what I was doing. I said that I was just about to write to John. He

eyed me suspiciously and sat all evening watching me write my letter while pretending to read. When I had finished my writing and put my things away Father went to his study, announcing that he had to finish his sermon. (He looked meaningfully at me when he said this.) Mother, Mary and I were left alone and for the first time I had an opportunity to tell them what had happened. Mother was afraid, for if Father had been so critical of me what would he be to her? Mary wanted to rush off at once to 'beard him in his den' as she put it. I persuaded them to let things lie. Father did not suspect that they knew anything about Susan's situation. He was most welcome to visit all his wrath upon me, for I did not care a jot for his disapproval (and as I said it I knew it to be true!). Mother thought that I was being extremely heroic. Mary was uncomfortable but was easily persuaded to let things pass.

We parted for the night determined that, whatever happened, we three would do our utmost to help Susan. My letter to John, written under such surveillance, I tore up and re-wrote, which is why, as I finish my diary entry for the day, it is one-thirty in the morning. My final hope as I go to sleep is that Susan has received my note and may be spared the inevitable denunciation which Father has so obviously prepared!

Sunday 3rd March 1918

I had hoped for a dull, wet day, thinking that such weather would keep people from church and so save poor Susan's denunciation before a large congregation. My wish was not granted for it was a beautiful spring morning, the early sunshine making rainbows of the dew in spiders' webs. I was purposely late for breakfast as I did not wish to meet Father and I knew that this first Sunday in the month he goes to church early for the communion service. Mary, Mother and I ate a solemn breakfast, all trying not to speak of the subject that was foremost in our minds.

The walk to church was splendid. I only wish that I had been in an appropriate state of mind to appreciate the beauties of nature. The wind was chilly, but the sunshine brightened everything. The hedgerows were alive with the small birds fluttering and twittering, the voles squeaking and rustling; making their new homes to welcome their coming families. The fresh green of the new growth throws the pale primroses and the rich purple dog violets into stark contrast. What a hopeful time spring is! I wish that life was as straightforwards for humans as it is for the rest of nature; how I would glory in nest building and home-making. Voles and chaffinches are not engaged in war and so their lives are simple. It was the sort of morning that is greeted with a smile, making one glad to be alive. A

great pity it was that the great black cloud of Father's sermon loomed over the sun and threatened storm!

Once in church I looked about me (furtively, for Father criticises those who openly survey all around them). Mrs. Farquharson was smugly in place, wrapped in her warm, fur coat - for I noticed that once out of the sun and inside the church, the temperature was decidedly cold. The sunshine had brought out most of the village and I anxiously scanned the pews, hoping that my note had reached Susan in time to prevent her attendance.

She was there! She sat with head erect, a slight pink spot on each cheek. By her look I knew that she had received my note but had determined to face it out. She acknowledged my glance with an almost imperceptible nod. The service proceeded as always and we seated ourselves for the sermon. I felt a small hand creep into mine and knew that Mary was feeling as anxious as I. On the other side of me Mother pressed my elbow. We were all full of trepidation.

Father started in a normal manner, describing the twin paths of virtue and vice. He spoke of duty; of obedience to God's law and to the laws of society. He dwelled for some time on the latter, convincing us that to break the rules and laws of society was to make oneself an outcast from that society.

"Society cannot," he said, "harbour rule breakers; for if we were to condone those who contravene the rules then society would break down." There was more in the same vein - much more, and then he paused: he paused for so long that some of the congregation thought it a lucky day - that they were to have a short sermon. We three knew better and held our breath. Father picked up his prayerbook and took a step forward. He cast his voice low - dangerously low, and almost whispered,

"I have heard things this week that I could scarcely credit; I have learned that one of our number - one of our society - has broken these sacred rules. The person has sinned before God and before us. She (for the sinner is a woman -as was Eve full of sin so is this woman) she has done what should not be done outside marriage. She has put herself above the law of God. God has decreed that marriage is sacred and that there are certain - duties - that should be carried out within the bounds of matrimony. This person has set aside those rules, she has flouted God. She has put herself above God in saying that those rules do not matter; she will behave in a married way without the blessing of the sacrament. This present day Eve has tempted a man to sin with her. She now bears the burden of that sin, to her public shame."

Father's voice had remained low throughout most of this diatribe, but had

risen towards the end in thunderous invective. Many in the congregation knew the identity of this 'present day Eve' but stared studiously ahead. Mrs. Farquharson had folded her arms and drawn herself up. I believe that if she had not considered it disrespectful to 'tut-tut' in church then she would have been tutting away! I dared not glance sideways at Susan. Her head was still erect but her colour was higher and her eyes glazed. She was staring at Father with all the fascination a rabbit has in a snake. She was absolutely still. Father suddenly slammed his prayerbook down on the edge of the pulpit, breaking the silence that had fallen and jolting everyone out of their stupor. His voice rose until it boomed around the church.

"Susan Bates, you have dared to flout the law of God and of society. I call upon everyone here to do their duty by God and by society and cast her out, cut out the canker of sin from our midst, shun the devil Eve and all her works. You must learn that you cannot disobey with impunity. You cannot be undutiful and expect to remain part of the society you have shunned!"

The congregation sat in silence, embarrassed by Father's harshness. There had always been such things happening in villages like Brabage, and such a catastrophe was understood by most in these troubled, insecure times. I am sure that they would have preferred Father not to have dragged this 'sin' into the cold light of day. They were in a dilemma, for they would have to choose to either side with Father and the church and shun Susan, or they could stand by Susan and be seen to be shunning the church.

The silence was broken by a slight 'clop' as a prayerbook fell to the floor. All eyes turned towards the source of the noise. Susan had stood up. She stood ramrod stiff, straight and tall. She looked Father in the eye, said (loud enough for all to hear)

"I am only guilty of love. God is Love!"

She turned on her heel and strode down the aisle, her manner lending dignity to her rather ragged appearance. How I admired her for standing up to Father like that. What great courage!

The silence was broken by Mr. Taylor playing the first faltering organ notes of our final hymn, 'Fight The Good Fight'. It took some time for the whole congregation to join in the singing.

After church I did not stay behind but walked towards home. Though the sun was still as bright, the flowers in the hedgerows just as beautiful, buds swollen with spring promise, a shadow had fallen over my world. Father's words had had the effect of making something beautiful (the act of pure love between a man and

a woman) into something shameful, sinful and mean. The wrath of Father's God gave no quarter; any that transgressed against His Holy Word would be outcast, unforgiven for eternity. Was God really like this? What of the sinners at the crucifixion? I could not reconcile my own logic and feelings with Father's sermon. Was Father's sermon the word of God or was it the utterance of a bitter, harsh man? I wanted some time to think. My instincts were to go to Susan, to stand by her. My heart urged me to rush to the Bates's cottage. My head instructed me to think before I stepped in, for to go now would be to alienate Father, irrevocably and for ever.

I have stayed in my room all day, missing Sunday School and Evensong. I have pleaded a sick headache, which is not exactly a lie for the matter has gone round and round so much in my mind that my poor brain is quite addled. I can see no way out. If only I had not delayed in writing to Mrs. Cooper. She will have only just received my letter and will, no doubt, take some time to reply. Poor Susan needs friends more that ever at this time.

I had retired after writing that last but was aroused by a slight tap at my door. Mary came in. She too had been turning the matter over in her mind. She has strengthened my resolve and we have determined that tomorrow we will go to Susan, no matter what the opinion of Father and the village of Brabage. We have decided that if challenged, our defence will be that we are being true Christians in not casting out the 'Mary Magdalene' in our midst.

My final thought on the whole business is that we are cowards to require a defence before we take action but, be that as it may, at least we will stand by Susan.

I will relate all to John in my next letter; perhaps he will be able to make things clearer.

Monday 4th March 1918

True to our resolve, Mary and I went to Susan early in the afternoon. Father was at the church, supervising the building works and so was oblivious to our whereabouts. Our courage did not have to be tested.

The cottage was quiet, Joe Bates being absent and about his work (doubtless receiving the benefit of Father's moral wisdom) and the children at school or out at play. Susan looked exhausted. Her efforts of yesterday had quite worn her out and she was sitting before the kitchen fire, weeping sadly. She soon brightened and bustled about to fetch us some tea. She had seen few people that morning for no-one had come to the cottage. I was surprised, for, knowing as

I do that Susan takes in washing and that Monday is the day that it is sent to her, I had expected her to be busy. It transpired that most people in the village had heeded Father and not sent their washing (presumably to keep it clear of contamination!). The few people whom Susan had seen had looked hastily away rather than shun her openly. She did not know how she would bear the next few months.

Mary and I tried making some suggestions, but to no avail. We thought that perhaps it would be best for Susan to return to her aunt in Northwich but she would not hear of it. She was determined to stay and look after the children. We lapsed into a thoughtful silence that was broken by a commotion outside. Miller's trap had arrived from the station and a busy woman was getting herself and her packages down from the high seat. Susan stared through the tiny window and was open-mouthed with amazement. The small figure bustled up to the front door and rapped sharply on it using the handle of a very stout umbrella she carried.

"Mrs. Cooper!" exclaimed Susan, and her face flushed with pleasure as she rushed to the front door.

My wishes were granted, for surely here was the help and support that Susan sorely needed.

Mrs. Cooper stepped indoors and I confess that I liked her immediately. She had a pleasant, open, round face with a ready smile. The twinkle in her eyes disclosed a cheerful nature and the hearty embrace in which she enclosed Susan showed her to be a warm and loving person. Susan introduced us. Mrs. Cooper looked me straight in the eye and shook my hand firmly,

"You'm be the lady what wrote to me 'bout Susan. I'm 'onoured t'meet yer ma'am and thank yer, 'ere an' now, fer doin' the kindness o' tellin' me about me new granchile t'be!"

Susan said nothing and I hoped that this abrupt disclosure was not going to upset our friendship.

I had no time to wonder, for Mrs. Cooper was directing Mr. Miller in the matter of the disposition of boxes and parcels. She opened a capacious bag and paid him for his services, accompanying the action with the comment,

"An' try ter save up man. Get yerself a motor car, yer might live in the back o' beyond but there's no need ter be so far behind the times!"

With that she dismissed him and turned to us.

"Now, I could do wi' a nice cup o' tea. My poor ol ' bones be quite shook up after that ride from the station!"

In the next hour and a half Mrs. Cooper informed us fully of the events leading up to her arrival in Brabage. She had received my letter on Friday and had immediately determined to come along to be with Susan. Her family is all grown up and away from home (Alfie is the 'baby' of the family). From her home in Northwich she had gone to see her eldest married daughter in Crewe. Ruth (her daughter) had dissuaded her from setting off that day as it was already late. She added that if Brabage was typical of many small country villages in the area Susan would be having a bad time if her neighbours knew of the baby. Rather than pay a visit she had suggested that her mother brought Susan back to the family home in Northwich for there was plenty of room for her to stay. Mrs. Cooper explained about Susan's eight brothers and sisters. Ruth and Mrs. Cooper put their heads together. The outcome of their deliberations was that Mrs. Cooper had packed her boxes, shut up her house and come to stay with Susan until the latest in a long line of grandchildren was born,

"Fer if Alfie doan come back Susan, yer'll need someone, an' if he does, I can just as easy go back 'ome again. So, 'ere I am m'dear, come ter stay!"

Susan's dismay was clear and knowing the cramped conditions in the cottage I understood her consternation. Mrs. Cooper was aware of the hesitation,

"Now, m'dear, I can see 'as 'ow there's not much room in this cottage fer you an' yer father, eight littl'uns an' busybodyin' ol' me, so, I'll be grateful if yer'll fix me up with some decent lodgin's, near as possible!"

By the time we left the Bates's house Mrs. Cooper had been introduced to Mrs. Edwards, won over her sulkiness and stowed her baggage in the tiny back bedroom of Mrs. Edwards's cottage. It is in Mrs. Cooper's nature to compel all within her sphere to do her bidding, for she is such an amiable woman that to satisfy her is to please oneself. Mrs. Edwards became a devoted convert and far from shunning Susan, as she had before, she was herself bustling in and out of the cottage, excited as a mother hen arranging and re-arranging affairs. I could see that from now on Joe Bates would be given little scope to use his bullying ways in this household!

On the way home Mary and I chatted excitedly about the advent of Mrs. Cooper. She was exactly what was needed and her 'no nonsense' manner would soon sort out the village of Brabage!

"I wonder," said Mary, 'how she will get on with Father, for they are sure to meet fairly soon."

We lapsed into silence, each imagining that meeting. I was certain that not even our Father could best Mrs. Cooper.

Mother was as pleased as we were to hear of the arrival of Alfie's Mother. Father remained uninformed, for no-one wished to broach the subject of Susan Bates.

Mrs. Farquharson camc to spend the evening at the vicarage. Although Mother was extremely polite and hospitable and conversed affably, I can tell that she dislikes her intensely. Mary and I were absorbed in our work and so the good lady spent the evening chatting to Father. From what I overheard they were agreeing on the general decline in the morals of society since the onset of war. I forbore to interrupt them to challenge with the concept that war itself is an immoral thing!

I am grateful tonight that Susan has a firm ally to stand by her when she needs support. Now that I have met Mrs. Cooper, and found her such a likeable person, I hope even more fervently that Alfie is alive and safe somewhere, for he must be a very nice young man to have such a mother. However I suppose that there is little hope of that, for so many have been killed. I hope that I have word of John very soon. Goodnight my love. I am thinking of you.

Thursday 21st March 1918

Tonight I am so full of anxiety about John that I do not know what to do, where to turn. I have thought for some time that his letters betrayed a change in him, a difference that was more an impression than something specific. Today I have had my fears confirmed.

This morning I was surprised to hear that while I was out in Brabage a young man called at the vicarage. It was young Arthur Mayfield (Thomas, his brother is John's batman, and of course it was Arthur's unseen hand that delivered John's secret letters to the summerhouse until last Christmas.) He was clearly taken aback at not finding me at home, and he would leave no message but told Edna that he would call again in the afternoon, if that was convenient.

When Edna told me of the visit I could not imagine what Arthur wanted of me. I knew that it must be something important to make him come over from Framley and insist on seeing me - to the extent of making a second call. I tried not to think of the possibilities, but the more I tried to put the matter from my mind, the larger it loomed in the forefront of my thoughts.

I was watching from the window when I saw Arthur come up the drive. I opened the door to him myself and brought him immediately into the small sitting room and invited him to sit down. Mary was in the corner, working away at some sewing and I could see Arthur glancing nervously at her. He was extremely ill

at ease and I tried my best to make him relax. I had not been to Framley since the New Year and was interested to hear how my many acquaintances there were faring. Arthur answered my enquiries in low tones, very self-conscious and fingering his cap nervously. At last Mary stood up and announced that she must go to fetch some more work. Once she had left the room, all that Arthur had come to tell me came out in a headlong rush.

It transpired that Arthur had received a letter from Thomas by that morning's post. Over the past two months Thomas has commented on the bravery, the courage, the boldness of John. At times he has obviously been worried at the daring feats that John had accomplished, but of late he had conveyed a general sense of unease to his brother about John's behaviour. However, in this morning's letter he had described to Arthur some particular raid that John had led. The raid had been successful and 'Thank God' all the party had returned alive, though some were quite badly injured. What had disturbed Thomas was that John, in inspiring his men to overcome their reluctance to continue war, had become so bold as to be reckless. At times his bravery is almost foolhardy. Thomas had advised Arthur to come and see me, for he felt that as I was the only person John has left in the world, my influence may pull him back from the brink of whatever calamity must be looming. 'For no-one,' Thomas wrote, 'can survive that kind of risk over and over again. Disaster must surely come and Miss Aubrey may be able to hold sway where we cannot.'

Without a word I passed Thomas's letter back to Arthur. I sat in silence, thinking over what I had just read. Arthur was most uncomfortable and eventually stammered out,

"I 'ope Miss, that I ain't done no wrong in comin' 'ere. Thomas asked me see, an' if Thomas asks me ter do somethin', I will."

His regard for Thomas shone out from his bright, clear eyes. I hastily reassured him that he had done the right thing and that he had been duty-bound to come. I told him that I would have to think things over carefully, but that yes, I would do something. He was clearly relieved and asked if he might tell Thomas about his visit. I consented and then offered him some refreshment. He declined and said that he must leave for he had absented himself from work and must return as soon as he could.

When he had gone I went up to my attic and sat and thought. What Arthur had told me confirmed my own unease. But what was I to do? I turned the problem over and over in my mind but after more than an hour was no nearer a solution than when I had come up there!

At our evening meal I was obviously distracted and Father called me to attention on more than one occasion. I pleaded a 'sick headache' (how frequently I use that convenient excuse) and came early to bed. After more than an hour Mother came to me on the excuse that I may need something. She sat on my bed and held me in a close embrace.

"Come on Elizabeth, what is the matter? You are my daughter and I know you so well."

I told her all - of Arthur's visit, Thomas's letter and John's recklessness. She sat silently for a time and eventually said,

"It is obvious Elizabeth, it's as clear as crystal what you must do. You must write to John, in your usual way, not letting him suspect that anything is out of the ordinary. In that letter you must make much of how deeply you love him, and how great is your need of him. Write about your engagement and forthcoming marriage, your excitement at it all. Finally you must ask him to promise you something. You must ask him to promise that he will do his best to keep safe for you; not to take any unnecessary risks; to avoid danger as much as possible. Tell him that any injury to him would be injury to you and that without him your own life would not be worth living."

Of course, I have taken up Mother's suggestion and have tonight written the required letter. I have poured all my feelings, all my love, into that letter. I hope that Mother is right and that John heeds my words.

I am grateful for Arthur's visit and Thomas's warning, though I have been made very anxious by them. With Thomas watching over John I feel that he is not entirely alone. I am with John in spirit, and if my own love, my own anxiety can be made into a protective arm, then that arm will encircle him, will hold him and will restrain him from the headlong rush to 'glory'.

My final thought tonight is gratitude to Mother. She has shown herself as my true ally. I had not realised how intuitive she is, how great her grasp of my own affairs. I feel that in future I can turn to her as I never have before.

Sunday 24th March 1918

Until today Father had not met Mrs. Cooper. He had heard that she had come to Brabage and was lodging with Mrs. Edwards. I think that he has learned that she has gradually turned the tide of opinion in Susan's favour. Mary and I have visited Susan regularly and each time Mrs. Cooper has expressed a desire to meet Father

"I 'as things ter say ter that Reverend - beggin' yer pardon ladies, for I know 'e's yer father, but 'e never ought ter 'ave spoken out like that 'gainst Susan!"

We neither agreed nor refuted her words and were content to wait patiently until she would be able to 'say things'.

Father stood at the door of the church to welcome the congregation, as is his customary practice. He was about to close the doors and take his place in the pulpit when there was a great bustling at the gate. Three figures walked noisily up the path. By this time the entire congregation had turned to discover the cause of such clattering. What we saw amazed us all for, advancing arm in arm, were Mrs. Cooper and Joe Bates. I do not know whether Mrs. Cooper is a regular churchgoer, but Joe Bates has been in the church but a dozen times in his life (his own baptism, his marriage, the baptisms of his nine children, and of course poor Catherine's funeral). Father stood at the doors wearing his most forbidding expression, indicating by his look that a noisy entrance was out of place in Brabage Church. Mrs. Cooper and Joe took not a jot of notice. It was only then that I realised that the third figure, coming up behind the couple, was Susan. She looked a little pale but, as usual, held her head high.

The three figures stopped in the porch, squarely in front of Father. Mrs. Cooper dropped Joe's arm. Father greeted her with a rather gruff 'Good Morning. Just in time I see!' Mrs. Cooper calmly looked Father up and down, taking in his grim expression, his clerical robes and the polished shoes, just peeping under the edge of his cassock. She allowed her gaze to return to his face. All the members of the congregation held their breath, knowing that something momentous was about to take place.

"Good mornin' sir," said Mrs. Cooper, holding out her hand. Father managed to convey the air of touching something distasteful (rotting fish or a leprous limb) as he carefully shook Mrs. Cooper's hand. Mrs. Cooper continued in a booming voice which rang through the vault of the roof,

"My name is Mrs. Cooper, Hannah Cooper. I'm the mother of Alfie Cooper - who yer've never met, an' if it wasn't fer this cursed war I'd be the mother-in-law of Susan Bates - who yer 'ave met."

Father was, by this time, trying to quieten them and shepherd the group inside. Hannah Cooper would have none of it.

"Wait a minute, yer Reverence, I mayn't want ter come into your church. I've come 'ere today ter see what kind o' man, what kind o' parson it is that calls vengeance on a poor young girl that 'as done no more than foller the course o' nature - like people've bin doin' since the dawn o' time. She would 've bin decently married too if 'er young man, my son, 'adden 'a bin away fightin' fer the likes o' you, ter keep you snug an' safe in yer comfy country vicarage!"

As she paused for breath Father, whose face was blood red to the roots of his hair, tried to stutter an argument. I was amazed, for I have never seen Father at such a loss. Before he could utter a coherent sentence Mrs. Cooper went on,

"Now, yer Reverence, I think we'll step inside, Mr. Bates, Susan an' me. I'd like to 'ear yer preach, see what yer 'ave ter say fer yerself. And, yer Reverence, I want yer ter know that from now until the birth o' my granchile (Father looked greatly discomfited at the mention of something so immodest as childbirth) I'll be stayin' 'ere in Brabage an' I'll be keepin' and eye on you! Now, shall we go in?"

The congregation turned, as a body, trying to hide their amusement at the interlude. Father swept down the aisle and whispered a brief word in the ear of Mr. Taylor. Mrs. Cooper, Joe and Susan took their places in the church and the service began. The order was all wrong for we sang three hymns before Father got to his feet to speak a word. How Mrs. Cooper must have upset him! The sermon was a very modest affair, urging us on to greater efforts with our war work, beating the drum of patriotism and reminding us once more of the great and noble sacrifice being made in our name by the armies overseas. Mrs. Cooper sat throughout it all, her gimlet eyes fixed implacably on Father's face. Our final hymn was the rousing and martial, 'Stand Up, Stand Up For Jesus'. Father almost gabbled his closing blessing, so keen was he to finish the service!

As Father stood at the door to see out the departing worshippers, Mrs. Cooper made sure that she was the first in line. (How the woman appreciates the importance of an audience.) She took Father's hand and said, in her clear, loud voice,

"Not a bad sermon, yer Reverence. I've 'eard better but I've 'eard worse 'uns too. Now remember, no more o' this nonsense about our Susan. I've made friends in this village so I'll soon 'ear if yer've bin thumpin' yer bible again. Good mornin' sir!"

With that she exited triumphally, leaving Father to do his best to regain his countenance with the rest of the congregation.

Mary and I walked home from church, our excited conversation buzzing like a swarm of bees. To see Father so vanquished had diminished his tyranny in our eyes; for if Mrs. Cooper could prevail why should we not do so?

Back at the vicarage we greeted Mother who had remained at home through general indisposition. We could hardly wait to tell her our tale and gabbled it out before Father returned.

Over the meal table Father was grim. Mother made all the conversation and

Mary and I had to turn away frequently to hide our amusement as she asked questions about who had been in church. Father was uncommunicative and said,

"Mrs. Cooper was in church today Sarah, and she brought with her Susan Bates and her Father."

Mother expressed astonishment and, turning to Father asked,

"And what did you think of Mrs. Cooper, Lewis, for I believe that it is the first time that you have met her?"

"Yes, that is so. What a nasty, low, vulgar woman she is. She has no more idea how to behave in church than has a... a.. a donkey! I do not wish to talk further on the matter Sarah. I do not wish to introduce the vulgar lower classes to our dinner table. I am only thankful that Mrs. Farquharson is away at present and so was not in church to witness events. What she would have thought I cannot imagine! Now, the subject is closed."

We could say no more.

The remainder of the day was all anti-climax after what had passed in the morning. In Sunday School the children were bursting with what they had heard about the morning service. Out of public loyalty to Father I had to quieten them.

Evensong was uneventful. The church was more full than usual and I am sure that the news had passed around the village and many had come hoping for Mrs. Cooper's attendance. They were disappointed, but I could see that Father was relieved by her absence.

During the evening Father caught Mary and I laughing together once or twice. He criticised us sternly, reminding us that the Sabbath was a solemn day and not given for merriment. The more that we tried to stifle our amusement the worse it was. Eventually Father went to his study and we were able to laugh openly.

I have rarely enjoyed a Sunday as much as this one. It has done me a great deal of good to see that someone can get the better of Father. It gives me hope in my own affairs.

Wednesday 3rd April 1918

It has been almost six weeks since I had a letter from John and I have become seriously worried. I decided today to go over to Framley. I told Father that I was going to visit Mrs. Fraser's grave, a purpose he accepted without question. However my true purpose was to visit Arthur to see if he had received any news from Thomas.

I had never been to the Mayfields' house and I planned to ask directions in the village. The first person I stopped looked rather uncomfortable. The old man told me that he could give me directions to the Mayfields, but asked if I was sure that I wished to visit a house of sorrow at the moment.

"Sorrow, what sorrow?" I asked, but my heart misgave me for I think that I perceived something of the truth.

"They'm 'ad news today - a letter from France. Their son, Thomas, bin killed in the war!"

I must have gone white for the old man dropped his stick and rushed to my aid, sure that I was about to faint. I sat down on a low stone wall and clenched my fists so tightly that my nails dug deep into the palms, releasing a trickle of blood. The old man called out and the next I was aware was that a young woman was bathing my temples with a cool cloth.

"Yer didden ought ter tell 'er like that Mr. Lee, you'm doan know who she is!" said the young woman, telling off the old man as if he were a schoolboy. He was about to protest when I muttered,

"No, please, do not blame him, it was I who asked the way!"

The old man looked a little shamefaced and fussed about. I took some deep breaths and felt my face regain some of its colour.

"However," I continued, "I would ask again for directions, for it is now more urgent than ever that I go there."

When I was fully restored I stood up and went off, following the directions I had been given. My pace was slow for I was reluctant to arrive at the Mayfields' house.

Their cottage was one of a pair, and both were neat and clean. The gardens to the front were beginning to break into their fresh spring colours. I would have known the Mayfield house even without being told for the curtains were close drawn and an ominous silence rested over all. I opened the gate and, taking a deep breath, walked up to the front door. My knock was answered by a young girl who, I discovered later, was the daughter of a neighbour. I was ushered into the small kitchen and found the family gathered together. Arthur sat at the table with an older woman whom I presumed to be his mother. Two younger women were seated each side of the fire and an old man was standing, leaning one hand on a stick and the other on the back of Mrs. Mayfield's chair. Arthur introduced me, first to his mother, then to his grandfather and finally to his two sisters. All eyes were red-rimmed with crying and Mrs. Mayfield's face was puffed and swollen. By the time the introductions were over Mrs. Mayfield had realised exactly who

I was and her attitude of quiet welcome had changed to a bitter, angry expression. Her eyes flashed fire.

"And what do you want 'ere my fine lady? Ter find out if yer fine Captain be safe, I'll be bound!"

I could not speak, for the sparks flashing from her eyes, the aggression displayed by her tense stance, took away any words I might have uttered. She continued "Well, never fret yerself, 'e's safe, tho' my poor Tom be dead an' gone, blew ter bits, an' no doubt on account o' that Captain!"

Arthur interrupted her tirade.

"Now Mother, you doan know that. I'm sure Miss Aubrey..." His speech was cut off by Mrs. Mayfield,

"Doan you 'Now Mother' me young man! I tole Tom as 'e'd best not go ter war, tole 'im that 'e didden need ter foller 'is master ter France. An' you know, well as me Arthur, you know 'cos yer read Tom's letters out to us all - an' you talked to 'im when 'e wus 'ere , you know 'ow Tom would 'a' risked 'is life fer that master of 'is, rushin' out 'eadlong inter battle. Well, now 'e's done fer an' you Miss, doan you fret, yer man'll be bound ter be safe, officers allus is ain't they?"

There was nothing that I could say. I could ask no questions, I could offer no sympathy, so choked was I by her grief and so shocked at her onslaught. I turned and left the room, letting myself quietly out of the front door.

As I reached the edge of the village I heard running steps behind me. I turned and there was Arthur.

"I'm sorry Miss Aubrey."

"There is nothing for you to be sorry for Arthur," I replied, "it is I who should be sorry for intruding at such a time."

"No, Miss Aubrey, no. I'm sorry Mother spoke to you like that, she doan mean it. It's just that we're all upset on account o' Thomas's death yer see, we only 'ad the news this mornin'."

"Yes, Arthur, I realise that. I am so sorry, perhaps when your mother quietens a little you will be able to convey my sympathy to her? She blames John, Captain Fraser, for Thomas's death then does she?"

"Well, Miss, she mun 'ave someone or somethin' ter blame."

"And you Arthur, do you think that Captain Fraser was to blame?" Arthur could not, or would not, meet my eyes.

"We doan know any o' the facts, only that poor Thomas is dead. Pr'aps we'll 'ear later 'ow things was fer him. We doan know who was killed an' when, only

the letter said 'killed in action' so Mother's just supposin 'ow things was. You've 'ad no word then?"

"No, Arthur, I've had no word, not for weeks," I replied.

Wc talkcd for some time but he had no information to give me and I had nothing for him, save sympathy. He was clearly impatient to be back home and eventually I sent him off there, reminding him to pass on my sympathies when he deemed it appropriate to do so.

I had some time to wait before Mr. Bell met me (he is our grocer and had been going to Framley on business and so had brought me there and was to take me home) and I sat and thought. I could make nothing of the situation. I did not know if John was dead or alive; if alive, was he injured? I knew nothing of the circumstances in which Thomas had been killed, only that he was dead and that death had taken some life from his family. I mused on these matters for some time and was eventually roused by Mr. Bell's shout of greeting on his arrival. I had got quite cold waiting and was chilled further by the drive home. I was glad to get inside the vicarage, though the fire was low (Father decrees reduced coals once April arrives!). I claimed the excuse of cold to explain my pallor and my trembling, but I knew from the way Mother looked at me that she was aware that I had received a shock. She fussed about me and insisted that I went off to bed in order to stave off the cold. I was grateful to be alone and away from Father's probing questions.

During the evening Mother came to me several times but I have been unable to tell her about Thomas. 'Oh John, where are you? What has happened to you? Why do you not write to me? I feel so helpless lying here, unable to do anything but wait. I cannot even pray for you John, only hope so fervently that you are safe. If Thomas is dead then what has happened to you and the rest of the company?'

Tuesday 9th April 1918

Today I received a letter from France in an unfamiliar hand. My hands shook as I opened it and all that preserved my hope was that if John had been killed I would have been more likely to have received a telegram.

The letter is from a Doctor Courtenay, who is a doctor in one of the large field hospitals near Le Havre. He has written to me at John's request. John was taken to the hospital almost two weeks ago after being in the thick of the fighting. His company has been 'blown up and half shot to pieces'. John however had only sustained superficial physical wounds. The main effect of the bombardment has been mental. He is suffering from 'shell shock' and is half demented some of the

time and possessed by an uncontrollable trembling at others. He is unable to write but his constant anxiety is that I should hear that many of his company have been killed and think that he too has perished. The doctor has written in order to ease the pressure on his patient and to reassure me that, physically, John is safe, but mentally and emotionally he 'is in a poor state'.

I put the letter aside and wept. I do not know whether I was relieved at John's deliverance or grieved at his sorry condition. In my heart I know that whatever his mental injuries I can help to restore him to health. Shell shock is curable, death is final. Poor Mrs. Mayfield, she blames John, but from what is implied in Dr. Courtenay's letter I think that much of the company was destroyed.

When I had collected my thoughts I went and told Mother what had happened. She was very upset but managed to make some positive suggestions of things that I may ask Dr. Courtenay in my reply to his letter.

After talking with Mother I sat and wrote to the doctor, asking him whether John was to be kept in France or sent home; whether he was to remain in hospital or may be allowed home on leave. I asked for a realistic assessment of his chances of a full recovery. I also requested brief details of the action in which John had been involved. Finally I asked if there was anything that I could send, or anything that I could do, to assist John's recovery. I posted my letter and now feel that I can do nothing until I receive a reply.

During the afternoon Mrs. Farquharson called. She sailed into the house with an expression of sympathy written large across her face. It appeared that Mrs. Jameson had heard from Mrs. Mariot who had in turn heard from a friend in Framley that Thomas Mayfield had been killed in action.

"And I knew, Elizabeth, that he was John's servant so I thought to myself, 'You'd better go and see Elizabeth, make sure that Captain Fraser is safe, for where a batman has been killed an officer may also have fallen.' So, here I am."

While she pretended sympathy and concern I could see that her expression was insincere and her motives purely to upset and worry me. Thank goodness that I had this morning received Dr. Courtenay's letter.

When she had gone Mother and I discussed her visit. We agreed that her concern was pretence and that she had rather gloried in being (as she had supposed) the bearer of bad tidings. We dismissed her from our minds.

During the evening Father brought up the subject of Mrs. Farquharson. She had told him of her visit and her reasons for it. He praised her concern.

Mother and I exchanged a single glance which conveyed all our meaning. Father can see nothing beyond the woman's superficial bustling, how blind he is!

I was able to tell Father of the doctor's letter and he shook his head, and spoke solemnly,

"Poor Captain Fraser, shell shock is a dreadful thing Elizabeth. He may never fully recover but may remain as a ruin of a man for the rest of his life. You must not feel irrevocably tied to him. Breaking an engagement in such circumstances is no dishonour. In fact I was saying to Mrs. Farquharson ..."

"Father, I do not wish to hear what you were saying to Mrs. Farquharson. John and I will marry. Whatever wreck this war leaves I will still love him. Nothing, no injury, physical or mental, could prevent me from marrying John!" With that I said goodnight and went to bed.

I cannot understand Father. How can true love be washed away by any injury? John's condition makes me love him even more deeply. All that I wish for tonight is that he was here, where I could look after him and nurse him back to health.

Thursday 25th April 1918

Today I received another letter from Dr. Courtenay. He apologises for the delay in replying to me, and for the brevity of his letter, but explains that they are so busy in the hospital that there is little time for anything but their duties. He tells me that John has already been returned to Britain by hospital train and indeed that by now should be a patient in Craiglockhart Hospital, just outside Edinburgh. This hospital specialises in treating neurological conditions. He has every expectation that, given time and care, John will make a full recovery. He expects that after treatment at Craiglockhart he will be allowed some home leave before returning to the Front. Of course I would be permitted to visit him at Craiglockhart on application to the hospital.

I have never heard of Craiglockhart Hospital! I do, of course, know where Edinburgh is situated and so am sure that I will be able to discover the exact location of the hospital. I intend to visit John and so discussed the matter with Mother. She does not wish me to go alone but fears that she is unable to accompany me. She suggested that we should discuss the entire subject with Father. However when I told Father of my proposed visit he was adamant that I should not go. No amount of argument, pleading, persuasion, would make him relent. When I persisted he flashed angrily,

"Elizabeth, I have refused my consent. I now consider the matter to be closed!"

As I went on with my usual duties today I felt a determination grow within me, for I will go to Craiglockhart to see John. At this precise moment I am

unable to see how that will be accomplished but that I will go I am certain!

I had some good news today. When I visited Susan Bates Mrs. Cooper was with her, as is her custom. They were both a-flutter for they have had news of Alfie. Apparently he was involved in some heavy enemy action and was caught in a bomb blast that not only removed all his clothes and left his uniform shredded, but also blew out his memory. For almost two months he has lain injured in a hospital, neither he nor anyone else knowing his identity. He was eventually read a list of the names of all the soldiers known to have been in that sector when he had been injured. Eventually one group of names awakened his mind. The doctor took that to be his own company. This narrowed the field quite considerably. They were able to eliminate two or three names as they had positive identification of the dead. Finally they were left with a choice of three and with patience, and by obtaining descriptions from the central records office, they identified Alfie. He is now well enough restored to return to duty. He has himself written a short letter to his mother which was only today delivered (by her daughter, Ruth, who came specially to Brabage to bring it).

They are full of plans to write back to Alfie, tell him about Susan and the fact that he is to be a father, and to make arrangements for a wedding. They are overjoyed. I can see only one black cloud and that is that I expect that Father will be too stiff-necked to marry them in Brabage Church. I mentioned the fact to Mrs. Cooper but she would have no hurdles placed in her way. She says that if Father will not marry them then she will sort things out so that they may be married in Northwich. They asked after 'Captain Fraser' and I was able to tell them that he was in Craiglockhart Hospital. Neither of them had ever heard the name before.

I am pleased that Susan's story would appear to be reaching a happy conclusion. Perhaps it augurs likewise for my own!

Saturday 27th April 1918

Father has heard the news of Alfie Cooper and has surprised us all by welcoming the expected marriage. Perhaps Mrs. Cooper has more influence than I credited. Oh that I had a Mrs. Cooper to advocate my case! I miss my staunch ally Mrs. Fraser so very dreadfully!

Today I managed to find out from Mrs. Farquharson the exact location of Craiglockhart. She likes to be seen to know everything about the army and its institutions, so when I asked her about the hospital, telling her that John was to spend some time there, she was only too delighted to go to great lengths to tell me

all that she knew. I told her that I required the exact address in order that I may write to John. (I fear that it will be a considerable time before he is fit enough to write to me.)

I have written a careful letter to John (for I do not know if he is able to read it for himself or must have someone to read it to him) telling him that I have heard from Dr. Courtenay and know his condition. I have told him that I intend to visit him as soon as I am able to do so. I enclosed a letter to the matron of Craiglockhart requesting information about visiting hours and asking her if she would be kind enough to recommend some local lodgings that I may take for a week or two. Of course this has all been done in secret for I do not wish Father to know of my determination. Now all that I need to do is to wait for matron's reply and find out which train I must take to get to Scotland!

I had time this afternoon to call on Susan. What a change there has been in that household since the advent of Mrs. Cooper. Joe Bates is seldom drunk. He does go to the 'Swan' with his companions, but only once or twice a week, and when there drinks only moderately. Not only does he look much better for the new life, but the family is thriving on his improved temper (and the increase in their finances!). He seems to have a great respect for, if not fear of, Mrs. Cooper and is happy to carry out her every whim in the most cheerful way imaginable. It may well be that there is more than one wedding in that household before too long! When I hinted the same to Mrs. Edwards she nodded her head in agreement and said that it was not only her but half of Brabage that had commented on the improvement that Mrs. Cooper had made in Joe Bates. The gossips buzz with the notion that a marriage is imminent, in spite of the difference in their ages.

During this evening Father commented that Mrs. Farquharson had told him about my enquiries concerning Craiglockhart. He was initially suspicious but was eventually content to accept my explanation. He told me that when I write I am to send John his best wishes for his recovery. He then spoiled all his concern by going on at some length, advising me how I was best to conduct my correspondence.

"You must bear in mind Elizabeth, John will be much changed. You should write in such a way that his expectations for the continuation of your engagement are not upheld."

I told Father that my opinion had not changed since I spoke last on the subject. Father frowned and was going to add more but, thankfully, Mother changed the subject.

I have though much about what Father has said, and about what Dr. Courtenay

wrote concerning the shell shock. Indeed, everyone who has heard of John's injuries tells me to expect him to be very different. I find, however, that I cannot believe that my own dear John will be so much changed!

Tuesday 30th April 1918

Today I asked, and was granted, Father's permission to go to Framley to visit Mrs. Fraser's grave once more. Mr. Preston, the joiner, was to drive over to collect some special wood from there and he would take me and bring me home again. I did as I had promised and visited Mrs. Fraser's grave, but only briefly. My main business was at the station where I discovered the time of the train I must catch to get to Scotland. I have found that if I leave early in the morning I may change trains at Crewe and be in Scotland by the evening. I have enough of my own money to pay for the ticket and my lodgings.

I had hoped to avoid any sight of the Mayfields for I do not wish Mrs. Mayfield's old wound to be re-opened. I did however see Arthur and he crossed the street in order to speak to me. He told me that the family has learned a little more about the circumstances surrounding Thomas's death. The Colonel of the regiment had written a very kind letter to Mrs. Mayfield, telling her that her son had died bravely in battle, doing his duty alongside his companions. He was a brave man and a good soldier and had given his life for his country. Many of his comrades had perished in the same battle and Colonel Tremling urged Mrs. Mayfield and her family to remember Thomas's name with honour. When she read the letter Mrs. Mayfield first cast it aside, saying that the Colonel 'did not know Thomas from Adam so how could he write like that about him?' Later, Arthur noticed that she had picked up the letter and put it safely away. The shock of Thomas's death had still not left them and Mrs. Mayfield, who was once an energetic woman, was now quiet and lethargic. Nothing would rouse her, as Arthur put it, 'All the heart has been knocked out of her'. The only thing that animated her at all was when Arthur spoke of his imminent departure to war. (He would be eighteen years old soon and so would be conscripted.) Mrs. Mayfield ranted and raved that he was not to go into the army,

"So, Miss Aubrey, I doan speak of it often, for, as yer know, I mun go ter war! What Mother'll be like when I go I doan know. P'raps my sisters will 'elp."

He asked about John and I told him the little I knew.

"So, 'e come out of it then! I'm glad fer your sake Miss, but I'd best not tell Mother, you understand?"

We parted and as I waited for Mr. Preston I reflected once again on the waste

that war represented. Nearly four years now and almost every young man had been snatched from his family as soon as he reached the age of eighteen to go to feed the great machine of war. So many had been chewed up and spat out by that machine; so many families had lost their sons; before long a whole generation would be wiped out.

My sad thoughts were interrupted by the arrival of Mr. Preston and I was glad of it. All the way home Mr. Preston chattered on about friends and acquaintances in Framley and so the journey passed quickly enough.

Once at home I immediately set about laying my plans and so when Father asked how I had got on in Framley I told him that Mrs. Fraser's grave was going to need a little more attention, and also that several of my acquaintances from Framley had asked me to call. Consequently I intended that one day next week I would go over to Framley early in the morning and get all my duties done in one day. To my consternation Father offered to drive me there but I said that I would most likely go on Wednesday (the day I know Father usually spends in the school) and that I could easily hire Mr. Miller to take me.

I have started to pack up a travelling bag and I have decided that I will tell Mother and Mary nothing for it will be better when they are questioned by Father that they are innocent. Instead I will write a letter and send it back to Father explaining what I have done. The letter will not be opened until he returns in the late afternoon (for after school he usually stops by the church to inspect the building works) and so I will have a full day's start on any pursuit Father may institute.

Perhaps what I am doing is disobedient and possibly undutiful, but I consider that my main loyalty now lies with John and I must go to see him and help him all I can.

Friday 3rd May 1918

I received a letter today from Craiglockhart. At first I thought that a companion was writing on John's behalf, but when I opened the letter I discovered that it was from Matron. I had not expected a reply so soon. She has kindly enclosed the name and address of a local 'respectable' lady who frequently has the relatives of officers staying with her when they visit the hospital. I am afraid that there is no time to write ahead and receive a reply, so I must trust to luck and arrive on Mrs. MacRae's doorstep hoping that there is a place for me! Matron informs me that John is 'as well as can be expected' and warns me that he is in a very poor state of health. He is too confused at the moment to write to

me himself, or even to make the effort to compose a letter to dictate to another. She is sure though that a visit by me will help enormously. She asks that when I come I go to see her first and she will explain all the visiting arrangements to me.

My hardest task now is to behave in a normal manner so that no-one will have their suspicions aroused about me. I tried so hard at this during the day that more than once I have found Father looking wonderingly at me. Tonight I have put all my old diaries, John's letters and other tokens into a tin box. I then placed this high up in the attic chimney. My current diary, and a photograph of John, goes with me but I dare not take the risk of anything being found. I read some of my old diaries and several of John's letters as I was packing them up. How grown up I feel to the girl of two years ago when I had not even been to an adult party, and of course neither had I met John! How I stood in awe of Father and never would have dared to defy him.

I have hidden my travelling bag and there is nothing remaining to be done until I go away next Wednesday. I am very tempted to tell Mother and Mary of my plan but feel it unwise to do so, for Mother may well try to dissuade me for my own safety (there can be some risk, I suppose, in a young woman travelling alone in these days) and Mary, I am sure would want to share my adventure and come with me. This, however, is something that I must take on my own shoulders and do alone!

I am sure that I will be unable to sleep any night until I am on my way. I am convinced that it is only my presence that will restore John to full health and so I feel justified in my actions.

Wednesday 8th May 1918

I am in Scotland. I am lodged in the house of the redoubtable Mrs. MacRae. My journey was long and wearisome and so I will write my diary properly tomorrow. In the morning I go to Craiglockhart Hospital and to John!

Thursday 9th May 1918

I have seen John and, oh God, what a change! He is a broken man and I cannot believe that he is the strong young man who returned to France in January. For his sake I have today remained quiet and calm, trying to appear unruffled by his altered state. Tonight, in the loneliness of my room in Mrs. MacRae's house, I have wept all the tears of Niobe. I think that Rachel weeping for her children could not have wept as I have tonight. However, now it is over and for John's

sake as well as my own I must don my brave mask and face the next few days. First the account of yesterday that I was too tired to record last night.

As arranged Mr. Miller called for me at seven thirty in the morning. I had hidden my travelling bag behind the summerhouse and if Mr. Miller thought it odd that I had him stop so that I could collect it, then he said nothing. I had imagined all sorts of reasons to excuse my behaviour, but as he was silent I offered none of them.

When we reached Framley I told him that he must leave me near the Mayfields' house. He assumed, as I had intended, that I was to visit there, but as the house is close to the station it suited my purpose well. Mr. Miller asked what time he would collect me. I informed him that I had arranged that someone else would take me home. This he accepted willingly enough and I paid him. As soon as the trap was out of sight I hurried to the station, pausing only to post my letter to Father. The letter informed him that I was going to Scotland and that I was determined to see John. I wrote that no-one else knew, of my escapade and assured him that I had made all the necessary arrangements and would be safe. I knew that the letter would be delivered that afternoon and that by the time Father read it I would be safe in Scotland.

I was soon in Crewe and, never having travelled alone, was at first rather bewildered by the hustle and bustle of the large, busy railway station. I used the services of a porter who soon put me on the right train. I put threepence in his hand at which he looked so disgusted that I pretended that I had mistaken the coin and hastily substituted a shilling. I am afraid that our modest country ways will not do in the town! I was amazed to see so many women working on the railways. In our little backwater of Brabage we are, of course, aware that women do all men's jobs now that such numbers have been conscripted, but I had not yet seen it with my own eyes.

I feel a fool - a sheltered, protected, uneducated idiot! To think that Father has managed to keep us away from all this. I simply did not realise that the whole world has changed. Clearly it would be quite easy, and doubtless quite respectable, for me to do some sort of job!

We were soon steaming our way north. I was glad that the day was bright and clear for I could see far and wide from the carriage window. I was alone in the carriage and I had taken the precaution of placing Mrs. Fraser's ring on my wedding finger so that no-one should think that a young, unmarried girl was travelling alone.

At each station we pulled into some people left the train and others joined it.

There were several soldiers on the train, obviously going home on leave. By early afternoon we had arrived in York and there were so many to join the train that I knew that I could not be alone for much longer. The door to the carriage slid open and two young girls looked in.

"Mind if we come in here?" one said.

"Of course not!" I replied, relieved to have such company.

They too were bound for Edinburgh. They were both nurses in France and were coming home for a short leave. The remainder of the journey to Edinburgh flashed by for I was enthralled by their conversation and asked them many questions about France and their work there. Oh how bitter I felt against Father who had never allowed me to do such useful work as they. Jean Smith and Mairi MacLeod were, in their turn, interested in me. I cannot believe it now but I found myself telling them the truth - all about John and about Father's refusal to let me go to Craiglockhart. I told them of my carefully planned flight. They regarded each other for a moment and then Jean reached out and clapped me heartily on the shoulder.

"Well done Elizabeth! What a pity it is that your strength has been wasted all these years. We desperately need people like you in France!" They told me the little they knew about Craiglockhart and then took some time and trouble to prepare me for the likely state of John. They had seen so many young officers in his condition that his symptoms were familiar to them.

Soon we were pulling into Edinburgh. Jean wrote her address on a small card and pressed it on me.

"If ye need any help Elizabeth, just get in touch and we'll do all that we can!'

With that they were gone, eager to commence their leave, and I was left to fight through the crowds and hope that I could find my way to Mrs. MacRae's house.

I took a taxi and in-less than half an hour Mrs. MacRae herself opened the door to me. I explained that the matron at Craiglockhart had given me her name as a reputable housekeeper who could perhaps give me somewhere to stay while I visited a patient at the hospital. She did not keep me on the doorstep, but once inside she wished to know who I was, where I had come from, who I was to visit, whether I was married - all sorts of questions. I was tired out by my journey (it was by then ten o'clock at night!) and so I merely handed over Matron's letter. This proved a magical passport and, having read it, she made me most welcome, fussing about to have the maid bring me tea and something to eat. She then showed me to my room and ensured that I was comfortable. Breakfast would be served at eight o'clock sharp, she said as she closed the door on me.

After writing the few lines in my diary recording my arrival it was all that I could do to remove my clothes and fall into bed. It was only as I was going to sleep that I realised that by then the inmates of Brabage Vicarage would know of my journey. My penultimate thought before sleep claimed me was to wonder about the reaction of Mary and Mother. My final thought was for John and the certain knowledge that the next day I would see him.

* * * * * * *

I slept heavily and, unusually for me, it was after seven when I awoke. I hastened down to breakfast. I was the only guest in Mrs. MacRae's house and so she kept me company over my meal. It turns out that the matron at Craiglockhart is her sister and so she was able to tell me much about the hospital. By the time that she had finished I confess that I was afraid of what I would see there. Mrs.- MacRae arranged a taxi and by ten o'clock I was stepping out of it to go through the doors of Craiglockhart and to see John!

I soon found the Matron's office but she was not in it. A Miss MacLeish was sitting in another office, almost submerged by a tide of papers. I knocked at the open door and the clerical Canute invited me inside. She had a high pitched voice and what I presume to be a 'refined' Scots accent. She spoke quickly and I had to concentrate carefully to follow her meaning. Matron would be about her rounds at the present time and would be back in approximately half an hour, she told me. In the meantime I was welcome to take a seat. Please excuse her if she did not stop for the hospital was so in demand that she had huge quantities of paper to deal with every day. As she spoke a great sheaf of papers fell to the floor and scattered. Instinctively I rushed forward to help and was pulled up sharply,

"Oh no Miss, please leave them. They are highly confidential and no eyes but mine and Matron's see what the doctors write. Also they have to go in a particular order y'see, so we cannae be too careful can we?"

I halted in my tracks as she bent and scooped up the precious papers and stuffed them back (no doubt in her very particular order) among the others, littering her desk. I sat back in my seat and watched as she continued with her work.

At the end of half an hour my confidence in the administrative system had sunk exceedingly low. Miss MacLeish seemed to deal cavalierly with her papers, boldly sorting, stacking, filing or discarding with great élan. To me everything looked muddled. I only hoped that, for the sake of the patients, Miss MacLeish could make sense of her apparently idiosyncratic system.

I heard quiet, authoritarian steps approach and I stood: Matron had returned. Miss MacLeish introduced me and Matron showed me into her office. She told me a little about the hospital, warning me that Craiglockhart was quite unlike any other hospital due to the nature of the injuries of its patients. She warned me that John was in a large ward and that while his appearance would be likely to shock me, I must also bear in mind that there were others in the ward to whom my reaction may cause upset. For the sake of her patients I must try to be strong and to remain calm at all times. If I became seriously alarmed than I must call a member of staff immediately. She then took me on a short tour of the hospital and I saw that she observed me closely when we came into contact with any of the patients. The dayroom was large and Matron told me that on good days many of the patients I could see sitting about in here would be outside, sitting or walking in the grounds, 'For we have beautiful gardens Miss Aubrey, which we take full advantage of when the weather allows us so to do.' I looked out of one of the large windows in the dayroom. The mist that had hung low that morning had turned into a steady drizzle which was pressing itself, claustrophobically against the glass.

As we toured the hospital my mood became as gloomy as the weather. There were so many young officers in there, some were obviously injured and walked with the aid of sticks or crutches. Others had arms in slings or dressing on hands, eyes or face. All though shared a common injury - their eyes were tense and they twitched visibly; they were nervous and jumped at the slightest noise; they could not sit still but were continually moving about restlessly. If these were the patients on the way to recovery then how was I going to find my poor John?

At last we paused before the double doors of a ward and Matron turned to me.

"I have been watching you closely Miss Aubrey. I think that you know what to expect and you certainly look to be a young woman strong enough to take what will greet you here. It is unusual to permit visitors out of the normal visiting hours, but I feel that your situation, the distance you have travelled, to be particular. Now, remember, do not show any outward signs of shock, horror or even sorrow; such feelings set the men back several weeks. Deep breath now dear and in we go!"

She suited her actions to her words and threw aside the double doors.

I had braced myself for what was to follow. Down each side of the long ward was a row of beds. Pyjama'd bodies tossed about, flung up their arms, cried out or lay stone still and grey in each bed. They all, every one of them, looked old and shrunken. I could not believe that before me lay the flower of their generation.

Our pause was only momentary and Matron propelled me down the central aisle between the two rows of hellish beds. I tried not to look to each side but the moans or screams, shouts and jerky movements, continually drew my eyes. Matron stopped at the foot of a bed.

"Now Captain Fraser, how are ye today? We've got a visitor for ye. Sit up now and try to look tidy."

My eyes had been on the lump made by feet under the bedclothes. Breathing steadily to still the anxious thump of my heart I allowed my gaze to travel up long legs, over an inert body. Matron bustled to the side of the bed and drew back the covers. The man in the bed raised his head and sat up. I wanted to scream out, to laugh, to shout, 'No, Matron, you've made a mistake, this is not Captain Fraser!' such a stranger was he. The stranger sat up; his tortured eyes met mine.

'L-L-L-Lizzie!" he stammered, "W-W-What are y-y-you d-d-doing here?" He held out his arms and before I knew it I was in his embrace. Matron tactfully withdrew.

Sitting on the low chair next to the bed I was able to see what ruin war had wrought. John was almost totally grey. The numerous small cuts on his face were still in the process of healing and his forehead and cheekbones betrayed the sallow yellowness of deep bruising just beginning to fade. One hand was bandaged heavily. Worse by far was the constant trembling. He could not hold himself still and when the doors at the end of the ward closed to suddenly with a low 'clap', he jumped almost out of his skin. I wanted to hold him in my arms and cradle him gently. I could not bear the haunted expression in his eyes, his inability to concentrate on anything for very long, his sudden lapses into total silence. When he did speak he would lose his train of thought part way through a sentence and his words would fade.

I told him that I had come without Father's permission; that I intended to stay for a while and that I would care for him on his discharge. He seemed oblivious to much of what I was saying and was content to lie back and hold my hand. On several occasions he fell into a troubled sleep, still clutching my hand fiercely. After some minutes of such sleep he would start up with an alarmed yell only to look dazedly about him and settle back again. Once he awoke and stared at me, his expression one of puzzlement,

"L-L-L-Lizzie, w-w-w-what on earth are y-y-y-you d-d-doing h-h-here?" he muttered before lapsing back into sleep. He had clearly not recalled any of the past half hour!

While John was asleep a young nurse came down the ward and spoke to me.

"Please miss, Matron has sent a message to say that she would like to see you."

I assumed that to be the signal that my visit was over and I loosed my hand from John's iron grip. He stirred and called out some indistinct words but did not waken.

The silence of Matron's office seemed worlds away from the noise and bustle of the wards. Matron did indeed consider my visit to have been of long enough duration. She asked my opinion of John's condition and I could not help but betray my sadness.

"They are all like that to start with my dear. In another few weeks you simply won't believe the recovery he will have made. Dr. Rivers is one of the finest specialists in the world. We enjoy a high success rate here. At the moment I feel that it is important for Captain Fraser to see you regularly. I understand that he has no close family at all?"

I confirmed the fact, briefly explaining the circumstances.

"Then it is more important than ever for you to visit him. We have found that one of the best aids to recovery is the patient's own determination to get well; they need a goal. I think that your presence, your urging, is exactly what is needed to stimulate Captain Fraser's determination. He has had such a bad time that at the moment he sees little point in recovery."

I asked what she knew of the circumstances of John's injury. She could tell me very little. He had been involved in heavy enemy action and as always had led his men forward. The bombardment had been dreadful and many of his men had fallen. No more was known and it was some time later that John was found wandering about in No-Man's Land, the body of his batman slung across his shoulders. His face was bruised and bleeding. His blood, and the blood of his dead companion had mingled and had run down and drenched his uniform. This fact had at first made his rescuers consider his injuries to be worse than they were. His right hand was badly torn and his mind was quite gone. He was raving; giving orders to imaginary troops which only his poor demented mind could see to his rear. They relieved him of his dead burden and he was taken off to a field hospital. He lay for some days ranting and raving, throwing himself about, re-living the battle. His brain had clearly been damaged and they were afraid to move him. Eventually he settled down somewhat and realising that his injuries were mental and too severe to be treated in France, they had sent him to Craiglockhart.

By the end of Matron's account, though my heart was torn and bleeding, I would not give way to tears. I had a shrewd idea that she had related these harsh details in order to test my mettle. If I failed then my visits to John may be denied.

“Thank you for telling me this Matron,” I said, “When may I come again?” She regarded me steadily.

“I think, Miss Aubrey, that you could make another visit later today. I think that for the time being we shall see how things go shall we, see what progress Captain Fraser makes?”

“Thank you Matron, I think that is all we can do. I will see you later today.” With that I left her office and the hospital.

I needed to think and so I spent some time walking about and considering all that had passed. That John needed me was obvious, a fact that Matron had herself admitted. I could not reconcile the wreck of a man I had just left with my own John. Eventually I thought of the family at Brabage and decided that it was my duty to send word to them. I sent off a telegram assuring them that I was safe and comfortably lodged. I added that John was most seriously ill and would need my presence for some time to come. That duty completed I returned to Mrs. MacRae's house.

On my later visit, John opened his eyes.

“Th-Th-There y-y-you are L-L-Lizzie! W-W-Where d-d-did y-y-you g-g-go t-t-to? W-W-When I w-w-woke up I th-th-thought I - h-h-had d-d-d-dreamt you b-b-but the n-n-nurses t-t-told me that y-y-you r-r-really had b-b-been here!”

I felt immediately better at these words for it demonstrated that he remembered my visit of the morning. Once more he lapsed into periods of disturbed sleep and again his sentences were disjointed. However I felt more positive when I left him, certain that he would recover.

Back at Mrs. MacRae's house I ate my evening meal and retired almost at once. I did not wish to face her probing questions and I was still very tired from my journey. In my room I sat and brought my diary up to date. As I look back over what I have written I feel a conviction that John <u>will</u> recover, he will find his right mind again. Somewhere under the shattered exterior of that stranger is my own John. I know that my presence here will help; we will together re-discover the old John. I think of Father’s words, voicing the likelihood of breaking our engagement. Even if I did not love John as I do, human compassion alone would make me continue with it. I think that if anything his condition makes me love him more, not less.

Goodnight John. Poor broken man that you are, I am glad that you are safe in hospital and such a short way away from me. You <u>will</u> get well, I promise you as I promise myself.

Friday 10th May 1918

I will write the events of today in the order in which they happened. After breakfast I went along to the hospital. Once again I met Matron but she had little to say to me except to remind me to ensure that I did not tire John. She proposed that I should spend an hour in the morning, an hour in the afternoon and an hour in the early evening with him. Though I would have preferred to stay all day at the hospital I readily consented to this most generous arrangement. She asked if I would go along to her office after my morning visit.

John was much the same as yesterday. He lapsed in and out of consciousness but trembled continuously, whether awake or asleep. When asleep he called and shouted. I was able to comprehend a few isolated words; I heard him call Thomas's name and shout orders to his men. I heard him tell them to 'Stand to' and 'fight to the last man'. Later I thought that I heard him call Charles's name but I may have been mistaken. Each time he awoke I was there at his bedside. Once or twice I think that he was startled by my presence, but by the time that I was due to leave I think that he had grown accustomed to it. He stuttered and his sentences were still disjointed, and I was distressed to see that at times the trembling was so great that he could not control himself at all. He was awake when I left him and seemed to understand that I was going but that I would return later in the day.

Matron was waiting for me and welcomed me most kindly. She had a proposition to place before me. She explained to me that most of the officers are far from home and have few, if any, visitors. Those who are very ill, like John, do not really feel the loss, but those who are on their way to recovery have the need for company - especially that of people unconnected to the staff of the hospital. Once she had recognised this need, Matron had enlisted the aid of a few of the local ladies. Under the leadership of Mrs. Scott the ladies organised small social events for the patients. This helped the men gain confidence and greatly hastened their recovery.

"So, Miss Aubrey, what I would like to propose to you is that if you intend to stay for some weeks (as you have already indicated to me) I hoped that I could prevail upon you to see Mrs. Scott and perhaps lend a hand in that direction?"

I required no time for consideration, for to be involved so with the hospital would surely allow me more opportunity to see John. I readily assented and Matron promised to make the necessary introductions as soon as possible.

When I returned to Craiglockhart in the afternoon the sun had come out and a number of patients were sitting in the dayroom. They called out a welcome to

me and shyly I returned their greeting. The fact that I felt that I already belonged to the hospital made my step light as I entered John's ward. He was awake and my optimistic mood was instantly banished when I saw his confused manner and his obvious struggle to recall why I was there. I would not let him see my dismay but immediately took his hand, sat down and began to talk of my morning visit. I talked of all the familiar things I could bring to mind, prattling on and on. John was quiet and when I looked at him, thinking that he had fallen asleep, he looked up at me and stammered out,

"L-L-L-Lizzie, you are w-w-w-w-wonderful I 1-1-love you s-s-so much my d-d-d-darling!"

He tried to pull me close to embrace me but there was no strength in his arms. I held him and we sat quietly.

For once everything in the ward was peaceful; the afternoon was warm and the window open slightly. It was so quiet that I could hear the occasional burst of birdsong. Suddenly there was a commotion from the end of the ward, raised voices, rapid steps, banging doors. The patients in the ward were instantly disturbed and began to call out, shout and tremble. The doors flew open and a familiar voice said,

"I will find my daughter. I know that she is here!" Father stood between the open doors and looked down the ward, straight at me. I rose from my place. Father strode between the beds, not caring about the disruption he caused. I took a step towards him. I have rarely seen such anger contorting any face, not even his. I held out my hand and was so icily calm that I surprised myself,

"Father! I am sorry but we cannot speak here for we are disturbing John, disturbing everyone."

"John?" Father looked around in bewilderment, "John? Where is he?" I pointed to the figure, huddled in the bed. Father's face fell, he shook his head in disbelief. "John, I did not recognise him. This, this, is John?" John opened his eyes as Father stepped up to the bed.

I have never seen such a change come over anyone as that which came over Father in those few minutes. He came in so aggressively, ready to drag me out should that be necessary, yet when he saw John the sharpness of his shock pricked the inflated bubble of his anger. He was instantly quiet and subdued.

The nurses had seen that Father had quietened and they went about their business. Matron stood alone.

"Mr. Aubrey, Reverend Aubrey, I do not think it advisable that Captain Fraser be so upset. May I suggest that you and Miss Aubrey talk outside."

"Of course Matron." Father was icily polite. He turned to John. "Sorry to see you like this, John. You'll be better soon old chap." He attempted heartiness as he added, "Buck up, we can't win this war without you, you know!" and with that he turned, took my arm in his and we walked together down the ward. Father did not deign to explain himself to anyone, not even Matron. Outside he was still angry with me but I had witnessed his shock, his compassion, and I knew it to be genuine.

Back at my lodgings I introduced Father to Mrs. MacRae and I could see that while he approved her strict correctness she looked admiringly at him, showing great respect for his clerical collar. Eventually Father conceded that we need not hurry back to Brabage immediately. He is to spend the weekend here and will return with me on Monday. I did not inform him that I have no intention of returning south on Monday! He has sent a telegram to the Reverend Spencer to arrange Sunday's service and after a splendid dinner cooked by Mrs. MacRae we spent the evening together.

Mother and Mary had been most upset by my departure. As I had guessed Mother was anxious for my safety but Mary actually had the courage to tell Father that she would have accompanied me had I given her the opportunity to do so! Father was furious that I had defied him and repeatedly listed my sins; the wicked, underhand way in which I had laid my plans; the wilfulness I had displayed; the disobedience to his authority. I was in no mood to listen, for I knew that I had been right to come.

I told Father that John had improved slightly since my arrival and that Matron thought that my presence would be of great benefit to him. I told Father of the suggestion made by Matron for my visiting other patients. At Father's frown of disapproval I argued that this would be 'war work' just as valid as any other. Father would not concede the point and we separated for the night still at loggerheads.

I am determined that I will stay here for at least two weeks and Father will not shake me from my purpose. John needs me and I will be here!

Sunday 12th May 1918

I have worked hard for my victory. Father is to return to Brabage tomorrow without me. He has held frequent meetings with Matron and visited John himself. At last he has agreed that there is a need for me to stay. He has spoken with Mrs. MacRae and left clear instructions as to the supervision of my welfare. He has allowed me two weeks and then I must return. He will himself come to fetch me.

I take the credit as my own but it is largely due to John's condition. Even Father cannot fail to notice that John is significantly better when I am by his side. I know that Father neither likes nor approves of my staying here but I am so glad that I am to remain.

I have written letters to Mother and Mary which I will send back with Father. I see him off on the morning train. I will then have two whole weeks of freedom when I can visit John and do as I wish without Father breathing down my neck.

Tonight I feel like a schoolgirl on the eve of a long vacation. I am sure that the improvement that I have discerned in John will continue. By the end of the month he will be almost his usual self! I can tell from Matron's expression that she does not share my confidence. She advises caution for, in her experience, these cases' always take a long time.

I now have a purpose in life, and I welcome it!

Thursday 30th May 1918

I had a final interview with Dr. Rivers today. I feel that he has been completely Frank and honest with me. With the truth known I am sure that I can face the future.

Dr. Rivers probably has more knowledge and experience of the mental 'trauma' and its associated physical condition brought on by war than any other doctor living today. He has made a special study of the officers in his care at Craiglockhart and I trust his judgement implicitly. He acknowledges that John has made a good recovery. His physical wounds healed long ago and his mind too has begun the painful progress back to health. Because nerves take so long to heal the trembling is still present, though not as noticeable as it once was. John's stammer is now more controllable and it is only on rare occasions that it is heard. The bad dreams continue and John's sleep is continually broken by his recurring nightmare. Dr. Rivers explained to me that this is the reason that John can not yet be passed fit for active service. He explained the situation to me in simple terms. An appalling experience has made John erect a barrier in his mind. He will not allow himself to recall that experience. It is, however, so deeply embedded in his mind that it cannot be shifted easily. Only when John is asleep does his subconscious mind take over and the experience surface in the form of a nightmare. To the observer this is evidenced by restlessness, shouts and general agitation.

I attempted to interrupt here, for I have read much in my long, lonely evenings of recent weeks about the nature of the mind. I was about to suggest

hypnotism as a method which would allow Dr. Rivers to reach John's subconscious mind.

Dr. Rivers held up an imperious hand,

"Let me finish Miss Aubrey. You may ask what questions you wish later." He continued with his explanation.

During his waking hours some of the words and phrases John had spoken in his sleep were quoted to him in an attempt to start his memory. His eyes glazed and his mind became blank. He trembled and stuttered that he could remember nothing until he woke up in the field hospital. Hypnotism has been tried but John has proved an unsuitable subject and all attempts have failed. Nevertheless, Dr. Rivers is convinced that there is something that will trigger the subconscious, something that will bring the wall tumbling down and allow the memories to come flooding out. Only such an occurrence will cure John completely.

He suggests that John remain here at Craiglockhart for one week more. He really feels that they have done all that is possible for John and can make no more progress at the moment. After that week he would like John to spend some time in convalescence. He has communicated with Father who has agreed that John may stay at Brabage Vicarage. For John to return to service is, at the moment, out of the question, for he is not fit to lead men. (Dr. Rivers has learned that John is to be promoted to Major on his return and is to be decorated once more for his actions on the battlefield.) He expects that, given John's current rate of progress he is likely to be fit by the end of July - by which time Dr. Rivers expects the war to be over. Oh that I could be as optimistic! He asks of me one thing: should anything happen, should the dam break, he would like to hear of it, for he has not yet met with a case quite so stubborn. He is sure that the unhappy events surrounding Charles's death, followed so closely by the death of Mrs. Fraser, have all taken their toll.

I thanked Dr. Rivers for all that he had done for John and assured him that I would write should John's memory be triggered.

I left Craiglockhart and returned to Mrs. MacRae's to complete my packing. In the time that I have spent here I have made many friends. I have enjoyed a degree of independence which will not be easy to relinquish. I look at the work that I have done at the hospital, and the work done by other women around me, and I wonder how I will live once more in the cloistered atmosphere of Brabage Vicarage under the discipline of Father!

Father arrived during this evening and made sure that I am ready to leave early in the morning. I told him that I had made arrangements at he hospital to visit early

and say my farewells to John and to the others I have met. Father began to object that this would delay us unacceptably.

"Then I will just arise a little earlier Father!" I retorted. He had nothing more to say but his expression told me that I could forget my independent ways once back at Brabage!

I cannot imagine taking up the reins of my old life once more. How far away Mrs. Jameson, Mrs. Farquharson, Susan Bates, Mrs. Cooper and all the others seem. I will be glad to see Mother and Mary, for I have sorely missed their company and letters only partially ease the separation.

After spending so long with John, day after day together, I am dreading our separation, even though it is only for one week. I have a conviction that it is only I who can help him, make him whole again. I do not wish to negate all that Craiglockhart has done but I am sure that his cure lies in our own hands. I am even more convinced of that fact after my meeting with Dr. Rivers.

I can only hope that the next week flies with the swiftness of the last three, for all I want in life is to be with John.

Friday 7th June 1918

John is here with us at last! I was so excited this morning that I could hardly eat my breakfast. Needless to say the morning dragged its feet but eventually it was lunchtime. Father criticised me more than once for the speed with which I devoured my meal.

With much urging I managed to make Father leave earlier than he had wanted to. All the way to Framley Station he criticised our lovely pony and trap. Because he has spent two or three days this week being driven about by Mrs. Farquharson's chauffeur, he has lost patience with our slow, plodding pace.

I must confess that today, in my excited mood, I too found Prince's pace to be tedious! Father would dearly love to own a motor car but I cannot foresee the day when he would make the necessary expenditure. I was tempted to utter something along the lines of 'Thou shalt not covet thy neighbour's motor car' but refrained, my mood being too happy to open an acrimonious debate!

Of course we were much too early at the station, but at last the train came in. John stepped off and walked towards us. I wanted to fling my arms around him, to hold him, to shout with joy and laughter. Father stepped in front of me and extended his hand. He shook John's proffered hand muttering sombrely about how much better John looked than when last they had met. Indeed he does! Physically he is much more robust than he has been for some time, although his

hand still betrays the trembles which once shook his entire body. It is only when you look into his eyes that the hurt, the misery, can be seen. His eyes are deep pools of anguish. I wonder whether he will ever be healed?

The journey back to the vicarage passed so quickly that I had not the opportunity to ask about half the people at Craiglockhart.

Mother and Mary welcomed John affectionately and in no time at all he was comfortably settled and we were at tea. The conversation started rather awkwardly and was somewhat stilted, for none of us wished to mention the war and the care we took to avoid any related subject laid a constraint upon us. The fact that John shows little physical evidence of his recent appalling injuries makes things harder. The more we tried to avoid the topic of war the more it arose. Father commented upon the extremely warm weather we were enjoying, which made Mother say,

"Mrs. Farquharson was telling me that the soldiers in the trenches find the heat intolerable!"

She immediately fell silent when she realised what she had said and her face reddened. John turned to her,

"Yes, Mrs. Aubrey, life is pretty awful in a trench at any time, but it is in the extremes of weather, heat or cold, when the men suffer most. I am aware that you have all, most kindly, tried to avoid the subject of war. You must not. Dr. Rivers tells me that it is better for me to talk."

Suddenly we were all talking at once. With that constraint removed we chatted in quite a relaxed manner and, most strangely, I noticed that we spoke very little of the war!

After tea John and I went walking in the garden. I was concerned that he should not over-tire himself for he has begun to use a walking stick again. The recent injuries have exacerbated his old injury and he feels a certain weakness. John insisted that we walk to the small lake, for he wanted to see the summerhouse. We sat on the steps for some time (I had not brought the keys with me for I had not imagined that we would walk so far.) John talked about his friends, his fellow officers, the men, and eventually about Charles and his mother. I listened quietly and without interruption, for I know that he must take things at his own pace.

"I must go back Lizzie," he said, "it is foul. We all hate it but I must go back where my duty lies."

I wanted to protest, to urge him to stay until the war is over, but I remained silent, merely gazing over the lake. Eventually his arm crept around my

shoulder and I turned. He kissed me so fiercely that I felt that my lips would surely bruise!

At last we broke apart and he was trembling violently.

"I am s-s-so s-s-sorry L-Lizzie. I should n-not h-have been rough w-with you," he managed to stammer out. I was dismayed to hear the return of this impediment and I put my arms around him and spoke softly. John listened to my comforting words and then responded,

"The war is so very far away, and yet when I speak of it I am right back there, right in the thick of battle. Guns, noise, smoke, flashes, gas, men yelling all around me, my feet slipping away from me." He choked, "I can't stand it Lizzie, and I am very much afraid that the longer I stay away the harder it will be to return."

I went to embrace him, but instead he took hold of my hand.

"No, Lizzie, there can be no comfort for me. I am painfully aware that. I am not doing my duty. I must pull myself together, get passed fit and return to the Front!"

I had nothing to say. This poor wreck of a man was speaking so bravely. Physically he probably was able to fight, but mentally he was ruined and would be totally unable to command men.

We sat in silence, his arms once again holding me close. I felt his trembling lessen and finally he took a deep breath and stood up, pulling me after him.

"Come along Miss Aubrey, we must get back or the Reverend will be sending search parties for us!"

We walked back but Father was away from home and so we need not have been anxious, for Mother and Mary understand that we need time together.

We dined early and Mother insisted that John went early to bed - she intends that he keeps hospital hours. After he had left us three alone (Father was in his study) Mother broke down and wept. When she had calmed down she apologised and explained that she cannot bear to see what war has done to John. Poor Mother! How much more upset she would have been had she seen some of John's fellow officers at Craiglockhart! It had been such a day that I too elected to retire early. Even though John is ill it is wonderful to have him here, to know that he lies sleeping, just two rooms away from me. After the week of separation I can now look forward to spending each day with him. Selfishly I hope that his recovery takes a long time!

* * * * * * *

I am writing this at three o'clock in the morning. We had all been in bed for some hours and were sound asleep when the calm of the night was shattered by shouts and screams which I knew came from John. I instantly leapt from my bed, threw a gown around my shoulders and went to his room. Father had got there before me. The door was open and Father was shaking John roughly by the shoulder.

"Wake up John! Wake up man! You are not in the trenches at Ypres now, you are in Brabage Vicarage. Wake up!"

Father was rough and his voice harsh as John awoke, confused. By this time I was in the room and John was beginning to gain some grasp on reality. He stammered,

"Oh God! W-W-What h-h-h-happened?" and seeing me and Father there, "I'm sorry, oh, I'm s-so s-sorry. I thought that I w-wwas over all th-this!" He was trembling violently, he managed to indicate a small bottle of medicine next to his bed and Father picked it up.

"L-Let me h-have s-some of th-that. I'm sorry, I should h-have taken a d-dose b-before I w-went to s-sleep"

Father handed over the medicine bottle immediately and John took some. Father turned to me,

"Go to your room Elizabeth! This is no place for you!" he snapped. I wanted to stay, to kiss away the hurt, the horror, fear and anguish in John's eyes. Instead I muttered,

"Yes Father," and came away meekly.

That all happened over an hour ago and everything is now quiet. I am too tense to sleep. John's road to recovery is to be a hard one. I only hope that Father will not be so rough with him. Father does not seem to understand that John needs kindness and gentleness, not firmness and bullying along. Worry as I may I know that only time will heal. If only there was something I could do to help ease those painful memories.

RUINED VILLAGE

The pounding of our marching feet
Has replaced the thunder of shell.
We marched along the cobbled street
Through the blackened ruins of Hell.

An eerie calm on every side,
Fear's icy fingers clutched my heart.
What horrors lurk, what terrors hide
In this village we've blown apart?

The ghosts of people long since fled
Echoes of joy, of love, of life.
Now the village itself is dead:
A victim of man's futile strife.

It's two weeks since we passed through here
The village was bright and gay.
Now charred remains fill us with fear
And smoke makes midnight of midday.

Where once stood cottage, church and shops,
Where people cheered and waved at us,
Now Death's sharp scythe has reaped its crops
And malice leers from skull-eyed house.

I wonder would this war rage on
If we fought it on English soil?
Would we let ruin and devastation
Run wild, our fair land to despoil?

This place can't ever be rebuilt.
A village is more than houses.
Bricks will never assuage the guilt
That death and destruction rouses.

When this war is finally done,
When all the carnage is over,
Nothing will be the same again:
Mankind can never recover.

John Fraser 1918

Saturday 8th June 1918

I looked around the table this morning at breakfast. We all looked a sorry sight! We were downcast and all had black shadows under our eyes. I suppose that everyone was like me - disturbed in the middle of the night and unable to get back to sleep easily for thinking of the horrors that John must have undergone.

Conversation was desultory and at the end of our meal John cleared his throat and spoke. He still stammered a little and his voice was low.

"I f-feel that I m-must apologise for l-last night. I felt so much better, s-so relaxed and so m-much more at ease than I w-was in the hospital that I did not take the medicine that is prescribed for bedtime. I th-thought that I c-could d-do without it. I obviously c-cannot and I apologise." He turned to Father, "Perhaps sir, it would be b-better if I w-went away s-somewhere else to c-convalesce. I do not w-wish to disturb your l-life here!" There was silence, total silence. Into that silence I dropped my knife with a clatter. Everyone turned to stare at me. I was white and trembled almost as much as John did. To think of John being elsewhere: I would have to go with him! A hundred thoughts and ideas flashed through my mind in the space of a moment.

Father turned back to John. We were all silent, waiting for the dreadful decision to fall. Father was embarrassed,

"No, no John, you must not think of that. The damage that the war has done to you must be repaired and Brabage Vicarage is a good place for that to happen. No, you must stay, but," (I held my breath) "but do remember to take your medicine each night as directed!"

I was so relieved that I could have cried. I stared, first at Father and then at John, and then back again at Father. What can have made the man discover his humanity. I was amazed!

Later in the day John and I went to Framley as John wished to visit his mother's grave once more. I recalled what Dr. Rivers had said, that if only the wall could be breached he was sure that John's mind would be made whole again. With this in mind I talked to John about the war. I asked him about his promotion. I was surprised when he was almost sneering in his discussion of it. He said that to make him a major showed how lacking was the army in good men! I tried to protest but he would not discuss the matter. I asked him about his company, his fellow officers. Each time he answered me but then steered towards other topics. It was clear that he was not yet ready to attempt an assault on the wall!

At Framley we visited Park House first. It was such a lonely, forlorn sight, all shuttered and closed up. John went from room to room, checking that all was

well. I was particularly sad in remembering just how these rooms were arranged when Mrs. Fraser was alive. How happy the house had always seemed, and how I loved the contrast it provided to Brabage! John became quite animated, putting forward ideas for changes that we would make when the war is over and we are married. I was sad however, unable to catch his mood. Eventually John locked the doors and after gathering flowers from the garden (rather neglected and a little overgrown now in spite of periodic maintenance) we went to the churchyard.

Next to his mother's grave, John stood in silence, hat in hand, for some time. The flowers we had gathered were gladioli and their bright, shining spears were thrown into contrast against the pale granite headstone. I walked back to the church porch in order to leave John time for contemplation. While I was standing there who should come along but Arthur Mayfield. I did not know how he would respond to John's presence. On seeing John, Arthur stopped and gazed over the wall, eyes fixed on John's back, taking in his slight stoop, the heavy leaning on the stick. John turned and on recognising Arthur he walked towards the gate. I too began to walk in that direction. Arthur turned, as if he would go away, but seemed to change his mind and turned back again. John advanced, hand outstretched. Arthur took it hesitantly.

"Good afternoon Arthur, how are you and your family?" I heard John ask as I came up.

"As yer'd expect sir," Arthur replied.

"I was wondering Arthur, if I could come along and see your mother? Thomas was my faithful servant for so many years and I would not wish his passing to go unmarked."

"I doan think that's a good idea sir, with respect. She's still very cut up about ... things and... and ..." Arthur stumbled over his words, unsure of how to continue.

"And, Thomas is dead and I am alive, eh Arthur?" John finished for him.

"That's about it sir!" Arthur was clearly relieved that John had grasped the situation so quickly.

"I can't tell you Arthur, how much I wish that I could bring Thomas back, and all of them. Most of the company fell. God knows how, or why, I am still alive!" John did not meet Arthur's eyes as he spoke.

"No sir, we 'ad a letter from the Colonel, told us 'ow bravely our Thomas fell sir. I think that's comforted Mother - she doan feel that it's all a waste."

John was lost in thought. Arthur shifted about awkwardly for a moment or two.

"I'd best go sir, Mother gets anxious if I'm away too long. Doan know what she's goin' ter do when I'm conscripted in a couple o' months!" John was still deep in thought, anxiety creasing his forehead. "Doan fret yersel' sir. No frettin's goin' ter bring back our Tom. Once they're gone, they're gone. This war's robbed so many mothers o' sons that our Tom's just one o' thousands."

I stepped forward and spoke.

"Not only robbed mothers of sons, Arthur, but brothers of brothers; sons of mothers." I looked significantly towards the Fraser grave.

"Aye, yer've 'ad yer troubles too sir. I'd best go. Goodbye now." He held out his hand and John shook it strongly. As John turned away I saw tears glisten in his eyes.

He was almost silent on our return journey. Eventually he roused himself from his reverie to say,

"It was madness Lizzie, madness. We were told to fight to the last man. The Germans were advancing on us and we didn't have a chance. The men were exhausted when I had to order them on. I felt that I was signing their execution order."

He had become agitated and was trembling. I listened in silence. I did not know whether it was better for him to talk, even though he was accusing himself, or to remain silent, blocking out the memory. He continued,

"Do you know Lizzie, to this day I do not remember all of that last day. There are g-g-great b-b-blanks in m-my mind." He was stuttering now and his whole body was trembling. " I r-remember g-giving orders; I r-remember g-going over the t-top. I c-can remember ep-episodes during the f-fighting, b-but s-somehow I am unable t-to p-piece these th-thii-ings t-together p-properly." He made his hand into a fist and in his frustration beat it against the side of the trap. He lapsed into silence. We were both silent, for what could we say?

The evening was quiet and John was very morose. Occasionally he spoke to say

"If only I c-could r-remember. If only m-my mind w-was not s-such a b-blank." I think that we all felt relieved when it was time to go to bed, for John's frustration and sadness oppressed us all.

I took charge of the medicine bottle and administered the dose to John. He laughed at this, playfully saying that he was not yet my husband and here I was treating him as a child! John instructed me to take great care of the medicine for it is dangerous. If I was to be 'in charge' then 'Nurse Aubrey, please ensure that I take the correct dose and keep the bottle locked away, for I am so forgetful that

I may take too much!' I turned pale at his joke but John laughed, telling me that he was only teasing me.

I love John so dearly that I cannot bear to think of anything happening to him. If only I could help him. To see him so depressed, so frustrated, makes me feel sad and helpless. If only I could discover the 'trigger' described by Dr. Rivers. If the wall could be breached then perhaps I would have the old John back again. I must try hard over the coming days to find the key.

Wednesday 12th June 1918

On our walk today John and I had a long discussion about what Father would refer to as 'married affairs'. It all started because I related to John the events of my parish visiting this morning. I went as usual to the Bates's house. Although Susan is now decently married there has been little change in circumstances, for Alfie is away again at the Front. I suppose that when the war is over he will make a home for himself with Susan and their child. At present she stays in Brabage, going along in her usual way, looking after the children. Mrs. Cooper remains with her still and is likely to do so until after the birth of the baby, which will be quite soon now. Susan is well, and in spite of the rationing of meat, seems to glow with health. In fact she looks better than she ever has before. With money from Alfie and the regular work Joe Bates has had on the church extension, I think that the family has never been so well off. I am sure that Mrs. Cooper contributes to ensure that Susan gets all that she requires.

John asked what my opinion was of Susan and what had happened. I replied, honestly, that although society condemned her I could easily understand what had happened, for when one loves sincerely one gives without counting the cost - or taking any cognizance of the consequences. John received my opinion silently and I began to fear that he thought less of me for my outspokenness. I tried to justify my opinion,

"It is not a view held only by myself John, I have met many young women over the past year or more who think likewise. The world is changing, society is changing. Even Mrs. Farquharson agrees that when the war is over things will never be the same again."

"Oh, Lizzie," he replied, squeezing my hand, "I am not condemning you. I am silent because I am thoughtful. In the army I meet so many different kinds of men. Some are terrified; some are foolhardy. Almost all have left loved ones behind. They carry their letter or photographs about with them all the time like some sort of talisman. Those loved ones are sometimes the only factor that can

spur the men on to superhuman feats of exertion or courage. They are fighting for a better world Lizzie. They believe this war to be a war for mankind, for civilisation. They believe it to be a war to liberate them. I censor the men's letters and so I know how important it is for them to have someone at home. The married men talk constantly of wives and children, the unmarried men of their sweethearts. What takes place between a man and a woman is not always merely lust. A bond is formed; love is complete. I suppose that the women give because it is the ultimate gift they can make to the man they love most. When he is away, serving in terrible conditions, she hopes that he will remember their time together, the passion, the tenderness, and that the memory will help him through his current misery and give him something to come home to. And it does, Lizzie, it does, for I have seen those men and I know that what their sweethearts give is not given in vain."

He fell silent. It was the longest speech he had made since his return from Craiglockhart and during its course he had not stammered once. It was my turn to remain silent.

"I suppose Lizzie that some people would condemn such behaviour, as they have done with Susan. I believe though that more will understand it in the future. These young men have gone off and many will never return; surely the least they can ask is that there is someone who loves them, enough to mourn their passing?"

I agreed with him, assuring him that my views concurred exactly with his. I gave the opinion that people like my father were increasingly in the minority and that when (eventually) the war was over they would be shown to be so.

John laughed,

"You know, Lizzie, it's a funny thing but our commanders are continually thinking up new ways to inspire the men, for at times they sink into the greatest lethargy and despondency. They send clergymen up and down the lines spurring the men on to fight in the name of God and all that is right; they have generals exhorting the troops to patriotism; they have sergeant-majors bullying the soldiers, and all the time I do believe that our men would be more effectively inspired by the young women of Britain!"

We laughed together at this thought and John hugged me close. I attempted to make him speak a little more about life at the Front, but he would have none of it. Instead he spoke of our marriage and promised to organise things with Father.

"For," he said, "I love you so much Lizzie that I cannot be complete until we are together, united as one."

I knew exactly what he implied by this and in spite of myself I coloured. John laughed,

"Sorry Lizzie, I have offended you. Come on, let's get back and I promise not to embarrass you by talking of this again!"

I would not for the world tell John that he had neither offended nor embarrassed me. My diary alone knows the truth of those blushes - it is simply that I desire John so much and to see that desire reflected in him only serves to inflame my own need. We must be married soon, for I cannot contain all the love I have for him!

As he had promised, John attempted to speak to Father but was unable to find the opportunity. Father seems forever busy at the moment!

The evening was passed quietly and only once was John disturbed. Mother happened to say that she had met Mrs. Hall from Framley earlier in the day. In speaking of joint acquaintances and other people in Framley Mrs. Hall mentioned the Mayfields. Mrs. Mayfield is creating a lot of fuss about Arthur going into the army. She wants him to be exempted. Arthur responds that there are no valid grounds for his exemption, and that in any case he would not wish to receive a white feather. Mrs. Mayfield's only response is that it is cruel that a woman who has lost one son must send another into danger.

As Mother related this tale John had become increasingly more agitated. Eventually Mother noticed his discomfort and hastily concluded with,

"Of course, war requires sacrifice of everyone. Mrs. Mayfield is by no means alone in being unable to come to terms with her loss." We fell into silence and shortly afterwards John excused himself to retire. I ensured that he had a good dose of medicine, for I read all the signs of his inner turmoil. If only he would speak of it, perhaps then I could help him. I suppose that Dr. Rivers is correct in saying that time is the only thing that will eventually provide the remedy.

Tuesday 18th June 1918

Today I have come of age, I am an adult, a woman and I am proud of it! Not only has a profound change taken place in me but John also has changed! The barrier is down, the trigger was found and while he is not entirely cured, he is almost there.

It all happened this afternoon. It has been a glorious day. After his morning duties in the school Father had taken Mother and Mary to Mrs. Farquharson's house. They were all to have an excursion in the motor car. It was considered wise that John should not go as anything noisy has such a detrimental effect on

him. I stayed with John, here at Brabage. Since the date of our wedding has been set for January Father is much more inclined to allow us time alone. Also I find that many days he is preoccupied, lost in thought about I know not what, and not noticing half of what happens around him. Enough of Father. This day belongs to John and to me!

We had walked down to the lake. The small boat was moored to the end of the jetty and it bobbed invitingly on the sparkling water. We walked down the jetty. John asked if I would trust him to take charge of the boat and row me around a little, on the water. I answered that of course I would, for would I not trust my entire life to him.

We were soon out in the middle of the lake. We had left the water lilies and rushes behind and were in clear water. There was the occasional 'plop' of a fish as it jumped to catch one of the myriad flies buzzing about just above the surface. The day was so warm and the sweet fragrance of the wild flowers filled the air. (Father had spoken of clearing the lake shores, but this year the flowers are so beautiful that I am glad that he has not yet done so.) A larger 'plop' than usual brought John towards me to peer over the side of the boat. With all the weight in one place the boat gave an abrupt lurch and John, still unsteady on his legs, stumbled. He put out an arm to save himself but was unable to prevent falling on to me. We lay for a moment, a confusion of arms and legs in the bottom of the boat. His face was next to mine, our bodies lying together, the sun warm and the air sweet. Suddenly his arms were, around me and we were kissing, long and passionately. A red madness swept over me; my desire was overwhelming. I kissed him as I had never done before.

He was holding me, running his hands down my body, over my breasts, pulling me closer. I could feel his desire, his urgency. I was ready to give ALL. The silence was shattered by a 'crack', the loud retort of a gun near at hand. Someone was shooting in the fields next to the vicarage. John was instantly tense and pulled away from me. I was confused in the abrupt parting and frustration of my desires. John was trembling as he sat upright. I put my arms around him, soothing his alarm. He apologised, adding that he could not yet bear the sound of gunfire. When he was calm we rowed to the shore and it was I who helped him from the boat. We sat for some moments on the pier. I suggested that we move to the summerhouse, where John could recover more comfortably.

Of course, it was there that it happened! We sat and, quite naturally, I held John in my arms. Gradually he calmed and he stroked my face lovingly. It seemed only a moment before he was stroking my arms, my shoulders, my back. Our

desire was fully re-awakened. It took but a moment for him to remove my blouse, to caress my naked shoulders. His hands moved to my breasts and gently, so very gently, he removed my underthings. I was bare to the waist and my only thought was that I wished to be totally naked! The unspoken desire communicated itself to John and as he kissed me tenderly he unfastened my skirt. Soon I was shamelessly naked and John too removed his clothes. We lay together on the old sofa, exploring each other's bodies with wonder intermingled with desire.

I could not tell exactly what happened but it seemed very suddenly that John was not alongside me but on top of me. My mind exploded. I felt desire overwhelm me. There was a hunger, a need, inside of me that cried out to be satisfied.

I had been led to believe that 'marital relations' were a painful duty to be undergone stoically by a dutiful wife. I had not been prepared for such joy, such fulfilment, such happiness. Even if I wished to describe what I felt there are not words in the language that would be adequate. I felt that my whole self had been laid bare, an offering to joy. I have never felt as happy as I did when our desire met and was fulfilled.

After the tumult was over I lay very still. John lay quiet, completely spent. Without warning John's whole body was convulsed and sobs racked him. I sat up, alarmed, and held him close. Slowly his sobs subsided and it was then that the dam broke. His words tumbled from him in a torrent, telling of his anguish, his torment, his guilt over the death of Thomas. He spoke of the horrors he had seen and undergone; his compassion for his men continually overridden by his duty to the command; his fears; his recklessness (particularly after Charles's death). It was in one such mood of recklessness that he took his men 'over the top' in that last assault. His men were tired and the Germans had been pushing them back, back towards the Somme. The command was insistent, they were to fight to the last man, to stand and deny the German advance. He had only just given the order that his company was to stand down, to take a short respite before taking up the assault once more. The men had sunk wearily where they stood. They were exhausted in the unseasonably warm weather and by the constant bombardment. It was then that the Colonel came on his tour of the line, ready to urge the men on. He was furious when he saw them at ease, and instructed John to issue orders to get them up again, for no such respite could be afforded. John opened his mouth to protest but the Colonel turned and stalked off. Instead of following him and explaining the situation, John resignedly ordered his men on once more. Thomas was at his side as he led the men over the parapet.

All was confusion, around him men were entangled in barbed wire. Machine guns were rattling, men were falling. Smoke made it impossible to see more than a few yards. The company floundered on, their ranks thinning as the German guns took their toll. The noise was unbearable. Men were shouting; casualties were screaming; bombs were exploding; John was yelling, screaming orders at his men, trying against all the odds to keep some sort of control. A young recruit fell to the ground on his knees, next to John, sobbing that he could not go on. He was whimpering, his eyes wide with terror. John paused for a moment, but the boy would not be roused. As he stumbled on, Thomas at his side, John heard one shot. He turned and through the murk could see the boy soldier, his head half shot away. He had put his own gun into his mouth and fired, considering instant death preferable to the continuing hell of which he was part.

Madness reigned, with bodies that seemed to be heaped all around him; barbed wire was everywhere. The men were yelling, shouting to each other and to the enemy. Shells were exploding and machine gun bullets filled the air around them. Trench Mortars were going off, throwing up showers of earth and, unspeakably, parts of bodies. His men were being massacred and John turned, ready to suffer the consequences of ordering a retreat. Before he could give that order the ground gave way beneath him and he fell into an old shell hole. It was partly flooded but his slide ceased at the edge of the water. He tried to climb out but each time he gained a few feet he slithered back. A head and shoulders loomed out of the smoke over the lip of the crater above him.

"Hang on Sir, have you out in a jif!" Thomas said. He went away and reappeared with a length of rope. He threw the end of it over the edge. In order to pull John up he had to stand and it was then that the bullets took him, right across the chest.

John fell back, stunned. After a while he roused himself, aware that he must get out of the shell hole. He grasped the rope which he tugged experimentally. It held so hand over hand he climbed out, scaling the slippery walls of his would -be muddy tomb. When he reached the top and slid carefully over the crumbling edge, he could see why the rope had held firm. Thomas had coiled it around his own body and it was that weight - that dead weight - which had anchored it. John untied the rope and felt for a pulse at Thomas's neck. Nothing. He knew that with all those injuries Thomas was surely dead, but all that he could think of was to take him back. This faithful servant had given his life for John; it was the very least John could do to take his body back. He may not be dead; there might still be hope. John shouldered his burden and staggered off into No-Man's Land. It

was more than an hour later that he arrived back at the lines and the burden was removed. The horrors he had witnessed, the perils he had experienced, had destroyed his mind: shells exploding close to him had destroyed his nerve so he was hospitalised.

When John finally finished speaking I could say nothing. His account had been so vivid that I had lived it as he had told it. I understood his broken mind. He put his fingers gently under my chin and lifted my face to his.

"I'm sorry Lizzie, I should not have told you all of this."

I was crying now, but not with sadness, for it was with such relief that I had looked into his eyes and recognised the old John.

We loved once more. Afterwards John apologised, "I should have had more control Lizzie, I'm so sorry. You must think me so awful!" I reassured him, referring back to our conversation of last week. It was the best gift, the only gift, that I could give him and I had given it gladly. He embraced me tenderly and sighed contentedly.

It was some time later when we emerged from the lake path. We were holding hands and on seeing Mother and Mary on the terrace, John dropped my hand quickly. I took his hand up again for I did not care. Our relationship was sealed; we were united for ever. We had, that afternoon, forged a link that would never be severed.

During the evening I saw Mother observing John closely from time to time. She too had perceived the difference. She looked from him to me and, shameless that I am, I did not blush. I am sure that Mother knows what has happened.

When I went to give John his medicine, he refused it. He told me that the medicine he had taken in the afternoon had assured him of peace. He kissed me tenderly, and there was in that kiss an element that there has never been before. Oh, how I love him - and I know that he loves me. I feel that I should shout our love aloud, proclaim it from the rooftops. I am married to John in all but name. It is wonderful. How can anything so wonderful, so joyous, so delightful, be wrong. When I see what the act of love has accomplished in John I feel that my actions can be justified - even to Father!

As I finish my diary tonight I am the happiest person alive. Even with the war and all that it involves, the world is a sunnier place. How I look forward to spending the rest of my life with my wonderful lover. My only regret is that I am too modest to write to Dr. Rivers to tell him how the wall was breached, what trigger was found. I will have to think of some other way to explain John's recovery.

POPPIES

Merciful poppies block out the mud,
The death, destruction and the blood.
They fill with beauty a place of death
I call them 'Nature's Wreath'.

John Fraser 1918

Wednesday 19th June 1918

John's broad smile and confident eye at breakfast this morning quickly dispelled my doubts and embarrassments at our first meeting. He is more like the John of two years ago than he has been for some time. When he went out with Father to discuss some arrangement for our marriage, Mother and Mary both commented on his great improvement.

We have spent most of the day together and I confess that, for the first time, I feel truly 'at one' with him. I now understand what is meant in the Bible by the words, 'one flesh'. I cannot believe that others have felt as we do, else why should there be such conflict in the world? I can even find it in my heart to be kind to Father, so happy am I.

During the afternoon John talked a little more about his army life. I was able to ask him questions and he answered me fully, evading nothing. Furthermore there is scarcely the trace of a tremble in his hands or a stammer in his words. We talked of the past year and all that has happened. I asked John about his worst times and his best times in the army. He maintains that the worst was the mud at Passchendale. None who were there will ever forget it. What made it more frustrating, for the officers at least, was the knowledge that the mud was caused largely by our own side. It appears that during the usual, preliminary bombardment intended to destroy enemy front line defences, the drainage system in the German trenches had been destroyed. Worse still was the fact that the Germans stood their ground and so when the infantry advanced, it was into a sea of mud in which they were easily cut down by enemy fire. Little wonder that there were over three hundred thousand casualties and yet only four miles of ground gained.

The best of times was when he was sharing the camaraderie of his men. After being through so much together he felt that he knew them all. He cannot believe that such sterling companions are all dead, wiped out at a single stroke. He was

silent for a time after he told me this, then, with an effort, he continued.

"Of course, when I return I will have a new company. One of the things that most upsets me is the knowledge that, as a major, I will be more distant from my men."

Although I assured him that he was the type of officer who would always be close to his soldiers, I do not know enough about the army to know if this was possible.

John spoke of Thomas once again and said that really he was being decorated for Thomas's bravery. He was promoted and Thomas had died in the course of rescuing John. We discussed the Mayfields at some length, but felt that there was no solution. However hard he tried John could never assuage the bitterness of Mrs. Mayfield's loss, neither could he prevent the inevitable call-up of Arthur.

During the evening Father asked John to step into his study for a time. They are certainly spending a considerable time together. Father also commented on John's improved health, adding that at such a rate he would soon be back at his duties.

When the time came to separate for bed it all felt so very unnatural, for I feel that I should never have to leave John's side again. Once more he refused his medicine. I am torn by delighting in his recovery but dreading the fact that it heralds his imminent return to duty. Perhaps the war will soon be over and he need never return. He carefully examines the newspapers each day, but is frustrated by the lack of real news. Since the Ministry Of Information has taken over the task of rallying morale, it is difficult to separate facts from propaganda. John suspects that things are not going well in France, but cannot know until he returns. God grant that his return will not be too soon!

Tuesday 9th July 1918

I found out today why father has been making so much of John. I had thought for a time that it was because Father had undergone a change of heart, or possibly because John, now that he is a major, offers a higher degree of status! I should have guessed that the sudden popularity is concerned solely with his church project. Father has always considered that, while Mrs. Farquharson is the main donor of funds for the extension, the villagers of Brabage would all contribute generously to enable him to fulfil his plans. They have, apparently, not done so. It could be that because times are hard that they have not been able to do so, but Father is bitter that he has been left with some shortfall in his funds. Subsequently

Father has courted John and John has agreed to supply the required amount. John did not tell me this himself, but I found it out by accident when Mrs. Farquharson visited the vicarage today. She was talking of our forthcoming marriage and commented that I was lucky to be marrying such a generous man. I agreed and she went on,

"Anyone who can find it in their heart to be so benevolent towards the church is surely good at heart."

Of course I would not give her the satisfaction of questioning her, but took the opportunity to talk to John later. He confirmed that Father had indeed secured a large donation from him, but that he did not care,

" Lizzie, I would give ten times as much to have you for my wife, my darling!"

He reached out for me and held me close to him as if I were the most precious object in the world. He asked me if I had not noticed how much more liberal Father had become towards us since early last month. (Indeed I had but I had not suspected the reasons.)

"If I had not been so generous my darling I doubt that we could be sitting here now!" (We were in the summerhouse.)

We discussed Father for a time and I amused John by relating another incident that had occurred during Mrs. Farquharson's visit. On stirring sugar into her tea, Mrs. Farquharson turned to Mother and asked how she was coping with the newly imposed rationing. Mother replied that it was something that we all had to get along with.

"But I know Sarah, just how much Lewis like his sugar in his tea! I hope that you are managing to provide well enough?"

Mother coloured and muttered some reply, for she was painfully aware that Father, a man of God, a supposed example of charity, self-denial and other Christian virtues, had forced her to buy up pounds and pounds of sugar in order to circumvent the rationing regulations. Her consternation deepened as Mrs. Farquharson added,

"It is all so very silly. Mr. Lloyd George has said that really there is no need for rationing, only that foolish people are panic buying and so causing shortages."

John and I laughed heartily over this and I told him what a huge relief it was for me to laugh at Father's ways instead of allowing his words and actions to anger me as they had done formerly. Cradling me close John said that he hoped that he would never anger me, but that if he did I must tell him immediately and he would mend his ways.

The day ended with a thunderstorm which, I was relieved to note, caused no

adverse reaction in John. I suppose that his return to France is inevitable. When I am alone here I will remember our long, warm days together; our loving (John calls it his 'Medicine'); and our sharing of all our thoughts, fears, hopes for the future. He has promised me that when he returns to duty he will take great care of himself,

"For now, Lizzie, I have something so precious to me that I cannot lose sight of it. I will come out of it alive - I promise you!"

I hope that he fulfils that promise for I cannot contemplate a life without John.

Thursday 18th July 1918

John was passed fit for active service today and will return to duty on Monday next. He is pleased to be returning, in spite of everything, for he says to stay at home makes him feel that he is 'letting the side down'. What utter nonsense. Why do men feel like this?

He has been busy since hearing the news for he must arrange all his affairs before his return. One of his major sorrows is that Thomas will not be at his side. Since going to war he has never been without Thomas and, John says, replacement will be impossible.

I have spent as much time as I could at his side, for I will be so alone when he goes. He insists on leaving the keys to Park House with me for he does not know when he will return on leave and he wishes me to go through the house and decide what I would like changed before January. I cannot believe that in six months I will be John's wife!

Although John does not want to leave me it is obvious that he is eager to return for, each time we have met anyone today, he has told them his news. Generally he is congratulated but I can see in the eyes of many people a new belief in the futility of war. When is it going to end? I cannot believe that almost four years have gone by and so many people have been slaughtered.

John is to go to Chester tomorrow, to his tailor, for he needs new uniforms and lots of other things. The trenches were so destroyed and the Germans advanced so far that even the billets behind the lines were overrun and few of John's possessions remain. Inevitably the next few days will be full of hustle and bustle, and when he is gone on Monday I will be so despondent. I must put it from my mind.

Mother has been helping me to make lists of things that I will require after I am married. How complicated it is to set up a household! She has promised to come to Park House with me and help in the plans. I think that she is more excited than I am myself! I look forwards to being John's wife. She looks

forward to me being mistress of Park House, at least these things will keep me busy when John goes back. I pray that the days until Monday will pass slowly, 'though I know from experience how they will fly!

LAST NIGHT YOU LAY IN MY ARMS

Last night you lay, soft in my arms.
I held you gently, yet so tight.
I was aware of all your charms,
In the shining silver moonlight.

Dark lake mirrored moon's stately grace,
Leaves stirred and whispered up above.
Together in our sacred place
United by triumphant love.

I breathed the sweet scent of your hair,
The sun in summer, flowers in spring.
Deep violet eyes, a skin so fair,
Poppy lips so ripe for kissing.

I brought your face up close to mine.
I kissed those lips. I closed my eyes
And felt my own heart beat with thine,
I entered into Paradise.

I open my eyes and you are gone.
You are in my embrace no more.
Cold in my dugout, all alone
I awake to the world of war.

Hardly light but guns are rattling,
The flares turn the night into day.
Down the line brave men are battling.
I push my sweet vision away.

Dreams keep me sane, help me endure
The mud and the filth and the stench.
Memories of you, our love so pure
Put to flight this hell in the trench.

So come to me love, please let me dream
Of the joy that shines in your face.
Just one more night, please let it seem
That I lie in your warm embrace.

John Fraser 1918

Wednesday 31st July 1918.

Today I received my first letter from 'Major Fraser'. Oh how I love and miss him! He has settled back into the routine at the Front with no adverse reactions. He has yet to command his first action but is confident that he has fully recovered. All is totally changed there, for the Germans drove our troops back almost to the Somme (and how dispirited the soldiers must be at the negation of all their past efforts). The first Americans have now arrived down the line and while many dislike them John finds them cheery, their confidence inspiring. The tanks are at last beginning to make a difference and John writes more confidently about the end of the war than he has ever done.

John has met with some of his fellows from Craiglockhart. They too look forward to the end. Some of them have had poems published about the war, which they believe has helped them to come to terms with their mental injuries. John comments that he does not reveal how his cure was effected! He assures me of his love and says that he will carry my 'gift' everywhere, for it lives in his heart.

It is a beautiful letter, so full of love and life. It is a letter that I will put away and treasure always. When we are a grey old couple I will bring it out and remind him how fresh and ardent our love once was.

I have carried out my usual duties but am extremely tired. I have noticed lately that the slightest exertion exhausts me and that I am glad to get to bed at night. I have also suffered periods of nausea, but am confident that there is nothing seriously wrong with me. I expect that I am missing John too much!

Each day I walk to the summerhouse - whatever the weather - just to sit and relive our past few months. With the lake outside and the stillness inside, I can (almost) recapture our happiness. Oh, how I miss him!

Sunday 4th August 1918

It is four years today since the war began. Everyone was so confident that it would be only of a few months duration that I can hardly credit that so long has passed.

Father made a special service in church today, to commemorate the fallen. The new extension is almost complete now and will be dedicated some time during the next month.

After church, Mrs. Farquharson commented that I looked a little 'off colour' and asked if I was quite well. I was about to tell her that I was in perfect health when Mother rushed to my defence,

"Elizabeth overtires herself Laura, she is hardly ever still." Mrs. Farquharson accepted Mother's answer and changed to other topics.

Later in the day Father commented on my poor appetite. I do not know the cause of it but I have found that, since John's return, there are certain foods that I cannot eat - indeed on some days I can eat nothing until the afternoon.

We passed our usual Sunday. I frequently wonder why I continue to supervise the Sunday School and yet cannot believe in God. A paradox! The children were livelier than ever today - Father's patriotism having stirred them. They were full of brave words; convinced that the war will end soon and victory be ours. I can only live in hope!

During the evening, Mary accompanied me on my walk. We went to the summerhouse. While we were standing at the edge of the lake I suffered a dizzy spell and Mary had to help me indoors to sit down until I could recover. Before we walked back she spoke of my health. She told me that both Mother and herself have noticed that I am not my usual self. She is unwilling to tell Mother of my dizziness, but has made me promise to see the doctor. I said that I would and I expect that I will. I was glad to retire early to bed. The longer I can sleep the more I can dream of John who fills my mind, awake or asleep.

Friday 9th August 1918.

I will not see Dr. Evans for I know what ails me. I am carrying John's child. I cannot understand why it has taken me so long to realise that fact!

I have done little today, pleading a sick headache to excuse me from company. I have sat, here in my room, and thought. When John and I indulged our love I was ready to proclaim it from the rooftops, ready to confront even Father! Now, though, I am not so sure.

Mother is aware that I am not myself and I suspect that she may have an inkling

of what is wrong. I have decided that I will write to John. I have heard nothing from him since his one letter, sent shortly after his return. There is no embarrassment between us and so I will write and tell him the truth. I will tell him that I expect his child, probably in March. In that case a January wedding will not be suitable. I will ask that we bring the wedding forward to October (I think that it is too late now for September). I am sure that he will be able to persuade Father. Once I have received John's reply I will tell Mother everything. I am sure that with our marriage in the offing, she will not condemn us too much. Indeed, knowing Mother as I do I expect that she will be excited at the prospect of a grandchild!

I have such mixed feelings. I am not ashamed of what we have done; my 'gift' to John was as much a delight to me. When two people love each other such a thing is inevitable. Part of my mind thinks that I owe a duty to Mother and Father to try to cover things as best I can, the other half is proud that I am bearing the physical proof of John's love for me.

As I lie in my bed I place my hands on my stomach. Though my baby can only be so very small, I tell him that he is loved; he has a wonderful father and such a life to look forward to.

In spite of the difficulties to come I think that I am happy. All that I hope for is that we may arrange things satisfactorily to protect Mother and Father's respectability and give me my husband and my baby his father. (How extraordinary it is to write of my baby!)

I am confident that John will be as excited as I on hearing my news!

* * * * * * *

EDITOR'S NOTE: AFTER THIS ENTRY THERE FOLLOWED MANY BLANK PAGES. THERE WERE NO FURTHER ENTRIES IN LIZZIE'S DIARY UNTIL NOVEMBER 1918

* * * * * * *

Sunday 17th November 1918.

I have decided to resume my diary today after such a long gap for several reasons. Primarily I would like to take the time to think over all that has happened in the last three months, for I need to come to terms with events. Secondly I feel that my story is incomplete, and it goes against my nature to leave anything

unfinished. Thirdly I require courage and a degree of calmness to face the end of today; ordering my thoughts may help me to achieve that. Finally I would like something, however small and insignificant, to be left behind me.

When last I wrote in this book I had realised that I was carrying John's child. I wrote to tell him the news and ask that we bring the wedding forward to October. He never received my letter. On the morning of 10th August I received a letter from John's Commanding Officer. The letter has long since gone, I know not where, but the contents are etched on my memory. It was dated 7th August. 'Dear Miss Aubrey,' it said, 'it is with great regret, indeed with deep sorrow, that I have to convey to you the sad news that your fiancé Major John Fraser, was killed in action two days ago.' There was more, but I cannot bring it to mind.

I was at breakfast when I received the letter and I could read no further. My eyes took in words such as 'courage' and 'bravery', 'duty' (of course). I was blinded by tears. I screwed the letter up, rose from my place at table and went outside.

I wandered about in the grounds, neither knowing nor caring where I went. I could not believe that John was killed and that I had known nothing of it. For one wild moment I thought the news to be untrue, that a mistake had been made. If John was dead I would surely know, I would surely have felt something. I realised that for the past week I had been ill and so entangled in my own selfish thoughts and feelings that I had given no attention to anything else.

I found myself at the edge of the lake. There was no point in being there alone. There was no purpose in living life without John. The baby was not the foremost subject in my mind, for all that I could think of was John and I could not contemplate a life without him - a life without love. Almost in a daze I walked down the jetty.

* * * * * * *

Some weeks later, when I had recovered, Mother and Mary kindly maintained that I must have lost my footing and slipped into the water. Father gave no opinion, for he has had little to do with me from that time forward. However kindly their explanations were meant, both my mother and my sister knew that I had wilfully intended to take my own life.

I remember seeing the sun reflected on the rippling water; the boat was where John had left it; the bees were buzzing; the air was once again filled with the scent of flowers. I had no part in it, for the world without John was an alien place.

I reached the end of the jetty and I stood. It took but a moment for all my time with John to flash through my mind: such joy, such happiness I had experienced, and now all that was dashed from me. How bitter were the dregs of my life. I rejected that bitterness so I abjured that life. Calmly, I hurled myself into the water. It was blackness. I was sinking, weeds were clutching at my legs, my skirt, my arms. I opened my eyes. I was dimly aware of light above me, sun on the surface of the water. I opened my mouth to cry out my sorrow, my anguish. It filled with water. Mud had been churned up by my movement and the water was clouded. It filled my eyes, my mouth, my mind. In spite of myself my body urged me to survive but I would not heed it. I grasped weeds at the lake bottom and I remember no more for I was swallowed into a sea of blackness.

When I recovered consciousness I was in my own bed. It was dark and the lamps were shaded. I was first aware of Mother sitting by my bed, a grave expression on her face. She realised that I was awake and started forward. She encircled me in her loving arms and held me close.

I do not need to detail my long and weary way to recovery. It was Father who had pulled my inert body from the lake. He must have realised that I had intended to die for he would have no doctor in attendance but insisted that Mother and Mary nurse me and keep the sinful secret of my attempted self-destruction. I suppose that it would not do for the vicar's daughter to commit suicide! Appearance is all that Father cares for.

I was much alone with Mother and several days into my reluctant convalescence I decided that I must grasp the nettle and tell her of my baby. I had started my story when she reached out, placing a finger across my lips to silence me.

"Do not speak of it Elizabeth. Before you go further I must tell you that you have no baby. The shock of your accident made you miscarry, which is one of the reasons why you have been so very ill."

I asked her what reaction there had been from Father. Mother looked shocked and told me that she alone knew my secret. Once she had seen how things were she had banished everyone, even Mary, from my sickroom.

I lay stunned. I had plenty of time to ponder on the events of the past few weeks. I had lost John for ever. If only I could have been strong then at least I would have had his baby in lasting memory of him. Now I had nothing. I would have been willing to face the world, to brazen out my 'shame', if only I had some remnant of John. I had asked Mother for the letter. She told me that she did not know where it was. She hastily reassured me that she had placed all my other letters and diaries into a safe place (how well she knew Father's snooping

habits!). When I had left the table on that fateful morning she had taken up the letter and read it. She was alarmed and went to follow me. Father and Mary went out with her to search the grounds. It was Mary who had thought of looking at the summerhouse. From the lake shore she had seen no signs that the summerhouse had been opened and she looked around the edges of the lake. She looked along the jetty and then it was that she saw the black space in the weeds. She screamed to Father who had pulled me from the lake, half drowned. I would that he had not.

It was some weeks before I was able to get out of bed. The fact that I did not want to live made slow work of recovery. Father refused to speak to me beyond the necessary communication of day to day life. He has never since referred to the incident and treats me coldly, speaking curtly. He has only once spoken of John. He received a letter from John's lawyers about the Fraser estate. Everything is to go to some distant cousins living near Inverness in Scotland. The letter asks that Father convey sympathy to me in my sad loss, but it goes on to request that he ascertains whether I have in my possession any Fraser family jewellery. If I have then it must, of course, be returned to the estate. Icily I told him that I had only Mrs. Fraser's rings. One of them had been given to me by Mrs. Fraser herself, and the other was a gift from John on our engagement. They are, I consider, absolute gifts and so need not be returned. Other gifts that I have received from John I consider likewise as unconditional gifts so I will return nothing. Father agreed with me and added that he was glad that the gift of money for the church fell into the same category. He would write in reply to the lawyers.

I was able to remain calm as I spoke to Father, for there is no feeling, no emotion left inside me. Since I had the news of John's death I am an empty shell, I have lived in a daze. I have no love, no hope, no emotion at all - or at least I thought at that time that I did not.

Since the 'accident' Father has kept me away from church; indeed he has ensured that I am isolated from everyone. Mary took over the whole of my duties and it was on her return from parish visiting in early September that she complained of feeling unwell. She had a high temperature and was flushed. Mother sent her off to bed, and when she had not improved the next day she sent for Dr. Evans. Mary had influenza and was terribly ill. Before Mother could nurse her back to health she too succumbed to the infection and there were two more invalids in the house. I was improved enough to get up from my bed and nurse them.

In spite of his reluctance to help Father had to lend a hand in caring for them. I was still quite weak and I could get no help from the village. Influenza had become an epidemic and no household was immune. Indeed, the infection still rages.

I will not dwell on what happened, for I can bear to think of it no more than I can think of John's death. Mother and Mary both died and were buried in Brabage churchyard. I thought that I had no emotion left in me but their deaths, the deaths of the only people left in the world who loved me, has seared my heart.

It was after the funeral that Father took to following me about, watching my every move. At first I thought that he feared that I would repeat my attempt at suicide, but I was wrong. Last Friday Father returned to the house unexpectedly. I was in my attic and Edna was the only other person in the vicarage. I was re-reading John's letters which I had taken from their hiding place. Suddenly, and without warning, Father was at the door. He burst in without even knocking and it was obvious that he was in a high temper. I can relate calmly in my diary what was, in reality, a whirlwind of events. During her illness Mother had been delirious and in one such bout she must have let slip my secret. In the circumstances Father had not challenged me immediately. He had just now returned from Mrs. Farquharson's house, having discussed the entire business with her. He shouted at me, almost screaming with rage. He accused me of deceit, of immorality, of disobedience - the list went on and on. His face was swollen and empurpled. Wicked and impious as I am, I wished at that moment that he would collapse and die of apoplexy! He demanded my diaries, my letters, anything that I had in my possession that was written by, or about, John,

"For," he said, "I will know, Elizabeth, I will know the very depths of your and his depravity!"

I do not know what incensed me most, that Father had discussed me and my affairs with Mrs. Farquharson or that he was daring to stand before me and denigrate John, a finer man in every way than he was.

Of course I refused his request, saying that he had no right to my things, that he only wished to pry - and, in my grief and anger, I said very much more. Father shouted; I screamed my replies. Father demanded; I refused. I had hold of a letter of John's and Father lunged at it, to take it from me. I picked up the nearest thing to me, the tin box in which I keep all my precious things, and I hit Father with it. He fell back, shocked and he stared at me in total disbelief.

"You struck me, Elizabeth. You struck ME, your father. I cannot believe it. I cannot ..."

I interrupted him, shouting once more my defiance. In silence, and clenching his fists tight by his side, he turned and left the room.

I did not see him again on Friday, but on Saturday he treated me with contemptuous silence.

This morning (Sunday) before he went to church, he told me that this evening he will interview me in his study. He intends to discuss my future. I will deny him that opportunity

I think over the past and wonder how I could have changed things. Perhaps, after all, there is a God and John and I are punished for our sinfulness. No, I cannot believe that, for what sin had Mrs. Fraser and Charles been guilty of? Also, I think of Susan Bates, thriving and happy, having committed the selfsame 'sin' that I did.

When my thoughts are at their lowest I think that if I had not indulged my desire with John he would not have recovered so soon; he would not have returned to France when he did; he would not have been in that place when that shell struck. When I think of John's love, his happiness in our mutual pleasure, I cannot believe it wrong.

I wonder about my baby - our baby, and how I grieve. If I had not dashed myself into the lake, if I had not been as impulsive as Mother always said that I was, then I would at least have his child to love and comfort me, something of John left behind.

Then there is the matter of Mother and Mary. They exhausted themselves on my account, Mother in nursing me, Mary in taking over the duties my actions had barred me from carrying out myself. Perhaps if they had not been so exhausted then they would not have succumbed so easily, and so fatally, to influenza.

I have no-one left in the world. I cannot live my life with Father, and I know that I will never love as I have loved John. Such love is given but once in a lifetime, if it is given at all. Life is bleak. Mother was my staunch friend, the barrier between me and the black despair of life. Now she has been cruelly swept away. I feel that everything is my fault. When I think of my past happiness it is as a pain inside me, and I cannot bear it. When I think of the future, I see only blackness.

It is because of this that I have decided on my course of action. Father is away much of today, and when he is home, such is his attitude towards me that he would not seek my company. I have in any case been in bed since midday yesterday, and I fear that I too have contracted influenza. I have still some of John's medicine. (Oh, how that word clutches at my heart, but I mean, of course, the bottle of medicine used as a sleeping draught.) When I have finished writing this entry in

my diary I will pack up everything that is precious to me, pack it in my tin box and hide it in the old place in the attic chimney. I will then return to bed, take the whole of the bottle of medicine, and hopefully never have to face the cruel world again.

I am thankful for the happiness that I have enjoyed with John. Perhaps, if there is an afterlife, I will share it with him. If my life were to be set out as a balance sheet I think that on the positive side would be John and our love. The negative side, though, would form a long list - Father; my impetuous, impatient nature; the deaths of Mother, Mary, Mrs. Fraser, Charles, and of course, John, the loss of my baby. I suppose that it is the war that has ruined everything.

In years to come, if these words are read, I hope that the reader will remember that although it is the end of my happy, sad life, I am only one of millions. There are countless others who have suffered as I have, whose lives have been blighted by war. Many have had the courage to face adverse circumstances and live on. I am so unhappy, so full of grief, that I cannot find that courage.

THIS WAS THE FINAL ENTRY IN
ELIZABETH ALICE AUBREY'S DIARIES.

EPILOGUE

Paul looked around the room and inwardly congratulated himself. It had been a brilliant idea to use the restored summerhouse for the party. The warm August evening was filled with happy chatter. In one corner he could see that Roger and Simon had homed in on Grandpa Shipton who was entertaining them animatedly with his store of memories. Watching them, Paul was convinced that Roger would soon be publishing another of his volumes of local history.

Of the fifty or so people in the room more than half were from the locality. Paul was pleased that they had managed to make so many friends. They seemed to be accepted as part of the community now. Of course, over the past few months Liz had mixed well. Her researches into village history had proved to be the passport to their welcome. He caught sight of his wife, flanked by Eileen Jenkins who was fussing over Liz's determination to carry around trays of drinks in spite of her advanced state of pregnancy. Their baby was due in less than a month now and Paul experienced a flood of warm anticipation as he contemplated fatherhood. Everything was wonderful - at last. He had worried and fretted over Liz for so long, even fearing for her sanity at one point, that it was sheer delight to see her so happy, so carefree, so serene.

Paul's anxiety had not ended with the discovery of Lizzie Aubrey's diaries. Liz had been the first to read them, hungrily devouring every detail. When she had finished Paul had judged it wise to tell her of his own recent experiences in the summerhouse and the attic. Naturally Liz had not been pleased that he had kept the information from her, but she grudgingly conceded that Paul's secrecy had been well-intentioned.

It was a few days later that Liz seemed to sink into a deep pit of depression. She mooned about the house, spent hours in the attic staring into the garden and was reluctant to leave the vicarage for any length of time. She immersed herself in every scrap of literature she could find dealing with the Great War. She spent long periods watching television and playing videos (including "Oh What A Lovely War!" he had noticed with disquiet). It was only when Paul had suggested the renovation and rehabilitation of the summerhouse that she had emerged from her cocoon of sadness.

Once the work on the summerhouse was underway, Liz had been galvanised into action. Announcing her intention to find the graves of Elizabeth, Mary and Mrs. Aubrey she had set out determinedly to the churchyard. In the new

extension, so well noted in Lizzie's diaries, Liz had found the sadly overgrown plot. The headstone was stark, detailing only names and dates. Patiently Liz had cleared and tended. Fittingly the first flowers she placed on the grave were violets. Paul knew that Liz regularly walked Sally down to the church to renew the flowers and that the Aubrey grave was now one of the best tended in the cemetery.

Discovery of the grave had led Liz back to the record office and Paul remembered her excitement on discovering traces of Susan Cooper (nee Bates), the Mayfields and the Frasers. Park House was sold, the distant cousins never taking up residence.

Neither he nor Liz had been surprised to discover that after moving to Framley the Reverend Aubrey had married the widowed Mrs. Farquharson.

"And I hope that she spent the remainder of her life as a thorn in the side of Lewis Aubrey!" Liz had said, for her hatred of the Reverend Aubrey was implacable.

She had discovered so much about him; little to his credit. He had even stopped the custom among the young couples of Brabage of carving their names on the birch in the vicarage grounds. He had gone further and prosecuted one local lad, Davy Martin, for trespass when he had found him on the vicarage wall. He was a real tyrant of a man who was not loved locally but who had been esteemed by his colleagues in the church.

It had been Liz's desire to see that Lizzie's story was told and the good vicar of Brabage exposed, that had finally made her approach Simon with the idea for editing Lizzie's diaries and publishing them. Now, here they were, celebrating the launch of Liz's book!

Shortly after starting work on the diaries Liz had discovered that she was pregnant, three months pregnant. Paul had heaved a sigh of relief. The pregnancy explained it all. Women's hormones changed so much in pregnancy, the emotional turmoil of accepting that a new being is growing inside you must create a tumult. What had happened at Brabage had been the result of it: some sort of poltergeist activity. Paul hastily stifled the treacherous question regarding his own involvement. He had Liz back now. She wasn't quite the Liz he had always known, how could she be? Pregnancy alters everyone.

Paul beamed across the room and Liz smiled back at him. She walked out onto the verandah of the summerhouse and sat, quietly contemplating the pool of dark water.

After reading Lizzie's diaries so much had become clear. The dreams of

drowning must have been part of poor Lizzie's experience. The attraction to the attic, to the summerhouse had all been part of Elizabeth Aubrey's life. Even the names carved on the tree had played their part. Now it was over, and Lizzie's story was told.

Since the discovery of the diaries there had been no more weird occurrences at the vicarage. Paul had explained it all away but Liz knew that it had all really happened. Lizzie Aubrey had been leading her to the discovery of the diaries. She wanted her story known and had chosen Liz to tell it.

Now it was done and Lizzie would be at peace.

Liz looked across the dark pool. It was all so easy to imagine, to re-create all that had happened here. She almost felt that she had become a part of the Aubrey family, as though Lizzie herself had been absorbed into Liz. She was happy, fulfilled and looking forward to the future. Lizzie Aubrey had added a new dimension to her life. She was a very different person from the Liz who had first seen the derelict vicarage.

Paul emerged from the summerhouse and stood behind Liz, his arm protectively around her shoulder. They gazed across the pool, enjoying their brief period of isolation from their guests. The inner kernel of knowledge within Liz, that essence that was Elizabeth Aubrey, thought about the poems that had been among the letters, poems that John Fraser had written to Lizzie. Why should she not organise their publication? Why should John Fraser's story not be told? She began to plan the work.

Above her Paul was lost in happy contemplation of the balmy evening. The night scents mingled with the fragrance of Liz's perfume - violets. Odd how, since becoming pregnant, Liz had taken to wearing that perfume.